# COMING OUT
# BLACK

by W. Edward Morton

**DORRANCE**
PUBLISHING CO
EST. 1920
PITTSBURGH, PENNSYLVANIA 15238

Dorrance Publishing Co
585 Alpha Drive
Pittsburgh, PA 15238
Visit our website at *www.dorrancebookstore.com*

ISBN: 978-1-6470-2184-9
eISBN: 978-1-6470-2761-2

# CHAPTER 1

"Carter, what are you doing? It's so quiet up here," his mother asked. She had come up the back stairs that placed her in the hallway right outside of his bedroom. He expected her to comment on the clothes he had taken off and discarded in the mud room when he came into the house via the back door. Whenever he came in from the stables in Cobblestone Creek Park, his mother had instructed him to always disrobe in the back kitchen and leave his smelly jeans in the laundry room.

This he had done, but he hadn't bothered to put them in the laundry basket. His mother had said many times that he should make sure they were in the basket because when left strewn on the floor, the whole area smelled of horse. A smell, by the way, that Carter didn't mind because he loved horses. In fact, at 16-years-old, he preferred the company of horses more than people.

In the summer, he was happy to spend his days at the stables. Jack and Sam, the owners, allowed him and his best friend Steve to hang out there to help with the horses. They saddled horses for riders who came to rent them by the hour or for the day. They also rode out with some of the parties that requested guides or even instructions. Usually when he arrived back home, he parked his bike in the backyard, went in through the back door, disrobed, and jumped into the old shower in the back shed. During that time, his mother would usually be in the main kitchen preparing dinner and she would know that he was home safely.

This time he had arrived and she hadn't heard him come in. When it dawned on her that she wasn't sure if he was at home, she went up to his room to check. Recently, she had become apprehensive. Carter seemed to be withdrawing more and more from the family. In previous years, they would invite one or two of his cousins to come and spend the summer, so that he would have companions his age when they moved to the shore for the season. This year he had been pleading with his parents to leave him at home and have Ann, their all-around housekeeper/babysitter, move into the house for the summer. She would then be in charge of the house and of him. His mother wasn't sure she liked this idea. Ann was a real gem, she worked hard and attended night school, but his mother, being a proper lady wasn't sure that would be appropriate. Now that Carter was 16, leaving him under the jurisdiction of a young woman who was only 27 might not be the best idea.

His mother was not aware of the fact that Ann had given him his first complete sexual experience four years ago when he was 12. Even before that, the previous babysitter Joyce, who was older than his mother, had fondled him and found every opportunity to press his face into her crotch while supposedly combing his hair. That began when he was only five and continued until he was 11 when she moved away and it was no longer convenient for her to continue working for Carter's parents.

As for his step-father Bob, whom Carter called Dad, if Carter didn't want to go to the shore for the summer, let him stay at home, and go down for visits when he wanted to join the family. He didn't see the harm in Carter being left alone with Ann. Bob was in Carter's corner for whatever he wanted. He saw Carter as his natural son. Carter's mother Lila had divorced his father when he was two-years-old and married his step-father Bob in the same year. Bob was very pleased to have a son. His first marriage had not produced any children and he had been divorced three years before marrying Lila.

Now it was the 26th of June ,1952, and Carter had been advanced to his senior year in high school with a B+ average. It was time to start really planning for the future, choosing a college, and having a social life, such as joining "The Top Notch Teens" (A group of teens who were considered the in-crowd) or at least dating some nice girls. Several of Lila's club members and friends had daughters that would have rated high on her list of girls that would be perfect choices for Carter.

Carter answered his mother with, "I was just fantasizing about being rich and owning a huge horse farm with a stable of champions."

Lila replied "Carter, I would rather hear that you were thinking of a great summer in Cape May."

"Mother, I don't want to go to Cape May and I don't want to socialize with all of those silly mush mouthed kids who are there every year, it's boring."

"Why have you suddenly become so anti-family and anti-social?" his mother asks.

"Because I have become more mature," he replies. "I would rather stay home and discuss books with Ann. We have a lot in common."

"Other than books, what on earth would you have in common with a 27-year-old woman who has already had one child out of wedlock? She is a very nice girl who has had a lot of ups and downs at an early age, but I think she might be a bit worldlier than someone you need to be in long discussions with. In addition to that, you are spending too much time alone. Your sister and I were discussing you this morning. She thinks it might be a good idea for you to come to stay with her and Gregory if you aren't going to Cape May."

Carter was quite upset by this idea. His sister Catherine would be a deterrent to his being with Ann. Catherine was a lot more aware about what might be happening with Carter. She was also on his case about dating and going to parties and dances like other kids his age. Everybody has ideas about what he should be doing.

His mother ends her statement by saying, "Dinner will be ready in 30 minutes. Try to come to the table in decent attire; your dad is in his shower now and will be dressed for work." His step-dad was the night manager of the largest auto parts manufacturer on the east coast, and five nights a week, he had dinner with Carter and his mother and left for work at 7 PM. His position was considered a very good one for a black business man at that time.

All Carter could think of was the coming Saturday when his parents were due to attend a formal affair at Bob's relatives' (well known in black circles) restaurant, The Crystal Inn. Ann had promised to hang around after she's finished cleaning the house, so that they could be together. That's how she put it. For him it was a chance to get his rocks off. She was always telling him it was fine for her to have sex with him because it was safe. After all, if she got pregnant, she was an adult and she could say it was a boyfriend's baby. That way Carter would be in the clear. He was kind of dubious about that theory, but he only wanted to think about the wonderful release that he experienced every time they were together. The only problem was that after two ejaculations, he was sated and simply wanted her to leave. She, however, would try for more often by sucking on him until he was sore. When that ended, she wanted to talk.

Dinner that night was the same old same. Lila wanted Bob to agree that Carter should accompany them to Cape May. Bob replied since he would be driving down every Friday night, Carter could ride with him and they would return to Philadelphia on Sundays. In fact, this would be a good time for Carter to practice driving the car. It would serve two purposes: giving Bob a chance to rest on the way and allowing experience for Carter. This idea didn't sit well with Carter either because he was looking forward to his trysts with Ann.

Finally, his mother gave in and agreed to every other weekend and having Carter's best friend Steve come with them. Lila liked Carter's friend Steve. Steve's mother and Lila saw everything about raising their sons the same way. Steve's mother was also remarried after divorcing Steve's father. She was determined to send Steve to the right schools and to have him associating with the right people. Steve was destined to attend college at Fisk University. Several members of his mother's family had gone there for undergrad and were now professionals who had a great deal of influence at the school.

When Carter called Steve that night, he told him that his mother would be calling Steve's mother to ask if the plan for the weekends at the Shore would be to her liking. Carter told Steve if he didn't want to come along, he didn't want to go either. Steve never liked the beach. He had been invited to spend the summer with his father who owned four horses and had a small farm in Chester County. His father was a whiz at cards and had taught the boys all kinds of games when they had both gone out to visit him. But Steve agreed to go to Cape May every other weekend. Ironically, Carter's step-dad wasn't that fond of Steve and Steve's step-father was outright unkind to Carter.

That might have been the reason that Lila and Jasmine (Steve's mother) didn't do more socially.

None of this affected the boys' relationship. They told each other everything. In fact, Carter confessed that night to Steve about Ann. He told him all of the gory details. Of course, being a horny teenager, Steve wanted to be counted in on the Saturday plans. He had often checked Ann out when he visited Carter's house. His attitude toward her was a bit disrespectful.

He made it obvious that he thought she was hot, and when Carter said "Cool it, she can hear you."

Steve replied, "Fuck her, she's a servant."

Carter corrected him by saying, "We don't have as much money as your parents have. She is Mother's helper and is paid by the hour."

Steve replied, "She's still a servant. It's part of her job to take care of the young squire." Carter was convinced to tell Ann she could at least be nice to Steve on Saturday.

When the day arrived, Carter was awakened by a hand that had slipped under the sheet that covered him. He opened his eyes and there was Ann. She was holding on to his penis, which was already so stiff, it ached.

He sat up, saying, "Hey, my mother is in the house."

Ann laughed and said, "No, she isn't. She went to the beauty salon. You know she wants to be glamorous tonight. I couldn't wait to grab onto this joy stick. Don't worry, your mom didn't want to drive, so your dad took her. You poor thing, I'll take care of you." She commenced to massaging and then taking his penis into her mouth. He gasped and fell back on the bed. In a matter of seconds, he ejaculated.

When he was able to catch his breath, he said "Steve wants to join us tonight."

"What? What do you think I am, a whore? I wouldn't let that snobby prick touch me. He looks at me like I'm dirt. I thought you and I were special, and you want to pass me off to that stuck up friend of yours."

"Wait a minute, Annie, it's just sex, I'm only 16."

"You little bastard, I'm going to tell your mother you raped me."

"Are you serious? My mother won't believe you. You better think twice about that. When I tell my parents you've been doing me since I was 12-years-old. My mother doesn't play, she will have you arrested. Better yet, I will call my sister right now. What do you think will happen then? I can talk to her, she won't be as shocked. She never liked you anyhow."

"Okay, I'm out of here, you little prick. I'm going to tell my new man about you and he will kick your narrow ass."

"Annie, you are irrational. I'll tell your new boyfriend you've been sucking me off since I was 12. You won't have him long. Get out of our house, I'll tell Mother you didn't feel well and left without doing your job. Wait a minute, I've got $50 hidden in my desk drawer. I'll give it to you for the blow job."

"That's ok, you're going to be sorry in a week or so. You're too much of a nerd to go out and get a girlfriend. Maybe you can fuck one of those horses you go out to play with every day."

With that last word, Ann ran down the steps and out of the house.

After Ann was gone, Carter began to panic. What's going to happen now? If she does tell someone, what will I do? She might lie to Mother and Dad. I won't have the nerve to tell either of them the truth. He decided to get himself together and go out to the stables. He jumped in the shower in his parents' bathroom. He stopped on his way out of the house in the kitchen where he found the breakfast table set for him with a half of a grapefruit and a bowl containing two boiled eggs. He wolfed down the eggs and went out the back door into the yard.

His bike was there where he left it. He decided to stop first at Steve's to first of all tell what happened, and secondly, to ask him if he wanted to go with him to the stables. It was Saturday and normally they would go out to the Bala Cynwyd Country Club. On Saturdays and Sundays, if they were not meeting the other members of The Jockey Club, they would go out on the polo field to help tend to the polo ponies.

When Carter arrived at Steve's, Mrs. Caster (Steve's mother) opened the door and hugged Carter.

"Go on upstairs, he's still in bed." Steve was groggy and squinting at Carter.

He said, "I went to that party in Yeadon last night. I told you about it. It was Sheila Edward's house, Dr. Edward's daughter."

"I know, I didn't want to go. How was it?"

"It was great. Anita Chaney asked for you. I told her you don't go to parties. You know she really likes you. She asked me if I could convince you to come to her party next week. I'm going to call your sister, Catherine. She'll make you go."

"Between my mother, your mother, and Catherine, I can't win. Those girls at those parties are not interested in me."

"You have no idea how wrong you are. They want you bad because you seem like the mysterious silent type to them. Most of those girls are nice, you are missing out. I'm your friend. I'm telling you those girls are ready."

"Well, I can tell you one other thing? I know those guys in that group don't like me."

"Carter, you really underrate yourself; the guys really want you there almost as much as the girls. Brice Winter asked me where you learned to ride a horse as well as you do when we go out with the Jockey Club. The other person that mentioned you directly was Joe Curtis, he remembers when you were in elementary school and your parents had your birthday parties at the upstairs of the Crystal Inn."

"Yes, my mother did all the inviting, my classmates and her club members' kids. Look, I didn't come here to hear about parties. I wanted to tell you to forget trying to get some of Ann. That's all over, she is threatening to tell my parents and her boyfriend to have me done in."

"Oh, crap, don't worry about that slut. She molested you when you were a little kid. Well, in age that is. She's a rapist and she's lower class. Your mother will put her in her place."

"Anyway, I'm going out riding, you want to come?"

"No way, I'm still trying to recover from last night. We had some gin in the punch. I'm hungover."

"Ok, I'm off."

Carter left Steve's house and biked off to the stables. When he arrived there, Tommy the manager was there. Carter sat in the Tack Room with Tommy. There were about eight stable hands running in and out, picking up bridles and saddles as they prepared horses for groups of riders who had reserved horses in advance. Saturdays and Sundays are the busiest days at the stables. Tommy informed each of them not to send Walking Jennie out with any of the groups or individuals because he knew when Carter came out to ride solo that he wanted to ride out on Walking Jennie. Tommy really liked Carter, so he made sure that Carter got his wish.

Tommy was described by most of the people at the stables, male and female as the Greek God, although Tommy was not Greek. He is a blond Irishman with a perfect body. He had a reputation for being a real favorite of the ladies, even though his live-in girlfriend also works at the stables in the office. Together, they occupy a farmhouse, which is on the property and is part of the deal with running the stables for the owners. As quiet as it's kept, Carter suspects something is different about Tommy because he always seems to treat Carter like he is special, which is ok, but he goes out of his way to wrestle with Carter and ends with a hug each time. It's not that Carter finds Tommy out of order. In fact, he enjoys these moments in some curious way.

Tommy is 25 and Carter decides maybe he can discuss the Ann relationship with him because he has had many experiences with women and might have some good advice.

Tommy responds with, "You don't need to take a chance on getting some older chick pregnant. Try some sessions with a buddy. You'll be getting your rocks off with no worries afterwards."

This advice surprises Carter and he replies, "I don't want to get it on with a buddy. I don't find any of my buddies attractive. I couldn't even get it up for a buddy."

Tommy came back with, "You won't know until you try it."

Carter retorted, "I don't want to try it."

"Listen, just about every guy that reaches manhood has had experiences in that direction. Come on back to the feed storage room and I'll give you lessons."

"I don't think so."

"Come on, don't I always save your favorite horse for you when you come out?"

"I'm sorry, Tommy, I'm not into guys, and besides, I'm only 16. I'm not ready for that kind of action. I thought you'd give me advice on handling a woman. I'm not desperate to have sex. I was getting plenty before Ann went off on me. I like you a lot. You never treat me like you treat the other kids out here. I've seen you yell at them and tell them to work or go home."

"Ok, Carter, don't go crazy, nothing has changed. I could say more, but we'll drop it right now and we'll forget it. One more thing though. Once you think about it and if you change your mind, I'm here."

"Now I get it, you think I'm a homo."

"I didn't say that. I know you're a sheltered kid, and besides, I definitely think your buddy Steve is light in the loafers."

"Ok, I'm out of here." Tommy stands up and Carter is alarmed. He knows that Tommy could really beat his ass if he wanted to and Carter is not a fighter, at least not since elementary school.

Carter starts for the door and Tommy manages to grab him and holding him tightly says, "Carter, calm down, I will never hurt you. I've watched you grow up in the last three years. I've been where you are. I know you feel like everybody is against you. Stop struggling, I don't want you to stop being my young buddy. Forget everything I said. Get Walking Jennie out of the corral, put the gear on her, and go out for your ride." He actually started crying, but he stopped struggling and he realized he wanted to remain friends with Tommy in spite of everything. Tommy released him now that he stopped resisting. Tommy is apologizing profusely.

He is saying, "I'm so sorry, I didn't mean to upset you like this. The power is in your hands. If you tell Jack or Sam, I will not only lose my job, but they will throw me and Dotty out of our house and off the property. You know Steve's father and Sam are good friends, and besides, I can imagine them thinking I'm some kind of kid molester."

Carter finally gathered himself together, stating, "I'll never tell anybody, not even my best friend Steve."

He ran out to the corral and singled out Walking Jennie. He led her into the smaller paddock and placed the short blanket on her back with the saddle on top. With Walking Jennie, he uses an English Saddle befitting her long graceful gait. She is a pure-bred Tennessee Walker Horse. He mounts and rides off, noticing Tommy watching him from the doorway of the Tack Shop. Carter rides out to the bridle path and continues aimlessly along passing other riders along the way. It's almost like Jennie already belongs to him and can sense his mood. He directs Jennie alongside the creek, which is pretty high up its banks since the night before there had been a heavy rainfall. When he comes out of the park at the Belmont Avenue crossroad, he decides to go to visit his father, who lives right at the edge of the park.

His father (Joseph Johnson) was an authentic professional gambler with many other sidelines. His mother said while they were married when things were good and he was winning, they lived the life with the best of everything. She shopped at Nan Duskin and Bonwit Teller and he was a

real dandy in suits from Wm H. Wanamaker, Jacob Reed, and even Brooks Brothers in New York. But when things were bad and he was losing, he even lost their house in a game. After seven years, Carter's sister was born. His mother felt it was time to think about stability. His father even got several legitimate jobs, but his real money was coming from banking numbers and other shady deals.

Three years later, another child was born. It was a boy, but he lived for one year and died of what was later to be determined as Crib Death. In another four years, Carter was born. After two more years of ups and downs, his mother moved out and acquired a well-known lawyer who was the husband of one of her best friends.

He rides Jennie right onto the front lawn, dismounts, and knocks on the front door. Ruby, his father's latest live-in girlfriend, opens the door and tells him his father is around the corner at the barber shop where he uses the back room and upstairs for his gambling operations. Carter leaves Jennie tethered to the railing leading to the porch. When he enters the barber shop, Andy, the head barber, and his assistant seem very nervous, and Andy tells him to wait in the shop. The young assistant goes through a door at the rear of the shop.

In a few minutes, his father emerges from the rear.

"My son, it's great to see you. How's your mother?" He always asks about Lila. He once told Carter that he likes young women, and as soon as they begin to grow old, he trades them in for a newer model. But the only woman he will ever love is Lila. He says "she is real class" and he had to formally beg Carter's grandfather for her hand in marriage.

He had arrived in Richmond a year before that driving a Stutz Bearcat (a snazzy sports car in those days). Lila met him at a party, given by her best friend at the time, Ella Mae Winters. All of the girls at the party were whispering about the handsome guy that was staying with Rodney James of the James Undertaker Family. Everyone knew that Lila and Rodney had been dating steadily for some time. Rodney even traveled to Sedalia, North Caroliina to visit Lila when she attended the finishing school there. Of course, those visits were always chaperoned by the house mother at the young lady's residence and they were allowed to take afternoon walks together around the small campus.

Rodney had made it known to friends that he was going to marry Lila, but here arrived this slick dude from Providence, Rhode Island with this clipped way of speaking. In fact, sounding almost as if he had an English accent. He kept asking Lila to dance and dancing was her weakness. She used to like practicing The Charleston, The Black Bottom, and other jazzy dances when she and her girlfriends got together. Unfortunately, Rodney and most of the other local young men didn't know much about the latest dances or any others, except for the waltz and the two step that they had to learn in order to escort the young ladies to the coming out parties and the "Colored Ball." Joseph, being what they considered as sophisticated and from the North was quite the dancer. He knew all of the latest steps. The girls were almost lining up to dance with him, but he kept coming back to Lila and she didn't seem to mind.

Rodney, however, became noticeably unhappy with the attention that Joseph was directing to Lila. He called Joseph aside and expressed his dismay with the goings on and emphasized his intention to make Lila his wife. In the end, when Joseph began visiting Richmond on a regular basis, he took a room at a boarding house in town. After some time, he went to Lila's father to ask for permission to call on her.

Lila's father finally consented after telling Joseph he would have to think about it before answering. He gave his permission, even though he and Lila's brother instinctively did not like Joseph. Lila was flattered by Joseph's efforts, but at first, she refused to be anything but a friend to Joseph. She even suggested that he should turn his attentions to her sister Ada, who was dating several other fellows and wasn't serious, she thought about any of them. Ada also loved to dance, and in addition, loved to flirt. In fact, she had been threatened several times by her father and her brother with being sent away to live in Washington D.C. with their Aunt Lola, who was known to be a very strict Episcopalian Woman that believed in tight curfews and proper conduct for unmarried young ladies.

However, Joseph prevailed. He succeeded in capturing Lila in the end, and when he asked her for her hand in marriage, Lila begged her father to give his blessing to the union.

# CHAPTER II

Carter had been fascinated by these stories that his mother had related to him as a young child. He sensed that his mother still had a special place in her heart for Joseph and the whirlwind days of their love affair and marriage.

Joseph was always glad to see his son Carter, but he didn't want him exposed to any of his dealings. First and foremost, he was pleased with the way Carter was being raised by Lila and Bob. As for their daughter Catherine, he knew that she worshiped him, in spite of the divorce when she was nine-years-old. He in turn adored his daughter. She never developed any affection for the step-father, Bob. She constantly reminded Carter that Bob had been one of Joseph's friends before Joseph and Lila broke up. She felt that this was not a coincidence after 16 years of marriage.

Carter and his father leave the barber shop and walk back around to his father's house. Joseph is impressed by Walking Jennie, who is still tethered to the railing outside of the house. They discuss horseback riding in detail, but Joseph is aware that something is seriously troubling Carter, so he questions him. Carter finally admits he has had this big fight with his ex-babysitter and she has threatened to accuse him of rape or at least to tell his mother and Bob, his step-father, about them having sex.

With more prompting from Joseph, he comes out with the whole story starting at age 12. He notes a change in his father's eyes as he relates his tale and he begins to worry that he should not have confided in his father. He is panicking and thinking his father is going to blame him and will call his mother to inform her of the situation. Instead his father replies with a razor-sharp edge to his words.

"Don't you worry about it! Did she leave the house right away?"

"Yes, she ran out and slammed the door after her. Daddy, are you going to tell Mother?"

"Listen, try to forget this happened," his father said, "get on your horse and be careful going back to the stables. I'll see you next week. Don't worry about anything. You're my son."

Carter mounted Walking Jennie and rode off. He reached the bridle path and urged Jennie into a canter and then a gallop. She moved as smoothly as any well-oiled machine. Going with her rhythm was so easy and fluid. He eased up as they approached a bend in the path. He knew that if they came upon a park guard, he would be cited for careless behavior on the park bridle path. Galloping your mount on this path was forbidden.

He proceeded back along the bank of the creek and his mind returned to the day's happenings. He still was very concerned about the Ann incident, but he decided to follow his father's advice. As for Tommy, he had ambivalent feelings. He knew he wanted to still be friends with Tommy, but he was confused about his reaction to Tommy's offer. The business about breaking out with tears, did he cry because he was afraid of Tommy or was it because Tommy thought he was queer, or was it that he felt the urge to consent? He agonized over this until he reached the stables. He worried that Tommy would come out to talk to him, but Tommy was not there. One of the other stable hands told him that Tommy had gone home to dinner. Carter was relieved and yet also disappointed.

He removed Walking Jennie's saddle and led her into her stall after a vigorous rub down with a towel. He took her bridle off and gave her a customary kiss on her muzzle, retrieved his bicycle from the tack room, and peddled off home.

Upon his arrival, he went through his usual motions, and after his shower, he ran into Bob, fully dressed in formal wear in the hallway.

Bob said, "Hey, buddy, I've convinced your mother that you are trustworthy enough to be in the house alone this evening. Annie won't be coming over. After all you are 16, and I believe a responsible young man."

"Uh, yeah, thanks, Dad," Carter replied.

"Your mother is just about ready. We are due at the Crystal Inn at 6:00 PM, so she fixed something for you to warm up for your dinner." He patted Carter on the shoulder, and looking Carter straight in the eyes, saying, "Remember, I am always going to be in your corner." Carter sensed something intrinsic in this statement and felt assured that things were going to be okay.

He went down the stairs and into the living room. This to him was the most formal room in the whole house. The only times that he spent in that room were usually when his mother was sitting in there and when his grandmother was visiting from Virginia. His grandmother always sat in the living room with the radio tuned to a music station. She was a piano teacher back in Richmond. She loved classical music. Perhaps that is how Carter's mother developed such a love for musicals in the theater. Also, as a result of his mother's great affection for the

Theater, Carter was the chosen one to accompany her to the Saturday Matinees in lieu of his step-father, who considered the theater a bore, especially musicals. Lila and her sister Ada were both members of an amateur theater group that performed in the original colored "Theater Royale." One of her writers was Richard Wright, the author of *Native Son*, a play which her company performed as one of their presentations.

Carter wanted to be in the living room when his mother came down the stairs in her gown dressed for the formal dinner party. This was a kind of a tradition with him and his mother when she dressed for a special event. As she finally descended the stairs, he swelled with pride and admiration. His mother possessed the ability to look chic in whatever she wore in those days and this time was the crème de la crème. She was wearing a pale blue sheath that flattered her complexion. Her hair was styled in a fashionable bob with a mini cloche made of pheasant feathers placed on the top of her head.

She came into the living room and did a spin for her loving son, who simply exploded with compliments.

"Mother, you look fantastic. You will make everyone else come in second." Lila adored her son, and seeing the pleasure on his face was thrilling to her.

She thanked him for his compliments and added, "You're a good son and we will go to any lengths to keep you safe and happy." Again, Carter detected an undercurrent message, this time from Lila.

After Bob and Lila drove off, Carter went up to his bedroom and picked up the mystery he was reading by his favorite author at the time, Mickey Spillane. Carter never heard or saw anything of Ann after that, even though she lived nearby.

Sunday morning arrived. Carter awoke with a voracious appetite since he hadn't eaten anything at dinner time the night before. It was customary for Carter to attend Mass at St. Thomas Episcopal Church on Sundays where he would take communion. Of course, one should not eat before taking communion, but this morning, he wasn't sure he would be able to make it that long, but he would try. After bathing and dressing, he went downstairs to find his mother in the kitchen still wearing her housecoat. This was unusual; his mother normally would be dressed on Sunday mornings and inspiring him to get to mass on time.

Lila had joined The Granite Rock Baptist Church to please her husband Bob, who was Baptist, but at heart, she was still an Episcopalian, along with the rest of her family going all the way back to her grandparents on her father's and her mother's sides of the family. She was determined in her own way to keep the faith through her children. It hadn't worked with Carter's sister Catherine. She had decided to become a Methodist and had joined St. Mathews AME Church. Catherine was extremely strong willed and always made her own decisions.

This Sunday morning was different; Lila was not her energetic self. She had made coffee and she sat at the kitchen table looking sleepy. If Carter hadn't known his mother better, he would have thought she had a hangover. He knew his mother did not drink, so he ruled that out. However, he later found out that Bob's brother, who was a chronic jokester, had given Lila a drink called a Top and Bottom disguised as a fruit punch, and Lila had become quite ill after drinking it.

Larry, Bob's brother, was very apologetic when he realized this was no joke. Bob had become quite angry and had even gone as far as telling Larry that he was not welcome at the house anymore. He relented after Larry apologized so profusely.

After seeing his mother looking so great when they left for the affair the night before, he was glad he wasn't awake when they returned home.

Carter left the house and walked to the church. As usual the mass lasted for an hour. Unlike a lot of the other churches in the area, 10:00 o'clock mass was well attended, especially by a lot of the other young people in the neighborhood. After stopping at the door and chatting with David and Fred, Father Jefferson's two sons, Carter walked down to the sidewalk where Louie and Denise from the "in crowd" were talking with a bunch of their cohorts.

Louie called to Carter, "Hey, the only place I see you is church. Don't you like parties and being social?"

Carter replies "I've been studying a lot."

"Studying! It's summer vacation, man. You don't need to be studying unless you're going to summer school."

"Well I'm thinking about the S.A.T.s" says Carter.

Louie says "Man, give it a rest. You'll be in Cape May soon, and I know you won't be studying down there."

Denise piped in with, "I hear you're going to be at Anita Chaney's party on Friday. I didn't think you liked parties, she must be special." Carter chose not to commit to either of these disguised questions.

When he arrived back home, his mother had perked up enough to fix breakfast. Bob was already at the table dressed for church. Carter went to the table and sat.

Bob quipped, "You enjoy your Latin lesson this morning?"

Carter answered, "Dad, all of Mass is not spoken in Latin. You know that." Bob laughs, and as usual, Lila speaks up with, "Bob don't make fun of ours and we won't make fun of yours." Carter adds, "I never could understand the ladies in their big hats who always get happy and dance and shout when your Preacher becomes more and more excited at your services." All of this exchange is made back and forth with a tinge of sarcastic repartee."

After a hasty breakfast, Bob leaves late for the 11:00 o'clock service at his church. Since Lila is not feeling up to par, she goes up to her bedroom. Carter goes to the hallway telephone, thinking he can call Steve without disturbing Steve's mother or step-father since Steve is privileged to have a phone extension in his bedroom. Steve does answer as it happens his parents have also left for church.

"Hey, Steve, I can't talk loud, but I think I'm in the clear with the Ann situation. Everybody is being mysterious. I'm getting these sort of indirect reassurances."

Steve answers "I told you not to worry, you did what comes naturally and you were led by that oversexed nympho witch. Throw it out of your mind. I'm feeling better today, are you going to the Bala Club?"

Carter says "I guess so, but I really feel like going to the Stables instead."

"Why," says Steve. "It's always crowded on Sundays and I'm not in the mood to ride out with some no riding jerk who wants to be coached." Carter would normally agree with these sentiments, but he realizes that he is anxious to see Tommy to make sure it's like Tommy said and nothing has changed. He knows that he still wants to be friends with Tommy and he wants to prove that he hasn't mentioned Tommy's offer to anyone.

Carter has to accept the truth in this matter. Two years ago, when he was 14, his cousin Vincent who was in the Navy, had come to join his mother Bernice for a visit at Carter's home. Vincent was stationed in Newport News, Virginia and had a weekend pass. His mother came out from their home in Los Angeles. They decided this would be a perfect opportunity for mother and son to see each other after Vincent's long stint in basic training. Vincent was 18 and seemed to Carter like a big brother.

They found time to go out bicycle riding and they went to the movies together. Vincent told Carter about training and getting fit in the Navy. This led to demonstrations of different exercises and finally to a wrestling match. As it turned out, Carter was of course the loser, but he didn't expect what happened during the wrestling match. Vincent became a vicious attacker, and not only did he become cruel, but he forced Carter into anal sex. After it was over, Carter was crying and Vincent threatened him.

"If you tell anyone, I'll get you. I mean you won't see another day." Carter believed him, he was afraid of Vincent after that and he never told on him. Carter was glad when Vincent and his mother left.

He had tried to put the experience with Vincent out of his mind, but Tommy's overtures had brought it racing back. It made him wonder if Vincent, and now Tommy, saw something in him that he was repressing. Or maybe Tommy was right about most guys going through that kind of stage on the way to adulthood. The other nagging question was why did he feel the need to explain all of this to Tommy?

Pushing these thoughts away, he gave in to Steve's plan to go to the polo field where they could watch the expert horsemanship and the beautiful trained polo ponies.

Steve and Carters' love of horses was demonstrated in the way they handled the polo ponies that they were trusted to walk and rub down as the horses were exchanged for fresh mounts. Most of the players had at least two horses, so that they could constantly change mounts at the end of each period or even each break.

One of the regular players, Glen Weatherby, was always accompanied by his girlfriend Alice DeWalt and his 21-year-old sister Felicia. To Carter, Felicia was the classiest and gorgeous girl he had ever seen, and she seemed to know he had a crush on her. She would always come over to say hello to Carter.

"How are you, Carter?" Carter would sometimes become speechless. Finally, after stumbling and bumping into the horse he was tending to, he would stammer a reply. This always made her laugh with that wonderful sound that made him feel like he would melt.

If Glen came pounding off the field to change mounts, Carter had to have the rested pony ready so that Glen could quickly dismount the winded horse and ride off on a fresh one.

He knew his sister enjoyed flirting with Carter and he joked with Carter about it, saying, "First of all, she's too old for you, and secondly, you don't have enough money. Wait till you finish college and get a career. By that time, she'll be tired of her married life, but even then, if I find out you are messing with my sister, I will punch your lights out."

Felicia replies in Carter's defense, "Glen, you stay out of this. Carter is cute. I'm going to make him my young Paramour. It'll be a lot of fun."

Of course, Carter knows there is no chance of any of this coming true, not with this pretty white girl from a prominent Mainline family. Steve has warned Carter that a few of the older polo players and attendees are observing these goings on and obviously are not pleased. Steve is afraid they will be banned from the club and will miss out on the tips, which can amount to as much as $50 per day. Also, just being there is like a privilege to have the opportunity to be a part of a high society event. Carter doesn't worry about that aspect of things, his father has always instilled a sense of pride in him.

"Nobody on this earth is any better than you are. Never feel inferior to anyone." So, the thought of those others having them banned because of a flirtation with a white girl didn't worry him. Besides, Glen always chose him to take care of resting his three ponies.

After the games, the boys rode their bikes back to their respective homes. When Carter finished cleaning up, he found his mother in the living room.

When he just briefly mentioned Felicia Weatherby, his mother said, "I just read about her in the society pages of the newspaper. She's getting married in September."

Carter asks, "Who is she marrying?"

"A very wealthy young man from France," answers Lila.

Carter says, "You'd never know it by the way she flirts with me."

"What? I know you are not serious about some older woman who is engaged to another man."

"Mother, please, I'm not interested in her or anybody else at this time." When he looks at his mother, he sees something in the expression on her face that tells him she is half serious. His mind drifts back to Ann. He thinks, now Mother may assume that I am going after grown women, she must know about Ann.

He decides to change the subject, "When are you leaving for Cape May?" He is immediately sorry he chose that as a topic change.

Lila says, "I've been thinking about that again and I really want you to go with us to stay for the entire summer."

"Mother, you promised."

"I did not promise, I was forced to agree."

"Forced? Dad said I could go down every other weekend with him. Please, Mother, I promised I could be at the Stables every day and we got Steve to agree to go with me to Cape May every other weekend. He will be at his father's the rest of the time."

His mother replies, "You won't even have Steve in town, he will be in West Chester."

"Yes, but I told him we can still go to parties on the weekends that we are in the area." He knew if he threw in the part about the parties, she might relent.

Lila gave in and agreed to the original plan. "I do want you to start a social life. It will be a good thing for you to go to parties and dances with people your own age. You spend too much time with horses and being alone. At least now your friend Steve goes to a lot of parties and he has a few nice girls that are calling him quite often. Jasmine says he already has been asked to accompany Patricia Roxbury, Judge Roxbury's daughter, to the Christmas Cotillion."

"I know, Mother. I'm not popular enough to be asked to the Cotillion. Besides, it's expensive." "Carter, you know very well that Bob and I would definitely make sure you had enough money to go," his mother replied.

He decided not to add any more reasons for not going because he was sure none of the pretty girls who were scheduled to come out at the affair would want him to be their escort. However, his mother was determined to go on with this conversation.

She went on to say, "Besides, even if we couldn't afford to send you, I would call your father. You know he would certainly be willing to pay for the whole evening." He did not reply to this statement, he knew his father would pay whatever the cost. He would be anxious to outdo Bob.

When Carter wanted to buy his Boxer puppy from the AKC Breeder three years ago, Bob had refused to give him the money because he felt that Carter would eventually lose interest in the dog and his mother would have to end up taking care of his pet. When Carter went to Joseph, his father had jumped at the chance to score points with his son. He not only paid the $75 for the purchase but also paid for Fawn's registration, bought supplies, food, and Veterinary services. This is probably one of the reasons Bob is now seriously considering buying Walking Jennie for Carter. This is the latest dearest wish. Carter has presented Bob with all of the details and requirements for owning a horse.

Carter knows his advantages, in fact he receives weekly allowances from both fathers. This also pleases his mother, who is aware of the rivalry and is happy that both men want Carter to favor them.

"As for Cape May, your cousins Renee and Peter are coming here from New York next Sunday, and Bob is going to drive us down on Monday. He was planning to take that week off for his vacation, but now he has decided to take the last two weeks of August instead."

Carter says, "Why did he change his mind?"

Lila replies, "He just thought it would be better to take the two weeks together."

Carter considers this answer and silently decides that the real reason is probably so that he won't be completely on his own.

"By the way, you will be going around to your sister's for your dinners and even your breakfasts if you like. Bob will be having his meals at Mrs. Kelly's house." (Mrs, Kelly is an older woman who had rented a room to Bob during his divorce from his first wife and the three years after until his marriage to Lila. Carter and his sister Catherine called her Momma Kelly. She was a wonderful cook. The huge kitchen in her house still contained the old-fashioned coal burning stove from which she turned out delicious baked goods. When Carter was much younger, his mother and Bob would take him with them to visit Momma Kelly; he would dance for her to the music from her old wind-up Victrola. She would reward him with huge slices of her scrumptious pound cake or tasty apple pie (She also always gave the family a bakers' box of her wonderful homemade cinnamon buns for his mother to serve along with their breakfasts).

Carter replied to his mother, "Mother, I can fix my own food. I know how to cook eggs and I can make sandwiches out of lunchmeat and cheese. For dinner I can have hot dogs and beans. Also, why can't I just have TV dinners to put in the oven?"

"What kind of mother would I be if I let my son shift for himself for his food?"

"Mother, I'm 16, I'm not a baby."

"Stop and listen to me, Carter, this is not a negotiation. There will be plenty in the refrigerator for you to snack on, Catherine will see to, that but you will have your dinners at her house every day that you spend in Philadelphia."

Carter realized that she was warning him that she could easily change back to his being ordered to go to Cape May for the entire summer.

His mother rose from the chair by the window and said, "Dinner in 30 minutes." She left the living room. Carter remained sitting in the chair opposite the one his mother had vacated. His mind drifted back to thoughts of Ann and the sex. He admitted those thoughts were making him wish she was still coming to his family's house to work. Remembering how he had scoffed at the idea of his missing their intimacy, he experienced a tinge of regret.

He decided that he had time before dinner to meet Madam Palm upstairs in his bedroom. The relief was temporary. He became angry with himself, feeling helpless was not his style; he always wanted to be in control. Being needy was out of character for him. When other guys at school in the gym talked about sex and whacking off, he always felt superior because he knew that most of the ones who boasted about having sex and being good at it through experience were exaggerating with a few exceptions.

Now it was apparent that being accustomed to it and suddenly being deprived was not fun. He hadn't been above masturbation, but it had seemed more satisfying because he could fantasize about a past meeting or about a near future one. He was about to start all over again when he heard his mother calling him to dinner.

When he came into the dining room (On Sundays dinner was always served in the dining room), his step-father was already seated at the table.

"Hey, buddy, why does your mother have to call you so many times before you answer?"

Carter replied, "I didn't hear her, my door was closed." Bob raised his eyebrows with a perplexed expression.

"Why do kids today need so much privacy? In my day, our bedroom doors were always open." For once Carter had no reply, he was suddenly embarrassed as if Bob would know what he was doing. When he sheepishly raised his eyes to Bob's face, he thought he saw a light go on and then Bob looked embarrassed, too.

Dinner progressed mostly in silence, except for comments made by his mother about neighborhood chatter and news headlines, most of which Bob answered with uh-huhs and "Is that so?" Bob did not believe in trading neighborhood gossip. In fact, he spoke to everyone he encountered with a friendly greeting, but it was not his style to welcome coffee clatches or conversations over the back fence. In fact, in their neighborhood, most of the adults seemed to feel the same. The Coopers were an older couple next door. Mrs. Cooper was an official in the Elks Assoc. and her husband a Commander at the lodge. She was a very proper lady and he was a slim elegant gentleman. On the other side were The Allens. Mrs. Allen was a wonderful lady who was very fond of Carter. She was very active in her church, and when Carter was younger, she had made him the groom in the Thom Thumb Weddings she presented at her church every spring. You could say that Carter was married many times. Mr. Allen was another tall, dignified gentleman who looked 20 years younger than he probably was. Most of the other neighbors were similar and most still had businesses, such as Smiths Roofing, Martin's Beauty Products, Morgans' Moving Co., Drummond's Candies, Nutley's Chicken Stores, Fillingaine's Groceries, and others, such as Mr. Powell the Banker, Reverend Anders, Councilman Sharp, Dr. Winston, and Mother McCullough of Crusaders for Christ.

In short most of the neighbors either had their own businesses or worked on jobs that afforded them what was considered a middle-class life in the "colored" world. The opposite side of the very wide street still had a smattering of White families that were gradually moving out. Basically, everyone owned the homes they occupied, including Carter's mother Lila. She had bought their house with help after leaving Carter's father Joseph.

After dinner, Lila and Bob sat in the living room listening to music, as was their Sunday custom. Bob was a staunch Jazz fan. In particular he loved Fats Waller. He had tried to encourage Carter to become a drummer. He bought Carter a set of drums one Christmas. Carter preferred banging on the upright piano in the living room, but when his mother and grandmother wanted him to take lessons, he begged off for the ridiculous reason that he thought that playing the piano was sissy.

This time Carter did not join them in the living room to listen to music. He went back up to his room and tried to read his latest Mickey Spillane novel. Spillane was his favorite mystery writer during that period of his life. Carter loved all kinds of books, he was reading 12$^{th}$ grade level books when he was in 7$^{th}$ grade. He is unable to concentrate on his book; his mind returns again and again to sex. Finally, he gives in. He promises himself this will not become a habit.

After the hand action, he thinks maybe the pillow might be better next time. He catches himself, he must be some kind of oversexed freak that has been unleashed by these immoral women. He is remembering the story of the Egyptian Boy King who was supposedly sexually assaulted by nurses, priests who were eunuchs, and palace guards from childhood until the time of his death at 17. Carter fell into a troubled sleep

Monday morning arrived. Carter is awake at 6:00 AM. The sun is streaming in through the window. He knows if he gets up and starts moving around, his mother is going to wonder if he is okay. He doesn't normally appear before 8:30 or so. He doesn't want to seem anxious to get to the stables. But why not? Lila knows how he feels about the stables and the horses.

When he comes into the kitchen, his mother is surprised to see him so early, but she attributes it to his desire to get to the stables early in order to put in a full day there. She wants him to eat a full breakfast, but Carter insists on a bowl of Raisin Bran. Somehow his system can tolerate a small amount of milk in a bowl of cereal in spite of his lactose intolerance. If he overdid the amount of milk, he would suffer from chest and stomach pain.

Once finished with breakfast, he went out and got his bike and pedaled off to the stables. He had told Steve he would see him there instead of stopping at Steve's house as usual. Steve was becoming such a party animal that he was always too tired to get started early. Upon his arrival, most of the other guys and girls were there. During the week, there were not as many Stable Hands. There were two girls, Patsy and Julie, who came out, plus a couple other guys who helped Tommy's assistant.

Julie, it was well known would give it up for a smile, but Patsy was a no-no, she almost didn't seem to like guys very much, except as buddies that she discussed baseball with. Carter went into the Tack Shed where he found Tommy talking to Julie, who was paying rapt attention to every word Tommy uttered. Carter was a little disappointed because he realized that he had rushed to get there early so that he and Tommy could talk more.

Tommy said, "Hey, buddy you're early, you trying to impress somebody?" For some reason, that made Carter defensive.

He replied, "There's no one here that I want to impress." He caught Tommy's expression, he looked like he had been wounded and Carter was immediately sorry he had answered the way he had. After all, he had rushed there so that he could make sure that he and Tommy were alright. Julie was so intent on vamping Tommy that she didn't even speak to Carter. He was cut by her non-response and he reacted with another caustic statement.

"Ok, Julie, better watch out. Dottie will kick your butt."

Julie retaliated with, "What's wrong, are you jealous?"

Carter was embarrassed and he meekly answered, "I'm just kidding cause you never smile at me."

She answered "I like a real man and you're just a boy."

Tommy decided to put an end to this repartee, "Ok, Julie, you can go help Dottie with the phone calls." Julie turned and glared at Carter as she flounced out of the shed.

Carter stood there awkwardly, not knowing whether to leave or stay.

Tommy spoke, "So, Carter, how are you doing?"

"Fine," said Carter. "Hey, Tommy, we're still okay, right?"

"Sure, you turkey, you're too serious, we're ok."

Carter went on, "I didn't mean what I said about not trying to impress anybody. I wasn't trying to cut you."

Tommy replied, "I know, buddy, don't worry about it. By the way, I don't need to go back to Julie for seconds. That was a one-time thing."

"Tommy, I didn't know anything about that. It's none of my business, I don't pay any attention to the stories that go around out here."

"Listen, Carter, you told me your secrets. That means you trust me, so I trust you. You know some of these women are easy and they are throwing it around. That goes for some of the ones that come out here to go riding, too."

Carter says, "What about Dottie?"

"She may have an idea, but I don't throw it in her face. I keep her happy, so I don't think she wants to know."

Carter turns to go out of the shed, saying, "I think I'll go and rub down Jennie."

Tommy says, "Come here, Carter." Carter had felt relaxed, but now he becomes tense. He approaches Tommy and Tommy grabs him in a hug. He is pressed hard against Tommy's body. At first, he is straining to pull away, but weakening, he stops resisting. Tommy takes his hand and presses it against his crotch. At this time, they hear Steve's voice right outside of the Tack Room and they jump apart.

Carter is literally gasping for breath.

Steve enters saying, "What are you guys doing?"

Carter chokes on his attempted reply, but Tommy answers sounding very calm, "We're minding our own fucking business." Steve is taken aback and gets a shocked expression on his face.

Carter finally finds his voice and says, "Come on and help me get Walking Jennie out of the corral, so I can give her a rub down."

Steve and Carter go out and over to the big corral where most of the horses have been let out to run and graze. Strangely, they don't see Jennie out there. They then check the other corral where the private owned horses are. There among all of the special horses is Walking Jennie, who upon sighting Carter, trots over to the fence. Carter is thrilled that she recognizes him.

He shouts, "She knows me."

Steve sneers, "Of course she does. Because of you, she gets plenty of special treatment by everybody else and you by order of the boss."

Carter glances at Steve and sees that sneer still on his face. He feels that Steve probably knows that he and Tommy are —- But wait, it's not him, Tommy is the one who is coming on to him.

Steve is his best friend and he doesn't want to lose his friendship, so he says, "What's wrong with you?"

Steve answers, "I'm pissed. I wanted to drive us to Anita Chaney's party in the Cadillac, but Manny (his step-father) says Benny, Manny's son, can drive us because he's older and he's been driving longer."

Carter was relieved, not because of the car situation but because he thought Steve knew what was happening with Tommy. Steve didn't call his step-father Dad or Father, he called him Manny. He was always upset with Manny because he felt that Manny was beneath him and his mother's family, which was composed of lawyers and doctors and was very influential back in Jacksonville, Florida.

This time he was super angry because he felt that Manny was trying to get his son accepted by the kids of the "nice class of colored folks" in Philadelphia and Bennie was not well spoken and didn't know much about the "Ivy

League Look" that was in fashion with the guys in most of the groups attending the affairs that Steve preferred. In short, he was a mechanic and was not college material. There was also an unspoken rivalry between Steve and Bennie.

As for Carter and how he felt about Bennie driving the car that would take them to a party, he could care less. He didn't want to go anyway.

So, Steve griped about that for a while, and Carter didn't try to change Steve's attitude because he knew that would never happen. Steve was pretty nice and outgoing to most people no matter their style, but as far as Bennie was concerned, he was adamant with his criticism.

Steve had been sitting on a bale of hay talking to Carter while Carter was brushing and grooming Walking Jennie. Julie came out of the office and sat next to Steve. She whispered into Steve's ear and they got up and wandered off in the direction of the woods that bordered the stable grounds. Carter thought to himself, Steve is going to get in trouble fooling around with that sex maniac.

It turns out that Carter's thinking is on target. A car drives up to the parking area and Carter recognizes that it is Sam, one of the stable owners. Sam goes directly into the tack room and Carter can hear him shouting at Tommy. Tommy comes out of the shed and heads off toward the woods where Steve and Julie headed earlier.

Shortly, Tommy comes back followed by Steve and Julie. Sam goes into the office where Dottie is answering the phone and taking reservations. Dottie and Sam come back out to where Tommy has told Julie and Steve to wait. Sam reads the riot act to everyone. It turns out that Dottie has complained to Sam about the girls, Julie in particular. Sam tells Julie she is not welcome at Creek Stables anymore. Although Julie usually has something to say to anyone who gives her flak, she doesn't have anything to say this time. Her face turns red and she runs off to find her friend Patsy.

Sam proceeds to read Steve the riot act and he threatens to tell Steve's father.

Steve answers, "Ok, I won't come here again."

Sam says, "I'm not telling you that you can't come here. I'm telling you that you can't come out here and get some easy lay pregnant. Your father would blame me for letting you kids use this place for a make out spot."

Steve is not repentant, he says, "Carter, you can stay, but I'm leaving."

Carter replies, "I want to take care of Jennie." Steve gets on his bike and pedals off.

Sam turns to Dottie, "Hey, Dot, I'm glad you let me know about this. I can't have parents coming out here accusing me of allowing kids to come here to get their jollies." Dottie gives Tommy a look and returns to the office.

Sam turns to Tommy again with, "Tommy, I don't want to hear that you let this kind of thing go on again." Carter knows that this is embarrassing for Tommy, so he pretends to concentrate on brushing Walking Jennie.

A few of the other helpers are standing around and Sam orders, "Ok, everybody, back to what you were doing." The others disperse and Tommy goes back to his desk in the tack shed. Sam goes into the office and chats with Dottie.

Carter leads Jennie over to the exercising ring and leaps on her bare back, trotting her around the ring. Sam comes out, and waving to Carter, gets into his car and drives off. As soon as the car disappears down the hill, Carter decides that Jennie has enough exercise and he leads her over to the Private Horse Corral, removes her bridle, and releases her. He goes into the tack shed where Tommy is sitting at his desk, going over feed charts. Carter stands there quietly waiting for Tommy to say something.

Finally, Tommy speaks, "Did you come in to make fun of me or to say I told you so?"

"No answers," Carter, "I just wanted to say it wasn't your fault."

Tommy replies, "I probably should have told Julie not to come out here to screw anybody she could get her hands on."

"The other thing is maybe Dottie is more aware than you thought," says Carter.

Tommy looks up at him and says, "She doesn't know about us; she just gets jealous of these young girls."

Carter answers, "What do you mean us? There is no us."

Tommy looks at Carter, "You came in here to cheer me up because you care about me."

"Yeah, I care about you as a friend, that's all."

"Ok, Carter, you don't give a shit about me."

Carter continued standing there in front of Tommy's desk. Tommy pretends to concentrate on the feed supply charts.

Finally, Tommy says, "What are you still here for? You don't care about me."

"I told you I do care about you but not the way you think."

"Me thinks you protest too much," replies Tommy.

"I'm not about to have Dottie coming after me for something I'm not guilty of."

"Okay, buddy, let's drop it."

"You still think I'm gay," says Carter.

"I think you are a normal kid who is maturing and who has needs. If there is someone who can fulfill those needs and you find that someone appealing, male or female, you don't have to be classified as abnormal."

"Tommy, why me, do I seem gay to you?"

"Maybe it's me, Carter, think of that. Why am I coming on to you?"

"I don't know why, maybe you think you can screw me or something, and that's not going to happen. That's an exit, not an entrance."

"Listen, Carter, when two people have sex, they do what comes natural." Suddenly, Carter is at a loss for words. He even feels weak and he sits down in the chair next to Tommy's desk. Tommy looks Carter in the eyes for a long moment. Carter is very disconcerted. Tommy takes his hand in his, but this time he rests his other hand on Carter's crotch. The response is immediate.

Carter already had the beginnings of an erection, but with the touch of Tommy's hand, it went full on. He tries to push Tommy's hand away, but Tommy keeps his hand there. Carter is finding it difficult to breathe normally.

He gasps, "Tommy, somebody is going to come in and catch us." Tommy rolled his chair closer and placed Carter's hand on his bulging crotch. Carter felt lost. He tried to stand to get away, but Tommy was stronger than he and he held him in the chair. Carter said, "Tommy, don't, somebody will find out." Tommy seemed to collect himself and he finally took his hand away.

He said, "We close up at 5:00 PM tonight, wait for me, I'll drive you home."

Carter replied, "It's only 4:30 and everybody knows I always ride my bike home."

"Don't sweat it," answered Tommy "We'll say you hurt your foot and I'm going to give you a lift."

Now Carter was anxious to comply with Tommy's directions. He told himself, if I'm going to get a blow job, I'll go along with the plan. He went out and sat on the bale of hay outside of the office. He even pretended to have a slight limp. Tommy came out, giving the other Stable Hands orders to drive all of the horses into their stalls. Carter was glad he had an excuse for not joining in the action because he couldn't seem to get his erection to subside completely. When Dottie came out and asked him if he wanted to wrap his foot, he told her he was afraid if he removed his shoe, he wouldn't be able to put it back on.

Tommy asked Dottie to lock up and went down the hill to his house to get his car. He drove up to where Carter was sitting and got out of the car and came around to help Carter into the passenger side. He then opened the trunk. Carter was sure his bike wouldn't fit into the trunk, but to his surprise, the bike went in easily. They drove off, and by this time, Carter couldn't understand why he couldn't stop shaking. He felt like such a kid and he was thinking to himself, I am a kid and he is an adult. He could get into a lot of trouble for fooling around with me.

Tommy didn't drive toward Carter's home; he turned in the direction of the airport. Carter didn't object, in fact, he was finding it hard to say anything. Tommy drove into one of the airport parking lots and all the way to the far end where most of the long-term cars were parked. He pulled into a space against a wall. Turning the car off, he pushed the seat back. They sat there in silence for a while. Suddenly, Tommy reached over and pulled Carter close to him. He hugged Carter tightly. Carter didn't resist this time, he was still anticipating the blow job. But Tommy started kissing him on the cheek and his neck, moving toward kissing him on the mouth.

Carter resisted, saying, "I'm not kissing any guy on the mouth." At this point, Tommy wasn't stopping; he not only kissed Carter on the mouth, he forced his tongue into Carter's mouth. At first, Carter was repulsed, but he began to respond almost as if he had no control over his actions. Tommy put his hands inside of Carter's shirt. He rubbed his chest and stomach, he unfastened Carter's jeans, and released his throbbing erection, which sprang free. He reached across Carter and dropped the seat all the way back and took Carter into his mouth. Carter erupted almost immediately.

Tommy reached onto the back seat, grabbed a towel, and spit into it. Carter sat up to start getting himself together, but Tommy wasn't ready to quit. He pulled Carter over and pressed his face into his crotch. Carter tried to keep his lips tightly closed, but Tommy forced his very large penis into Carter's mouth. Tommy didn't last long either, he was coming in gushes it seemed and Carter was choking and struggling to get him out of his mouth, but Tommy held him tight and he was forced to swallow.

When Tommy finally loosened his grip, Carter pulled away sputtering and wiping his mouth.

He yelled at Tommy, "I'm not your cocksucker, you made me swallow your juice and you spit mine out. I thought you brought me out here to blow me and you end up stuffing your dick in my mouth." Tommy had lain back in his seat. He didn't seem upset at all by Carter's tirade.

He answered calmly, "I've never blown any guy before. I've gone down on girls lots of times, clean ones that is, but I never even had complete sex with a guy before. Yeah, when I was a teenager, a couple of my buddies and me would have jerk off sessions and there was one guy who wanted to suck my cock, but I wouldn't let him. I just wasn't into that, but I got carried away with you. I didn't want you to go unsatisfied and it was almost natural for me to get my thing, too. You shot off so fast, I wasn't ready for all of that, I wouldn't do any of this for anybody else. I don't know why I started wanting you so bad. You've got that smooth brown skin. You feel smoother than any woman I ever had." Carter has been taking this all in but refuses to admit it.

He simply says, "I want to go home."

Tommy sits up and replies, "Ok, I'll take you home." He starts up the car and drives to the parking lot exit.

Carter is still struggling to get his clothes together. They drive in silence, but Carter's mind is racing; he has to admit to himself that after what just happened, he should be more upset. Instead he is thinking about what Tommy said and it makes him feel strangely proud because of the comment about his brown skin and its texture. He keeps stealing glances at Tommy, who is concentrating on his driving. Tommy is really a good-looking guy. The girls that come out to ride at the stables flirt with him all the time and he seems to treat them like he could take them or leave them. He does respect Dottie, however.

When they arrive at Carter's house, Carter opens the door on his side and gets out of the car. Tommy jumps out, opens the trunk, and starts to get Carter's bike, but Carter pushes him aside and struggles to get the bike out himself.

Tommy says, "Carter, don't be like that. We had a mutual experience and we both enjoyed it, whether you admit it or not." Carter simply wheels his bike around to the back of the house without another word. Tommy is left standing next to his car.

Carter locks his bike to the tree in the backyard and enters the house through the back door as usual, but this time he proceeds through the kitchen and up the back stairs to the second floor. He proceeds up the hallway to the front bedroom, which used to belong to his sister but is now the extra room. He can see the street from the front windows. He doesn't see Tommy out front, so he knows that Tommy has left. Carter goes back down the hall to his bedroom and removes all of his clothing. Tonight, he doesn't feel that he needs to bathe. After all, he wasn't riding horses, and other than administering to Walking Jennie, he hadn't even been around horses that much. He wouldn't admit to himself that he wanted to preserve the aftermath of a sexual experience.

After putting on fresh clothing, he went downstairs. He looked into the living room, his mother was sitting there with only a dim light on next to her favorite Queen Anne Chair.

She spoke, "Carter, you're late. Why did you get out of a car?"

He replied without hesitation, "It was getting late, so Tommy, the manager, gave some of us kids a lift home."

"I don't like your being out in that area too late," Lila replied. "You are riding that bicycle through wooded areas and heavy traffic. I worry a lot about you."

"Mother, don't worry about me. I'm always very careful."

Lila next asks, "What's this Tommy like? Does he make sure you boys are careful around the horses?"

"Mother, Tommy and his lady Dottie watch out for us all the time."

"That's interesting because I spoke to Steve's mother today and she said Steve came home early and he wouldn't tell her why. The only thing he did say was he couldn't stand the stable manager and he wasn't going out there again."

Carter replied, "He'll get over it, he's angry because he doesn't want anyone to tell him what to do."

Lila looks dubious, "You and Steve are close friends. I'm surprised you didn't leave with him."

"Yes, Mother, Steve is my best friend, but I don't always have to agree with him."

"Yes, you are right, you don't have to dislike someone because he does. I have kept your dinner warm, so go sit at the table."

Carter asks, "Where is my Fawn? (his Boxer who would normally be following him everywhere)"

His mother answers, "I'm sorry, I put her in the basement when the new helper Maria came to clean. She's afraid of dogs."

"Then how is she going to work here?"

Lila answers, "She is a nice older woman and I like her, so we will make an exception and put Fawn downstairs or in the yard when she comes to clean." Carter started to protest but thought better of it. No need of putting his mother in a mood.

When Carter was finished, he got up and took his plate to the sink.

Lila said, "Don't worry, I'll clean up." She had been sitting across the table from Carter, watching him eat. He had tried to make conversation, asking what book she was reading.

She replied, "From Here to Eternity."

He said, "Wow, that's an old one."

"I know, I've read it before. I was just in the mood to reread it." Normally, he and Lila would discuss whatever book he or she was reading, but this time she only said, "Most of the characters in the story are only a year or two older than you. They are rushed into manhood as soldiers in a major war."

"Yeah, well, life is very different for guys who go into the service right after high school."

"Well, I hope and pray that you will not be drafted."

"The plan for me is to go on to college, right?"

"Of course, that is definite, even if I have to go to work."

"What do you mean, Mother, why would you have to go to work, and what would you know how to do?"

"Are you being fresh? I can become a saleslady in a dress shop. I know clothes and how to wear them."

"Yes, you know that pretty well, but you know Dad would never permit you to go to work, he's too proud."

"Bob doesn't have to give me permission to do anything. I can make my own decisions. Besides, there are reasons we may have to cut back."

"What reasons, Mother?"

"I don't want you to worry, but Bob is going to have to go into the hospital."

"What, but why?"

"They have discovered a tumor in his bladder."

"Oh, no, where is he now?" His mother started to cry.

"He went to work. You know nothing stops Bob from going to work."

"Oh, Mother, I'm so sorry. Don't cry, don't worry, if it's just a tumor, it can be removed. These days they can do anything." He wanted to comfort his mother, but hugging and holding were not customary in this household. It was even surprising that his mother was shedding tears in his presence. She was always a sweet, gentle person but showing affection and other personal feelings wasn't proper.

Carter knew his mother loved him dearly, but she just was not the gushy type. She stood up and went to the sink to wash Carter's plate and silverware. Carter went back up to his bedroom. With Fawn now released from the basement, following close at his heels, he sat in his chair by the window, rubbing Fawn's ears. He knew he should have been thinking about Bob's condition, but his mind drifted back to Tommy and what had happened between them earlier. Thinking about it made him become aroused all over again and he ended up pulling one of the pillows off of his bed and masturbating into a towel that he placed over it.

Afterwards, he thought to himself, I must be gay because all I can think about is Tommy and the sex. Maybe it's like he said, it's he who is gay and I'm just human." He took all of his clothes off and got into bed. He tossed and turned for a while and eventually fell into a sound sleep.

He awoke in the morning to a pleasant aroma of coffee wafting up from the kitchen. He suddenly remembered Bob's problem and decided he would jump up quickly, so that he could run into him at breakfast, but when he was dressed and entering the kitchen, he saw that Bob was not there. His mother sat alone at the table.

"Where's Dad?"

"He already went up to rest. He had to show Bill Marshall how to do his reports. Bill is going to fill in for him while he is out. He is pleased though because the company is going to pay him full salary for the whole period of time that he will be out."

Carter quips, "They should, he runs that place like a smooth machine."

"The company is grateful for his service. Since he is management, they are also picking up his hospital bills." Lila continues, "I don't know why I'm telling you all of this, but I have to tell someone in the family. Your aunt and your sister unfortunately do not wish Bob well."

"Mother, I'm 16, I'm almost a man. I need to face the facts when necessary."

His mother then says, "If you are going to those stables, I'm going to ask your cousin Henry to take you for your drivers' test. You need to be able to drive yourself, so that you don't need to wait for someone else to bring you home when it's late."

"What will I drive?"

"Your father called and said he bought a used car from a friend and he wants you to have it."

Carter had to control himself to keep from leaping for joy. He was going to have his own car at 16. Even Steve didn't have his own car.

His mother went on to say, "I told your father he should be planning to help send you to college instead of buying you a car. He says he is doing well now and he will pay your tuition and expenses. I shouldn't be telling you this because knowing your father and his dealings, everything could come crashing down next week. You know he doesn't believe in bank accounts." She seemed to catch herself at this point. She had always spoken to Carter like an adult but never to this extreme. Carter told his mother he was not going to the stables today. She replied, "Oh, so you've decided to side with your friend, Steve."

"Not really. I'm going over to his house to talk about next week and maybe the party this Friday." Lila smiled at hearing this. The mention of the party naturally sounded encouraging to her.

Carter decided to walk to Steve's house since he wasn't going to the stables and Steve's house wasn't very far away. When he arrived at Steve's, Miss Adele the housekeeper let him in. Steve was up in his bedroom as usual. His bedroom was twice the size of Carter's and Steve had been allowed to pick his own furniture and to even decide on the color scheme. Whenever Carter visited, he always thought to himself that Steve had excellent taste. There were nice paintings and posters on the walls. Steve's younger brother Randy's room was next to Steve's. It was just a typical young boy's room with the usual sports stars posters and such. Randy had already left for their father's place for the summer.

Steve was sitting on the floor polishing his shoes.

When Carter came in and sat on the bed, Steve said, "I thought you'd be out at the stables sucking up to your idol, Tommy."

"What do you mean sucking up?" answered Carter.

Steve's eyebrows shot up and he said, "That's just an expression, don't get up-tight."

"I know it's an expression, but I don't suck up to anybody. I thought I'd come over to see what you're up to."

Steve said, "I'm still steaming over that bastard, Tommy. He's playing like he never fucked any of those girls that hang around him like ants. He has screwed Julie at least three times right in the back room. She told me all about it. She even says he has a really big dick. He is also screwing a lot of those women that come out there to supposedly go horseback riding. I hate his guts; he should have stood up for me."

"Steve, you know the guy couldn't do anything but follow Sam's orders. You know Dottie called Sam because she was jealous. What was he supposed to do? He couldn't call her a liar and mess up their relationship."

"Carter, why are you defending that piece of shit? I thought you were my friend."

"I am your friend, that's why I'm here."

Steve calmed down, but in dropping the subject, he said, "You'd better watch it with that guy. I think he's a big freak." Carter started to say more, but he thought he was in dangerous territory. They changed over to Carter's news about a car. Steve was genuinely pleased. He said, "That's great, it means we won't have to put up with my classy step-brother in order to get the Cadillac."

"We won't have it by Friday, I have to pass my drivers' test first."

"Call your father and tell him I already have my license, I can drive the car until you get yours."

"I guess I could do that, but I don't really care about that party."

"Listen, Carter, I promised Anita I would get you there."

"That's the main reason I don't want to go. Anita Chaney is a fox and her father is a professor at Lincoln University. I don't want to be her Jester, she's always laughing at me and saying, 'Oh, Carter, you're so funny.'"

"She's not laughing at you, she's laughing with you. Girls love guys with a sense of humor. The other thing is you treat all of the girls at school and at the Jockey Club with respect, they like that. The last thing is, have you looked in the mirror lately? You're a good-looking guy. You outclass a lot of those phony guys that are at all of those parties."

Carter laughed at this and asked, "Steve, are you coming on to me?"

Steve replied, "You're not my type, but you are my buddy and I tell you the truth. I know I'm fine, but you are ok, too." They both laughed at Steve's remark.

They spent the rest of the day playing cards and joking. Steve's neighbor James came up to the bedroom after Miss Adele let him and called upstairs to say he was coming up. James did not like Carter. He constantly made sarcastic remarks in Carter's direction. Carter simply considered him strange and mostly ignored him. He had horned in on Steve and Carter's deal at the stables and he led the criticism of Carter and Tommy's friendship.

He would find every opportunity to come into the tack room when Carter was there talking to Tommy until Tommy finally told him, "If you are going to keep coming out here for tips from customers and free rides, you will have to make yourself useful."

This really infuriated James because Tommy never seemed to tell Carter to get busy. In fact, he wasn't hard on Steve either, and James felt that was due to Steve being Carter's friend. Actually, that was probably because of Steve's father's clout with Sam the co-owner of the stables.

When he came into the bedroom that day, he glared at Carter, saying, "Man, don't you ever stay at home?"

Carter calmly replied, "Since I'm not in your house, it's none of your business."

Steve quickly interrupted what could have become nasty back and forth insults by saying, "James, I thought you had a part-time job, what brings you over?" James mumbled something about the drug store where he worked being closed by a power failure. Carter always wondered about Steve being friendly with James. James was always frowning and trying to look tough. He knew that James was jealous of him because he got along so well with Tommy and with his best friend Steve.

James was older than the two boys and his mother worked for different families in the area. That was not a problem for Carter; they had other school-mates and acquaintances whose parents worked for private families. However, Steve was a little more selective. He did not want to spend much time with kids who weren't part of the "in crowd" and were not invited to parties and social functions.

James was never invited; the story was he had gotten some girl pregnant and the girl's father was going to do him in if he came around again. The other thing was at this point, most of the guys in their age group were into "the ivy look" and "Quo Vadis" haircuts. This was not James' look. He wore dungarees all the time and that wasn't in during that time, except of course out at the stables. Carter and Steve usually wore dungarees out there, but when they rode out of The Bala Cynwyd Stables with the Jockey Club, they wore jodhpurs and English Riding Boots.

Steve's mother had come home from the office where she managed accounts and other details for Steve's step-father's business. She called upstairs for Steve and Carter to come down for something to eat. James told Steve he would come back later when "you've gotten rid of your buddy" as he put it. Steve's mother had fixed fried chicken and potato salad. Nobody could out do her on these dishes. Carter never said no when he was invited to stay for dinner when it was chicken and potato salad. Steve's mother had called Carter's mother to say he would be having dinner with Steve.

Steve's mother didn't join them at the table. She would wait for her husband, Bennie, to get home. The boys had freedom to discuss any topics they chose at the table. Carter asked Steve what he and James had in common.

Steve answered, "Oh, he just likes to hang around here when he's not at his father's house in Jersey."

"Well, it's pretty obvious that he doesn't like me and I don't know why. I've never done anything to him."

"Don't worry about it, he isn't going to be running around with us. He doesn't count, he's just amusing to me, that's all."

"He acts like he can tell me to get out of your house. Even out at the stables, he's on my case. When I'm talking to Tommy, he's hovering around," says Carter.

Steve replies, "Speaking of Tommy Turkey, he treats me like I'm in the way when you two are talking."

"Are you kidding? Tommy never yells at you or gives you orders like he does the other guys."

"No because he can't give us orders because he's not paying us, but he was glad to have an excuse to jump on me the other day. I don't like him."

"You don't have to worry about him when you come out, just do your thing."

"Hey, I'm not going out there again, I don't need any of them. You shouldn't go out there either; that guy is lame. He'll turn on you, too, if you mess with one of his slutty women."

"Oh, please, he knows I don't want one of those hungry hoes."

"Oh, yeah, that might change now that you don't have your servant girl anymore." Carter was embarrassed by this last remark. He hadn't thought of Annie since Tommy had moved into his sexual fantasy land.

They finished eating, and after a little more conversation, Carter decided to head home. Steve had mentioned that his mother wanted him to spend his high school senior year in Florida. Steve's family had a lot of influence in Jacksonville, Florida and could help him qualify as a shoo in at Fisk University in Tennessee. Carter walked off toward home. He almost bumped into James, who was on his way back into Steve's house. James just glared at him and brushed by without a word. Carter was amused; he made a note to totally ignore James the next time.

When Carter arrived home, his mother was in the kitchen.

He went into the kitchen and his mother said jokingly, "So, you don't want any of my cooking?"

Carter answered, "Mrs. Caster said she called you and she insisted I have dinner with Steve."

"I don't mind, you know that. I'm glad you and Steve are not having a dispute over those stables. You'll probably snack later. Your dad will be down in a few minutes. I told him you know about the operation."

Carter said, "Should I sit and talk to him when he comes down to eat?"

"No, wait a while; he will probably talk to you before Monday."

"What about Cape May?" Carter asked.

"He wants us to go down on Wednesday. He believes he will be fine and recuperating by then."

Carter went up to his bedroom. Fawn was on his bed asleep, and when he came in, she leaped on him, almost knocking him down. It was nice to have an animal that just adored him and whom he adored in return. His mother's Siamese cat Moody (Samooda) was not interested in showing affection for anyone but his mother. The cat didn't mind being around him, but she could take him or leave him. However, Moody hated Bob. She would hiss at him and leave the area when Bob came into the room where she might be resting. Luckily, she had been declawed when she was a kitten.

He sat in the chair and Fawn was at his feet. He was just about to turn on his radio to listen to music when he heard the phone ringing. His mother called to him from downstairs to say that the Stable Manager Tommy was on the phone for him. He went into the hallway to pick up the phone.

"Hello."

"Hey, Carter, what happened to you today, are you staying away because of what happened?" Carter called down to his mother who hadn't hung up.

"Mother, I have it." At this his mother hung up the phone. "Hey, Tommy. I don't talk on the phone much."

"Ok, I'm sorry to call you at your house, but I was afraid you were upset."

"I'm thinking about not coming out there again," replied Carter.

"Carter, please, can't we talk about it?"

"I don't want to talk about it anymore. We talked enough and it will only get me into more trouble with you."

"What kind of trouble?"

"You know what I mean, more trouble with you."

"Carter, listen, Dottie left me. We had a big fight over her calling Sam. I'm all alone."

"So, what am I supposed to do about that? I can't help you."

"I know that; I just wanted you to know."

"Tommy, I can't stay on the phone."

"Okay, but please say you'll come out tomorrow." Carter was silent. Tommy said, "If you don't come out, I'm going to quit the stables and leave town. You won't see me again."

"What, are you crazy? What am I supposed to say, please don't go?"

"Okay, Carter, I told you I'm at your mercy, you have all of the control. It's up to you." At this Tommy hung up. Carter was perplexed. He stood there in the hallway for another minute holding the now silent phone.

Suddenly, he realized his mother was coming up the back stairs. He pretended to just be finishing the call.

"Okay, I'll come out to help tomorrow." He hung up the receiver. Lila followed him back into his room.

She asked "What did he mean by 'After what happened?'"

"Oh, he was talking about the dispute with Steve."

She stood there for a moment and then asked, "Since when do they call you from the stables to ask you why you didn't come out there? You don't work there, you go when you want to and I thought it was mostly because of the horse you care so much for."

"It is because I love Walking Jennie but also because I just like being around horses and I like to ride, water, and feed them."

"Well, I'm glad you are an animal lover. It promotes respect and compassion for living things, even for people, but you know Bob wants you to a have relaxing summer so that when you return to school in the fall, you will be ready to concentrate on your studies. This is your senior year, it's most important to get good grades."

"Mother, going out to the stables is relaxing for me because I enjoy it."

"Alright, but remember, if it's going to mean you're coming home after dark, we will have to rethink this. Also, if I'm not going to be here to check the time you get home, I will have to make sure that someone is checking on you."

"Mother, I thought we always had trust between us."

"We still do, Carter, but what kind of mother would I be if I allowed you to be completely on your own at 16? Besides, it's not you I don't trust, it's the others."

"Okay, Mother. I will make sure I get home before dark."

His mother returns to the first floor and Carter turns on his radio and lies across his bed. His favorite station at the time is WHAT.

Jocko the Disc Jockey is reciting his well-known intro, "E Tiddly OP, this is The Jock" and announcing the latest record by The Platters. Thinking about the phone call and his response, he drifts off to sleep. He awakens in the middle of the night. The radio is still playing softly. Carter rises from the bed, removes his clothing, and turns off the radio. Returning to bed, he pulls the sheet over him and falls asleep again.

In the morning, the sun is streaming in the windows. He gets up and goes into the hall bathroom where he decides to get into the bathtub to soak for a while. It's Wednesday and he would normally call Steve on the hall phone to make sure he was going to the Stables, but since Steve has said he won't be going out there again, he doesn't call him. After getting dressed, he goes down to the kitchen where his mother is fixing breakfast. When his breakfast is finished, he takes Fawn out for her morning walk. As usual Fawn is frisky and happy to be out walking with Carter. He has been so busy lately that he hasn't been spending much time with his beloved dog.

When he comes back into the house, Bob has arrived home from work and is having his breakfast before going up to sleep.

Bob says, "Well, hello, stranger, where have you been keeping yourself?"

"Hi, Dad, I've been out taking care of my horse, Walking Jennie," said Carter with a smile. "She's not yours yet, and I'm still thinking about it," replied Bob.

"I know, Dad, I'm just kidding. I know especially now that things have changed."

"What do you mean especially now?"

"Well, Dad, I know about the operation."

"Listen, I don't want you worrying about that. It's going to be very safe and simple. I'm going through a procedure they call freezing the tumor. It will just go away and that will be that."

"Dad, that doesn't sound right. If they don't remove it, it might get worse."

"Look, I don't want you worrying about such things. Your mother shouldn't have told you."

At this his mother turned from the sink where she was rinsing dishes and said, "I want my son to face reality. In my family, boys are taught to be men and to be strong."

"Okay, but first, let him enjoy being a boy; he will have to be a man for much longer than he will be a boy. I know your father and your brother are big important men in their town, but let him have a carefree youth first."

"Yes, but I want him to know that he needs to appreciate all that you do for him and even how much his father does for him, too."

"Okay, I'm not going to get on that subject; his father is another story. I'm his father," and Bob laughs.

Lila gives Bob a stern look and says, "That's why we love you." Bob rises from the table and reaches for Lila. She draws away, saying, "My son is here." Bob sits down again.

Carter breaks the silence by saying, "Speaking of Walking Jennie, I promised I'd be out there today."

Lila speaks then, "Make sure you're back home by 6:00 o'clock."

"Okay, Mother, I'll be back by 6:00."

Carter gets his bike and pedals off to the stables. Arriving there he locks his bike to a fence where other Stable Hands who are already at work mucking out the stalls in the big horse barn have placed theirs. He sees Walking Jennie standing at the fence of the smaller corral. She has seen Carter and is waiting for him to come over to pat her on the neck and kiss her on the nose as is his habit when he arrives and sees her. As he is greeting Jennie, Troy, Tommy's assistant, comes over and tells him that Tommy wants to see him.

Carter reluctantly goes into the tack room and Troy shouts, "He's in the office." So, Carter walks over to the office.

As he walks in, he remembers that Tommy mentioned that Dottie had left him and the stables. He thought, Oh, shit, now what? Tommy was at the desk on the phone. He motioned for Carter to sit in the chair next to the desk. When Tommy was off of the phone, he looked at Carter with that intense stare that he lately affected when he looked at Carter. As usual Carter became un-comfortable.

"Tommy, cut it out."

"Cut what out?"

"You know what you're doing." Tommy got out of his chair and went to lock the office door. Carter jumped, saying, "Don't lock that door. I'm not going to mess around with you again." Tommy left the door unlocked and sat back down again.

Tommy said, "Okay then, let's talk business."

"What business?"

"Well, you know Dottie's gone, so I wanted to ask you to take over the office. You can answer the phone, take reservations, and schedule the horses I can do the rest. I just come out here because I like riding, and most of all, I like horses."

"Carter, I don't understand why you always try to say things to hurt me. I'm asking you to help me by working in the office for the summer or at least until I find someone else."

"Oh, you mean until you find some hot chick to fuck whenever you want or maybe now some good-looking guy and then you can throw me out like you probably did Dottie?"

"Hey, Carter, first of all, I begged Dottie to stay and she refused. Second, I didn't lie when I told you I never had another guy and I don't want to. It happened with you and I want it to happen again, I admit it."

"Please, now I guess we're in love?" said Carter.

Tommy replied, "Are you?"

"Fuck you!" said Carter. At this Tommy stood up and Carter thought, This is it, he's going to beat my ass. But Tommy stood over him and grabbed his shoulders.

"What's wrong with you? I've never heard you use this kind of language before."

"That's because you don't really know me. I'm not nice, I can be a real nasty guy."

"Carter, cut it out, this is not you talking. You're scared to admit you liked it, and just like me, you want more or you wouldn't be here. You don't want me? Tell me you don't want me." Carter couldn't look at Tommy, he diverted his eyes off to the side.

"Okay, just take your hands off of me. Suppose I tell on you?"

"Tell who?"

"My parents or Jack and Sam."

"If you want to tell on me, do it."

"You know what, Tommy, you're crazy. I'm only 16 and I just wanted my dick sucked; you think I'm gay and I'm going to be your fag. Well, you've got another thing coming."

"Okay, Carter, you want to destroy me, go out there and tell Troy I'm trying to have sex with you. He will love that because he wants my job. I don't know what happened. I started thinking about you and I know you're just a kid. I only tell myself you must have it in you because you went for it pretty easily. I like sex, in fact I love it, but all I ever thought about was women. Then you start coming around. I even thought you were coming on to me. Sometimes I would catch you looking at my crotch."

"You're out of your mind. I never looked at your crotch."

"Carter, I didn't imagine it, you did." Carter was thinking to himself, I did. The girls around here always said he had a big one and so did some of the guys. In fact, Steve was one of the guys. Carter said, "If I looked, it was just male curiosity."

"Well, it got so that I wanted you to look. I wanted to give it to you. Let's talk about the job you'll be helping me if you take over the phones." Carter calmed down; he knew if he said he would do it, he would be obligated to show up every day and he would have to lie to his parents. But he did like money, and truthfully, he liked the fact that Tommy really liked him.

He didn't know where this was all going. He was thinking about the episode with Tommy. He knew he still liked girls, but if he had a choice, which one would he choose first? Suddenly, he realized he had been thinking and Tommy was sitting there waiting, looking at him for an answer. He felt really warm with the thought that Tommy was implying that he cared a lot for him. Why did he enjoy torturing Tommy? Excitement was welling up inside. This guy that everyone thought was handsome and sexy could be his secret, what?

He answered Tommy's offer with, "I'll answer the phones when I'm here, but I'm not going to be a regular employee. I'll just come out during the week, not weekends. I promised my mother I would go down to Cape May on weekends to join the family."

"Okay, I'll show you how I want the reservations kept in the log book. I'll pay you by the hour in cash and you can decide whether to tell your parents or not."

"In other words, you're telling me to lie to my mother and father?"

"Carter, why do you always want me to be the bad guy? I just want you to be okay with it and to do the right thing."

"Oh, yeah, by having sex with a 25-year-old guy who wants to make me his jerk off."

"Are we going back to that?" said Tommy, "Let's drop it."

"I can tell you the next time it's going to be you doing me."

"Hey, Carter, I thought you said never again. You want me, just say it." Carter didn't answer. Tommy continued, "You brought it up again, so that tells me you want more."

"I didn't say that, I just meant if it happened again."

"So, you're saying it can happen again?"

Carter was confused with his own feelings. He decided it was best not to say anything; he was getting that shaky feeling again. In fact, he was actually having trouble keeping his legs from visibly trembling.

Tommy was aware of his discomfort and he said in a lowered voice, "Let's tell Troy to take over, so we can go out for coffee. I'll tell him I've got to get your mother's permission for you to work here officially." Carter knew what would happen if he left with Tommy, but he now knew he wanted it to happen. He was thinking I must be gay because I want to go with him.

Tommy went to the door and Troy was just sending two young girls off for their hour of riding. One of the girls, a 20-year-old pretty blonde saw Tommy come out of the office. She turned her horse around and called to Tommy to come and ride with them.

Tommy answered, "You know I can't go out this early. I have to make sure things are running well here."

She laughed and riding off said, "It's your loss."

Troy said, "See what happens when you screw these young girls? They get possessive."

Tommy replied, "Cool it, don't say that in front of the kid."

Troy answered, "Why not? He can get his head wet, too, with all these hot chicks around here begging for it."

Tommy said, "Carter is not ready to be screwing around with these girls. I gotta go with him now to ask his mom's permission to let him work in the office every day."

"What are you talking about? Carter is here almost every day anyway," said Troy.

"That's okay, he just wants his mother to know he's supposed to be here."

"Okay, I'll hang tight and answer the phone. The other guys can take care of the customers." Tommy turned to Carter, saying, "Okay, come on, Carter, we'll go down to get my car." Carter followed Tommy down to his house. "Come on in, Carter." Carter stood by the gate for a few seconds and then decided that he couldn't play games anymore. Tommy had him pegged; he wanted what was about to happen. When he stepped inside, Tommy reached behind him and closed the door.

Carter's breath was coming in gasps again. Tommy went into the living room.

He turned and said, "What do I have to do coax you all the way?" Carter followed him into the room and Tommy sat on the couch. Carter sat down a space away from Tommy. Tommy moved over and forcefully pulled Carter closer to him.

Carter said, "Hey, suppose Dottie comes back?"

"She's not coming back." Carter felt his control slipping and he let Tommy start putting his mouth against his neck. He knew he wanted Tommy to kiss him on the lips like the last time. When Tommy took his time about kissing, Carter took Tommy's face in his hands and kissed him first. Tommy responded, and again, Carter found out what a real French kiss was. Tommy took Carter's hand and put it inside his Levi's. This time Carter did not pull away. Tommy was not being cautious this time. He had Carter's T-shirt up in front and he was kissing Carter's chest and licking his neck. Carter realized that Tommy had not even touched his penis, but he had climaxed anyway and he was still very excited.

When Tommy did touch him there, he said, "We're going to have to dry your pants. Come on, we'll go up to the bedroom."

Carter briefly protested, "I don't want to be screwed."

Tommy said, "Stop worrying about details, just let everything happen naturally."

"There's nothing natural about that it hurts."

"How do you know?" Carter had promised himself he would never tell anyone about his cousin, "So, he said I've heard it hurts and that would make me a real homo." Tommy kissed him on the mouth again, Carter melted but said, "After you get what you want, you will toss me aside like you do all those girls you've had."

"It's different with you. I don't know why, but I just want to be with you. I know you're a young kid, and if anyone found out, I'd be in a lot of trouble, but I just want to be with you. I will never hurt you; if you say so, I will leave you alone until you come back and tell me you are ready." Carter felt completely overwhelmed. He didn't know what to say. Tommy stood up and pulled Carter to his feet. He led him to the second-floor bedroom. They sat down on the side of the bed. Tommy pushed Carter back and started first pulling Carter's T-shirt over his head. Next, he removed Carter's Desert Boots and socks. The Dungarees and under shorts came off last.

Tommy hurriedly took off his clothes and he was on top of Carter, kissing him and moving down his body. He ended at Carter's throbbing erection. This time he slowly massaged the head of Carter's penis with his tongue. Carter was in ecstasy, he was moaning and thrashing around on the bed. Tommy's excitement mounted, too; he physically lifted Carter's body up while taking his penis as far into his throat as possible without choking. When Carter felt he was going to explode, he wrapped his legs tightly around Tommy as he turned on his side. He held onto Tommy's head, and in spite of Tommy's superior strength, he was able to keep his penis in Tommy's mouth as he came in spurts. He continued to hold Tommy tight and Tommy had to swallow. He felt Tommy's resistance subside and he rolled over on his back.

He was surprised when Tommy seemed to follow his turns and was still keeping his penis in his mouth.

He was able to whisper, "You made me swallow yours, so I made you swallow mine." At this point, Tommy let his penis go and lay his head on Carter's stomach.

"You don't understand yet, Carter. You're too young to know what happens with passion."

Carter replied, "I'm not that young. I know you got carried away."

"Okay, Carter, put it that way." Carter felt that he had to show Tommy that he had feelings, so he started rubbing Tommy's chest and following the golden line of hair running down over Tommy's stomach. Tommy's already semi erection rose to stand as straight and as hard as steel. When Carter thought he would reciprocate by jerking Tommy off, Tommy pushed Carter back and was on top of him in a flash. He elevated Carter's legs and pinned them back with his arms, so that Carter's anus was exposed. Right away he had gotten the head of his penis into Carter's rectum. Carter tried to stop Tommy, but Tommy was much stronger than Carter and he had him totally under his power.

As Tommy tried to thrust deeper inside, Carter cried out, "It hurts, it hurts, take it out please, please."

Tommy seemed to come to his senses and he stopped applying pressure. He let his erection slip out and he released Carter's legs, so that he could straighten them out, but he remained on top of Carter, kissing him deeply on the mouth. He let his erection rest between Carter's legs, and when Carter could finally breathe, he told Tommy to let him up.

Tommy repeated his old promise, "I'll never hurt you, just hold me." With more kisses, Carter was again compliant and Tommy reached an explosive climax between Carter's legs.

Afterwards, they lay there for some time just holding on to each other. Carter's mind was racing. He knew that he could not tell anyone about Tommy and him, not even Steve, especially Steve because he felt protective of Tommy and he thought that Steve would drop their friendship like a hot potato. What kind of future did Tommy have? After all he only had a high school diploma. He thought about his classmates who mostly all plan to attend college. The party that he was invited to on Friday would be full of kids who would look down on Tommy. He asked himself if he cared because he was gay and he was in love with Tommy.

"Wait a minute, of course I'm gay. Here I am lying in bed with a naked man and we just had wild sex like in some of the books I've read. But I don't think I'm in love with Tommy, he's just another person to have sex with like Annie was. He sure is good-looking and strong. He cares about me. At least now he does. Maybe after this he will tell me to go fuck myself because I wouldn't let him screw me. I hope he still likes me because I always want to be his friend. He thinks I'm immature, but I really felt carried away when he made love to me. I have to admit, I liked it and I will do it again if he wants to."

With this thought, he started rubbing Tommy all over and again they had body to body sex.

Afterwards, they realized a lot of time had elapsed and they got up and put their clothes back on. Carter's jeans didn't show the stain, so he didn't feel that anyone would notice anything.

Carter and Tommy returned to the stable office. Troy was there looking stressed. He told Tommy that they had gotten busy with a lot of customers, both on the phone and in person.

Tommy replied, "I'll oversee Carter for today, but he'll be able to handle reservations by tomorrow." Carter sat down at the desk and Troy left the office. Tommy stood over Carter, showing him how to register the reservations in the record book and told him to answer the phone with the name of the stables and his name followed by, "How can I help you?" Tommy knew that Carter could handle it; in fact, Carter spoke so well that Tommy felt his voice and manner of speaking would add class to the place.

Tommy was thinking how much he cared for Carter and wasn't worried about categorizing his feelings as being gay, bisexual, or straight. He just knew he cared deeply for this young kid. After listening to Carter answer the phone a few times, he left the office and went to his desk in the tack room. At the end of the day, he told Carter he would drive him home. Carter answered he would rather ride his bike home. Tommy reminded him that he should actually speak to Carter's mother about him working at the stables. This made Carter nervous because he knew that his step-father Bob did not like the idea of him having a summer job.

When they arrived at his house, Tommy lifted Carter's bike out of his car's trunk and they wheeled it around to the backyard. When Carter started for the back door, his mother opened it, looking worried.

She said "What happened?"

Carter replied, "Nothing, Mother, Tommy just wanted to talk to you, so he brought me home." Lila answered "Alright," turned to Tommy and said, "I'm glad to meet you. Please come in." Carter saw that Tommy was acting very nervous and he wanted to try to put him at ease. He knew his mother would be kind as she was to everyone. Unlike Bob, he knew Bob would be very abrupt and was even rude to white people who came to the house.

Tommy followed Carter into the kitchen and Lila said, "Come into the living room and have a seat."

Tommy answered, "Oh, no, Mrs. Hawkins. I've been working around horses all day and I haven't had chance to clean up."

Carter joked, "Well, she won't make you take off your clothes in the back kitchen and shower before you come into the main part of the house like she does me." His mother gave him a look that silenced him immediately.

She said, "If you insist, Tommy. We can sit here at the kitchen table. Carter, give Tommy a glass, so that he can have some iced tea."

Tommy said, "Oh, no, I don't want to impose. I just want to ask your permission to let Carter come to the stables every day during the week so that he can answer the phones and take reservations for customers who want to hire horses. I plan to pay him by the hour."

Lila answered, "Oh, Tommy, I don't know about that. I can tell you his dad would definitely not like that. He wants Carter to enjoy his summer so that he will do well in his senior year at high school. You understand Carter is going to college and we want him to be accepted at a school that we all agree on." Tommy was shifting from one foot to the other and searching for a reply.

Carter spoke up, "But, Mother, I told you I enjoy being at the stables. It's my kind of relaxation and I like spending time with my friend Tommy."

She looked at Carter and said, "I'm sure that Tommy being much older than you enjoys an occasional conversation with you but would probably enjoy being with friends his own age and being with his wife."

At this point, Tommy speaks, "I don't have a wife. I had a girlfriend, but we had some problems. Carter is my young buddy. He's like a kid brother to me; he is very smart and mature for his age. I get a lot from our conversations, in fact I learn from him."

"Yes, I agree he is a smart young man and we are proud of him, but he might be a little too serious for his age. We want him to be more social and to spend more time with people his own age. However, I personally don't mind his wanting to work at the stables; in fact it will be good for him to develop a sense of responsibility. I think I can handle my husband, so I give you my permission. Just one request: take care of my son. He is so impetuous and this will give him something to occupy his mind. I am glad to meet you, Tommy. I can tell you like my son and that means I like you."

Tommy just beams, "I will look after him. He is like my own flesh and blood. My mom and dad were killed in a car accident when I was 17 and I don't have a brother or sister, so he has all of my affection."

"Well, I'm sorry to hear about your parents, but it's nice to hear how you feel about my son. Would you like to stay for dinner?"

"Oh, no, I'd better get back home and do some things around there."

Lila says "I'll fix you a plate, you can take it with you."

Tommy exclaimed, "Wow, no wonder Carter is so great; he has you for a mom." Carter's mother fixes a big plate of food for Tommy, and Carter is so pleased with his mother, but they can hear Bob moving around upstairs and he is glad Tommy is not staying for dinner.

Carter walks out with Tommy, helping him carry the take home dinner.

He says, "That turned out differently than I expected."

Tommy replied, "Your mother is beautiful and really nice. I should have known after knowing you she was like the elegant lady that you might see in a movie, it makes me care even more for you. I haven't met colored women like her before and most of the white women I've known, especially the main line types, are second to her."

Carter said, "First of all, I don't like that term 'colored,' and second, my mother is just like any other cultured lady who attended finishing schools no matter what color."

"Hey, wait a minute, you know me. I'm not talking about anything racial, give me a break. I don't mean to say anything that would make you think I'm prejudiced. I'm trying to make you care about me like I care about you. I was trying to say I've never been in the company of a lady with that much class. If anything, I feel like I'm not high class enough for you."

Carter is incensed, "Don't be crazy. I'm not into that kind of stuff. You must be thinking of Steve."

"Yeah, you got that right. I can tell he's a snob, but I'll bet he would like to suck my dick."

"What are you talking about? Steve isn't into that kind of mess."

"Oh, yeah, I used to catch him looking at my crotch, too; he is probably mad because I let him know it will never happen."

"Are you trying to turn me against my best friend?"

"No, but I don't want you to become more than just friends."

"Tommy, go home and get some rest, you're not thinking clearly. I know that I will never see Steve that way."

"You didn't see me that way and look what happened."

"You're different."

"How?"

"I don't know, go home. I'll see you tomorrow."

"Maybe someday you can tell me how and why." When Tommy says this, his eyes change to a dreamy look and Carter is affected by the loving gaze. He quickly turns and walks back toward his yard. Tommy gets inside his car and sits there for a long moment, thinking I'm falling for this kid, I must be crazy.

When Carter comes back inside, Bob has come down to have dinner before going off to work.

He says, "Carter, your mother tells me you brought the white guy from the stables here."

"Yes, he was here to ask permission for me to come to the stables every day."

"Why? You already go out there every day."

"Yes, Dad, but he wanted to make sure I had my parent's permission."

"Ok, that's good but don't make bringing whites into this house a habit."

Before Carter could reply, Lila said, "Bob, I don't want my son to be taught to make differences in anyone. He can have friends from any background if he thinks they are worthwhile."

Bob answered, "Well, that's up to you and Carter, but I have to work for them and with them, but I don't have to have them in my home."

"Bob. you are forgetting this was my home first and my son can have any of his friends over."

Carter realized that this could be the beginning of a rare dispute between his parents, so he says, "First of all, Dad, he won't be coming here. He is the boss at the stables and he is 25-years-old. He is not my age, so he won't be coming here often." This put an end to the discussion, but the thoughts lingered in Carter's mind. He got that protective feeling for Tommy again and he was secretly angry at Bob for his small-minded attitude. He knew that Bob was full of prejudices. Bob also didn't like dark skinned colored people and often made disparaging remarks about them. His mother was constantly correcting Bob's remarks about other people he looked down upon. Lila obviously was not color conscious; Carter's father would be described as very dark and handsome. In fact, that was an issue with Lila's father and brother when Lila married Joseph. It seemed to Carter that a lot of the older people in his family were prejudiced.

Bob, his step-father, and even his grandmother were constantly reminding him that he should be careful who he married in the future because he just made it as far as complexion and marrying too dark would ruin his children.

His grandmother's favorite saying was, "The blacker the berry, the sweeter the juice, but nobody wants sugar diabetes."

Bob would say, "You just made it be careful go lighter." Luckily, none of this rubbed off on Carter probably because of his mother and also his sister Catherine's influence.

Carter sat at the table quietly eating his dinner, which happened to be one of his favorites, steak with onion gravy, mashed potatoes, and green peas. When he was finished, he went up to his bedroom. His mind strayed again to the afternoon with Tommy. He thought about how Tommy had tried to get him to say that he liked him. He knew he was not ready for deep feelings, but he did want to please Tommy. He soon drifted off to sleep with his radio playing music in the background.

When Carter woke again, his dog Fawn was in his bed, and even though his mother would scold him for allowing Fawn to climb on his bed, he rolled over and put his arms around her and fell back into a deep sleep, imagining that his arms were enfolding a person.

Thursday morning, he was up and bathed early. His mother was in the kitchen when he went down. He ate a hearty breakfast and left for his new job at the stables. When he arrived, Sam the owner was in the office. He asked Carter if he would enjoy his new assignment. Of course, Carter was very enthusiastic about answering the phone and taking reservations. Sam told Carter to call him directly if he changed his mind about the job. He wasn't undercutting Tommy and Troy, but he knew a young kid might get bored with a regular job.

When Tommy came into the office, Sam told him to come into the back to go over the books with him to get ready for the Accountant who comes once a month. With Tommy occupied all day with Sam, Carter and Tommy only had time for an occasional question or comment, so the day passed with Carter answering the phone and consulting with Tommy's assistant Troy for information about availability of horses etc. At five o'clock, Carter went back to tell Sam and Tommy he was leaving.

Tommy was about to say something, but Sam said, "Ok, kid, be careful going home." So, Carter left.

When Carter arrived home, his mother told him Steve had called and said he hadn't talked to Carter since Tuesday and he thought Carter was thinking of not going to Anita Chaney's party.

"I talked to your sister, she is coming over tomorrow evening to make sure you go." Carter was a little annoyed with Steve for his reporting on him. He called Steve, and when Steve heard his voice on the other end of the line, he started laughing.

"Hey, your sister is going to dress you and kick your ass out of the house tomorrow night."

Carter replied, "You didn't need to get them involved. I said I would go."

"Yeah, I was just making sure. How come you didn't call me yesterday? Did you go out there with your trashy boyfriend?"

"What do you mean boyfriend? And he's not trashy, you didn't call him trashy when you were still going out there."

"Man, you are getting too sensitive. I'm beginning to wonder if you will ever realize that some people are born lower class and they will always be lower class. That guy is nothing but a Stable Hand."

"Why are you on his case? He didn't make you go out into the woods with that nympho."

"Oh, yeah, well, who has been screwing around with the maid in his mother's house?"

"Oh, low blow. I should never have told you."

"Yeah, well, it's a good thing I'm your best friend or…"

"Or what?"

"Ha-ha, I would wait until I went to the party tomorrow, and if you don't go, I could tell the story to everyone there. But wait a minute, that would make all of the girls really go after you. They would think that's exciting. You know most of the guys who are supposed to be so with it have never had any. It's funny the guys think you are so shy and quiet, and here you are, screwing grown women."

"Okay," said Carter "What time should we meet?"

"Meet, I'm coming to pick you up in my chauffer driven limo since you haven't taken the time to get your license so that your father would turn over your car."

"Oh, so that means you will have to put up with your step-brother."

"Yeah, speaking of lower class."

"Give him a break. He drives you around with all of your girlfriends and doesn't complain." "Yes, he gets to go to all of the in affairs and to pretend that he is accepted. Anyway, we'll pick you up at 8:00 PM; that should give you enough time to wash the horse and trash off of you." "Ok, wise guy." Carter had dinner with his mother and went to bed early.

Friday morning arrived in a blaze of sunshine. Carter arose early and went down to breakfast. His mother had a cup of coffee while he ate. She would wait for his step-dad to get home to have her breakfast. She mentioned to Carter that his cousin Henry would be available on Sunday to take him out for driving lessons. Carter replied that he could probably get Tommy to take him out for lessons.

Lila answered, "Don't impose on that young man asking him to do that. How would he find time, doesn't he have to be at the stables every day? Besides, we would probably have to pay him to give you lessons."

"Mother, he is my friend and he can put Troy his assistant in charge while we are out."

"Friend or not, I'm sure the owners of the stables would not allow him to go out to teach you to drive on their time. Don't ask him to jeopardize his position. He is a very nice fellow and that would be unfair to him."

"Well, it was an idea and I wouldn't have to rely on Henry keeping his promise."

"Promise me you won't ask Tommy."

"Okay, Mother, I promise."

Carter went out to the back yard, unlocked his bicycle, and peddled off to the stables.

Tommy was in the office when he arrived.

"Hey, buddy, you left before I had a chance to tell you I would take you home last night."

"That was okay, you were busy with Sam."

"I'm never too busy to take care of you."

"Are you kidding? I've been riding both ways on my bike since I first started coming out here." "I know. I just wanted you to know you can get a ride whenever you want." Tommy was smiling at him, and again, he felt that familiar warm feeling. He thought to himself, I know if I ask Tommy to take me out for driving lessons, he will do it, and as Mother said, that would probably get Tommy in trouble. He stood over Tommy's chair and put his hands on Tommy's shoulders. He was rubbing the shoulders and Tommy leaned his head back against Carter. Carter felt the urge to kiss Tommy but instead moved quickly away.

Tommy swiveled his chair around and said, "Carter, you don't have to be embarrassed if you want to touch me." Carter started to deny any desire to get a chance to touch Tommy but decided that he didn't need to keep up any pretense of not wanting Tommy.

Instead he replied, "I know we can't be fooling around all the time."

Tommy answered, "What we did was not just fooling around; we made love. I know you are a young kid, but you've got me anytime you want me."

Again, Carter wanted to disagree about feeling anything but sexual desire for Tommy but surprise! That definitely meant he was gay. If you want to have sex with another male, you are a homo. He sat down at the other desk and took the appointment book out of the drawer.

Tommy stood up saying, "I'd better get over to the tack room to check on the gear. If you need me, let me know. On the other subject, maybe we can get together after 5:00 PM. I'll call your mother and tell her we're working late."

"Not tonight, I promised I'd go to a party and my sister is involved in getting me to go."

"Whose idea was that, your friend Steve?"

"Yeah, he told my mother and sister I was turning down invites."

"So that means I'm by myself tonight?"

"Tommy, what did you do before the other night?"

"I hadn't been with you. I'll go out and find some girl at the bar I go to sometimes, don't worry about me." Tommy left the office. Carter was left sitting there thinking about Tommy being with someone else, not because it might be a woman but because it could be anyone else. He realizes he is actually jealous, but he doesn't know what he can do about it.

Carter also does not like the feeling. What's going to happen to me? I'm supposed to be thinking about girls and I'm thinking about a guy. I know he likes me, but he just said he can go and get somebody else if I'm not available. Here I am turning gay because of him. But that's ridiculous because I was already gay. I never really thought about it seriously before. I can't blame Tommy. I've always had symptoms. That's probably what my cousin sensed.

The day progressed with a lot of calls and reservations for riding parties for Saturday and Sunday. In addition, Troy came into the office a few times to give Carter information on available mounts for appointments. Tommy did not come back into the office until 4:30 PM when it was a half an hour before Carter was scheduled to leave. Tommy asked Carter if he wanted a ride home.

Carter answered he was fine. He could get home in plenty of time to get ready for the party. Tommy stood in front of the desk, staring at him for at least five minutes. Carter was nervous as usual and was about to say if I get in the car with you, I might not make it home.

But Tommy turned to leave the office, saying, "I'll have Troy pay you for the time you worked this week."

"Why can't you pay me, it's only about two days?"

"I am the one who is paying you, but Troy will give it to you just to make sure the bosses know you are being paid fairly."

"Tommy, I'm sorry. I promised everyone I would go to the party tonight."

"Look, kid, I don't care. Don't start thinking that I'm lost if you don't spend time with me. I think you said one time it's only sex."

"Tommy, wait!" Tommy went out and shut the door behind him. Carter was upset at first and then he thought, What do I care if he gets mad at me? He's right, I did say it's just sex and I don't need him. I can find somebody my own age."

When Carter was leaving, he stopped to pat Walking Jennie and to nuzzle noses with her. He hadn't been paying as much attention to her for the last few days and he felt a little guilty about being so distracted.

As he arrived home, his sister Catherine was already there accompanied by his two-year-old niece, her daughter, and her one-year-old son. He was glad to see his little niece; she was his favorite. His nephew was already walking and speaking some words. He was a cute kid that the whole family spoiled. Carter spent some time playing with his niece and nephew. Catherine started right in telling him to get ready for the party. He reminded her that Steve would not be there to pick him up until 8:00 o'clock and it was only 6:30.

She said, "That's only an hour and a half away, and you need a lot of work."

His mother joined in, saying, "Yes, honey, go take a shower in our bathroom."

"Mother, I spent the whole day in the office. I only stopped to say goodbye to Jennie on the way home."

"You will still need more grooming. I don't want people to think my son is sloppy and unkempt. Besides, your friend Steve is already very conscious of his appearance, so you need to look your best to keep up."

Carter replied, "Do you all know that I am considered one of the best dressed guys in my class at school?"

Catherine agreed, "You got it honestly. Our father is always dressed to the nines in expensive suits and J&M shoes on his feet."

Lila, too, admitted, "Yes, he is quite the Dapper Dan, even when those expensive pockets are empty."

Of course, Catherine objected to the last comment with, "Mother, you know that Daddy does very well most of the time."

His mother replies soothingly, "We know, dear, most of the time but not all of the time."

Carter nipped further commentary in the bud by saying, "Okay, I'll go take my shower and get dressed for your approval."

By the time Steve and his step-brother arrived, Carter's mother and his sister had supervised his attire. Carter had been correct when he mentioned earlier that he was considered one of the best students in his class. He was known for his cashmere sweaters, flannel trousers, and buttoned-down collared oxford cloth shirts. His mother who was usually fashionably chic herself, was largely responsible for his acquired tastes. In addition, he had always admired his father's ability to always look neat and well dressed.

This evening he was wearing a Harris Tweed Jacket over a cashmere vest and blue oxford cloth shirt with grey flannel pants. His shoes were J&M tassel loafers. When he came down into the living room where Catherine and Lila sat waiting to see him off, Catherine added a silk handkerchief to his jacket breast pocket. Carter accepted the addition and the approval of the ladies.

Catherine quipped, "If I were a young girl at the party and you came in looking so fine, I would definitely make myself available for at least a dance." Steve was telling Catherine about Anita Chaney, whose party they were going to attend.

"She is always asking for Carter. Anita and Carter are meant for each other; she loves reading and listening to music just like someone else we know (named Carter)," said Steve.

"Sounds perfect, let's hope," replied Catherine.

Carter's mother asked Steve's step-brother if he was planning to go to college since he had finished high school in South Carolina three years ago.

"No, ma'am," he answered "I'm working in the stock room at one of my father's stores."

Lila, smiling, said, "Oh, then you will have a future in retail by working your way up."

"Yes, ma'am."

The boys left for the party, which was taking place in Yeadon, Pennsylvania. Steve and Carter were glad to be able to ride in the car instead of having to take a train and then a bus. The most trying part would have been after the party. They would have had to check the suburban bus schedule and would have to be at the bus stop on time.

When they got to the party, it was in full swing. Dr. and Mrs. Chaney were at the door admitting the attendees. Carter had heard this was customary with most of the parents of kids who gave some of the best parties. If the parents didn't approve of anyone or that person, or those persons were not invited, they did not gain admittance. Sometimes the party giver was summoned to the door to verify a person's invite.

Mrs. Chaney spoke to Steve directly since she had seen him at TNT affairs where she was one of the chaperones and she thought he was a nice young man. Steve was the epitome of mannerly teens.

He introduced Carter to Mrs. Chaney and she exclaimed, "Oh, I know your mother, we were friends years ago and I still see her occasionally at affairs. How nice to meet you."

Carter responded with, "It's nice to meet you also."

Mrs. Chaney was a very impressive woman. She and Dr, Chaney had met in Detroit when her parents had given her a Debutantes' Ball, eligible up and coming bachelors from all over the country at the time just happened to be invited. Her family was one of the most prominent black families. Her forebears had migrated to Detroit by way of Canada like many of the black families that willingly came to the U.S. in the 1800's after the Civil War.

Carter was so impressed by Mrs. Chaney that it almost seemed like he had come to the party to meet her. He and Mrs. Chaney spent so much time talking that Steve came back up to the entrance hallway to find him.

"Anita is looking for you. I'm sure she didn't expect you to come and try to make it with her mother."

"Very funny," answered Carter, "You are just full of jokes."

"Well, maybe it's a good idea to impress the parents of the girl you are going to date," said Steve. "

Wait a minute, don't try to rush me into anything, I told you she just finds me amusing." At this time, Anita discovers them in the hallway.

Anita says, "Carter, I'm honored that you have decided to come to my party. Come on out to the sun room and meet some of my other guests." She took Carter's arm and led him out to the large sun room where loads of young people were talking and sipping punch, which was spouting from drink fountains located in three strategically located spots in the room. The French doors were open all around the room, leading out to a patio where steps led down to an expansive back lawn. A temporary dance floor was assembled over a swimming pool where there were girls and guys dancing to the latest music supplied by a Disc Jockey coming from four oversized speakers placed at the corners of the deck.

Carter felt his spirits rise in this party atmosphere. He was glad he had come. Anita took him around introducing him to guests from New York, Delaware, Washington D.C., and of course, from Detroit.

When she presented him to one of her female cousins, she said, "Clara, this is Carter."

Clara replied, "So, you are Carter. I have heard so much about you and now I see why."

Anita quipped, "Alright, back off, girl, this one is going to be mine." Carter was thinking he was going to wake from this dream any minute. Here were two gorgeous girls talking about him like he was special. He was immediately smitten with Anita, who he had never thought would be interested in him.

Anita took his hand and said, "Carter, please dance with me?" Surprisingly, this was a perfect chance to help Carter with overcoming any shyness he felt. His sister Catherine had used him as a practice partner from the time he was ten-years-old and he had become a great dancer as a result. They went to the center of the dance floor and Carter was so taken with the music and Anita that he danced with so much enthusiasm that he suddenly realized the other dancers were forming a circle around Anita and him. They were clapping and stamping along with the music. He heard several shouts of, "Get it, Carter."

Carter thought to himself, Wow, what I've been missing. The night progressed with Anita constantly by his side. When the party was breaking up, it was almost 11:00 PM and time to go. Steve had latched onto another girl whose name was Alice Windsor and they were heavy petting in the back seat of the car. Anita came out with Carter to the car where Benny had it idling, waiting for Carter.

"Call me tomorrow and we can just talk," said Anita.

Carter said, "I really had a great time; thanks for inviting me."

"You were first on the list," she answered.

"I will call you tomorrow. I got your number from your cousin Clara."

"Oh, that is super it served two purposes, one, you got my number, and two, you let her know you wanted to talk more to me. I was afraid she was giving you her number."

Carter laughed and said, "No, I asked her for yours right away."

He started to get into the front seat of the car and Anita said, "Carter?" He turned and put his arms around her and they kissed. He felt like many of the romantics describe like he heard music. When he settled into the seat and closed the car door, Benny drove off.

Benny chuckled, "You look like you're in a trance."

Carter answered, "I am."

Alice spoke from the back seat, "Everyone will be glad you and Anita finally got together. All she ever does is question everybody about you." Steve pulled Alice back and continued kissing and touching her.

Between kissing and groping, he mumbled, "Let them work it out; they don't need us."

When they got to Carter's house, he looked in the back of the car to say goodnight but realized that the couple wouldn't hear him because they had moved on to actual coitus. He thanked Benny and went inside. He was still thinking about Anita. He wondered if he needed to formally ask her to be his girlfriend. It seemed like that would not be necessary. The house was quiet. Fawn came down the stairs to meet him in the hallway and followed him back up to his bedroom. It occurred to him that he had not walked her at all that day. She didn't seem anxious as she would have been had she not been walked. In fact, she jumped on the bed. Carter hung his clothes in the closet and got into bed, pushing his dog over to make room. He lay there in the dark thinking about the party and Anita. He really liked her; she was the type of girl he had always pictured as one he would end up with.

The interesting thing was that his reaction to the kiss and being close to her was different from the uncontrollable feeling that arose when Tommy mentioned sex. He knew he would enjoy sex with Anita, but he felt more reserved and paramount in his thinking was a feeling of respect. He would never try to have sex with her in the presence of others like Steve had done with Alice in the back seat of a car. He also would never tell others about their intimacy. Not even to Steve.

So, that would be another secret to keep away from his best friend. Finally, his last thoughts before sleep landed on Tommy. I wonder if he did what he said he would, picking up some woman who hangs around bars. That could be dangerous to one's health; he could end up with a venereal disease. That would sure turn me off. I'm going to ask him if he fooled around with some-body else. If he did, it will give me an excuse to say no next time. Besides, maybe he won't want to again. Carter turned his radio on soft and soon drifted off to sleep.

Anita's party turned out to be the beginning of a whirlwind of parties, dances, and summer romance. Anita was very popular, she was invited to parties almost weekly, and of course, Carter was her escort at all of the func-tions, starting the very next day, Saturday.

Carter called her and she answered with, "Oh, Carter, you must say you will go with me to Denise's lawn party in Germantown tonight."

He answered, "I would love to, but I'm not sure she would welcome me uninvited."

"Don't be silly. You will be with me and I'm sure Steve and Alice will be there." Carter was surprised to hear that his friend Steve hadn't mentioned this party to him. Anita continued with her plan, "I can ask my mother or father to drive us there and we can get back home by grabbing a ride with someone at the party."

Carter realized this was a chance to impress Anita. "I'll ask my cousin Henry to drive my car. I don't have my license yet, but he has his."

"Carter, you have a car?"

"Yes, my father bought it for me."

"Oh, super, that solves the transportation problem. Why don't you call your cousin and then call me back with the time for me to be ready." Carter thought, why did I open my big mouth about the car? Now I've got to call Daddy to ask him to let Henry come to get the car, so that I can take the driver's test in it. First, I have to find Henry. Aunt Ada says he is never at home and he is between jobs. Besides, Daddy never personally told me that he bought the car for me.

So, Carter called his father at the barber shop.

When his father picked up the phone, Carter said, "Daddy, Mother told me you got me a car."

His father answered, "Well, you get right to the point. It's a nice two-door 98 Olds. Andy bought it and his wife has been complaining about it because she wanted a four-door sedan. She feels that the car is too young for them. I thought it would be a nice car for my son to drive all the young pretty girls wild with."

"Thank you, Daddy. I am so grateful, thank you."

"Listen, son, I am proud of you, even though I can't be with you every day. I want to be a part of your life. I want you to have the best of everything."

Carter filled his father in on the plan for the night, having his cousin Henry drive his date and him to the party. His father agreed to have the car ready for Henry and him to pick up. He told Carter he would have driven them himself if he didn't have some business to attend to. Carter knew that business was probably a big game of poker with a group of big spenders.

He answered, "Maybe when I'm driving myself, I can pick you up to demonstrate my driving abilities."

"I'm going to hold you to that, son," his father replied.

Now Carter had to find Henry. He called his Aunt Ada. She informed him that Henry had just left the house. Carter had to think, what now? Then he remembered Henry often hung out at a corner store a few blocks away. There were pin ball machines inside the store; Henry and his buddies were usually playing the machines. Carter was five years younger than Henry but a bit more mature. Henry was very fond of Carter, but he liked to tease him about being a good boy and a momma's boy.

Henry's buddies were kind of rough and consisted of ages from 17 through their 20's. One guy in particular, Skippy Benson, the neighborhood bully, didn't like Carter because he thought Carter was "stuck up" and that his parents gave him everything he desired.

When Carter went to the corner store looking for Henry, Skippy was standing outside with three other thugs. Skippy put out his arm to block Carter's way into the store.

Carter said, "Excuse me."

Skippy repeated, "Pay a dollar to go inside or get your ass kicked, mother fucker." The store door opened and his cousin Henry came out.

"What the fuck are you doing to my cousin?" he asked.

"I'm telling him no faggots allowed."

"If you don't get out of his way, everybody out here is going to find out who is the real faggot." At this Skippy glared at Henry but backed off and said to his three buddies, "Come on, boys, let's go where we don't have to be around this punk."

Henry called out as they retreated, "If I ever hear you bothered Carter again, your ass is mine, mother fucker." Skippy and his colleagues kept walking.

Carter said, "I wasn't afraid of him, Henry."

"That guy is dangerous; he and his pals are dirty fighters. You wouldn't stand a chance. What brings you down here?" replied his cousin. Carter filled him in on the car plan. Henry said, "Let's go get it, cuz." They went back to Carter's house, picked up his bike, and rode off to Joseph's home. Henry pedaled with Carter on the back of the bike.

When they arrived at the house, Ruby answered the door and told Carter his father was at the barber shop waiting for him. She was very abrupt and Carter asked if she was feeling ok.

She replied, "I don't think no kid 16-years-old should be getting his own car when I don't even have one myself." Carter was surprised at her vehement reply but didn't say anything in return. He and Henry wheeled the bicycle around the corner to the barber shop.

On the way, Henry said, "Your father will whip that bitch's ass when you tell him what she said."

"I'm not going to tell him what she said. I don't want to cause any trouble for anybody. If she wants to say that to him, it's between them."

Henry shook his head, saying, "I don't believe you, cuz, you're too nice to people when you should stand up to them. Your father owes you everything he can do to make up for not being there when you need him."

"Oh, come on, Henry, he is always good to me."

"You need a father when you're growing up."

"Hey, I've got two fathers. I'm really lucky." Henry was going to comment further but decided not to.

They entered the shop. Andy and the other two barbers were all busy and the chairs in the waiting area were all occupied; it was a typical Saturday.

Andy spoke, "Hey, kid, congratulations." Carter knew he was referring to the gift of the car.

He answered "Thanks, is my father back there?"

"Yeah, hold on, I'll get him."

"That's ok. I'll go find him, you're busy."

"No way, your father would have me skinned alive if I sent you back there." Carter stood there while Andy rushed through the door at the rear of the shop.

Almost immediately, Andy returned with Joseph, who greeted Carter with the usual show of affection.

He put his arm around Carter's shoulders, saying to everyone in the shop, "This is my handsome son. He is at the top of his class and he is going to college next year."

Carter was embarrassed and he corrected, "Not quite at the top."

Joseph continued, "On top of everything, he has humility." He then turned to Henry, saying, "How you doing, Henry?"

Henry replied, "Tryin' to make it."

"Ok, let's go check out the love buggy," said Joseph.

Henry laughed, "Yeah, don't say that to his Mom."

Joseph replied, "No way, she would not let him have a car if she thought that would be the case."

They went outside where there stood the two-door Oldsmobile in two shades of green, a dark top with a light-colored lower half. Carter was ecstatic; he wanted to jump up and down with joy. However, he contained his enthusiasm. He hugged his father, he even kissed him on the cheek. His father was pleased with his reaction, but he reminded him that as a young man, you show your gratitude with a handshake.

When Carter drew back, Joseph laughed and said, "Son, I'm joking, nothing makes me happier than the way you are expressing your thanks. I'm kidding you because I know the men on your mother's side of the family would tell you to contain yourself in public." At this Henry reminded Joseph that he was from that side of the family.

Joseph replied, "Oh, I'm not including you in that group. Your father was like me a regular guy."

After more back and forth conversation about family, Carter said, "Daddy, we have to go. I'm supposed to pick up my date. Henry and I have to get home to get dressed." Henry asked Joseph if he could speak to him in private.

Joseph answered, "Ok, but what's so private that my son can't hear?" They stepped away from the parked car. Carter was so involved in checking out his new car that he didn't even look their way at first.

When he did look over, his father was shaking his head and saying, "No way that's all your mother and the rest of the family would need." Henry looked very disappointed and started to walk away when Joseph grabbed his arm while reaching in his own pocket. Carter saw him pull out a wad of bills and press them into Henry's hand, saying, "You know if it wasn't for your family, I'd be glad to say yes. I'm grateful to you for taking care of my son." Henry seemed to perk up with the passage of the money to him; he shook Joseph's hand and they came back over to where Carter was about to get into the passenger seat of the car.

Henry said, "You've got your permit, right?"

Carter answered, "Yes."

"Well, said Henry, "you can drive us home." Carter's father agreed. "You're not nervous, are you?"

"A little," replied Carter. "Don't be," said Joseph. "It's all yours." He had been holding a brown letter-sized envelope which he handed to Carter. "Here's your title, owners' card, and insurance papers all made out in your name at your address."

Carter wanted to hug him again but instead this time shook his hand, saying, "Thank you, Daddy, with all my heart."

His father replied, "If I can make you happy, I'm happy."

Carter went to the driver's side of the car and got in behind the wheel. Henry got into the other side and they drove off. Carter felt instantly confident driving without any nervousness.

Henry said, "Well, it looks like I can just relax and enjoy the ride. You've got it, but you can't drive tonight."

"Yes, I know," said Carter, "but maybe by next week."

Henry added, "Don't rush it. I'm looking forward to some of your kiddie parties."

"Wise guy," said Carter. "By the way, what did my father tell you 'No' about?"

"I'm not going to tell you about that."

"Hey, listen, I know my father has all kinds of business deals."

"Yeah, everybody in the family knows, but they don't discuss it. I can't tell you because you're the young, innocent kid and you don't need to know. Hey, slow down!"

"I'm in control, I'm not going fast. He didn't need to give you money. I've got money for gas, plus extra for whatever."

"Okay, I'll tell you. I asked him to let me work for him." Carter was silent after this; he knew that his father was probably a Numbers Banker and he also knew he was considered a professional gambler in addition. He didn't want to think of how much more of his father's dealings were illegal. He only knew in spite of it all, he loved his father and he was even a little proud of him in that Joseph was a very handsome, dark skinned man who was a snazzy dresser.

Carter drove right up the driveway at his house.

He turned to Henry and said, "Now you take the car, go to your house, and get dressed."

Henry replied, "I can walk home. I'll be back by 7:00 o'clock and we'll go pick up your girl by 8:00."

"Hey, cousin, you won"t stand me up, right?"

"I told you I'm glad to drive you and your sweetie around tonight."

"Okay, I'm counting on you. I'm going to call Anita and tell her the time for pick up."

"Listen, my man, I will be here on time." Henry went to the back door and Lila was just coming out. He said, "Hi, Aunt Lila. I was coming in to speak to you." Lila knew that Henry and his two siblings, Marie and Donald, adored and respected her. In fact, she was the adult they always came to with their problems because Ada, their mother, was usually preoccupied with her own issues.

After Ada's husband's death years ago when Henry was four-years-old, she returned to dating potential replacements. Donald and Marie were both older than Henry. Marie was the oldest now at 26 and Donald was 23. Henry walked around the car with Lila.

Lila said, "This is a very nice car; did you tell your father how much you appreciated it, Carter?" Carter had been standing there in the driveway next to his new car.

He answered his mother, "Of course, I told him that I am very grateful."

"You should also remind him if you decide to go to Penn State, you will not be able to take the car with you."

"I didn't think of that, but if I get accepted at Penn State, I will tell him. He has said he will help with tuition and other costs."

Henry left for his house to get ready for the evening. Lila and Carter went inside. His mother was telling him that his step-dad was not happy about him having his own car before his high school graduation; she did not mention that her subconscious was telling her Bob was a little jealous that Joseph had won brownie points with Carter because of the car gift.

Carter went straight to the phone in the hallway and called Anita. He told her he would pick her up at 8:00 PM. Anita was excited; she said she was look-ing forward to seeing him. When he hung the phone up, he sat there next to it, thinking about Anita. He knew some of the other guys would love to be in his shoes. He did like her a lot and he was still floating on a cloud of surprise and pleasure that she liked him in return.

He next dialed Steve's number.

Steve answered, and when he realized it was Carter, he said, "Hey, Cart, good work. I already heard you're taking Anita to Denise's party."

"Yeah," answered Carter. "Do you and Alice want to ride with us?"

"I would love it, but Alice is all excited about Benny driving us in the Cadillac; she wants to impress everybody at the party."

"That's stupid, most of those kids have seen Cadillacs before."

"I know, and they probably won't see what we drive up in anyway."

"Well, you can tell Benny that he doesn't need to stay because you can ride back with us."

"Yeah, that is a great idea. I won't have to be embarrassed to have Benny trying to hit on all of those girls who wouldn't even let him kiss their asses."

"They might let him do that," Carter laughed.

"Okay, we'll see you at the party."

Carter was dressed and ready at 7:00 o'clock. He went out to the driveway to wait for Henry, who finally showed up at 7:20. Carter, by this time, was nervous, thinking maybe Henry wasn't going to come at all. Henry strolled up the driveway dressed in casual slacks and a sport jacket. Carter thought, well, he decided to wear a jacket, that's good.

Henry said, "Okay, cuz, let's get this show on the road." Carter realized he had been drinking but didn't seem intoxicated.

He said, "Hey, Henry, I smell liquor on your breath. That's going to be a problem for Anita and her parents."

"Don't sweat it, cuz. I got lifesavers."

"They don't help much. I guess I've got my father to thank for giving you all that money."

"How do you know how much money he gave me?"

"I don't know how much it was, but it looked like a lot. I didn't think you would go out and drink when you agreed to drive us tonight."

"You're the only one who can talk to me like this besides your mother. That's because you are my special cousin. You are just like your mother, she has all of the class in the family. My mom always talks about her being the favorite because she has the lightest complexion and the best manners. Even our uncle, their brother, liked Auntie the most. Between Granddad and Uncle Richard, they wanted her to marry the big undertaker in Richmond and become the Colored Society Queen.

Then along comes Joseph Johnson to mess up the plan. At least that's what my mom says. She gloats over it like that was the big disappointment and it served them right. It's funny because I'm a lot like your father, except he's good at everything, unlike me. I'm a loser and he's a hustler who wins."

"Oh, Henry," said Carter, "don't say that. You're okay, you just need to find yourself. Mother always says you have a heart of gold, you are a good person."

"Oh, no. I'm not, I'm crazy about Aunt Lila and I think of you as my young brother. Nobody had better ever do anything to hurt you, but I don't give a shit about a lot of these other people, I don't mean my mom, my brother, and sister, but as for the rest, fuck 'em!"

Henry, then changing the subject, said, "You drive, and when we pick up your girl, I'll take the wheel cause you'll be nervous." Carter got in on the driver's side and they drove off. Henry continued his testimony, "If anything or anyone is bothering you, come to me and we can deal with it together."

"Okay," Carter answered. "I do care a lot about you, and if I am successful in life, you won't have to worry about anything." With this kind of sincere affection exchange, Carter's mind strayed to Tommy as he drove. He wondered how Henry would react if he told him about Tommy. He answered his own question in his mind. Henry would probably go after Tommy. That would be bad; he felt protective of Tommy. He wouldn't want him to get hurt. He decided again to put Tommy out of his mind.

He drove up to Anita's house. He and Henry got out of the car.

Henry said, "I'll wait out here and have a cigarette." Carter went up to the door and rang the bell.

Dr. Chaney opened the door, "Come in, Carter. Anita will be down shortly." Mrs. Chaney came into the center hallway. She greeted Carter.

"Oh, Carter, you look so handsome. How is your mother doing?"

Carter answered, "She is fine; she said to tell you hello."

"Good, we must get together soon. Come into the living room and have a seat." The three of them go into the living room on the right-hand side of the hallway.

Dr. Chaney says, "Sit over here and let's chat while Mrs. Chaney gets us some iced tea. So, what do you plan to major in at college?"

"Well, I plan to major in Journalism."

"Aha, excellent, to what end?"

"I have this nagging desire to be a writer."

"Well, that's impressive; with being an English Major, there are so many avenues you can travel to assist you in reaching your destination. Have you applied at many schools?"

"Yes, I'm a dreamer. Michigan University, University of Ohio, Penn State, and Temple."

"Those are great schools, but what about Lincoln?" Dr. Chaney questioned.

"Well, Lincoln is a good school, but I want to attend a school that has a reputable school of Journalism or at least with a separate program and not just Liberal Arts with an English major." "Well, of course, you know I will trumpet Lincoln. I'm sure you would be an asset in one of our freshman classes. I'm told you are a good student."

"Thank you, sir. I'm still shopping, so if I don't get positive responses from the ones I've already applied to, I will be trying for others."

"I notice you didn't mention any of the negro colleges; do you feel that none of them can give you adequate training and background?"

"Oh, no, sir, it isn't that at all; a few of my friends and acquaintances plan to attend black schools. In fact, my best friend Steve will be going to Fisk University. It's almost a family tradition for him."

"Well, our Anita will be going to Howard," Dr. Chaney added. Carter thought. I'm not making a hit with Anita's father.

At this moment, Anita sails into the room looking great and apologizing for keeping Carter waiting.

Her father spoke up with, "I've been keeping Carter company."

Anita laughed and said, "That's what I'm afraid of, Daddy."

He replied to Carter's surprise, "You don't have to worry, Carter is a fine young man with very sensible goals. Your mother and I both approve." Anita took Carter's hand and led him out to the hallway where she had thrown a silk scarf over the bench by the front door. She picked it up and Carter took it from her hands draped it around her shoulders.

She said, "Carter, you always know what to do and what to say at the right times." He responded with a kiss on her cheek. They went out to where Henry waited by the car.

Anita exclaimed, "Oh, Carter, this car is divine."

Carter introduced Anita to his cousin Henry and they got into the back seat as Henry directed saying jokingly, "I'm your chauffeur this evening." Henry drove the car with careful aplomb. Approaching the party from the road, they could see the string lights already sparkling in the fading daylight. There were groups of young people laughing and talking all over the back lawn. As they drew closer, Carter saw many familiar faces, most of the kids he would never have thought would ever socialize with him.

Denise was standing with Louie and she exclaimed, "Anita, I see you got what you wanted as usual. Welcome, Carter and who is this distinguished older man?"

Carter replied, "Thanks for having me; this is my cousin Henry, he is our adult for tonight." Denise responded, "I haven't had you yet, but I'm impressed by this older man."

Henry laughed and said, "Wow, I thought this was a kiddie party, but that's grown up talk." Louie spoke up with, "And that's all it is, talk."

Henry replied, "Ok, guy, don't get up tight. I don't rob the cradle." Carter had to put an end to this repartee; he didn't want his new venture into "the social life" to start with a clash between his uninvited kin and one of the members of the group that he chose to mingle with. Denise instead said to Louie, "Listen, dear, it's my party and I don't need anyone explaining my words."

Louie looked at her with a surprised expression and said, "Ok." With that he turned and walked away toward another group standing nearby.

Denise went on with, "You will have to excuse him. I keep telling him we're just friends. He's stuck with all of this nonsense about whose father does what. My father started as a plain old fireman and now he is the Head Commissioner of the Fire Department, but he had to work to get there."

Anita said, "Yes, but you are his princess since your sister dropped out of school and married a policeman; he is concentrating on you to have the cream of the crop."

Henry turned to Carter, saying, "You kids have fun. I'm going to the car. I'll probably take a nap. Just come out when you're ready to leave."

Carter answered, "Ok, we will."

Denise quipped, "I may come out to make sure you're alright." Everyone laughed, but Carter grew even more nervous.

Anita noticed his discomfort and whispered, "Don't worry, Denise is a big flirt, but she won't actually follow up on her playful advances."

"Yes, she might just be flirting, but my cousin is not the type to play with."

"Don't worry, she can handle the situation," Anita said.

After a while, Carter relaxed and they proceeded to have a good time. The lawn party was a big success, and by the end of the night, Carter felt completely accepted by the other guests. Steve and Alice joined Carter and Anita for the balance of the evening, and at the end of the party, they rode home in Carter's car, but there was no hanky panky on the way because Steve rode in the front passenger seat next to Henry, who was driving. After the girls were dropped off at their homes, Steve brought up his earlier encounter with Patricia Roxbury, who was also at the party and whom he was due to escort to the Christmas Cotillion. Evidently, Patricia had assumed that Steve was only dating her. He had explained to her that he thought they were both free to date others. Anyway, their planned date for the Cotillion had really been arranged by their parents. Carter told Steve that he thought it could have been handled with more consideration for Patricia's feelings.

Steve asked, "How would you have handled it?"

Carter replied, "I would have told her I thought she already had a date for Denise's party, so you accepted Alice's offer to go with her."

"Carter, you don't live in the real world; she needed to be set straight right up front. Don't you agree, Henry?"

Henry answered, "Don't include me in this conversation. I believe in feel 'em, fuck 'em, and forget 'em. The skanks I mess with don't go to Cotillions and lawn parties."

Carter said, "Yes, and I hope you don't decide to change and fool around with Denise."

"Yo, cuz, don't worry. I'm not that interested in busting a cherry. I prefer something more seasoned and experienced. You boys wouldn't know what to do with the chicks I know."

Steve replied, "I wish you would introduce me to some. I'm sure I could handle it, in fact, your little innocent cousin here probably can outdo both of us with experience." Carter froze; he had never told Henry about Annie or about before Annie. When they arrived at Steve's house, he thanked Henry for the ride and went inside. Henry turned the car around and drove toward Carter's house.

They were silent at first and then Henry spoke, "What did your buddy mean by you having experience?"

Carter replied, "Oh, he's just talking trash; he kids a lot."

"Listen, Carter, I wasn't born yesterday I've been there, done that."

Carter thought, Well, I guess I can tell him, he won't tell anyone. So, Carter told Henry about Anne. By this time, they were parked in Carter's driveway.

Henry exclaimed, "Carter, you don't need to be fooling around with no grown woman, especially one who has already got kids and no husband. If she would get pregnant, you'd have some shit on your hands."

"I know, but she always said if she got pregnant, she could blame it on her boyfriend."

"Cuz, I'm surprised at you don't you know they lie? You'd be the first one she would blame and claim you jumped her or something. Why didn't you come to me for advice? I know how these women operate."

"Don't worry, it's all over now, she won't be coming back."

"That's good; all she probably wanted was to get this young stud. She's really a rapist, you're just a kid. Next time you come to me for advice."

"I know. I talked to a friend about it; he gave me advice and he's older, so he knows things." "What friend?" Carter was immediately sorry he mentioned "the friend" (Tommy). He was afraid Henry might get that story out of him and he was determined not to let that happen.

Henry repeated the question and Carter finally said, "Oh, a really nice guy at the stables where I go riding."

"Is he white?"

"Yes, he manages the stables, we talk a lot."

"Listen, nobody who is white can give you advice about anything they don't know shit about us and they don't care."

"Henry, that's not true. Most of my classmates are white and I get along fine with them. We all have the same kind of problems growing up. Tommy really likes me and I like him, it doesn't have anything to do with race; that's one thing Dad and my father agree on. We're all the same, nobody is better than anybody else."

"Oh, yeah, well, I don't know this guy Tommy, but I'll bet he is lower class and isn't worth anything." Carter realized he was growing very angry and decided he'd better end the conversation.

He said, "You know, Henry, you are a great person, but prejudice is just as bad on your side as it would be on their side."

"Ok, little brother, don't get so uptight, maybe it's good that you feel that way. It will help you to be successful in their world."

Carter said, "On another topic, you can take the car to your house and maybe you can find time to take me out on a practice run tomorrow, so that I can take my driver's test on Monday or Tuesday."

"I can walk home; keep your car here and I'll come tomorrow afternoon to take you out." Sunday came and went with no Henry. Carter was disappointed but not surprised he knew that Henry smelling of alcohol on Saturday meant the beginning of a bender, which would last until Henry ran out of money, and from what he could see of the roll of bills his father had given Henry, that might take a while. His cousin meant well but was not in control when it came to drinking. Carter decided to get someone else to take him for his test in the coming week.

It was going to be a difficult week with his step-father's procedure scheduled for Monday and the family planning to leave for Cape May on Wednesday if things went smoothly for Bob. Just as he sat thinking about the coming week, his mother called upstairs to say that his cousins had arrived from New York.

Carter went down to greet his cousins. Peter was one year older than Carter and Renee, Peter's sister was one year younger than Carter. At 15, Renee had really blossomed and Carter was uncomfortably aware of her shapely body; in particular he noticed her breasts, which seemed to be ready to burst through the polo top that she was wearing with a gabardine pencil skirt that hugged her hips. Carter stammered out his greetings and told them both to come upstairs to put their bags into the bedrooms.

Renee quipped, "Are we all sleeping in your bedroom?" Carter knew she was joking, but he reacted with a self-conscious mumble and his mother spoke from where she was standing in the hallway.

"Renee, dear, you will have the front bedroom and Peter will bunk in with Carter."

Renee laughed and Lila said, "You'll have to forgive your cousin, he spends most of his time with horses." Carter regained some of his composure, but he was having trouble with his pants growing tight.

Peter and Carter sat and talked in Carter's bedroom.

Peter was saying, "I guess you heard about my scandal?"

"What scandal?" asked Carter.

"Oh, I should realize that your mom would never burn your tender ears with my escapades."

"What happened?"

"The girl I've been dating got pregnant."

"Wow, is it yours?"

"Of course it is. Are you that innocent? I'm her man." Carter was amazed at Peter's attitude. He would be devastated if it were he who was in this predicament. Peter continued, "I told my mom I wanted to marry her, but her folks and my dad won't let us see each other. I think they are going to take her to one of those doctors to get rid of the baby."

Carter could not believe what he was hearing, and most of all, he couldn't believe that Peter could be so matter of fact about it.

"Peter, I would be going crazy thinking about the girl and my baby. The other thing is you're only 17 and you haven't finished high school, how would you make it if you got married now?" "Yeah, well, that's why they shipped me off down here to get me away and they probably sent her somewhere, too."

"But don't you care about her?"

"I guess so, I don't really know now. I thought I did before; now that I don't see her, I don't know."

Carter looked at his cousin, he was another nice-looking guy. He had gotten into some trouble a couple of years ago and he flunked some classes in school, putting him back. His mother was Lila's favorite first cousin, so they talked a lot by phone and saw each other often, even though Cousin Rita lived in New York City. Earlier that year, Cousin Rita had been diagnosed with cancer and had been in and out of the hospital. Lila had offered to have Cousin Rita and the two children that were still at home to spend the summer in Cape May. That would have made the small house really crowded, but a lot of the summer people had crowded arrangements at the beach in those days and it made it more campy and fun. Cousin Rita could not come, but Peter and Renee were sent down. Of course, they expected that Carter would be there the entire time also. When Carter mentioned that he would only be down every other weekend, Peter was disappointed. Renee would be fine because she could help Aunt Lila with the house and Catherine's two children.

Peter decided to ask if he could stay in Philadelphia and come down to Cape May every other weekend with Carter. Carter didn't want Lila to agree to this plan because he didn't want to have Peter with him all of the time. Peter was ok, but he didn't want to be responsible for entertaining and keeping Peter happy all summer. Under it all, he knew he didn't want Peter to get in the way and he wanted to continue to work at the stables. He had to admit to himself he wanted to be able to be with Tommy if Tommy wanted to be with him. The other thing was having him tag along with Carter and Anita. That would not work at all, he didn't feel that Peter would be interested in the same activities they enjoyed.

As it happened, Lila did not consent to Peter's plan. She told him that she would like having a male family member at the house in Cape May for the entire time because Carter and Bob would only be there on weekends. Otherwise it would be a house full of women and children for a lot of the time. Carter wondered about this explanation; he realized that his mother might not want the two boys to be in Philadelphia together without supervision. He was sure she knew about Anne, and also Peter had his saga back in New York. Putting the two together without an overseer where they could compare notes might not be a good idea. So, by the time they sat down to dinner that night, most of the conversation was between Bob, Lila, and Renee. Bob was eating lightly due to his scheduled surgery on Monday. He had to finish eating by 6:00 PM and have nothing else before the operation.

Carter kept stealing glances at his Cousin Renee and he got the impression that she knew it. She kept smiling at him and he was getting that feeling again that his pants were too tight. As Lila was serving the dessert, the phone rang and she went out into the hallway to answer it.

She came back into the dining room, saying, "Carter, it's the stable manager, Tommy."

Bob spoke up, saying, "Didn't you tell him we're having dinner?"

"No, he's a nice young man and I didn't want to embarrass him." Bob just grunted at this. Carter went out to the phone trying to look calm; actually he was pleased because he had thought maybe Tommy wasn't interested in talking to him anymore.

He picked up the phone and said, "Hello, Tommy."

Tommy asked on the other end, "Are you coming to work tomorrow?"

"I'm not sure, my dad is going for an operation tomorrow morning and my mother might need me to be with her."

"Oh, Carter, I didn't know. I hope he'll be ok. I, uh, I missed you, Carter."

"What? I was there on Friday. I told you I wouldn't be there on weekends."

"I know, but I thought you might come out on Saturday to tell me about the party."

"Why? It was just a party. I went to another one last night."

"Oh, I see now you're the popular big guy on campus."

"On campus? I'm not in college yet."

"It's just an expression, give me a break."

"Yes, well, anyway, I can call you tomorrow to let you know if I can make it out there." Tommy was silent on the other end. Carter asked, "Are you there?"

"Yeah, I'm here, listen, Carter, even if you can't come to work in the office, I can pick you up later."

Carter knew exactly what he was talking about, he replied, "I thought you were going to go out and get one of your women to have fun with."

"I know what I said, but I didn't mean it, I was just kidding."

"You didn't sound like you were kidding, so I just decided you meant it."

"Hey, Carter, please don't give me a bunch of shit. I didn't want to pick up anybody. I want to just talk with you. I promise I won't try anything you don't want."

"Listen, Tommy, I got to go; my family is at the dinner table waiting for me."

"I'm sorry I interrupted your dinner, tell your mother I'm sorry."

"She would probably tell you to join us, she is such a softie."

"Yeah, and your step-dad would kick my ass out."

"Yes, you're probably right."

"Okay, please call me tomorrow I'll be looking for your call."

Carter felt really warm and excited. He decided it was like he was developing deep feelings for Tommy and he knew Tommy liked him a lot.

When he went back into the dining room, his mother said, "Tommy must have had a lot to tell you."

"Yes," he answered "He was telling me about one of the mares that foaled over the weekend." His step-father said, "He's white, he has no manners." Lila cleared her throat, giving Bob the signal to drop that subject. Bob then said to Carter, "I've been thinking maybe I'll buy that horse you like so much; everything is going to be fine tomorrow and the company is paying for everything. Since you're out at their stables all the time, maybe they'll give us a discount on feed and boarding."

Carter answered, "No, Dad. I'm too busy now to give Walking Jennie a lot of attention."

"When did you change your mind?" Bob seemed disappointed, even though this decision would save him money.

"I've gotten really interested in Anita Chaney, so I'll be going out to her house once I get my license and I won't be spending as much time at the stables."

Peter spoke up now that he was getting over Lila's denial of his request.

"Listen, I can help with the horse and I wish somebody would just give me a car."

Bob said, "We ought to give you that one that's in the driveway, at least you are 17. He's only 16 and he hasn't finished high school."

Carter said, "My father gave me that car, so nobody else can decide they are going to give my car away."

Bob answered, "I would have waited until you graduated from high school."

Lila spoke now, stating, "Carter is a responsible son and he will be a very sensible automobile owner."

Bob backed off by saying, "Carter is a wonderful son and I'm glad to help giving him the best of everything."

Carter turned to Peter, saying, "Do you ride?"

Peter answered, "No, but I can learn, it can't be that hard."

"Well, maybe in the fall when you come back from the Shore. We may not be going out there tomorrow. I want to be with Mother."

Bob said, "You boys can go ahead and make your plans. Your mother will be fine; they'll have me in and out in no time and she won't need moral support. We might even be able to leave for Cape May on Tuesday."

Lila commented, "Peter and Renee already know that tomorrow can be a movie day for them. Catherine and the children will be here, she will be preparing the meals for everyone since I will be at the hospital with you."

"Don't make such a fuss about this minor procedure. I'm told it will be simple, the doctor is just going to zap it. They call it freezing the growth until it will just shrink away with no lingering problems."

Lila agreed, "Yes, I'm sure everything will be alright." But at this, she excused herself from the table and rushed into the kitchen. Everyone left at the table was silent. Carter was upset; he knew his mother had left the table and gone into the kitchen to hide her emotional turmoil.

After dinner Carter and both of his cousins went up to his bedroom. They talked about their classes at their schools and their friends.

Carter mentioned his new girlfriend Anita again and Peter joked, "I thought you only liked horses."

Carter laughed, answering, "Anita is no horse, she's a fox." Peter asked if he had gotten any of that and Carter let him know that Anita wasn't that type.

"She has class, and when that happens, it will be special." Peter yawned and looked bored. Carter turned to Renee, asking her about her plans for the future. He found it difficult to look directly at her, and when he did, he got the impression that she was teasing him. He became painfully aroused. He swallowed hard, and the more uncomfortable he became, the more she seemed to taunt him.

Peter had flopped across the bed and fallen asleep.

Renee rose from the chair where she was sitting and said, "I think I'll go into my room and read." She went up the hall to the front bedroom. Carter sat there on the floor, thinking about Renee's breasts. He seemed to have thoughts about sex all the time anymore. Everything seems to lead to sexual fantasy or even to finally masturbation. He got up and went into the bathroom where he sat on the side of the tub. Courage came from somewhere and he got up and went to the front bedroom. Renee was laying on the big double bed reading.

He knocked on the door jamb and she looked up in surprise. He had his hands jammed in his pants pockets. She saw what he was trying to hide.

She said, "You know we're third cousins."

He answered, "Of course I do, why are you bringing that up?"

"Because I know what's on your mind."

"No, I just came to ask what you are reading."

"You've been looking at my breasts like you want to eat them or something." Carter felt weak in the knees and he found it impossible to hide his bulging crotch.

He confessed, "I'm sorry, Renee, that's all I can think about lately, don't tell on me. I'll go and leave you alone."

She said, "Don't worry, Carter, you're cute, but I don't want to get in trouble with anyone. I plan to go to college and on to nursing school. I don't need to be distracted."

Carter went over to the bed and knelt down next to it. He kissed Renee on the cheek, and when she turned her face toward him, he put his mouth on hers. He placed his left hand on her breast. She kept her lips tightly closed, so that he could not insert his tongue inside her mouth. She let him gently massage her breasts for a time and then she pushed his hand away. He realized that she was breathing as fast as he was.

He tried to put his hand up her skirt and she sat up saying, "No, I mean it," softly. He drew back and stood up; he didn't know what to say or do.

She smiled up at him, saying, "Someday when we are both with someone else, we'll laugh about this." He backed away to the door. She got off the bed, and pressing her hand against his chest, urged him out of the room and shut the door.

He went back to his bedroom and Cousin Peter, who was snoring, already undressed, and in bed. Carter decided to put blankets on the floor to sleep on. He didn't want to sleep in the same bed with Peter after all of the arousal with Renee.

In the morning, he was awakened by Lila with a gentle shake.

She said, "It's 5:00 AM and Bob needs to check in by 6:30. We'll take your car, Henry says you are a good driver, so you can drive us since Bob and I are both licensed drivers. We don't have to wake Peter and Renee. Catherine will be here with the children by 8:00 o'clock. I didn't realize that you didn't want to sleep with your cousin; your bed is certainly big enough for two."

Carter, still half asleep, mumbled, "He snores and he's all over the bed."

"Well, at the Shore, you will have to make do; we don't have a lot of space down there."

"I won't be there much anyway." Lila didn't want to get into specifics at this time, so she simply left the room, saying, "Hurry now."

They left for the hospital in Carter's car. He felt proud to be able to drive his parents to an important appointment. When Bob had gotten checked in and assigned to a room in the hospital, they were dismayed to discover that Bob's procedure was not scheduled until Tuesday morning and that he would be in the hospital overnight to be prepped for surgery. Bob convinced Lila to go back home with Carter and come back to the hospital on Tuesday morning. She really protested, but Bob was adamant and finally won out by pointing out that a licensed driver had to accompany Carter on his return home. In addition, she had all of the preparations to complete for the move to Cape May. "You can get those things out of the way, and tomorrow you can come to get me after the surgery."

Carter wasn't sure about what happens on the same day of an operation, but he didn't think Bob would be able to go home on Tuesday. When they left the hospital, his mother was very quiet. He tried to talk about other things to get her mind off of Bob's operation, but then Cousin Rita's condition came up and Lila was more depressed. He could tell that she was holding back tears.

When they arrived back home, it was already about 12:00. Catherine and her children were there. The children were glad to see their Nana and Uncle. Carter played with them for a few minutes while Catherine helped Lila fix sandwiches for lunch. Carter was a little hungry since they hadn't had breakfast that morning. Catherine told them that Peter and Renee had gone to see a movie.

After lunch Catherine went upstairs to Lila's den to put the children down for a nap. Carter decided to go out to the stables. He wished that he could drive his car but that would be taking a chance on being pulled over by the police, who were always ready to stop a young person of color who was driving a decent car. Besides, his mother would have a heart attack if he slipped out and drove off alone. So, he went out to the yard and unlocked his bike and rode off. He remembered as he rode along he hadn't told his mother he was leaving; he decided he would call her from the stables when he arrived.

Lila answered the phone on the first ring, "Carter, this isn't like you. You would normally have told me you planned to go to the stables today."

"Yes, Mother, but I thought there was still time to help out here and then to get back before dark."

"I don't need more to worry about Carter. Be careful."

"I will, Mother."

Tommy walked into the office, "Hey, Carter, you decided to give us a break."

Carter answered, "You know I told you about my dad."

"Yeah, I know, I was just trying to cheer you up. You look sad."

"No, I just called my mother to tell her where I am." Tommy came closer with his arms outstretched as if to hug Carter and Carter stepped away.

"Hey, Buddy, I'm just glad you came out. I've had a hectic morning and we've only got three other guys here today." Carter knew if he let Tommy hug him, it might cause a problem. He sat down at the desk and opened the log book.

"You've only got four reservations written in here for late afternoon."

"Yeah, but I needed to order feed again and schedule the Vet for the pregnant mare."

"Yes, in fact, I told my mother she already foaled over the weekend."

"Why did you tell her that?"

"Because we were on the phone so long, I made up an excuse." Tommy gave him one of those long stares that Carter was getting used to.

Tommy finally looked away, saying, "I'd better go over to the tack room to check the gear. I'll give you a ride home later when you're ready." Carter didn't object; in fact, he admitted to himself he was looking forward to the ride home in Tommy's car.

The rest of the day went by quickly. The riders who reserved horses came and went. It turned out to be a slow Monday, which was typical. Tommy came in and out of the office several times. At 5:45 PM, Tommy and the three stable hands drove the horses out of the corrals and into their stalls. Carter remembered his special Walking Jennie and went out to pat her neck and whisper in her perked ears. He told her he was sorry he had been so busy lately and that he would see her the next day. Tommy came over as Carter walked Jennie into her stall.

He said, "You know, I think she understands what you are saying."

Carter laughed, "Of course, she does, she knows I love her."

Tommy replied, "Then you should show it by coming out to see us more."

Carter didn't pick up on the obvious; he turned to Tommy and said, "Are you still going to give me a lift home?"

Tommy answered, "Of course, let's lock up. Phillip the Night Guy has his keys." After they locked the tack room and the office Carter got his bike and they went down the hill wheeling the bike alongside them. At Tommy's house, he said, "Come on in. I'll take a shower and then I'll drive you home." Carter parked his bike by the fence and followed Tommy into the house. He was already feeling nervous. Tommy asked him if he wanted a soda or anything.

He answered, "Just anything?"

Tommy turned and looked at him, "What?"

Carter laughed nervously and said, "Nothing."

"Come on upstairs while I shower." Carter went up the stairs behind him, he was actually shaking. In the bedroom, Tommy took off the T-shirt he was wearing. For the first time, Carter looked at his body with interest, or was it desire? Tommy had a fine patch of silky hair covering his well-developed chest, a line of hair ran down over his stomach to the top of his jeans. As Tommy unbuttoned his jeans and pulled down the zipper, the hairline widened, and when the jockey shorts came down, a sea of hair was exposed surrounding his abundant manhood semi erect. Carter was acutely aware of Tommy's beautiful body.

Tommy seemed to be reading his thoughts; he said, "Carter, do you want to touch me?" Carter was transfixed, but his mind was racing and he was so aroused that he didn't know what to do. Tommy almost whispered "Come on, Carter, take off your clothes." But Carter continued to stand there. Tommy came close to him and undid his belt buckle. He then unfastened Carter's jeans and pulled them down, followed by his underwear. When the jockeys came down, Carter's erection sprang forward. Tommy put his muscular arms around Carter, pulling him tight against his body. Carter closed his eyes. Tommy walked him toward the big double bed in the corner of the room, he sat him down on the side of the bed, and in one motion, pulled Carter's polo shirt over his head.

Tommy threw the shirt aside and pressed Carter back across the bed with his body against his. Carter wrapped his arms tightly around Tommy, their bodies were crushed against each other. Tommy was murmuring, "Carter," and Carter couldn't seem to hold him tight enough. This time when Tommy put his mouth on Carter's mouth, Carter's tongue met Tommy's and they were kissing passionately. Tommy rose up and lifted Carter onto the center of the bed and began kissing him all over his body. He ended by taking Carter into his mouth, making Carter climax almost immediately with his body jerking in response. Tommy continued kissing and sucking in Carter's release. Carter was in the thralls of another orgasm and Tommy turned him over onto his stomach and kissed Carter's back from his shoulders down to his buttocks. Next, Tommy had moved into position and inserted the head of his penis into Carter. Carter tried to move up and away, but Tommy's strength was greater than Carter's and he succeeded in going all the way.

Carter was suddenly struggling to get away and exclaiming, "It hurts, take it out." But Tommy put his mouth over Carter's and slowly the pain eased until there was none. When Tommy finally came to a crashing climax, he continued to hold Carter and did not pull out.

"Carter, am I hurting you, do you want me to let you up?"

"It doesn't hurt anymore."

"Do you know what's happening between us, Carter?"

"I know I wanted it."

"Yes, but that's only part of what's happening."

"If you're talking about love, I'm not in love with you, it's still just sex. I really care about the girl I've been dating, she is the kind of girl I would like to marry someday. But I'm not thinking about that any time soon. We can have fun, but I'm not going to fall in love with a guy. I like you a lot but just as a buddy."

"What you mean is as a fuck buddy. I know you are very young, so you don't understand feelings yet. You don't want to say you care about me as much and maybe more than your new girlfriend."

"Hey, Tommy, we'd better get up. I should get home. My cousins are in town and my dad is in the hospital, so I need to go."

"You don't want to admit the truth, that's why you are in a hurry all of a sudden."

"I don't want to talk about it anymore," said Carter.

"Okay, I'm coming on too strong, but I've been thinking about you all weekend. I didn't want to go anywhere or do anything else but see you. I know I'm a man over 21 and you're still just a kid, but you've got me spinning."

"What about Dottie? A month ago, you and she were together and we had never even talked more than 15 minutes at a time."

"Yeah, that's true, but I already had a thing for you as quiet as it was kept."

"You had all of the girls and women giving you sex whenever you wanted it"

"Yeah, but I wanted you."

"You know they would call you a child molester if anybody found out about us."

"Are you going to tell them?"

"Of course not."

"Why won't you tell them?"

"Because."

Tommy repeated, "Because what?"

"Because I don't want to get you in trouble."

"Why?"

"Because I don't want you to get hurt."

"Aha, see what I mean?" Tommy proceeded to kiss Carter on the mouth again and Carter responded with feeling.

Tommy held Carter off, saying, "No more tonight, I'm giving you something to come back for. You can think about our talk when you get home." Carter got off of the bed as Tommy went into the bathroom to shower.

He wanted to shower, too, but Tommy said, "No, your mother will notice if you don't need to wash up when you get home."

"I told her I'm only answering the phone in the office. It's not the same as being close to the horses all day."

When Tommy finished showering, he came back into the bedroom and put on clean clothes. Carter tried to look unconcerned, but he admitted to himself that Tommy was really a good-looking guy and he liked him a lot. It felt good to know that Tommy cared about him in return. They went out to Tommy's car parked in the back of the house. Tommy opened the trunk and they put Carter's bike inside.

On the way to Carter's house, Tommy said, "I can take you out for your driver's test and you'll be able to drive my car if you want to any time." It dawned on Carter that he hadn't mentioned his new car and that it was at his house. Tommy said, "Oh, that's great, but I was looking forward to letting you share mine."

Carter answered, "Well, we can trade back and forth. I like this car, too."

Tommy smiled, "What's mine is yours."

Carter laughed "What about your body?"

Tommy said, "You've already got that whenever you want it."

"I meant make my body as nice as yours, you have a great body."

Tommy replied, "You have a perfect body, what are you talking about? I told you your skin is like smooth silk, none of the women I've been with have skin as smooth as yours."

"I don't want to hear about who you've been with," said Carter.

"I didn't mean it that way and I don't want you to go with anyone else either," Tommy replied. "Wait a minute," said Carter, "I didn't promise not to see anyone else. I'm dating Anita."

"Yes, but she's a girl. I meant other guys."

"What! I've never been with any other guys because I wanted to. My cousin forced me, I don't find guys attractive." Tommy glanced at him. Carter added, "I admit you have a nice body."

"You told me earlier that you wanted it."

"Yes, I did. I don't want to talk about it anymore."

"Okay, Carter, I'm pressing you too much. I'll shut up."

Before they got out of the car, Tommy grabbed Carter's hand and held it for a few seconds. He then got out and opened the trunk to take Carter's bike out.

Carter said, "You can come in if you want to. Dad is not at home tonight."

Tommy replied, "So, the only time I can come to your house is when your step-father isn't there?"

"Why are you asking a question you know the answer to?"

"It's not a question, it's a statement."

"My mother might offer you dinner again."

"It's eight o'clock, dinner time is passed."

"That's okay, she will probably have mine warming."

"No, I'll go back home, I'll see you tomorrow."

"Maybe, I might have to be with Mother, and besides, my cousins are here so, I don't know." "You can bring them out. If you want me to come and get you, I will."

"Tommy, I don't know, I'll call you."

At this moment, Peter walked down the driveway.

Carter turned and said, "Hey, Peter, this is my boss Tommy from the stables." Peter and Tommy shook hands.

Peter said, "Glad to meet you. Can I come out with Carter to help out or something?"

Tommy answered, "I was just telling Carter I can come pick you all up tomorrow since he doesn't have his license yet."

"Hey, that would be great," said Peter.

Carter cut in with, "Peter doesn't know how to ride."

"That's okay, you can take some time to give him lessons in the practice ring."

"Well, Renee will have to come, too; we can't leave her at home with nothing to do that wouldn't be fair," said Carter.

Tommy said, "Okay, it's a plan," and got into the car and backed out of the driveway.

Peter and Carter went inside through the back door. Lila was in the kitchen talking to Renee. She asked Carter why he was so late and he told her there was so much to do in the office.

"I hope Tommy isn't giving you too much responsibility; you are supposed to relax on your summer vacation, both mind and body."

"I'm fine, Mother, I enjoy working there."

"Alright, go and wash up, I'll take your dinner out of the oven."

Renee smiled at Carter, saying, "I'm going to the hospital with Aunt Lila tomorrow since you have to work."

Carter replied, "Tommy was going to come and pick us up if I decide to go to the stables, so that you can go, too."

"I would rather go with Aunt Lila, I'm afraid to get too close to horses, and besides, I'll keep Aunty company." Carter went up to the bathroom thinking that no one ever corrects Renee about his mother being her second cousin and not her aunt. Then he secretly chastised himself for knit picking, it was merely a title of respect for an adult relative.

He would like to have bathed, but that would take too much time and he was anxious to get back to spend time with his mother and cousins. He washed his hands and splashed water on his face. He was drying his face and hands on the thick hand towel hanging on the rack and thinking about the day. He again got an erection. He locked the bathroom door and took care of it. That seemed to be the only way to get it to go down. While he was massaging, he fantasized about Tommy. He had to control himself to keep from crying out when he climaxed into the towel. He told himself he was a sex maniac or something. If Tommy was there at that moment, he would jump his bones.

"He wouldn't have to start anything I would, but the other thing is if Annie were here or if Renee was available, I'd take either one of them. All I think about is sex and I can't seem to get enough. Is it because I'm 16 and I started too early?"

He washed up again, this time not just his hands. He rushed back down to the kitchen where his mother waited with his dinner. She looked at him with concern.

"Are you alright?" she asked.

"Yes, Mother, I'm fine."

"Peter was telling me that you will be taking him with you tomorrow, that's good; we didn't expect to have to delay everything with Bob going into the hospital and you having a summer job. Your cousins would not enjoy just staying here and waiting for us to be ready for Cape May."

"Yes, it was Tommy's idea; he's going to pick us up. I wasn't sure because I thought you might want me to go with you to the hospital."

"Don't worry about me. Renee and I will be riding with Larry. He will be with us and he wants to drive Bob back home when he is released."

"Tommy is also going to take me for my driving test sometime this week, maybe Saturday." "That Tommy is such a nice young man and a wonderful friend. I just wish your dad would realize that white people can be just as nice as any other people. He deals with them in business, but he doesn't think they can be trusted as friends."

"Mother, we are all just people; a lot of my classmates are nicer to me than a lot of the so called African-Americans. In fact, a lot of the African-Americans don't like me because I am friendly with whites."

Peter had been sitting at the table listening to the conversation.

He said, "We New Yorkers don't get into this race business. My girlfriend is Italian, I used to go to her house all the time because her brothers and I are buddies. We play a lot of football and we go to the beach together."

Carter said, "I don't know about that. What about Harlem?"

"What do you mean, we live in Queens."

"I know, but Harlem is known as the Black Mecca."

"Listen, the clubs in Harlem are full of whites every night."

Lila added, "Dear, that's part of the Café Society. Many of the social types travel up there for the music and shows. Your mother and father and Carter's father and I used to go to Harlem quite a lot when we traveled to New York. All of the big stars appeared in Harlem at one time or another. There is also Sugar Hill where the Harlem Elite live."

Carter added, "Those were probably exciting times and still are today in 1952."

Renee spoke, "Yes, Mother has pictures of you all at night clubs and dances, even with some of the celebrities, like Pearl Bailey and Lena Horne, you were some glamorous ladies."

Lila admitted, "We had wonderful times in those days." Carter looked at his mother, she always seemed to brighten when she talked about the "old days." He had also seen the pictures from the good times when his mother and father were married. They talked more about New York and old times that Lila and Carter's father had experienced.

On Tuesday morning, Peter and Carter were ready for Tommy to pick them up early. Carter had ended the night before talking to Anita. They had stayed on the phone for at least an hour before parents on both ends had asked them to release the phones and save some conversation for when they see each other in person.

When Tommy arrived, Lila and Renee had already left the house with Bob's brother Larry. Carter made sure the house was locked up and went out to Tommy's car. On the way to the stables, Peter brought up Carter's phone call to Anita.

"Hey, Cuz, you stayed on the phone all night with your girlfriend."

Carter glanced at Tommy before he answered Peter, "It wasn't all night, we just like the same things, so we find a lot to talk about."

"Oh, come on, man, you're crazy about that girl. You were sitting on the floor in the hallway all that time looking like you were in another world."

Carter laughed, "Well, yeah, I like her, but we're not going together yet, I haven't asked her." Tommy spoke, "Are you going to ask her?" Carter looked at Tommy and thought he detected a look of disappointment on Tommy's face. He thought to himself, I know I'm imagining things because he must know I prefer to be with Anita, and once she and I get really close, I probably won't be spending much time with him.

When they arrived at Cobblestone Creek, Tommy and Carter got busy with their separate tasks and Peter decided to walk around checking out the place, looking at the horses in the corrals and introducing himself to some of the Stable Hands. One of the ones he met was Steve's neighbor James. Peter walked into the big barn where James was pushing bales of hay out in a wheelbarrow.

"Hey, how you doing? I'm Peter, just visiting from New York." James stopped, they shook hands.

"Yeah, I'm James, glad to meet you. Who are you with, did you come out to ride?"

"Yeah, I want to learn as soon as Carter has time to help me."

"That stuck up ass! He's not the one you want to ask for help. He's always sucking up to Tommy the manager, and he's a prick. I can take you out and give you pointers."

Peter answered, "Oh, really? Well, that prick is my cousin and one of the nicest guys I know. Also, I don't like anybody calling him names."

James was surprised by this response but didn't back down.

Instead he said, "Well, if he's your cousin, you don't have a choice, but I do and I'll call him names if I feel like it."

"Hey, man, I'm a visitor here and I don't want to cause trouble, but I will knock you on your ass, so get out of my face." At this time, Tommy came into the barn.

"What's happening, fellows?"

Peter answered, "Nothing yet."

James went back to the bales of hay, saying, "I was just filling him in on what we think of that nerd Carter."

Tommy answered, "First of all, who is we and why are you calling Carter a nerd?"

"I'm sure all of the others will agree with me because he is a nerd and a suck up."

"Carter is well liked around here, he's helpful and he even put in a good word for you. That's why you're allowed to hang around here."

"Steve put in a good word for me. Carter didn't have anything to do with it."

Tommy replied, "I'm not going to argue with you. If you don't like the way things are run around here or the people, you can get the fuck out."

James dropped the hook he was using to lift the bales of hay and started out of the barn.

"Fuck you and that faggot, I don't need you." Peter suddenly stepped up and punched James in the mouth. James fell to the ground.

Tommy held Peter back and James got up, saying, "The next time I see your sissy cousin, I'm going to take it out on him."

Peter, still struggling to get at James, warned him, "You touch Carter and I will come down from New York to whip your ass."

Tommy, still holding Peter back, said. "By the time you get here from New York, there won't be anything left of him for you to beat. I will kill him if he even looks at Carter." James stormed off.

Carter by this time had heard some of the commotion outside and some of the other stable workers had gathered around to watch the altercation. When Carter came into the barn, Tommy had released Peter and was telling him not to worry about Carter because he would never let anyone touch him. Carter was embarrassed.

"Tommy, you don't have to protect me. I can take care of myself."

"You won't have to as long as I am around."

Peter had a quizzical look on his face when he said, "I'd be grateful if somebody cared that much about me."

Tommy spoke, "Ok, it's all over; let's get one of the guys to take Peter out to the practice ring to get him used to mounting and riding one of the gentle horses." Carter offered to work free for the day in order to pay for the time it would take for Peter's instructions. "Don't worry about it," said Tommy "I'll take care of it." Carter wanted to protest, but Tommy walked out of the barn to get one of the Stable Hands to help Peter. Carter went to answer the phone in the office. Afterwards, Carter sat at the desk thinking maybe Tommy was being too obvious. Peter might have gotten some ideas about Carter and Tommy's relationship. Peter's older brother Johnnie was the family secret. He and his lover had met in college, and after graduation, had decided to live together in the Village in New York City.

When Carter had gone with his mother to visit Cousin Rita and her family, he had avoided Johnnie because he secretly thought that Johnnie would detect something different about him. Johnnie and his partner Carl became very successful interior decorators who were very sought after by very wealthy clients, even some of the big celebrities.

Carter's thoughts were interrupted by Tommy's entrance into the office. "You okay, Carter?"

"Of course, I'm okay, you don't have to watch over me. I'm fine."

Tommy replied gently, "I know you can take care of yourself, but I'm not going to let anybody do anything to hurt you." Carter looked at him and became a little overwhelmed; he fought the urge to tell Tommy that he cared a lot for him, in fact now as he looked up at him, he felt like he wanted to hold him. Tommy seemed to read his thoughts because he walked around behind the desk and put his hands on Carter's shoulders. He leaned down and put his face next to Carter's cheek to cheek. Carter contained himself.

"Tommy, don't, somebody will come in."

"I don't care what anyone else thinks! It doesn't bother me."

"Well, I do, especially if it's my cousin. I don't need my parents finding out I've been kissing a guy."

Tommy quipped, "It's not just kissing." Carter let that remark pass. Tommy walked to the office door, saying, "I'll treat you and Peter to lunch, think about what you want me to order."

"Okay, but I already think pizza would be good. Peter thinks New York has the best. We can prove him wrong."

The rest of the day went by quickly. They had pizza with the works for lunch and Peter admitted it was almost as good as New York's. Tracy, Tommy's assistant, joined them for lunch in the office. He was teasing and bragging about Tommy's prowess with the girls and women around the stables, and in fact, in the area bars. Carter was pleased by the comments from Tracy thinking that this might make Peter realize that both he and Tommy were only into girls.

Peter was in a good mood as a result of his riding instructions. When Tommy drove them home, Peter got out of the car and thanked Tommy for a great day. Carter lingered by the car, leaning into the window.

Tommy said, "Get in, so we can talk." As usual Carter was reluctant to give an appearance of being too close to Tommy.

He answered, "No, we can talk another time."

"I only wanted to tell you not to pay any attention to what Tracy was saying about the girls. I haven't been with anyone else since our first time."

"Are you kidding? I told you it's only sex with me; I don't care if you screw some girl or anybody else."

Tommy looked at him without speaking at first and then said, "Carter, I know you're young and maybe you don't feel anything for me, but I do feel a lot for you and I'm always thinking about you."

Carter cut him off, "Look, I'm going to finish high school and I'm going away to college, probably to Penn State. After college, I'll probably get married and move away somewhere. I'll remember you as one of my growing up experiences."

"Boy, you don't pull any punches, do you? I think you might change your mind one of these days. Suppose I told you no more sex, in fact suppose I quit the stables and left town? You might miss me."

"Tommy, I'll see you tomorrow. I don't want to talk anymore."

Carter went up the driveway to the back door of his house. Inside, he walked into the kitchen, his sister Catherine was there with Peter and Renee.

Carter said, "Hi, where's Mother?"

"She is still at the hospital with Bob," said Catherine, "Renee had to take a cab home because Uncle Larry stayed there with Mother."

"Oh, that's what I thought would happen, I didn't believe they would let Dad come home on the same day as the operation."

"That's true, but I think it has turned out to be more serious than they thought," replied Catherine.

Carter was a little stunned at the sound of forbidding in Catherine's voice.

He answered, "How do they know? It's supposed to take time to determine the results."

"Well, I think the x-rays show a lot more than they expected. At any rate, we won't be driving down to Cape May tomorrow." Carter was very upset by this news. The other side of the thing was Renee and Peter would still be there on Wednesday, which might mean he would have to keep them entertained. At least as far as Peter was concerned.

Catherine spoke again, "I asked Renee to come with me tomorrow shopping for beachwear and do. In fact, Peter might go with us, too. We'll spend most of the day in town." In spite of the news about his step-father, Carter was relieved to hear his cousins might spend the next day with his sister Catherine. They had a quiet dinner prepared by Catherine. Carter's niece and nephew were at home being cared for by Catherine's mother-in-law. After dinner, they played Monopoly.

Lila and Larry came in late that evening. After a short time, Larry left for his home, promising Lila he would pick her up the next morning to go back to the hospital during visiting hours. Carter asked his mother to give him the prognosis on Bob. She seemed to be reluctant to talk about his condition in front of Peter and Renee; instead she informed them that Catherine would be going down to the Shore. She would take Peter and Renee with her on Thursday, there was no need to delay their summer vacation because of Lila's need to stay in Philadelphia.

Carter said, "I'll go to the hospital with you tomorrow."

"No, you are due at the stables, and right now Bob is not ready to see too many visitors." Carter was going to object but thought better of it because he didn't want to distress his mother any further.

Catherine rose from the sofa, saying she would be back in the morning to pick up the cousins for their planned shopping trip. Peter and Renee decided to go upstairs to their bedrooms. Carter sat in the chair facing his mother's. Again, he asked her to tell him about Bob's condition.

She responded after a brief hesitation, "Bob has bladder cancer. The surgery that was done was exploratory. They are going to try treatments to see if they can contain it's progress and then they plan to perform major surgery."

"Oh, gosh, Mother, I'm really sorry. When will the treatments begin?"

"They have already begun; as a result, he is quite weak, uncomfortable because there are tubes attached to his body. I am exhausted, so I am going up to bed."

Carter remained there in the living room for a while, thinking about his step-father. He would really miss him if this illness turned out to be fatal, Bob was his moral support. He made Carter feel ready to tackle any obstacles that might stand in the way of any success.

When he went up to bed, Peter was already asleep and Carter decided no floor tonight. He slipped into bed next to Peter and fell into a deep sleep. In the morning, when he awoke, Peter was still asleep; he had one arm and a leg thrown over Carter. Normally, he would have simply shoved Peter over to his side of the bed, but this morning it disturbed him, and he sprang out of the bed. Peter woke up and looked at him, still half asleep and rolled over. Carter was embarrassed; he was glad Peter seemed unaffected by his reaction.

He went into the bathroom and closed the door. He stood looking at himself in the mirror.

"Why the hell did I do that? I've slept in the bed many times with my cousins, it must be because of this relationship with Tommy. It makes me conscious of another guy sleeping in the same bed with me. Now all I can think about is Peter has a nice body and he is pretty decent looking. In fact, he is handsome and very masculine. I have to face it: I'm gay. If I wasn't gay, Tommy would never have convinced me to have sex with him, and what about Tommy? He said he never did this before. Is it that there is one person somewhere that can bring it out in you? So, I brought it out in Tommy and he brought it out in me. Does this also mean that I am in love with Tommy? I think he's trying to tell me he's in love with me. The other side of this whole mess is maybe I want to be faithful to Tommy and I don't want to fool around with other guys. But it's okay to have girls. I'm so confused, I don't know who I can confide in, certainly not my best friend Steve, he is a regular cunt hound and he wouldn't understand."

Carter is snapped out of his reverie by knocking on the bathroom door.

He calls out, "Okay, just a minute."

Peter answers, "Hey, come on, Cuz, I've got to go." Carter had been standing there in the nude.

He said, "Wait, I'm naked."

Peter replies, "So what, we got the same equipment." Carter grabbed his towel from the rack and wrapped it around his body. He opened the door and Peter came in and went directly to the toilet to urinate. He teased Carter, "What happened, did it shrink and you don't want me to see it?"

Carter stammered, "No, I'm older now, so I am modest." Peter finished and flushed the toilet; he was grinning at Carter. He reached and yanked the towel off of Carter. They struggled with Peter now laughing. Peter was taller and much stronger than Carter.

He easily held Carter in a Half Nelson, saying, "Say uncle! Hey, Cuz, you sure didn't shrink, in fact you got a hard-on. What's this do, I turn you on?"

Carter was mortified, he couldn't answer. Peter released him, picked the towel up off of the floor, and handed it to Carter. Carter quickly wrapped it around his waist again. Peter stood there, staring at him.

Finally, Peter spoke, "Hey, Carter, are you gay?"

Carter answered "Are you crazy? No!"

"Look, Cuz, you know it wouldn't make any difference to me; you're still my favorite cousin and you know Jimmy is gay. He came out of the closet in college. I don't care if you like guys, I'm not into it, but to each his own. Did that flake at the stables mess with you? I'll go find him and kick his ass."

"Who, Tommy? No, Tommy is the nicest guy I know." Peter got a knowing look on his face.

"No, I meant that motherfucker I punched in the mouth. I didn't mean Tommy, he seems like a cool guy, but he's a lot older than you."

"I know, are you kidding? Tommy is just a nice guy that I've known and always talked to about girls and all. He had a girlfriend that lived with him. They just broke up."

Peter seemed to accept this, but he continued with, "I mean what I say, Carter. I wouldn't tell anyone if you want to talk about it. I'm only a little older than you, but I know what Jimmie went through before he just accepted it."

"So, you've decided I'm gay without me telling you?"

"No, I haven't. I'm saying if you want to discuss it, we can. It's not something you decide. I think that if you are gay, you were born that way." Peter left the bathroom, Carter was relieved. He had thought Peter was going to shout the alarm to the family, but now he had the urge to tell him everything. However, he had picked up one warning. Peter would not agree with the situation with Tommy due to the adult/teen relationship. The racial thing wouldn't faze Peter; he was a well-rounded guy. Besides his oldest sister, Bernice was married to a wealthy white Texas Rancher, and in a way, he was biracial because his father, Uncle Eduardo, was Puerto Rican. Cousin Rita herself was very light skinned, like most of Lila's family.

Carter made up his mind; he would confide in Peter. He rushed through his bath. When he came out of the bathroom, he went back into his bedroom. Peter was reclining on the bed, waiting his turn in the bathroom.

Carter said, "You can go in now."

"Thanks, your majesty."

"Why did you call me that?" said Carter.

"Because you do seem like the young prince. You are pretty special to the family and especially to me." This answer just solidified Carter's decision to talk to Peter. He knew that Peter was sincere and he realized he was very mature in his thinking.

When Peter came out of the bathroom wrapped in his towel, he went to his bag that was spread open on the stool at the foot of the bed. He pulled out a clean pair of jockey shorts, dropped the bath towel from his waist, and stood there naked, not hurrying to put the underwear on. He didn't seem to be flaunting his body, it was just natural motion, but Carter was transfixed. He had certainly seen his cousin naked before, but he hadn't really looked. He was suddenly aware of how nice Peter's body was and also how well-endowed he was. Peter caught him staring and seemed to speed up getting into his clothes.

He said, "Listen, Cuz, when I said you could talk to me, I didn't mean anything would happen between us. I am not into that. I'm hung up on women."

Carter was embarrassed, "I'm sorry. I didn't mean to stare, I was just thinking that I guess I am gay. I know we are family and everything. I just never had that thought about another guy before."

"Why do you think you've started now?"

"I don't know, lately all I think about is sex. I just feel like I want it all the time. I'm crazy about sex with women and lately it's sex with anybody. I look at guys now as sexual objects just as much as girls."

"Well, Cuz, I would say thinking about sex all the time at 16 is natural, but I think it would be with girls only. If you are thinking about guys, too, maybe you are bisexual."

Carter answered, "I don't think there is any such thing as bisexual. I read about this; there's a lot of theories but most agree you are either homo or you're not. There is no in between."

"That's bullshit, everybody is an individual, so you don't have to be labeled," said Peter.

"I don't know, Peter. I think soon all I will want is a guy. What happened with Jimmie, did he go through this stage?"

"Are you kidding? Jimmie always liked guys and he admitted it, no doubt there. Look, Carter, don't stress about it. If it turns out that you are into guys, don't feel that you are some sort of freak; just relax and live your life, man. It's your life, just be careful not to go off the deep end. Jimmie has told me some real nightmare stuff that happens in the gay world. In fact, why don't you talk to Jimmie sometime in the future if you decide it's not just a phase you're going through. I know you don't know him as well as you know me, but he is a great person and I'm not saying that just because he's my brother."

"I know Jimmie has always been nice to me, but I'm not ready to discuss this with anybody else but you right now."

Peter replied, "You can trust me. I won't say anything to anyone else. Just tell me have you actually had sex with another guy? Is that why you suddenly are so interested in other guys?" Carter was stymied, he finally answered truthfully, "Yes, I have."

Peter asked "Who was it?"

"I'd rather not say." Peter looked at him without saying anything else.

At this moment, Renee knocked on the bedroom door, "Peter, Catherine is waiting for us downstairs; she says we can get something to eat in town."

Peter answered, "Ok, Carter and I were just talking, we'll be down in a few minutes." Carter was overwhelmed with affection for his cousin.

"Peter, do you mind if I just hug you? No funny business, just a hug."

"Hey, Cuz, don't get yourself so uptight, of course you can hug me." Carter put his arms around Peter and thanked him profusely for listening and not judging. They went down stairs where Catherine and Renee were waiting.

Catherine spoke to Carter, "I think it's wonderful that you plan to stay home with Mother while she tends to this business of Bob and his illness." Carter didn't mention that he didn't want to go to Cape May anyway.

"Did Mother leave for the hospital already?"

"Yes," answered Catherine, "Uncle Larry picked her up. I should drive your car today, it's nicer than mine."

"No, I think Tommy is going to come to take me for my driver's test."

"They only give the tests on Fridays and Saturdays at the State Police Barracks," replied Catherine.

"Oh, well, he might just let me drive to the stables and back this evening."

"Anything to keep me from driving your car, don't forget my father gave you that car."

"He's my father, too, that's why he gave it to me."

"You don't even care about Daddy, Bob is your idol."

"I don't know where this is coming from, but I don't have to prove how much I care about our father to you."

"You've got both of them twisted around your little finger," replies Catherine.

"That's not true, you barely talk to Dad, so how can you expect him to adore you, and Daddy wasn't allowed to bring his girlfriend Ruby to your wedding, so he didn't come."

Peter was staring at Carter and subtly shaking his head to signal to Carter to stop.

Carter ended the discussion, which was growing more heated, by saying, "I am not saying another word." He turned to Renee and Peter to apologize for Catherine and his behavior. Catherine was wound up to continue the argument, but Carter walked out of the kitchen to pick up the phone in the hallway. Catherine and the two cousins left for their shopping trip.

Carter dialed Tommy's home number and got no answer, so he called the stable office phone.

Tommy answered, "Hey, Carter, you want me to come and get you?"

"You promised to let me drive my car today."

"You can drive mine, what difference does it make as long as you're driving?"

"I want to drive my own car."

"Okay, I'll be there soon; you're a spoiled brat," Tommy said jokingly. Carter hung up the phone, thinking, Maybe I'm getting too demanding. I better check myself. I don't want to take advantage of anyone, especially Tommy. I want him to keep liking me. As for Dad and Daddy, if they found out that I was making it with a guy, they definitely would not be twisted around my finger like Catherine said, in fact Bob would definitely disown me for being gay, and worse, being with a white guy.

Tommy rang the front door bell &and Carter went to let him in. He told Tommy that he would move his car out of the driveway, so that Tommy could park his car behind his parent's car. Tommy answered he would leave his car parked in front of the house. They went out to Carter's car and Carter got in on the driver's side; he backed the car out of the driveway almost expertly.

Tommy got in the passenger seat, saying, "Somehow I knew you would be a good driver. You are so cool and calm that I knew you would just get in and drive. I think that's part of the reason I care for you like I do."

"Okay, don't start. I'm having enough trouble keeping some details from my cousin Peter." "What do you mean? Did you tell him about us?"

"No, I didn't and I won't, but I did tell him I have had sex with another guy."

"Why did you tell him that, are you trying to get him to have sex with you?"

"What? He's family! What do you think I am?"

"It doesn't matter if he's your cousin, he's still a good-looking guy and that kind of stuff happens all the time, especially with young guys."

"Look, I never thought about any other guys before and especially not members of my family, besides if I did, so what? You don't own me."

"I know I don't, and I don't have a right to ask you that question, but I'm so confused about what's happening with us that I keep thinking you will give in to someone else."

"Tommy, I told you it's just sex, so I don't need to go to any other guys. If anything, I will do it with girls."

"Carter, when you say it's just sex, that hurts. I feel a lot more than just sex with you and I think you feel more for me, but you won't admit it."

Carter didn't reply to Tommy's last statement; he was thinking that Tommy might be right. He didn't want to hurt Tommy and he did feel something for Tommy. He knew he didn't want their relationship to end. He almost said I think I'm gay and I'm only going to be with you, but he controlled the urge.

Instead he said, "I don't want guys, I want girls." Tommy didn't find that comforting either, but he didn't want to push any further.

When Carter turned the car onto the road leading up to the stables, Tommy said, "Park at my house and we'll walk up."

Carter replied, "Tommy, we need to get up there. Troy is going to start wondering about us."

"I'm not worried about Troy; he likes playing boss, and besides, he's the kind of a guy that couldn't care less about what we are doing. I'm just talking about us getting together later." Carter turned up the dirt road to Tommy's house.

They got out of the car and Tommy said, "Come in for a minute." Carter followed Tommy into the house. As soon as he shut the door behind them, Tommy turned and pulled Carter close.

He tightened his arms until Carter said, "You're squeezing the breath out of me." Tommy cupped his hands around Carter's face and pressed his lips to Carter's. His tongue slipped into Carter's mouth and Carter didn't resist. In fact, Carter felt like the heat had turned on all over his body.

When the kiss finally ended, Tommy continued to hold on to Carter.

He buried his face against Carter's neck, murmuring, "I don't know how I fell in love with a 16-year-old kid." Carter was overwhelmed by Tommy's passion; he felt completely submissive. Tommy seemed to collect himself and he stepped away, asking, "Do you want orange juice or something before we leave?"

"No, thanks," answered Carter. He was still gasping for breath.

They went out and walked up the hill to the stables' office. Carter was in a pensive mood and Tommy was being quiet also.

Carter went to the desk and Tommy said, "I'll be in the tack shed if you need me."

Troy came out of the restroom, "Hey, Carter, how you doing?"

Carter brightened a bit, replying, "I'm okay, thanks for answering the phone for me."

"I didn't mind. Tommy tells me you'll be driving yourself soon. Where's your new car?"

"It's down at Tommy's."

"You afraid to drive up the hill?"

"No, it's just easier to leave it down there."

"Well, take your time, soon you'll be driving up and down the hill doing 80."

"I don't think so," answered Carter, "I'm a careful driver. I like going fast but on a safe, straight road."

Troy answered, "We'll see about that once you get used to driving."

Carter spent the rest of the day taking phone calls, reservations, and scheduling horses. He did take a break for a short time with Walking Jennie, who responded by nuzzling her nose against his neck. She made him a little sad because he had told his step-father he was no longer interested in owning her.

When his work day was over, he went to find Tommy, so that he could ride back to his house with him. Tommy told Troy to take over until 6:00 PM and then to shut everything down. Carter and Tommy walked back down to Tommy's house. Carter announced that he had better go right home since his cousins would expect to spend some time with him since they were leaving the next day for the Shore. Also, he wanted to check on the latest about his step-dad. Tommy looked disappointed, but he didn't protest too much because he understood.

"I feel kind of selfish because I wanted you to be with me for a while this evening."

"Even if it weren't for my Dad's condition, I still wouldn't be late tonight because I think Peter would figure out what's happening between us."

Tommy replied, "If he asks me about us, I'll tell him the truth."

"What! Are you nuts? He might tell the family, or worse, he might get violent; he already hinted that it better not be you because of our ages."

"You told him you had sex with someone. I'm not going to lie if he asks if it was me."

"Tommy, my parents would call the police or something. You'd be in a lot of trouble because I'm only 16. Please tell me you won't tell him or anybody."

"Okay, calm down, he probably won't ask me, but if he does, I'll play dumb."

Carter continued driving during this conversation and he said, "You're making me nervous. If you think about telling anybody, I will stop coming out to the stables." Tommy became very quiet. When they arrived at Carter's house, Carter parked in the driveway. Tommy got out of the car and walked toward his car.

Carter asked if he was coming inside and Tommy replied, "No, you would probably be ashamed to have me come in."

"Are you mad at me, Tommy?" said Carter, "You know what I said makes sense."

"That doesn't make it right, I don't like feeling like some freak," said Tommy.

"Let's talk about it tomorrow; they'll be gone and we'll have more time," replied Carter. Tommy got into his car and drove off without another word. Carter went inside.

Peter, Renee, and Catherine were in the kitchen. Catherine and Renee were preparing dinner. Peter asked Carter if the stables were busy that day. Carter answered that it had been a busy day.

Peter continued, "Maybe I should stay in Philly with you and I could go to the stables every day to help out. I like the beach, but if you're only coming down now and then, I'd rather stay here with you. Then we can go down to the beach together." Carter was caught off guard. Any other time, he would have liked that idea since Steve wouldn't be around most of the summer; he would still have a "running buddy" to join him in his forays into the teenage summer party scene. However, he felt he would be deserting Tommy. He was fighting his feelings of deep affection for Tommy.

He replied, "I don't think Sam the owner would like me bringing someone with me to work every day. That would make it seem like I wasn't paying attention to the phone calls or whatever."

Peter looked a little disappointed, but he seemed to accept Carter's explanation. After dinner, Lila had still not gotten home, so Renee went home with Catherine to see the kids. Peter and Carter were left playing cards and listening to WHAT FM Radio.

Peter started the conversation, "I think you don't want me to stay here with you so that you can mess around with whoever the guy is that you had fun with before."

"Peter, that's not true. I just want to work at the stables, talk to Anita a lot, and figure things out."

Peter replied, "You don't want me to know who it is. I just don't want you to be influenced by some sex maniac who is taking advantage of you."

"I'm not being taken advantage of, it's only happening because I want it to."

"Well, I guess you can't be more upfront than that. I'll back off, but you still can always talk to me when you want to."

"Hey," exclaimed Carter, "let's go down and raid Dad's bar. I like to mix some of each bottle with ginger ale or grape soda." They went downstairs to the alcove between the dining room and the kitchen that Bob called his bar. They opened the cabinet where the ample supply of liquor was kept. There were bottles of White Horse Scotch, Gilbeys Gin, Old Hickory Bourbon, and Schenley Blended Whiskey. Carter got a bottle of grape soda out of the refrigerator and poured equal amounts in two glasses. He then poured a small amount out of each of the open bottles of liquor into each glass. Using one of the stirrers in the bar, he stirred the concoctions and handed one glass to Peter and they both drank.

Peter said, "Wow, this is great." His glass was soon empty and they mixed two more. Peter gulped his drink down again. Carter hurried his to keep up with Peter. He noticed that Peter was beginning to slur his words and he was feeling woozy himself. He knew he had made a mistake by deciding to drink alcohol.

Lila would know right away if he tried to talk to her about Bob's condition when she came home. Peter laid back on the bed and quickly fell asleep. Carter decided to get into bed himself, and if Lila came to his room, he could feign sleep. He went into the bathroom and brushed his teeth, thinking that might get rid of some of the smell of liquor. He went back into the bedroom and undressed. By this time, Peter was in a deep sleep, snoring loudly. Carter decided to try to move Peter over, so that he could get into the bed. This proved to be a major undertaking because Peter was completely passed out and he probably weighed 20 pounds more than Carter. That was 20 pounds more of muscle because he had a very developed body.

Carter removed Peter's shoes and socks and proceeded to pull his pants off. Peter stirred and mumbled something unintelligible. Carter finally succeeded in getting Peter into the bed and climbed in himself. He turned the light off and laid there feeling drowsy and touching Peter, but Peter was a restless sleeper and he soon had an arm and a leg thrown over Carter. Now Carter was wide awake, and to his dismay, he became aroused.

He attempted to move Peter off of him, but as he placed his hands on Peter to move him, Peter woke up and said, "Hey, Cuz, I'm not having sex with you."

This angered Carter; he thought, I'm being accused of it, so I'll try it. They struggled a bit and Peter didn't seem to be trying to get away from him.

Peter stopped resisting and said, "What do you want to do to me?" Carter couldn't find words; he just hugged Peter tightly and put his face against Peter's neck. Peter said, "If you want to make love to me, nothing is going to happen on my part. I told you I like girls." Carter knew he should stop, but he couldn't. He kissed Peter's chest and he was on top of him. He lifted up enough to get his jockey shorts down far enough, so that his erection was against Peter. Peter wasn't resisting at all, so Carter was able to also get Peter's underwear down, and when his crotch was pressed against Peter's, he went into motion. When he tightened his arms around Peter, Peter turned his face to the side away from Carter, and Carter was telling himself again to stop when he realized that Peter also had an erection. This gave him impetus to continue. He moved down Peter's body, kissing his chest, his stomach, and finally he took Peter's penis into his mouth.

When it was all over, Peter simply turned over on his side away from Carter.

Carter said, "Peter, I'm sorry. I took advantage of you." Peter was silent.

Carter awoke the next morning feeling ashamed of what had transpired the night before. He got quietly out of the bed, so as not to disturb Peter who was sleeping soundly. He went into the bathroom and bathed in the big claw footed tub. When he finished his bath, he went back into the bedroom with his big bath towel wrapped around his body. Peter was still in bed, laying face up staring at the ceiling. He didn't look at Carter. Carter proceeded to put on his clothes. Peter remained in the same position, not speaking. Carter thought, I've got to say something. I can't just act like nothing happened.

Carter spoke, "Aren't you going to get up and get ready to leave for the beach? Catherine will be here soon with the kids and Renee." Peter turned his head and stared at Carter.

"Why do you care? Now that you raped me, you want to get me out of here as soon as possible." "Hey, Peter, I said I was sorry, but I didn't rape you. You were willing. You're much stronger than me. I couldn't make you do anything you didn't want to do…"

"Wait a minute, are you trying to say I wanted you to do me?"

"No, I'm just saying that you enjoyed what I did to you." Peter leaped out of bed and grabbed Carter's arm. He was poised to punch Carter in the face when Carter burst into tears. Peter stopped mid thrust and dropped his fist to his side.

"Carter, what the hell are you crying for? I didn't hit you yet and I'm not going to, you're still my family, and maybe you couldn't help it, but you planned the whole thing. You got me drunk and then you took advantage of me. You admitted it yourself last night." Carter sat on the bed and continued weeping.

"I didn't mean for it to happen. I was just trying to be cool by offering you booze. I'm always trying to impress you. When you started climbing all over me in bed and then accusing me of trying to have sex, I got mad and decided to do it. I guess I can't help it. I know I'm gay now, I know it."

"Listen, Cuz, I know I told you before. I don't care, but I didn't mean I was going to be your boyfriend or anything, besides we're cousins. Look, it bothers me that you're crying. I don't want to hurt you, so stop crying and let's forget it."

Peter sat next to Carter on the bed and put his arm around Carter's shoulder. Carter pulled away and stood up because this comforting touch made him feel like he was going to get that sensation again. Peter looked at him in surprise and then seemed to realize what caused this reaction. He went into the bathroom to get ready to leave for the Shore.

When Carter walked into the kitchen, his mother was sitting at the table sipping from a cup of coffee. His sister Catherine sat across from Lila. He could hear his niece and nephew playing in the backyard. His mother looked tired and she had obviously been crying. It made Carter very sad to see his mother looking so depressed. He felt so helpless; he wanted to do something to make her feel better, but he didn't know what that could be. He sat down at the table and joined in the conversation between Lila and Catherine.

Renee entered the kitchen. She had arrived with Catherine and had gone up to her bedroom to gather her things to take to Cape May. Carter soon learned from his sister that she was pregnant again. He thought, Wow, she doesn't get a chance to breathe before she is having another baby. Lila answered Catherine's news, "Well, I suppose it is best to build your family in the beginning by having your children all together." Carter thought his mother always looked at the positive side of everything; that was part of what made her special.

Peter came into the kitchen saying, "I put our bags in the front hallway, so we're all set."

Lila said, "Peter, you could stay here and go down with us. When Bob is able, we'll be going down and he will be convalescing in Cape May."

Peter replied, "Carter doesn't want me to stay."

Carter said, "Peter, that's not true. I said I'd be going to the stables every day and you would be by yourself most of the time."

Lila, sensing some dissension, says, "Are you boys alright? I thought you would want to spend the summer together."

"It's okay, Cousin Lila, he just doesn't want me around his girlfriends." Carter stared at him and Peter looked away.

Carter said, "Ok, stay here if you want to, but I know you don't want to hang around the stables." "I'll go with you sometime and I'll help here with Bob until they go to the Shore." Carter realized that Peter really wanted to stay in Philadelphia, so he felt guilty all over again because he felt he was betraying his relationship with Peter and now he wanted him to go, so he wouldn't have to face it.

Peter was looking at him when he glanced in his direction.

He said, "Peter, I want you to stay."

There was a look of real affection on Peter's face when he answered, "If you want me to stay, I will."

"Okay, maybe you can fill in for me today on the phones if Tommy will let you while he takes me for my driver's test."

"Let me? Are you serious? He should be happy I'll be doing it for free. I'm doing it for you, not him."

"Oh, I'm sure Tommy will insist on paying you under the table. That's how Tommy is."

Peter started to say more but instead he rose from the table and went out to the front hallway, saying, "I'm going to put my bags back into your room." Carter didn't bother to remind him that he could move into the front bedroom since Renee was leaving for Cape May.

The front doorbell rang, Tommy was there to drive back to work with Carter. Carter answered the door and invited Tommy to come inside to say hello to his mother. When they went into the kitchen, Catherine was gathering her crew together to leave for the Shore. She looked at Tommy when he entered with Carter. Carter sensed right away that Catherine didn't like Tommy on sight. When Carter introduced Tommy to Catherine, she only gave a slight nod in his direction and immediately turned to Lila, saying she would call when they got to Cape May. It was the kind of slight that doesn't go unnoticed.

Tommy looked very uncomfortable, and when he was introduced to Renee, he didn't offer his hand as he had to Catherine. Fortunately, Renee didn't notice.

She responded by saying, "I'm looking forward to coming out for riding lessons." Lila offered Tommy coffee and a Danish. He accepted the coffee but explained that he had asked his assistant Troy to order breakfast for him and Carter when they got back to the stables. At this point, Carter mentioned that Peter was coming with them to fill in for him while they went for the driving test. He caught Tommy's surprised expression that quickly disappeared.

Tommy said, "Oh, I was thinking we'd go Saturday morning early; you could stay over at my place and we could go directly to the testing station since it's closer to my house."

Before Carter could respond, his mother spoke, "We usually expect Carter to be at home at night, sleeping in his own bed." Tommy was immediately very flustered.

He stammered, "Oh, I only meant that would maybe place us at the head of the line of other applicants."

Lila replied, "Tommy, you are so kind to offer to take Carter for his driver's test, but he knows that you are busy managing your riding stables. His older cousin Henry can take him. He has a lot of time on his hands and that was the original plan anyway."

Carter spoke up, saying, "Mother, Henry didn't show up for the driving lessons last time and Tommy volunteered because it will be great when I can get to work on time. And I don't have to worry about riding my bike home when we work late."

"I agree that would make me feel better, but you should not impose on Tommy's kindness; he has other responsibilities."

Carter was afraid he was sounding too defensive, "I don't need to stay at Tommy's. I can get up real early on Saturday."

Tommy cut him off, "No problem, I'll get here early to pick you up."

Lila added, "We should really pay you something for your time." Carter was upset by his mother's decision to treat Tommy like a hired helper.

Tommy's reaction to her offer was a simple, "No, thanks. I'm doing this because Carter is my friend." Peter was watching Carter during this whole exchange. Carter, sensing Peter's attention, kept his urge to comment under control.

They left for the stables in Carter's car. When they arrived, Troy had ordered two breakfasts for Carter and Tommy. Carter shared his eggs and sausage with Peter. Tommy agreed that it would be okay for Peter to handle the phones, so that they could go to get Carter tested for driving. Troy was available for any questions that Peter might have.

As expected Carter passed his driving test easily.

They were on the way back to the stables when Tommy finally said, "So, your cousin is going to stay with you all summer?"

"Yes, he didn't want to be at the Shore with just the girls and the kids."

"So, what about us?"

"What do you mean, what about us?"

"I thought you might have more time to be with me when your cousin left for the shore."

"He won't be coming with me every day; we can have fun now and then."

Tommy says, "Fun now and then? I keep forgetting you're just a young kid. To me it's more than just fun." Carter didn't respond with his usual bravado. He realized that he understood what Tommy was feeling. He didn't feel it was casual sex anymore either. In fact, his confusion had increased. He felt happy when he was with Tommy and he even wanted to hear Tommy say he wanted to be together more. He still thought about Anita, but now he found himself comparing his feelings for Tommy with his affection for Anita.

Carter broke the silence with, "We can stop at your house if you want to. They won't expect us back for a while."

Tommy answered, "What for, just a hug?" He was smiling. Carter didn't answer; instead of driving up the hill, he turned onto the road to Tommy's house.

Afterwards, when they continued driving up the hill, Carter was sure that he cared a lot for Tommy, and Tommy had told him he loved him during their passionate session.

Tommy broke his reverie, saying, "I'm jealous of Peter." Carter was not prepared to respond to this; he was caught off guard. He regained his composure as he parked in a space behind the office.

"Tommy, he's my cousin and he's only into girls."

"I see how he looks at you," said Tommy, "he really likes you a lot."

"I hope so, he's family and my family members are all close; we care for each other as cousins." "I can't help it. I want you to only be with me."

Carter realized he was telling a lie when he answered, "I'm never going to have relations with any other guy."

That was the beginning of summer vacation, 1952. It was the first summer of awareness. During those hectic and even exciting days, Carter at 16 years of age discovered he could have deep feelings for another male, and in conjunction with those feelings, truly care for a sweet, innocent, pretty girl while also initiating a male cousin into enjoyable consensual sex. The latter happened when Peter insisted on staying with Carter in Philadelphia instead of going to Cape May with the family.

When Carter's step-father Bob was able, Lila took him to the Shore to convalesce. Carter convinced her to trust Peter and him to stay at the house alone, considering that Peter was 18 and had demonstrated a maturity that Lila admired. That first Saturday night when they got back home, Peter asked Carter if Tommy was the person who had been with him and Carter lied again answering no. Peter kept lingering in Carter's bedroom when it was time to call it a night, so Carter finally suggested that he sleep in the bed with him.

When they were settled in bed, it became obvious that Peter wanted Carter to initiate sex with him when he kept pressing his body against Carter. After that night, the sex continued for the rest of Peter's stay. Carter still spent time with Tommy when possible. Actually, Peter was his excuse for having to get home at a reasonable time from his job at the stables. Tommy seemed to become more and more possessive and this made Carter more determined to be uncommitted to their relationship.

As summer waned, Carter spent more time with Anita and Peter. Anita liked Peter right away and often suggested that he date one of her friends. Peter seemed to enjoy being with them for parties, and they even spent a few weekends at the Shore. Anita's parents had a house in Morris Beach, an enclave of black upper middle-class summer homes near Cape May. She and one of her girlfriends would stay in Morris Beach, and Peter and Carter would drive over from Cape May. On these weekends, when they offered to take Renee with them, she refused. After meeting Anita once, she decided that Anita was affected and that any of her friends were probably stuck-up, too. Carter would have been angry at anyone else who said those things about his girlfriend, but he was so fond of his cousin Renee that he let it go.

Suddenly, it was mid-August; the hallway phone was ringing incessantly at 6:00 AM on a Tuesday morning. Carter went sleepily to answer. His mother was on the other end. He was immediately wide awake. She sounded like she was crying. She told him to wake Peter and tell him to get ready to go back to New York right away. Carter knew without asking that it was about Cousin Rita, Peter and Renee's mother. Lila told Carter to be sure to comfort Peter. She said she, Renee, and Bob were leaving Cape May within the hour. Bob would be coming home to stay in Philadelphia and she, Renee, and Peter would be going on to New York.

Carter went back into the bedroom and shook Peter awake. Peter sat up in bed. Carter just put his arms around him.

Peter said, "Cart, I don't want all this hugging and stuff just because we've been screwing around all summer." Carter stopped him with the news about his mother. Peter was overcome with sadness and shock. He cried uncontrollably as Carter held him close and he, too, cried for beautiful Cousin Rita.

Later, they sat in the living room waiting for Lila and Renee to come downstairs. Renee had been inconsolable and had wept profusely all the way up from the Shore. Luckily, Bob had been strong enough to drive because Lila would not have made it. Carter was looking at Peter and wondering about the intense emotion he felt right now toward his cousin. Was it love for a family member, or was it something more? He wanted to hold Peter again to comfort him in his sorrow and he wanted to tell him he loved him. He was sure Peter would tell him to back off because he didn't accept the fact that they had been intimate all summer and were actually "fuck buddies."

Carter finally decided that he had to tell Peter that he loved him and he would always remember this summer. He rose from the chair, and at the same time, Peter stood up. When Carter hugged him, he didn't resist. Carter brushed his lips against Peter's cheek, and when Peter didn't pull away, he pressed his lips against Peter's lips. The kiss on the lips became a passionate tongue on tongue merging of the mouths. On hearing the sound of Renee and Lila descending the stairs, the two boys stepped away from each other.

Carter drove them to 30th Street Station. His mother gave him the money to go buy the train tickets for her and his two cousins. The next train to New York was already boarding, so they went down to the platform. The baggage handler took their bags and the ladies boarded the train.

Peter turned around to Carter, saying, "I'll see you, Cuz." He grabbed Carter's hand and squeezed it tightly.

Carter said it, "Peter, I love you."

Peter answered, "I know, but we won't do anything about it. Take it easy, I love you, too, Cuz." Peter got on the train that was already starting to move. Carter drove back home and went straight to his room.

Carter awoke the next morning; it was Wednesday the last day of August. The events of the last few days came rushing back. He remembered that he hadn't even spoken to Bob the night before to even see if he needed anything. He went into the bathroom, jumped in the tub, and bathed. When he was dressed in his Levi's, he went up the hall to his parents' bedroom and knocked on the door.

Bob answered, "Come in, Carter." Bob was still in the big four-poster brass bed. Carter felt panic realizing that the bed seemed to dwarf his stepfather, who had lost a lot of weight. Bob had been a tall, well-proportioned man before his recent illness, but now he almost seemed to have lost in height as well as weight.

Carter asked, "Can I bring you anything from the kitchen?"

Bob answered, "I'll come down after I wash up and get dressed." He noted Carter's worried expression and added, "Carter, I'm okay. I can fix something for myself. I'm able to move around. I'm getting better. You go ahead and do what you need to do."

Carter backed out of the room, mumbling, "I'll be downstairs if you need me." He was in shock; he had a premonition that Bob was not going to get better. His whole life was changing and this summer had been a major turning point.

When he went into the kitchen, there were dishes in the sink. These were from Bob having to fix soup for himself the night before. Carter was ashamed that he had only thought of himself when he came in last night. He washed the soup bowl and bread plate and put them away. He fixed himself a bowl of corn flakes and sat at the table. The phone rang in the front hallway. He went up to answer it. Tommy was calling to ask if he planned to come to work.

"You didn't show up yesterday and you didn't call. You're so tied up with your cousin that you don't give a shit about me or your job." Carter was determined not to get angry, but now Tommy was being too much.

"Tommy, Peter's mother, my cousin, died and too much was going on yesterday I forgot to call to say I wouldn't be coming out." Tommy was immediately apologetic.

"Oh, Carter, I'm so sorry, I really am. I had all kinds of crazy thoughts. I felt I wouldn't see you again; maybe you and Peter were you know what I mean."

"Tommy, I don't want to talk about that right now and maybe we ought to stop all of it anyway. My father is at home, he is not well enough to go to New York with my mother, so I need to stay home to make sure he's okay."

"What can you do? You can't cook or anything."

"How do you know what I can and can't do? I can be here if he needs me."

"What about me?"

"What do you mean? You guys can run the stables without me and I don't think I'm going to be able to come out to work there anymore."

"I don't care if you work or not. I want to see you."

"Tommy, I don't think I want to do that anymore."

"What do you mean do what?"

"I've got a lot to think about and I need to get ready to take my S.A.T. test to make sure I get a good score."

"If you don't come out to see me, I'll come to your house."

"Tommy, I don't think my dad would like that."

"Carter, what are you saying, don't you want to be my friend anymore?"

"Listen, I'll call you later. I've got to think about everything." Carter hung the phone up and was surprised to see Bob standing there in the hallway.

"Is that the white boy who runs the stables you go to all the time?"

"Yes, Dad, that was Tommy; he just wanted to know if I'm coming out to help today."

"It sounds to me like he was insisting that you come out there. I told you I don't want you working during your summer vacation. What did he say I wouldn't like?"

"Oh, he was just saying I could work there part-time." Carter answered Bob's questions calmly, hoping that Bob didn't hear his whole side of the phone conversation.

Bob walked slowly to the kitchen, saying, "I think you were right when you told him you needed to get ready for your test and your future. He doesn't care if you make a good life for yourself; he's white and he probably thinks you should plan on cleaning out stables for a living."

This statement really angered Carter, but he kept quiet. He knew that Tommy would want the best for him because he knew that Tommy cared deeply for him. With this thought, he also knew he still wanted to be with Tommy. Luckily, Bob had not detected anything unusual about what he overheard in the hallway. He made up his mind to call Tommy when the coast was clear.

Now his thoughts came back to Bob's condition. Bob sat at the table with a cup of instant coffee.

Carter said, "Dad, if Mother were here, you would be drinking fresh perked coffee; she hates instant."

"Yes, she makes the best coffee in the land, but it's easier for me to just drink instant."

"Dad, how do you feel, what did the doctor say?"

"Don't you worry, boy. I'm going to be here a long time. You just get good grades and get accepted at a good college, so you can get a degree. It's getting so that if you don't have a degree, you won't get a decent job. Your uncles, Irving and Larry, both got their degrees and I at least attended college, even though I didn't finish, also your aunts Rainey and Irene finished with Bachelors. As you know, Rainey became a principal in the school system in Atlanta and Irene is a dietician and actually runs the restaurant. As soon as I can, I'll go back to work. The company has been good to me, but I know soon they will be asking me to just quit, so that they can get me off the books."

"I've been thinking," said Carter, "I can apply at Temple or Chaney College and I can commute back and forth that way. I can get a part-time job to pay part of the expenses."

"Oh, no, you won't! You make your plans to go away to college. Even if something happens to me, your mother will get insurance and I've saved good money in the bank, so you both will be okay. Also, the owners of my company have a deal where they promised to consider granting an assistance for my kids to go to college."

"You mean a scholarship? That would be great if I can qualify."

"I'm going to approach them about it. We'll see. You know, Carter, I love you like my own flesh and blood. I want you to have the world. When you graduate, get married, and have a family, I hope you will also look after your mother when I'm gone."

"Dad, you aren't going anywhere. You'll be here with us like you said for a long time." Bob became silent and Carter knew that Bob would not be with the family much longer. For the rest of the day, Bob spent his time upstairs in the middle bedrooms.

Carter found time to call Tommy again. He told Tommy he would find a way to come out to the stables the next day (Thursday). The stables would be busy with Labor Day approaching. Carter wanted to be there to help out, but more than that, he wanted to see Tommy.

The next morning, he awoke with anticipation. After dressing in his Levi's and putting on his Desert Boots, he went up to check on Bob. The bedroom was empty. He became alarmed and went downstairs. Bob was sitting in one of the chairs in the living room. He asked Bob if he was okay.

Bob replied, "I've had too much rest, so I can't sleep."

"I'll fix something to eat," Carter said.

"No," answered Bob, "Bert (Bob's sister) is coming over. She's going to fix food for us and then Mrs. Miller (the new cleaning lady) will come tomorrow and the rest of the weekend to take care of the house and us."

His mother called; the viewing was scheduled for the next evening and the funeral mass on Saturday morning. She also mentioned that the family understood that Carter would not be attending since he was staying in Philadelphia in order to be available if his dad needed help. Carter went into the kitchen and had a bowl of cereal. When Aunt Bert arrived, Carter let her in. She immediately went into the kitchen after speaking with Bob. Carter told her he was going to his part-time job; if she needed him, she could call him at the stables and he gave her the phone number. He went into the living room to tell Bob he would be back by 5:30 PM, but Bob had fallen asleep in the chair by the window. Carter stood there quietly, looking at his step-father. He was very sad; he knew Bob would never be the same again.

Carter drove off to the stables. When he entered the office, Troy was at the desk talking on the phone, taking reservations for a riding party. When he was finished with the call, he jumped up and grabbed Carter in a hug.

"I sure am glad to see you for two reasons. First of all, it's busy as shit, and second, Tommy has been downright evil." At this second, Tommy came into the office.

He yelled at Troy, "Get your hands off of him!" Troy released Carter and stared at Tommy in amazement.

Carter spoke quickly, "Troy was pretending to beat me up for not being here lately." Troy didn't say another word; he just turned and left the office. Carter said, "Tommy, what's wrong with you? Troy wasn't hurting me, he was just saying he was glad to see me."

Tommy answered, "You're driving me crazy, you're nice to everybody but me."

"Tommy, you are losing it I don't even look in Troy's direction, you need to get a grip. I came out here to try to cheer up. With everything that's happening with my family, you start right out giving me a hard time."

Tommy was very apologetic, "I'm sorry, Carter. I don't know why I think you will just go with someone else." Carter felt like the adult in this situation. He looked at Tommy and he could see how upset Tommy was.

"Why are you upset? I told you I was coming out today. You know I'm only here because of you." Tommy started toward him and he held up his hands to stop him from hugging him. "Tommy, we've got to be careful. You've got Troy wondering what's going on with us."

"Fuck Troy, he would probably love to get his hands on you."

"What makes you think that?"

"I don't know. I'm jealous of everybody."

"You don't have to be. I don't mess around with anybody but you, and I don't want to mess around with anybody but you." At this Tommy did grab Carter and he hugged him tightly against his body. Carter said, "I'll stop by your house on the way home." Now Carter felt genuine desire for Tommy; he was thinking, I'm only 16, but I know I really like Tommy and I don't care about anyone else as much as I like Tommy.

The day progressed. There were a lot of other guys and girls, riders and helpers all over the place. Carter was busy with the phones and scheduling. Tommy was saddling horses and assigning some of the experienced riders to go out with people who requested guides or just moral support. When things began to die down, Carter went to find Tommy to tell him he was going to leave. Tommy was in the big barn checking the feed bins and bales of hay. He gave his keys to Carter, telling him to let himself into his house.

Carter drove down to Tommy's house and parked in the back. He went inside and was just sitting down in the living room when Tommy came in. Carter tried to stay calm, but Tommy didn't give him time to sit down quietly. They were together first in the living room and then upstairs in the bedroom. Afterwards, they lay together in Tommy's bed.

Tommy spoke, "Carter, I've tried to go out with girls since we've been together, but I just can't get that interested. If you go away to college, I will be here alone. I don't know what I'll do with you out of reach." Carter didn't respond with his usual, "This is just sex." He was feeling very much of what Tommy was describing, but he also thought about Anita, plus he was looking forward to the college experience, living in a dormitory on his own.

He knew he was getting in deep.

"I will probably end up at Penn State if I'm accepted since I'm a Pennsylvania resident that will be way less expensive than the University of Michigan or Ohio State, my dream schools. My father says he will pay my tuition, but I don't think he has any idea of what it will cost to go to a top ten school."

Tommy said, "I know you are talking about your real father. He has a lot of money, doesn't he? First, you get your own car at 16 and then he tells you he'll pay for your college."

"Please, my father is a genius at making money and at losing money, that's why my mother left him. She never knew what would happen next. That's why I think about the least expensive of the schools I've considered."

"After meeting your mother, she doesn't seem like the type that would talk against your father." "Oh, no, she isn't; when she speaks of him, it's with a kind of affection. She was just used to a more stable life. My grandfather was always very sensible and he ran his farms wisely."

"Carter, when I'm with you, I feel like I'm the inexperienced kid. You seem so mature about everything, even about what's happening with us."

"I don't know what's happening with us, but I know now it's not just sex."

It was 8:30 in the evening when Carter finally left, promising Tommy he would see him Saturday early. When he arrived home, he found a note on the kitchen table telling him his baked blue fish was in the oven. He knew it would be delicious. Aunt Bert was a fabulous cook. Before sitting down to eat, he went upstairs to check on Bob. The bedroom door was closed, but this time, he didn't knock. The room was dim; there was a night light that didn't afford much illumination. His step-father was in the bed seemingly asleep. Carter stood there not wanting to disturb Bob but making sure he was breathing normally.

When he turned to leave the room, his dad spoke weakly, "What time is it?"

Carter answered, "About 9:15."

"What kind of stables are open this late?"

"Dad, this is Labor Day weekend, there are all kinds of activities going on out there."

Bob replied, "Carter, I want you to get back home from there earlier than this. If your mother were here, you know she would expect you home sooner."

Carter didn't want to have a dispute with his step-dad, so he simply answered, "Dad, I'll make sure I'm home by 6:00 tomorrow evening."

He sensed that Bob didn't feel up to continuing with the questioning, so he said, "Dad, I'll be downstairs eating if you need me." While he was enjoying his baked blue fish, the phone rang. When he answered, Steve was at the other end.

"Hey, Cart. I've been trying to reach you. Someone answered earlier, she said she was your aunt."

"Yes, that's Aunt Bert; she's here to fix dinner and stuff."

"Why, where's your mother?"

"Steve, a lot has happened" Carter went on to fill Steve in on what had been going on while he was away in Westchester. Of course, several details were omitted.

Steve had news, too; it had been decided that Steve should spend his senior year attending high school in Jacksonville, Florida. As mentioned before, he had relatives in Florida who had a lot of influence in the community and who would like for Steve to follow family traditions, including continuing on to Fisk University in Nashville, Tennessee. He would be leaving the following week. This gave Carter more reason to think about how his life was changing.

He had been counting on Steve to help provide him with distractions from his affair with Tommy. He thought that with Steve being the social animal, they would always have parties and other social events to attend. Without Steve, he felt that he would not be included by the group of friends and associates they had acquired as best buddies.

Also, this being their senior year in high school would mean that social functions would flourish. The Christmas Cotillion was something else that would be different for Carter, who planned to escort Anita for her coming out and for Steve, who was to escort Alice for her's. They decided after the ball, they would have a suite at the Penn Sheraton Hotel, where they would host an after the ball party. These plans even outdid preparations for the senior proms planned for in May, but they, too, would be memorable affairs. Steve seemed to hear his thoughts.

He said, "Mom says I will come home for Christmas vacation, so we can still plan on the Cotillion." Carter felt a little better hearing this.

"Well, we'll miss you at the parties, but I guess it will be up to me to make the reservations for the Cotillion since I will be here."

"Yes, I'll ask my mom to go with your mom to make reservations for the hotel thing."

"We gotta talk more about that, you know, especially since Annie my mother will worry about a hotel room."

"Oh, yeah, that's right, you're the big-time stud now. You're a bad influence, you have to be watched. Ha-ha."

"What do you mean does your mother know?"

"Are you kidding? Of course not." After Steve left town for Florida, Carter and Anita saw a lot of each other. They were together every Saturday and even attended Mass together some Sundays. However, Carter made excuses for Friday nights to Anita for having to study and telling his mother that he and Anita were together those nights, when in fact he was with Tommy every Friday. His mother was distracted during those days tending to her husband Bob, who seemed worse as time went by.

Carter told himself that he was in control, but deep down he knew that Tommy was his first real love. He also knew that Tommy felt the same for him. He struggled with the homosexual aspect of the whole affair. It felt so natural to be in love with Tommy, he couldn't accept that it was abnormal. In fact, Tommy kept talking about after Carter finished school, they could live together. Carter didn't want to think about that; he faced one day at a time. He still had feelings for Anita. They had come close to going all the way several times, but she had stopped him with the promise that they might for his birthday, which was in November. Carter didn't put any stock in that promise. Girls like Anita didn't go all the way in those days, not before marriage or at least engagement.

When November rolled around, Carter celebrated his 17th birthday. In previous years, his mother made him a cake and they would have a family dinner. He would be allowed to choose the menu. Carter had been able to convince his parents that parties at the restaurant were for kiddie birthdays. This year was different from all of the others because Bob was quite ill and spending most of the time in his bedroom. Now a visiting nurse came twice a week to change the dressings on his surgical wound. His mother was in constant movement fussing over her husband. His sister Catherine rarely came over anymore. She and Bob had had another big blow up that started over something minor and grew to explosive proportions.

So, Anita invited Carter over for dinner with she and her parents. After dinner they each gave Carter a gift, ties, and shirts from the parents and a nice friendship bracelet from Anita. Carter was very grateful. When he and Anita were alone later, he was aware that Anita was very jumpy. We certainly can't fulfill it tonight.

The Christmas season was fast approaching. Carter and his mother had gone to Thanksgiving at Catherine's. Bob's nurse sat with him and served him a meal he didn't eat. Rehearsals began for the Debutants Waltz. After the first session with the debs and their escorts being coached by a flamboyant professional choreographer, Carter felt he would never learn to waltz. When he arrived back at home, his mother asked how the rehearsal had gone. He told her he would never learn. His mother took him into the living room and put Strauss on the record player in the big floor console. She stood him there in the middle of the room and she demonstrated the simple steps of the Waltz 1, 2, 3, 1,2,3, step, and turn. She then told him to place his right hand on her waist, and with his left hand, take her right hand. In no time, they were whirling around the living room. His mother seemed to become young and carefree again.

After that day, when Carter went to the rehearsals, the instructor was very impressed with his progress and Anita was very pleased with her boyfriend's style. As promised, his friend Steve came home for Christmas and they made their plans for the Cotillion, which was held during Christmas week at the Convention Hall. It was a grand social event the young people in formal wear mingled with the adults in their evening finery. Of course, the parents of the debs were all there dining, dancing, and seated at huge circular tables that were placed all around the ballroom at the edge of the dance floor.

The debutantes and their escorts were each presented on a stage at one end of the dance floor. When their names were announced, they stepped to the front of the stage. The debs curtsied and the young men bowed. The couple then walked down the steps to the dance floor where they formed circles. When the announcements were complete and the circles formed, the Grand Waltz began. It was quite impressive with the gentlemen in tails and the young ladies in white ball gowns. Carter was sorry his mother and Bob could not be there because of Bob's condition. Steve's mother was not able to convince his step-father Benny to attend the affair.

However, Dr. and Mrs Chaney were there beaming with pride. It was true their daughter Anita looked beautiful in her ball gown and it made Carter feel on top of the world to be her escort. On that night, Carter fell in love, at least for that night. Steve and Carter had managed to rent a suite of two rooms at the hotel for a gathering after the ball. Two other guys had chipped in, so they invited all of the other couples to come over. They had also wangled a few bottles of alcohol from mysterious sources. Steve ended up on the bathroom floor with his rented tux soiled and wrinkled after starting out looking like he stepped out of Esquire Magazine. Luckily, of course, the adults had all gone elsewhere after the dance trusting their offspring to behave like well brought up gentlemen and ladies. At least there were no serious casualties that night.

During the Christmas vacation, Carter didn't see Tommy and he was surprised to realize he was not sad. There were parties every day and every night; by New Years Eve, the tradition was to drive out to Norristown to Shirley Sherman's house for a huge party to climax the holidays. There was no hanky panky there because Dr. Sherman was there moving through the groups snapping pictures, and Shirley's mother was at the punch bowl serving and replenishing it when needed.

If anyone decided to grind in a corner of the recreation room, Dr. Sherman's deep voice would boom over the music, "No slow dancing!" At most of the parties during those times, chaperones were present somewhere in the houses where the parties were given. Soon the holidays were over and Steve left again for Florida.

The following Friday, Carter resumed his regular session with Tommy. He was surprised to discover that Tommy was upset with him. He informed Carter that he had spent most of the holidays alone and hoping that Carter would at least come out and spend a day with him now that he no longer came to the stables to work. His mother had told him he could not go to work at the stables now that school was back in session. He needed to concentrate on getting good grades. The S.A.T.'s were scheduled for February and he would need to spend a lot of time studying.

Tommy told him he had started seeing another girl that he and Dottie had known when they were together; her name was Nancy. She had called Tommy on one of his loneliest nights and invited him to her place. It turned out that she had been interested in him all along but didn't let him know because of Dottie. Tommy asked Carter how that made him feel.

Carter answered, "What do you mean?"

Tommy replied, "Does it bother you that I've been seeing Nancy?"

"Why, are you having sex with her already?"

"Yes, we have had sex." Carter and Tommy were sitting across from each other at the kitchen table in Tommy's house. Carter didn't react at first.

Finally, he said, "I don't care. I don't own you. Besides, it's okay if you make it with a girl, that's different." Tommy looked perplexed.

He said, "It makes a difference to me, I don't like your being with anyone else."

"Are you serious? You sit there and tell me I can't do it with anyone else and you say you've had this Nancy?"

"I was angry with you because you didn't even call to say Merry Christmas or anything. I didn't say you can't have anyone else. I said it bothers me if you do. If you say so, I won't touch Nancy again."

"Tommy, you are messing up my mind again. I can't think about this stuff. I'm about to go away to college. I probably won't see you for months. What will you do then?"

"I'll wait for you to come back." Carter stood up.

"I'm going home."

"What? It's early, wait, I haven't seen you for two weeks." Tommy got out of his chair and came around the table and grabbed Carter. He wrapped his arms around him and tried to kiss him. Carter resisted and pulled away. Tommy said, "I want to show you your Christmas gift."

"What? I didn't get you a gift, I didn't even think of it."

"That's okay, you've given me a lot. I told you, Carter, I'm crazy about you."

"Oh, sure, but you couldn't wait to fuck somebody else."

"Wait a minute, you just said you don't care if I screw a woman."

"Yeah, I said that, but when you did it, you didn't know how I would feel."

"Carter, please come out to the shed, so I can show you the gift." Carter again felt like the adult in this alliance. Tommy seemed so immature to him suddenly, but instead of being repelled, it made him feel like he wanted to hold Tommy and reassure him. He thought, I need to take care of him because he isn't capable of doing that for himself.

He said, "Okay, Tommy, let's go and look at the gift.."

It was a beautiful English saddle. Tommy must have paid a lot for it.

Carter exclaimed, "Tommy, you shouldn't have spent all this money for me. I didn't even get you anything."

"I told you that you don't have to give me anything. I'm being corny when I say I want to give you everything. You've already got me." Carter turned and hugged Tommy. That night turned into the most passionate one that either of them had ever experienced.

When Carter was dressing in preparation to leave, Tommy said, "Carter, I'm sorry I cheated on you with Nancy. I'm going to stop seeing her." Carter wanted to say don't do that, but he couldn't because he didn't want Tommy to keep seeing her.

Carter arrived home about 11:30, only to find the house empty. The lights were on in every room. He became alarmed something was wrong. He went back into the kitchen and realized he had walked right past a note on the table. His mother had written the note telling him they had to rush Bob to the hospital. He was frightened.

"Oh, God, is Bob dead, what should I do? Maybe I should drive to the University Hospital." He read it again.

His mother had ended it with, "I'll call as soon as I can. But suppose she already called and I wasn't here." The phone rang and he almost jumped out of his skin. Catherine was at the other end.

"Where were you? Mother called Anita's house and she said you weren't there, so if you're cheating on her, she knows now. We're at the hospital. Bob became very ill and he passed out. Mother called the ambulance and I drove down, so she would have someone here. Now Uncle Larry is here. Mother is in with Bob. He is stable now; he will probably have to stay in the hospital. Mother says for you to stay home, there's nothing you can do here. If there are any other developments, we'll call you."

Carter was devastated. Bob was probably not going to survive. He was very fond of his step-father. Bob had always been good to him. He had felt very lucky because he had two strong male role models at each end of the spectrum. Suddenly, in the midst of thinking about Bob, he remembered that Catherine had said his mother called Anita. How much had been said? He felt trapped, he had lied to both of the special females in his life and now he was undone. Lies had led to more lies until finally the original lie explodes.

He went up his room to bed, but he couldn't sleep. Finally, when the weak sunrays of dawn crept through the window blinds, Carter fell into a fitful sleep. He was awakened later by Catherine knocking on his bedroom door.

"I've come to get a change of clothes for Mother. She has a bed in Bob's room, she is going to stay by his side. The doctor told her it won't be long now." Carter didn't want his sister to see him cry, but he felt like he was losing control. He knew that at times Catherine could be cold, especially when it came to caring about Bob. She might even taunt him about his crying over Bob's condition and not caring as much for their father. This, of course, was not true; he cared deeply for his father. He had a sort of idol fascination for him, although he didn't have a desire to follow in his father's footsteps. He admired his way of playing on the edge. He viewed his father's life as exciting.

Bob, by contrast, represented stability and dependability. Catherine went up to their mother's bedroom to pack an overnight bag. While she was gone, Carter managed to get out of bed and into the bathroom with Fawn at his heels. He shut the door behind them sat on the side of the tub and put his arms around his dog and buried his face against her neck and cried. Fawn seemed to know that he was upset, so she stood quietly while he cried softly, so that his sister wouldn't hear him. He almost felt that he heard is step-father telling him to stop crying and be a man. He would now have to step up and be strong for his mother's sake. Thinking this way, he pulled himself together.

When he was finished in the bathroom, he dressed and went down to the kitchen. Catherine was waiting there to tell him to come around to her house later to eat if he wanted to. He answered he could fix his breakfast, and for dinner, he would just warm up some leftovers from the refrigerator.

After Catherine left, Carter contemplated his next move with Anita. Should he call her now to discuss their plans for the evening, or should he wait till later and maybe suggest a movie. If she brings up last night, what should he say he did? He can't say he went to the library; it would have closed by 9:00 PM and he wasn't sure what time his mother talked to her. She will ask why his mother would think he was with her.

"I'm just not a good liar. I'll call her and say I'm going to the hospital to spend time with Dad, so I won't see her tonight."

When Anita answered the phone, she said, "I am so sorry to hear your step-father is ill."

Carter stammered, "Thanks. I'm calling to say that I will be going to see him, so I won't be coming out to your house tonight."

Anita paused for what seemed like a long time before she finally said, "Of course, you should spend time with him, I understand. We can talk tomorrow."

"Yes, I'll call you tomorrow," Carter answered. After he hung the phone up, he sat thinking, Anita had sounded different. She normally would have been more talkative. He was sure she was feeling angry and curious about Friday. Carter had always prided himself for telling the truth. Now he was feeling ashamed and guilty. He knew he would never be able to explain his confusion about his sexuality to anyone. It would just not be acceptable to explain it to his friends and family that he had equal feelings for Tommy and Anita. He decided to put these thoughts aside and to go to visit his step-father at The U. of P. Hospital.

Upon arrival at the hospital, he saw that Bob's minister Reverend Price was there along with Bob's sisters and his brother, Larry. Carter's mother was at Bob's bedside. Reverend Price was giving Last Absolution on the opposite side of the bed. The family was all in the room with heads bowed in prayer. Carter was horrified to realize he had arrived at the point of Bob's departure from this life. He wanted to run to escape this devastating scene. He had never seen anyone die before and he wanted to avoid seeing it now. Suddenly, Bob, who had been laying there breathing intermittently, opened his eyes and looked directly at Carter. He weakly held out his hand toward Carter, who was at the foot of the bed.

Carter, as if in a trance, went to the side of the bed where his mother sat and took Bob's hand. He had tears running down his face. He didn't care if everyone saw his tears. He was crying for the loss of his step-father, which he knew was happening, and he was crying for the loss of his carefree young life.

Bob spoke in a whisper, "My son, be a man for me. Take care of your mother."

Carter leaned down and replied, "Don't worry, Dad, we'll be alright. I love you, Dad." His step-father was still looking at him when he drew his last breath that sounded more like a deep sigh.

The room was suddenly silent, except for the sound of soft crying.

Reverend Price came around and embraced Lila, and then turning to Carter, who stood transfixed staring at his step-father's peaceful face, hugged Carter, saying, "He is with the Lord now, be thankful, no more suffering." Carter pushed away and went out into the hallway. He was in a state of shock. He never really expected Bob to go so quickly. He was thinking, he won't even be here to see me graduate.

Carter left the hospital. He got into his car and sat there staring straight ahead. Finally, he started the engine and pulled out of the parking lot. He drove aimlessly until he realized the park was ahead of him. Without thinking of where he was going, he drove to Cobblestone Park and to Tommy's house. He sat in the driveway, suppose Tommy has company. He had never gone to Tommy's house unexpected. He thought, If he has someone else here, I won't be able to be cool and calm. I know I don't have a right to care, but I do. Before he could decide to just leave, Tommy came out to the car and opened the passenger side door.

"Hey, did you decide to give me a treat and come out here on a Saturday?" On seeing Tommy, Carter just lost it. He started crying. Tommy exclaimed, "Carter, what's the matter?" As he came around to the other side of the car, Carter couldn't answer him at first. Tommy opened the driver side door and leaned into the car, putting his arms around Carter.

Carter was finally able to say, "My dad just died."

Tommy responded, "Oh, man, come on inside, Carter. I'm so sorry, come on."

Carter followed Tommy inside; he shut the door and they went into the living room. Tommy sat next to Carter on the couch.

He started to put his arm around Carter's shoulder, but Carter put up his hand, saying, "Please don't. I didn't come here for that, my step-dad just died."

Tommy said, "Carter, I know, but I just wanted to hold you. I'm not trying anything."

"I know you're not. I want to get myself together that's all." Tommy sat there looking as sad as Carter felt.

He stood up and said "How about a Coke?"

Carter looked up at him, saying, "Yes, I would like a soda, but I'd rather have a drink."

"What? You're not getting a drink here and I'd better not hear of you having a drink anywhere else."

"Why, what will you do about it?"

"Never mind, just remember, you don't need a drink." Tommy went out to the kitchen to get Cokes for both of them.

When he came back, Carter said, "You know you don't have to drink soda because I'm here. You can go ahead and drink whatever you were having when I barged in."

"What do you mean what I was having?"

"Come on, Tommy. I can smell it on your breath. For all I know, you were probably expecting company."

"I wasn't expecting anybody. I thought when you drove up, I was getting a pleasant surprise." Carter put his hand up to his head and said, "I shouldn't just come here without any warning." "Carter, do I have to tell you again? I'm not interested in anyone else. You can feel free to come here any time. I don't need to bother with anyone else."

Carter said, "Okay, I hear you. I know I give you a hard time, but you better find someone to fill in the blanks because I'm going away to college soon."

"You don't understand, Carter. I'm older than you, so I'm more mature."

"Are you saying I'm a child and I don't have feelings?"

"No, I'm saying I take things more seriously than you do, that's all."

Carter was looking at Tommy lounging at the other end of the couch. He was now wishing that Tommy would try to hug him again.

Tommy said, "Will you kiss me now?"

"What? With that alcohol breath?"

"I'll wash my mouth out," said Tommy. He sat up to go to wash out his mouth. Carter stopped him before he could stand and pressed his mouth to Tommy's. This progressed into full on love making. Carter pushed Tommy's T-shirt up and kissed his chest and stomach.

When Tommy reached for him, he said, "No, let me take over." Tommy laid back and Carter continued to kiss his chest and neck.

He pulled Tommy's shirt over his head and unfastened his Levi's. He got out of his own clothes and pulled Tommy's pants off. By the time he had their clothes completely off, he was on top of Tommy making love by just their bodies thrashing together. When the seizure of passion abated, Carter was in tears again. He didn't know why he couldn't control his emotions. He wasn't sure it was all due to the loss of Bob or if there were more reasons. Tommy locked his arms around Carter, comforting him. He didn't say anything, although he wanted to tell Carter how much he loved him.

After Carter had quieted and was sitting up, Tommy started talking, "You know I'm here for you always, Carter, you go ahead and cry as much as you need to, get it all out.

Carter replied, "I don't know what's going to happen now that Dad is gone. I won't be able to go away to school because it will be too expensive, and besides, my mother will be alone."

Tommy answered, "I'll help you with money, but I don't want you to go away, anyhow you said you could consider a local college. Why not the University of Penn or Drexel or Temple?"

"Are you kidding? First of all, I could never get accepted by The Wharton School at Penn, and second, Drexel is a good school overall, but I want to major in Journalism and Drexel doesn't offer a strong course currently in English Comp or English Lit. Besides, I probably would not be accepted at Drexel either. Temple's School of Journalism would be a great choice and I have been accepted at Temple, but I really want to go to Penn State and I want to live on campus. That will feel like the real college experience."

"Yes, but Penn State is a bit of a hike from here."

"Tommy, I could never expect you to help me go to college, you know you can't afford it."

"I've been saving a lot of money. I never know when my bosses might decide to close the stables and sell this land. I need to be able to find a new job and a place to live. Dottie and I were going to try to buy a house somewhere nearby."

At the mention of Dottie, Carter felt pangs of guilt. He asked Tommy if he hears from her. Tommy answered, "She used to call during the first couple of weeks after she left. I finally told her there was no chance of us getting back together. I think she left town."

Carter said, "I feel like it was my fault."

"How could it be your fault? I was screwing all those other women and she knew it. Besides, I came after you, you didn't come after me."

"Yeah, but maybe you would have taken her back if it wasn't for me."

"Look, Carter. I cared for her, but I didn't love her, so let's drop it." Carter became quiet.

Tommy asked about Carter's mother, "Is your mother alone, or is someone at home with her? Maybe she's worried about you, maybe you'd better call her."

"Yeah, I know, I don't know what to say."

"Tell her you'll be home soon. Tell her you're with me."

"I don't think I should, she might think I should have gone to Anita's house."

"Why? She knows we're friends and I'm the person you confide in."

"I'm going to call in a few minutes, let me think first. I hope she didn't call Anita's house again." "Come on, I'll take you home and you can get your car tomorrow. You're too upset to drive."

Actually, Carter felt better and much calmer than he had when he arrived, but he let Tommy convince him to go home in Tommy's car. When they arrived, the house was full of people, neighbors, friends, and family. At first, Carter was concerned about walking in with a white person with all of the people that were there because of his dad's death, but his mother was sitting in the living room surrounded by the bosses from the company that Bob worked for.

Lila looked up when Carter walked into the room and held out her hand. Before he could react, his sister Catherine sprang from the corner of the room.

"Where on earth were you when Mother needs you? You're nothing but a spoiled brat who only thinks of himself."

Carter's mother spoke firmly, "Catherine! Carter has suffered a loss, too; he cared a great deal for his dad."

Catherine answered, "He doesn't even care enough for his own father, let alone his step-father. He's out running around with his buddies or probably cheating on his girlfriend when he should be here helping you."

Lila again said very firmly, "Catherine, please!" At this his sister turned and stormed out of the living room.

Carter went over and leaned down to hug his mother.

One of the men who was there to comfort his mother stood and squeezed Carter's shoulder and said, "So, you are Bob's son? He was proud of you. I'm

Addison Hampton, the president of Bob's company. These other three gents are my brothers. Bob was our best manager. In fact, we were going to place him in charge as the day time manager at the store. We want you to know how sorry we are for your loss. We will miss Bob. I understand you plan to go to Penn State?"

"Thank you, sir, but I told him I'm not sure about Penn State. I may decide on Temple University, so that I can live at home with Mother; she will be alone here in this house."

Mr. Hampton answered, "I'm keeping my promise to Bob. Your college tuition and expenses will be taken care of by the company. We've established a trust for you to draw from as you see fit."

Carter was overwhelmed, "Sir, I'm so grateful. Thank you, thank all of you." He shook hands with all of the men.

His mother spoke also, "Thank you, Addison. Carter will keep you posted on his grades and progress." Tommy had been standing behind Carter the whole time. Carter introduced Tommy to Mr. Hampton, telling him that Tommy had been his summertime boss at the stables. It turned out that the Hamptons owned race horses and had a huge horse farm in Maryland. This revelation led to much conversation between Tommy, Addison, and Carter. Later, when the Hamptons were saying goodbye, Addison gave his card to Tommy and told him to look him up if he was interested in changing jobs.

After the Hamptons were gone, Tommy angled close to Carter's mother, "Mrs. Hawkins, my deepest sympathy. May I hug you?"

Lila responded, "Oh, Tommy, I should have realized Carter would come to you. Of course, you can hug me. I am so pleased that you are here to support my son during our sad time." Tommy leaned down and hugged her and kissed her cheek. Catherine came back into the room, excusing herself from Bob's sisters who were sitting around the living room. She took Carter's arm and led him out into the front hallway.

She whispered, "What do you think Bob would say about you bringing that red neck into this house and letting him touch Mother?" Carter was furious.

"He's not a red neck, he's my friend and Mother likes him. He isn't a bigot. He doesn't make any differences in how he treats anyone."

"What do you mean make any differences? He is lower class, he doesn't belong here. Why in the Hell would you go running to him at a time like this? I don't like the way he acts as though he owns you or something."

"Catherine, he has given me a lot of good advice and he treated me well as an employee." Carter walked back into the living room, leaving Catherine standing in the hall.

His mother was still sitting in her chair by the window and Tommy was standing off near the mantle over the old fireplace. There were more of the church people and members of Bob's family talking all at once. His mother looked tired. He wanted to get her out of there and up to her bedroom for peace and quiet. In strutted his Aunt Ada, she went and hugged Lila. Lila began to cry and her sister Ada told everyone that Lila needed to go upstairs to her room to rest. She asked Carter to help her with his mother.

Lila stood and said, "I'm alright, I can manage." Ada insisted on taking charge and Lila submitted to being led from the room and up the stairs.

On the way, Carter motioned to Tommy to follow him up the stairs with them. When his mother had been situated in her room and some of the other ardent family members had been ushered from the room, his aunt seemed to just notice Tommy.

"You can wait downstairs, we don't need help."

Carter spoke, "Oh, Aunty, I told Tommy to come up. He's my boss from the stables where I worked last summer."

Ada glared at Tommy, saying, "Your mother told me you spend all of your time with horses. You should be going out with some nice young ladies."

Carter should have let the remark pass, but instead he answered, "I am going steady with Anita Chaney, Dr. Chaney's daughter."

"Oh, I see you're hob nobbing with top drawer."

"No, they are nice people, very down to earth."

"I know them and they are top drawer. I saw your Cotillion pictures in the Tribune. You're going to have to make something of yourself in order to be accepted by them."

Carter decided not to respond to the last remark. Tommy was standing in the hallway looking uncomfortable.

Carter said, "Come on, Tommy. I'll show you my room." He could feel his aunt's eyes boring into his back.

When they went into his room, Tommy said, "Wow, your sister and your aunt are different from your mother."

"Oh, yes, but don't ever tell them that they are anything alike; they don't see eye to eye about anything in discussions. My aunt is always implying that this one or that one is a snob and she doesn't admit she is more of a snob than any of the people she accuses. Also, my sister is very critical, but she thinks she doesn't need suggestions about anything."

Tommy sat down in the chair facing Carter's bed.

"I guess you don't want to close the bedroom door," Carter replied

"Definitely not. The next thing I'll hear is Carter had this older guy in his bedroom with the door closed, who knows what they were doing."

Tommy said, "Don't you think that's a little exaggerated?"

"No, my aunt is something else and my sister doesn't trust anyone, especially anyone white."

"I noticed you said older guy."

"You know what I mean, although you look younger than you are."

"Thanks a lot."

"I know they know how old you are. My mother probably mentioned it."

Tommy changed the subject, "It feels good to sit here in your bedroom. Now when I think of you, I can form a real picture of your room." Carter looked at Tommy, thinking, he must be telling me the truth when he says he cares for me, but I don't want to think about that right now.

They went back downstairs and Tommy said, "I'll come tomorrow to pick you up, so that you can get your car."

"Okay, I'm going to have to stay close to home now that arrangements have to be made for the funeral and everything." Tommy and Carter shook hands as Tommy left. The next day came and went. Carter had his car again and was able to assist at home with errands and such. The house was full of relatives, friends, church members, and co-workers of Bob's during the whole week. The viewing and funeral took place on the following Thursday and Friday. The burial was in Bob's family plot in West Chester, Pennsylvania.

In the following weeks, Carter was glad that Lila's friends stepped in and kept her busy with activities to prevent her from sitting at home being sad. But things changed for Carter. Although Anita and her mother had attended Bob's funeral, Anita had avoided talking privately with Carter. She and her mother did not come to the repast, which was held at the Crystal Inn and not to their house afterward. When Carter called Anita the next day, she came to the phone after what seemed a long time. She told Carter she had been thinking and maybe they should give it a rest for a while.

Carter, being his usual self, said, "Okay, fine, if you feel like talking any time soon, give me a call." He could sense her distress over the phone.

After that he spent more time at home and continued his meetings with Tommy on Fridays. His mother was distracted during those days and didn't seem to notice. Carter was sad at times missing Anita, but he started looking forward more and more to being with Tommy.

So, graduation day arrived. Carter managed to get all A's and B's, giving him a 3.8 average, so he finished in the upper half of his class. That was pretty good since his high school had one of the higher rates in the city. He was amazed when it turned out that he was the only "colored male" to get a full scholarship for the college of his choice presented by Addison Hampton from Hampton Auto Supply. There was one more scholarship presented to a "colored female" for nursing school. Other awards were all presented to Caucasian kids with the exception of those sponsored by some of the wealthy Jewish students' parents who owned businesses.

He was accepted at Penn State University. As it turned out, he was more comfortable about going away to school. His sister Catherine had separated from her husband and divorced him. As a result, she and her children had moved in with Lila. This provided Carter with relief from worry about his mother being alone when he went off to college. Carter went to live on campus in State College, Pennsylvania. As a freshman at Penn State, he was required to live in a dorm on campus.

He had one roommate who turned out to be the regular Joe College type whose name was Ted Hughes. Ted was a member of the famed Nittany Lions football team. Carter didn't feel they had much in common. Ted resembled the actor Tod Hunter, blond crewcut and all. He tried to interest Carter in beer drinking at Otto's with some of the other students (fraternity types). Carter instead connected more with other freshman students, amateur actors, future journalists, and musicians at their gatherings.

Tommy drove up on some weekends and stayed at the local inn. At times when Ted was away at his family's home in Long Island, Tommy stayed in Carter's room. Eventually, Carter became paranoid about Tommy visiting so often and he asked Tommy to stay at a motel that was further from campus. Ted mentioned something to him about other guys in the dorm wondering who his friend Tommy was and why he visited so often. Tommy wasn't fazed by their curiosity but Carter was.

It was close to spring break when Ted was hanging around the room more than usual that he finally asked Carter if he was gay. Carter had been expecting him to ask eventually, so he didn't feign indignity nor did he worry that Ted would start spreading the rumor.

He simply answered with the question "Why?"

This threw Ted off guard; he stammered, "I don't care, it doesn't bother me. I just want to know if I should expect you to come sneaking into my bed one night." Carter though not admitting he was gay assured Ted that he was not his type. At this reply, Ted laughed and said "Why? Am I not rough enough for you?" Carter started to reply sarcastically when he realized that Ted was not belittling him, he was simply wondering why Carter wasn't interested in him. He went on to say, "It can't be because I'm white because your buddy is white."

Carter was baffled; he wondered if everybody was gay. He had thought he was all alone with his sexual proclivities.

He answered, "So, if I was gay, I should be coming on to you?" Ted looked confused.

"I don't mean you should fall in love with me or anything, but gays don't usually think about anything but having sex with anybody they can get." This really set Carter off. He found himself defending the gay life, even though he didn't know that much about it.

"Gay people are just like everybody else, except they chose to be with someone who is of the same sex. Which means they can fall in love with one person just like anybody else."

"Carter, I'm not trying to put gay people down. Look at me and my buddies, we have gone down to the Village in New York and hooked up with guys who like to give blow jobs for kicks. I enjoy it. I can get my rocks off without getting some girl pregnant."

"Listen, Ted, I'm sure there are all kinds of people on both sides, so you can't say that all gays or all straight people are the same."

"Okay, Carter, you're getting pissed off at me and I'm not trying to condemn anyone. I just like to party. I can get serious when I finish undergrad and go on to law school."

Carter realized that he was being too sensitive and he was sure that now Ted knew his story or he would not have told him about the visits to the Village. Ted was sitting on his bed and Carter was at the small desk that they shared. They both became quiet and uncomfortable.

Ted finally spoke, "Carter, I'm sorry if I insulted you, it's none of my business anyway. I would never discuss anything about this with anyone else here at school. In fact, if anyone says you are gay to me, I'll punch 'em in the mouth." Carter's first impulse was to tell Ted he didn't need him taking up for him, but he held his tongue. He thought, I had no idea Ted was so cool, he really is a nice guy.

Ted went on to say, "If you and your buddy have something going, that's between you two. I'm just about getting my kicks." Carter realized that Ted was offering him sex and he felt weak. What is it am I so weak that all anyone has to do is offer and I jump in? His appraisal of Ted now turned to: He is really good-looking and well built, he has intense blue eyes, and he is very blond. All of this aroused a beginning of desire in Carter. A battle was going on inside him. He thought of Tommy and how they had now become what? Lovers? Partners? A couple that was faithful to each other? Maybe if he was gay, he should try others and it didn't affect whatever he had with Tommy. He would never tell Tommy there were others, he knew that would upset Tommy.

He had immense curiosity about Ted all of a sudden. He knew if he had Ted, it would be a one-time thing. It would just be like what happened between him and his cousin Peter, and just like with Peter, he would have to be the aggressor. The tension in the room seemed to increase as did the uncomfortable silence. Carter felt like he wanted to get out of the room, and yet he knew he wouldn't because the longer this tension was allowed to mount, the more likely he was going to make love to Ted. He knew the invitation had been given and he couldn't resist it. He felt he was the experienced participant in spite of Ted's Village episodes. Those had only been quick releases. What was about to happen now would be a complete sexual relationship.

When he locked eyes with Ted, he felt there was no way out. He rose from the desk chair and stood over Ted. Ted didn't look up at him; he just sat there on the bed with his eyes averted from Carter.

Carter murmured, "Do you want to?" Ted looked up at him now with a nervous smile.

"Yeah, if you do." Carter went down in front of Ted, and in the same motion, pushed him back on the bed. Ted had his arms spread wide and Carter was on top of him. To Carter's surprise, Ted didn't object to Carter's face against his, and with Ted's submissive attitude, Carter took complete control. He grinded his body against Ted's and he felt that he would have released in his clothes, but he got up and locked the door, getting out of his pants and T-shirt in a flash. He knelt down and pulled off Ted's pants and his jockeys. He buried his face in Ted's crotch, kissing him along his thighs, finally taking him into his mouth. Ted responded with his body writhing and making moaning sounds. The response just inspired Carter and he made passionate love to Ted.

Their love making went on until they were both exhausted. They fell asleep in Ted's single bed. Carter woke first, the actions from the night before came rushing back; he was full of regret, a pall of guilt settled on him. He slipped out of bed, trying not to disturb Ted who still slept soundly. He gathered his discarded clothes from the floor and went to his closet, tossing his dungarees onto the closet floor. He grabbed his towel and shower things and went out to the floor bathroom where he showered and dressed.

Walking out onto the quad, his thoughts were only of a sense of betrayal to Tommy. He didn't really care if Ted told anyone, he only cared if Tommy found out by someone else telling him, as if that could happen since Tommy didn't know anyone at Penn State. He just felt he couldn't go through the same feelings that were prompted by his relations with Peter and his response to Tommy's questions.

For the rest of the week, Carter agonized over how he would seem when he met with Tommy on the weekend. During that time, Ted was obviously avoiding him. He was relieved in a way because he knew that if Ted was in the room every night, it would happen again and that would make facing Tommy even more difficult.

Friday arrived and Carter went into town after his last class to meet Tommy outside of the bus station. Carter was glad to see him; he looked great and he was smiling so brightly at seeing Carter. They drove to a motel on the outskirts of town where Tommy had made a reservation. When they had settled in the room, Tommy held on to Carter for a long time.

"Carter, a lot has happened this week." Carter was jolted by Tommy's statement.

He asked "Like what?"

"I quit the stables and I rented an apartment in the city. I also called your dad's old boss and he gave me a job at the auto supply store."

"Why would you leave the stables, you love the horses."

"Yes, but I care more for you than I do for horses and Sam was giving me flak about taking off weekends." This news made Carter feel worse than before.

"Tommy, you shouldn't be making drastic changes in your life because of me. You don't know what I may decide to do in the future. I might decide I want to move to another city after I graduate. Besides, I probably will get married, and if and when I do, I won't be playing around with you anymore."

Tommy didn't seem perturbed by this statement; he answered, "What we do with each other is not playing around, it is serious, and besides, where you go, I go."

Carter was incensed by Tommy's reply and he blurted out, "I had sex with someone else!" Tommy stood stark still.

"What do you mean someone else? Who? A girl?"

"No," answered Carter. "A guy!" Tommy sat down on the bed, which dominated the small room. He buried his face in his hands. Carter remained standing, immediately regretting his outburst. Tommy finally stood up and started for the door.

Carter reached out and grabbed his arm, but Tommy jerked away, saying through his teeth, "Don't touch me. I don't want to hurt you." He went out slamming the door behind him.

Carter was truly shaken by Tommy's reaction. He thought, maybe I should leave and go back to the campus." Instead he sat on the bed. After some time, he laid back on the bed; not knowing what else to do, he fell asleep. He was awakened later abruptly by the door slamming and Tommy was standing over him, looking bleary eyed and disheveled. Carter started to sit up, but Tommy pushed him back and was on top of him.

"Carter, I'm so in love with you that I can't think straight. You belong to me, I made you. I know you are still a kid and you need to be able to grow up. You're only 19 and I'm 28, but I don't want anybody but you. I never felt this way before. I never made love to a guy before, but it came naturally with you. I know there might be others for you, male and female, but don't tell me about them. I can't think of you with anybody else, just always be there for me."

Carter was overwhelmed by Tommy's passionate declarations; he was obviously drunk. He smelled of alcohol but even that was not unpleasant to Carter. He knew that he was in love with Tommy, too, although he didn't want to be, and even though he didn't know much about being in love. Tommy was still on top of him and beginning to fall asleep. Carter eased him off and pulled him fully on to the bed. He turned him over onto his back and proceeded to undress him. After he had all of Tommy's clothes off down to his jockeys, he pulled back the covers on the bed. By this time, Tommy was completely passed out. Carter, looking at Tommy's beautiful body, decided to massage him all over, thinking again, why would I want anyone else when this is all mine? Nobody else can understand why two guys can actually fall in love with each other and want to be together for the rest of their lives. My friends, my family, and all of society will look down on us."

They spent the rest of that weekend avoiding any further discussion of other people. When Tommy drove Carter back to his dorm on that Sunday, Carter found his room empty. Ted was not there. Carter undressed and got in bed. He was sound asleep in seconds.

The next morning, Carter was on his way to his first class when he ran into Ted going in the direction of their dorm. Ted looked sheepishly at Carter.

"Hey, Carter."

Carter stopped, answering, "Hey, I haven't seen you, haven't you been up in the room all week?"

Ted didn't look directly at Carter, saying, "Yeah, I've been there, but I've been staying with one of the girls I know off campus."

"Ted, we've got to talk. I've got a class now, but I will be back at the room by 1:00 PM."

"Okay, we can talk, but I know what you are going to say already. I know you and your buddy have a thing. No harm, no foul."

"That's not what I was going to say, but let's talk later."

Carter arrived back at the dorm at 12:45. Ted was not there yet and Carter wondered if he would show up at all. He was thinking he had to say something to Ted due to the roommate situation. They could not spend the rest of the semester avoiding each other and being uncomfortable when they ran into each other. He needed to bring it out in the open with Ted.

Ted finally came into the room. It was almost 2:00 PM and Carter had another class at 2:30.

Ted mumbled, "Hi, Carter, I'm here."

"So, I see," Carter quipped.

Ted immediately started talking, "Look, I'm not gay, so you don't have to worry about me trying to break you and your boyfriend up. It was just a sexual release and I admit I wanted it, but like I said, you don't need to think I want to be your lover or anything." Carter found that he felt surprisingly calm.

He answered, "You took the words out of my mouth, except for the part about not being gay. I'm not sure about what category I fit into, gay or straight. By the way, I never told you that Tommy is my lover, maybe he is and maybe he's not. Also, maybe we have sex and maybe we don't."

"I don't care, Carter, I like girls; in fact, I love them, and if I had to choose between you and a girl, I would definitely choose the girl."

"Listen, Ted, I'm not trying to tell you that you have to be one or the other. I'm just saying that I don't expect anything to be written in stone between us. It was just an experience that we both wanted at the time and it doesn't have to happen again. I do appreciate your admitting that you wanted it as much as I did and not taking the usual 'You made me do it.' Thanks for that. Now I've got to get to my class."

Ted remained there sitting on his bed. He had another class to go to, but he didn't feel like going to a class right now. He was thinking that now that they had the talk, he could face the truth. He really did like Carter a lot and he did feel a slight desire for more physical contact with him, but he didn't lie about wanting sex with girls more. He also knew if Carter wanted to again, he would. He now felt relaxed about their previous encounter because Carter had been so laid back about the whole thing and wasn't judging him.

Spring break had arrived and Carter had accepted an invitation from one of his classmates from Puerto Rico to visit San Juan during their time off. They flew off to Puerto Rico via Pan Am Airways in first class on tickets sent by Juan's mother, Donna Felicia. When they arrived at Luis Munoz (SJ Int'l), Juan's mother had his car in the parking area, ready for him to pick up. Carter was impressed by the beautiful island and friendly people. Juan drove them into San Juan, chattering all the way. They would be staying in Con Dado Beach in the Rodriquez penthouse apartment overlooking the ocean. Carter felt very lucky to have made such a great friendship. Juan and Carter had hit it off right away as freshmen. As it turned out, their interests were similar and they had often listened to classical music and discussed books they had read and it turned out that Juan loved Philadelphia. Of course, that was all Carter needed to know. The other plus was being able to converse in Spanish, which allowed Carter to have a chance to expand his limited language skills from the class rooms to actually being able to hold conversations.

Carter had no idea that his friend was from one of the wealthiest families on the island. They owned just about half of the island, which included a huge resort on the Caribbean. As it turned out, for that week, they would have the apartment to themselves since Donna Felicia would be at her home in Bayamon.

Juan said, "The first thing we must do is have a party. I will call some of my friends and have them over this evening. Tomorrow, Mother wants us to come to dinner in Bayamon. After that we will go out to the clubs. They are not as strict about age, they are only cautious about riffraff (Puta's)".

Carter commented, "I don't think I've actually heard that term used in real life. Do you mean lower class?"

"You might say that, but I am referring to hustlers."

Carter was confused, "Do you mean prostitutes?"

"Si, amigo, putas."

"Why? Are these clubs you speak of full of desperate guys?"

"Cartercito, are you that naïve? You must know I'm talking about gay clubs." It now dawned on Carter Juan had decided that he was gay without even asking. He wasn't sure how he should react. He sensed that Juan felt the same way about him as he felt about Juan. It was absolutely plutonic, although Juan was very good looking. The sexual thing was not a part of their affection for each other, it was more like brotherly love. They had never discussed it at all.

Carter decided to go along with the plans. He realized suddenly that he actually felt a sense of relief, in fact, he was happy he had someone he could confide in, someone who was like him.

Am I admitting to myself I'm gay? I know I love Tommy and I know I like sex with Ted and I no longer really miss Anita. In fact, I feel less stressed about not making time to be with her. Speaking of Tommy, I wish he was here to enjoy all of this with me. Juan had been watching him as if he was reading his mind.

"Cartercito, you don't have to be uptight here. We are going to have a great week, and when you return to Ted, you can enjoy your being with him even more."

"Juan, Ted is not the one, Tommy is my friend."

"Oh, mi amigo, you are busy. I thought you and your roommate were the item. I see him watching you a lot of times when we are gabbing away and you are not even aware."

"That doesn't make me feel very good. I do like Ted, but I have been close to Tommy for two years now. I keep getting all of these other opportunities and I can't seem to pass them up. Also, until almost just now, I wasn't admitting to myself that I'm gay. Somehow, I know instinctively that I can talk to you about all of this. I get the feeling that maybe you have knowledge about this stuff that I don't and the other thing is even though we've only known each other a little over a year, I feel like I can discuss it with you instead of my other best friend Steve, who I've known since middle school."

"I am flattered, I do care for you as my good friend, but I knew you were gay when we first met. I thought you knew that I was also in our society in PR; it's supposed to be macho all the way. Luckily, I have an older brother whom you will meet tomorrow. He takes the weight of the heritage off of me. He can carry on the legacy."

Carter accepted all of this with little surprise. He knew that he and Juan were drawn to each other as friends because they understood each other. Later that evening, others began to arrive at the apartment. Juan and Carter had worked along with Ricardo, the very flighty housekeeper who had been instructed to make hors d'oeuvres. The first to arrive was Vincent Calderon, a very good-looking guy who, so Juan explained, was adored by a very famous singer who comes to Puerto Rico to perform at one of the hotels along Con Dado Beach. Whenever he is in town, Vincent visits him at his penthouse condo at the top of that hotel. Vincent was already out of college and working in his mother's real estate business. As it turned out, most of the party attendees were already employed by the airlines. It seemed that most of the children of the middle class and above families ended up either working in their parents' businesses or for the airlines. At that time, there weren't many areas of employment for the offspring who had higher education backgrounds.

The get together was in full swing by 7:30 PM. Carter was conversing with Louis, one of Juan's cousins. Louis was already a doctor and a very interesting guy. Carter felt drawn to him because he had told another guy who was coming on to Carter, to the extreme of being annoying, to leave Carter alone and the person had backed off. Of course, the other reason he was drawn to him was that he found him extremely attractive. He was having difficulty with his conscience again, thinking of Tommy back home. There was great music on the stereo and some of the guys started dancing together in the living room, which opened out onto the terrace that ran the length of the apartment. This was the first time he had seen guys dance with each other and he thought it was too much.

The stereo changed to a slow record with soft Latin drums and Louis took his hand and led him out to the middle of the other dancers. Carter was so surprised, he didn't have time to refuse. When Louis put his arm around Carter and attempted to lead him in the dance, Carter stumbled and he told Louis he couldn't follow anybody in dancing. Louis just laughed and pressed himself against Carter and they fell into perfect rhythm. The champagne that Carter had been drinking helped to add to the pervasive mood that was overcoming any resistance that he felt.

Louis spoke. "Let's leave. I want to show you my place." Carter didn't protest.

They were almost out of the door when Juan appeared, saying, "Don't kidnap my friend, we have a busy day tomorrow."

Louis answered, "I am taking Carter to see my place. I will bring him back." Juan looked at Carter as if to say, "Are you sure?" By this time, Carter was anxious to go and he simply went out with Louis.

Carter and Louis went down on the elevator to the parking area where Louis' car was parked. Carter had always been into cars, and when Louis opened his Mercedes, Carter was taken with the gull wing doors. They drove down Calle McCleary to Ashford Avenue, which is really just around a curve, and made a left onto the first street they came to. From there Louis turned the car into a garage marked private. The building was slightly smaller than Juan's building, but as it turned out, there were three floors with only two apartments on each floor and they took the private elevator to the top floor penthouse, which rose from the rooftop and had two floors itself. The rooftop served as a very large terrace completely surrounding the penthouse.

Carter had always been taught to believe that there are really wealthy people in other places, just like there were on the Main Line in Philadelphia, and they are not all Caucasian. Seeing the great place that Louis occupied by himself proved the fact. In conversation as they sat in front of sliding glass doors that led out to the terrace, he discovered that Louis was being cautious with his approach to the goal of the night.

He said, "Juan tells me you have a friend." Carter was surprised that Juan had told Louis about his attachments. He wasn't sure he liked the fact that his personal business had been discussed without his permission. Louis was looking at him and he knew what Carter was thinking.

"You know, we Latins are very serious in our love lives. We don't believe in being unfaithful to our lovers and we especially don't like for our lovers to be unfaithful to us, that is part of the reason Juan told me about your partner. Juan was trying to discreetly tell me not to tell you that I find you very appealing."

Carter didn't know how to respond, he wanted to try to explain that he was new at this. With Louis speaking the way he was, he felt overwhelming guilt. He wanted to leave; now he was ashamed of his willingness to come with Louis to his home knowing that sex might happen between them.

Louis now continued with, "I wanted to have you no matter what Juan said. So, I'm asking will you stay with me tonight?" The cool and calm attitude of Louis made Carter feel really special. He felt desire return and he became almost speechless, but he managed to mumble a response of yes. It was everything about that night that made him want to be with Louis.

He woke in the morning from a dream about commencement day. It was really strange because Anita was the one who was in the crowd of friends and family. She was smiling and waiting for him to come down from the platform where he had received his degree.

He sat up in the huge bed as Louis came out of the bathroom wrapped in a bath towel. Louis let the towel drop from around his waist, exposing his great body. Carter couldn't pull his eyes away; he knew that Louis was proud of his body and he wanted Carter to admire him.

He said, "Do you like what you see?"

Carter answered, "Of course, you're terrific."

"Maybe while you're here you will decide that I am the only one."

Carter laughed, saying, "I don't know why Juan insists that I have a lover. Tommy and I are just close friends. I've just realized that I like guys and I'm not sure that I only like guys."

"I made love to you last night and you made it back to me; it was wonderful by the way. I must tell you that you are very into a guy."

"I don't deny it. I enjoyed it, too, but I used to enjoy girls also."

Carter jumped out of the bed remembering the plans that Juan had for the day.

"I'd better shower and get back to Juan's, he will be upset with me."

"Don't worry, Juan understands."

"It was rude of me to leave and stay out all night. He had arranged the gathering, so that I could meet some of his friends."

"Listen, any one of those friends would like to have what we had last night. Take your shower and we will meet Juan for breakfast."

When Carter was dressed and ready to leave, Louis said, "Before we go, I would like a good morning kiss." He hugged Carter tightly and kissed him on the mouth and the kiss turned into a passionate tongue on tongue.

Carter finally pulled away, saying, "I've got to catch my breath in a lot of ways. I'm getting confused again."

Louis answered, "I'll give you time, but I already have feelings for you I suppose that is obvious."

Louis had arranged to meet Juan further up Ashford Avenue at one of the hotels for breakfast. Louis and Carter arrived first and were just being seated at a table by the hotel pool when Juan arrived with Jonnie, who Carter realized was Juan's special person. Juan proceeded to address the new affair between Carter and Louis.

"So, are you two an item?"

Louis answered, "We are just friends, as Carter wishes."

"You took my friend away from his party, leaving a lot of his guests without the opportunity to even talk to him."

"Oh, stop being dramatic, Juan. I told you how I felt about Carter."

"It's a good thing I am such a nice cousin, or I might be angry with you," said Juan with laughter. Carter had been afraid that Juan was serious but now realized he was joking.

They had a great breakfast, and afterwards, Louis explained to Carter that he had to see patients and he would join them later at Donna Felicia's for dinner. Juan, Carter, and Jonnie went back to Juan's apartment to change into beach wear. From there they went out on the beach, which was directly across from Juan's building. Quite a few of the people that had been at the gathering the night before were out on the beach. One of those people was the person who had been so persistent at the party, his name was Carlos. He moved over next to where Carter was sitting. Carter was prepared to be nice but to let him know that he was not interested. Carlos, however, was different this time.

He said, "Well, you made your choice for the rich and handsome doctor. I know I don't stand a chance next to him congratulations. I guess he will be your Novio now."

Carter answered in Spanish, "No, no es verdad mi amigo, Louis tambein es mi amigo."

"Maybe you don't know it yet, but that is how it will be," replied Carlos.

After this he moved away and Juan, who had been listening, said, "Don't worry, Carter, when we get back to school, you will still be yourself with two boyfriends. You must understand these boys here are very possessive. It doesn't matter you are not the type to sleep around with just anyone. I can tell."

After the beach, they all decided to stop at Arcos Blanco for cocktails. Carter felt like an adult, so he never thought about being too young to drink. He finally asked what the age limits were and was surprised to hear that the age requirement was 18 in Puerto Rico. This was a surprise because everything else is so strict there with Catholicism being the major religion on the island. By the time they got back to the apartment, Carter was feeling mellow and relaxed. They sat and talked for a while before getting ready for the dinner at Donna Felicia's.

Juan said jokingly, "Welcome to the family."

Carter answered, "Juan, Louis and I just had a night together. I don't think that means we are going to be together for life. I don't even know what I will be doing one year from now, but I doubt that I will be with Louis and living here."

Juan smiled and said, "I understand since I have spent a great deal of time in the States, but it is sort of like Carlos said. Louis will now expect you to either tell him no or he will expect you to only be with him for the rest of the time we are here and maybe he will even visit you at school."

Carter made up his mind; he would tell Louis that he is not his lover and that he will probably not become his lover.

When they arrived in Bayamon at Donna Felicia's home, quite a few of Juan's family members were there. Juan introduced Carter to his gorgeous sister Marisa, who was recently married to Freddy, who Juan whispered was from Mexico. The family was unhappy with the alliance because Freddy didn't have a job until Donna Felicia influenced her son to employ him to oversee some of the properties that the family owned. Juan's brother Tony was obviously the member of the family with authority. He had a law degree from the U of P Law school and was essentially running the family interests since their father's demise. Donna Felicia also seemed to be very capable and handled a lot of the decisions.

All of Juan's family was very gracious and kind to Carter. Everyone was interested in Carter's plans for the future. They all seemed to think that the place for him to consider as a place to live was Puerto Rico.

"Come and join us here, we need young people with talent." It occurred to him that perhaps they all knew intrinsically that Juan was gay and this was like an offspring bringing a potential love interest home for approval. They of course didn't realize that Juan and Carter were just friends. Carter was finding out that most heterosexual people have no real idea of gay life and their relationships. This was even more true in a semi-strict Catholic Society. Juan's family obviously adored him and were accepting of his life style.

When Louis arrived late, the family sit down meal was halfway through. Donna Felicia was definitely into a traditional setting. There was beautiful crystal and china with heavy silverware set on an extended dining table that accommodated the whole family of at least 15 and the housekeeper and her husband were serving. One of the charming things about Donna Felicia was her down-to-earth attitude. She loved to cook and relished seeing everyone enjoy the food. She did require everyone to come to the table in decent attire. Of course, jackets and ties were not necessary, but no shorts allowed. In conversation there was joking about that requirement, but Carter mentioned that his mother was kind of particular about how you came to the table at dinner time also. One of the others reminded that most of the decent restaurants required jackets in the evenings.

Now everyone's attention turned to Louis, who had just been seated at the table and served. "Louis, how are you, we don't see you often enough," stated Donna Felicia.

"I am well, Aunty, but very busy all the time, so I don't get to visit often."

"Yes, well, I am glad you have found time to come and greet our dear friend Carter."

Louis replied, "I was determined to join in today to welcome him to our family."

Carter spoke up, "I feel most welcome. I hope that maybe someday you will all come to visit me and my family in Philadelphia."

"I for one look forward to that," replied Donna Felicia.

Louis added, "It depends on whether you accept my hospitality while you are here."

Donna Felicia said as if perplexed, "He is staying with Juan; he is Juan's guest." Louis didn't explain; he glanced briefly at Carter and continued eating.

After dinner was finished, everyone drifted out to the back patio overlooking a sumptuous, lush garden complete with a swan fountain flowing softly at one end. Carter was talking to Juan's sister Marisa when Louis drifted over and joined in the conversation. Marisa was describing the short time she spent in Mexico after her marriage to Freddy. Louis seemed almost parental when he spoke directly to Marisa, and Carter was feeling a little resentful in his direction because he liked Marisa immediately and he felt Louis was being rude to her.

Later, when he mentioned it, Louis said, "She needs to be told that she made a mistake when she married him. We believe he has already raised his hand against her, and if that is found to be true, the men in this family will have to severely punish him."

Carter was aware of a lot of tradition connected to this family. They seemed to adhere to very old customs in spite of the young offspring that were in charge in most areas. Juan announced that it was time for them to get back to the city.

Louis said, "Carter will ride with me."

Juan turned to Carter and asked, "Is that ok with you?" Carter wanted to say I'll ride with you but felt that might cause a problem, so he answered yes.

When he and Louis drove off, Louis said, "We'll go straight to my place." Carter didn't protest; he felt that excitement again just being close to Louis in the car. When they entered the condo, they went straight to the bedroom.

Later, they were talking about the evening and Carter decided this was the best time to explain that he was not starting a lover relationship with Louis. He definitely found him attractive and sexually exciting, but he didn't want to commit to anyone at this time, and especially someone so far away from home.

Louis answered, "Let's just see what happens this week and then we'll decide. As for the distance, that's what planes are for and I know you want to finish school, so we'll see." Carter could not believe he was allowing this to go on. He knew he should say this is it, it's over, it was just sex, but Louis seemed to have some sort of power over him and he knew it wasn't good for him, but he couldn't break the spell.

He got out of the bed and started to get dressed and Louis said, "Where are you going?"

"I'm going to Juan's."

"I will take you in the morning. Get back in bed."

"Hold up, Louis. I don't take orders from anyone, not even my mother if she gave them." Louis got out of the bed.

"I'm sorry, I guess I'm used to having my way. I don't mean to order you around."

"Good, I know you have to work tomorrow, so I will wait until morning. I don't want to go barging in on Juan and Jonnie this late."

"Ok, please get back in bed." Carter was tired, so he got back in the bed, but he stayed on the opposite edge away from Louis.

In the morning, when Louis came out of the bathroom, Carter rose from the bed without a word and went in to take a shower. When he had finished his shower, he went out and dressed.

Louis came over and tried to hug him, but he stepped away, saying, "I'm ready if you will drop me off at Juan's, I would appreciate it." Louis was upset.

"Of course, I'll take you, but I thought we would have breakfast again like yesterday."

"No, I'm not hungry after that great meal last night, but thanks for the offer."

"Please, Carter, let me give you a hug, don't be angry with me." Carter stood stiffly and let Louis hold him, but he was warming to the embrace, so he pushed him away.

Louis had called Juan to tell him Carter was coming, so when he dropped Carter off at the entrance to Juan's building, the doorman was expecting him and he let him in. Juan was waiting for him upstairs in the apartment.

"Well, good morning, love bird, when is the ceremony?"

"Please," answered Carter, "I am sorry, but there will be no ceremony, in fact, the party is over. I know he is your cousin, but I had to tell him to cool it. He is already acting like he owns me and I feel shaky about the whole thing. Louis says let's go and I obey before I can think about what I want."

"I tried to tell you that we Puerto Ricans can be very possessive. You have to understand that even though you are young and inexperienced, he expects you to only want to be with him." Juan changed his tone to a cheerful one, "Come, let's get ready for the beach and tonight we are invited to George's for cocktails and then to Old San Juan for dinner."

The beach was great and even more fun than the day before. Carter was accepted as one of the crowd. He knew that the feeling was any friend of Juan's was everyone's friend in the group. There was constant banter on all sorts of topics. These were the young offspring of the more influential population of San Juan and the surrounding areas. Much of their conversation was about politics, statehood, or independence. Many of them resented the Mainland

Dominance and so-called welfare programs administered by the government. They thought most of those programs fostered incompetence and insecurity. The resentment ran deep, especially when the fact that in order to get the kind of complete schooling that they had all had the advantage of receiving your parents needed to have enough money to send you to private schools. Carter did not have to struggle with Spanish. Most of the conversations were in English.

After the beach, they again stopped at Arcos Blancos where they enjoyed wine coolers. Carter thought to himself, I'm sure drinking a lot, but I'm on break, why not? They spent only about an hour there. The owner came down from his apartment and joined the group. He was a very interesting person. He had traveled extensively all over the world and he had interesting stories.

When they left, they went back to Juan's apartment to shower and change. When Carter came out of his bedroom all cleaned up and dressed, Louis was sitting with Juan talking. Carter was surprised at first, but realizing how foolish it was to be surprised, after all he was Juan's cousin and would certainly be welcome to come by any time when Juan is in town.

Juan said, "Louis will be driving us in his car tonight."

"Oh, he only has two seats in his car,"

Louis said laughing, "There's a jump seat in the rear, and besides, you can sit on my lap." Carter laughed along with Juan and Louis; he wasn't going to ruin the evening by being sour. They left in Louis' car with Juan crouching in the jump seat.

George (Jorge)'s house was on the other side of Santurce. It was a cottage situated on a beautiful estate off a driveway that led to the main house, which belonged to his parents. All around the outside were beautiful plantings and there was a garden in the center of the Hacienda full of lush flowers and plants. George was from a family of patricians; their roots were heavily intertwined with Castilian Spain. Of course, Juan's mother would also say there was at least a mix of approximately ten to twenty percent of the other Puerto Rican backgrounds. The family had had a family of servants that had served them since the first ancestors had arrived on the island. All of the members of the servants' family were born and lived on the estate and had duties of essentially running the estate from the landscaping to maintaining the houses and cars.

This, of course, was all new to Carter, and in a way, it was quite alien to his thinking. He even mentioned to Juan that the so-called servant family was really akin to slaves who had no avenues to independence.

Juan replied, "Don't ever say that to Jorge, his family believes that they treat that family as part of their family and that they are very good to them. He will be very upset with you. They have their own house on the estate and their parents and grandparents and all of those before them have lived in that house.

George's house was full of guys and girls who all seemed to have stepped out of a vogue magazine. There was intermingling of gays and straights according to Juan's description. Louis was obviously well known to everyone as the eligible successful male that the girls and the guys would like to appeal to. It was whispered around that he had been hooked by Carter. Some of the attendees even gave a little attitude to Carter treating him as though he had come to town and ruined their chances. This was making Carter uncomfortable and he mentioned to Juan that he didn't want these people believing he and Louis were lovers or anything but friends.

Juan answered, "I told you how it is here. One-night stands are not real common here; when someone like Louis is accepted by you, that means you two are together. When we leave for school, you can let him down easy."

When Louis was finally able to get away from the different people who were seeking to speak to him, he came back to Carter's side. Carter kept feeling as if he was a possession of Louis.

When George came over to ask Carter if he was enjoying his first visit to Puerto Rico, Louis spoke up with, "I am making sure he enjoys being here."

George answered, "I can see that Carter is very lucky to have someone so attentive." In spite of everything, the party was great and the guests overall were very friendly and kind to Carter. He was included in a lot of the conversations about politics and careers in business for the future. When he talked about wanting to be a journalist, they were all very encouraging.

When Louis was ready to leave, he told Carter they were leaving and Juan would be getting a ride back with some of the others who would be going in that direction. Carter didn't bother protesting. He simply followed Louis out, thanking George for a wonderful time as they left. Louis drove straight to his place and they sat out on the terrace talking until very late. Louis was ready to discuss his feelings for Carter.

He said, "Carter, I know I came on strong, but I do care for you very much already. I know we just met, but I would like to ask you if you are interested in being my friend. I want to know you. I can tell you I can wait for you to complete your studies at Penn State or we can have you transfer to the University here and you can live here with me."

Carter was very careful with his answer to Louis' offer; he really felt very special to be asked by this really handsome, already successful young guy to be his partner. He even felt affection for Louis. He, too, wanted to know Louis better, but he also thought of Tommy and he realized more than ever if he was going to choose to be with anyone permanently, it would be with Tommy. That is if Tommy still wanted him after all of his other experiments. He remembered that Tommy said he didn't want to be told about Carter's other forays into the gay life, but he wasn't sure if he was asked if he would be able to withhold the truth. Suddenly, he was aware that he was actually considering being lovers with a male instead of a female. He thought, I had to come all the way to Puerto Rico to finally admit to myself I'm definitely gay.

The rest of the week was filled with pleasant gatherings and great beach days. Juan's mother even took Carter and Juan to dinner at one of the exclusive restaurants in San Juan; it was just the three of them and Carter enjoyed it immensely. Donna Felicia was so gracious and kind that Carter became extremely fond of her; it was also obvious that she, too, was fond of him. She had insisted that she should have the opportunity to spend an evening with her two favorite young men.

When Sunday arrived, it was time to return to reality back at school. Louis drove Juan and Carter to the airport and Juan went inside to see that their bags were checked in and to arrange for them to wait in the VIP lounge before boarding. Louis drove the car off into a temporary parking area.

He turned to Carter, saying, "I'm not going inside with you. I don't like goodbyes. I want to hold you for a moment here. I will wait for your call when you get settled back at school."

Carter replied, "Louis, I really like you and I've enjoyed being with you, but I don't want to be serious about anyone right now, so I think we should just say it was nice and move on."

Louis said, "Don't say it now. Call me if you want to continue a relationship. If not, don't call." Carter felt awkward, but he reached out and hugged Louis, who responded with a kiss on his lips. Carter got out of the car and went inside to find Juan.

Back at school the following week, Carter was again involved in his studies. He was thinking, I can't waste time. I need to get my degree and put my life on track. Ted was back from Long Island with the news that he had become engaged to a girl whom he had known since childhood. Carter congratulated him and asked when they were getting married.

Ted answered, "Aren't you going to say you're sorry to lose me?"

Carter replied, "Of course, I know you're joking, but I am very happy for you."

"I'm not joking. I'm not going to keep having sex with you; after tonight, this will be the last time."

Carter laughed at this information and said, "Who says we are going to have sex tonight? I'm thinking about not doing that anymore."

"Look, Carter, I've been thinking about you and me. It's getting to be a habit and I just want to one more time and then we'll agree to stop."

Carter is amazed by this plan if they were going to stop the relationship why have sex one more time that didn't make sense to him. However, as he thought about it, he was very willing to have sex with Ted, but he doubted it would be the last time. Ted stood up from the desk chair where he had been sitting and came over to where Carter was sitting on his bed. He leaned down and kissed Carter on the mouth. Carter responded by pulling him down on top of him.

After much passion on both sides, they were lying nude in Carter's bed when Ted said, "We forgot to lock the door." At the same time, there was a knock on the door.

Ted leaped out of the bed, and Carter not knowing what else to do, pulled the top sheet on the bed over him. Juan opened the door and started in. Ted was still nude and grabbing for a towel to cover himself. Juan stopped midway in the room with a shocked expression on his face, which quickly turned to an embarrassed one.

Juan mumbled, "Oh, I am so sorry, I thought Carter was alone."

Ted replied angrily, "You know he has a roommate. I'm not on display." Ted wrapped the towel around himself, and taking his clothes with him, stormed out of the room pushing Juan aside.

Carter was still in his bed with the sheet over him.

Juan said, "Oh my God, you were having sex." Carter couldn't deny what was pretty obvious.

He sheepishly answered, "We were talking."

Juan said, "Wow, no wonder you couldn't commit to Louis; you're involved with three different guys and this one is gorgeous all over."

Carter answered, "It just happened, it wasn't planned and we said this will be the last time."

Juan said, "I'll meet you downstairs in the community room. I just came over to talk about next semester. We will be allowed to live off campus and I thought we might get an apartment together."

"That sounds like a good idea. I hadn't even thought about it, but I guess it would be a good idea to start planning now. I am sure Ted will be looking to move into his frat house and away from me."

Juan answered, "I know we are close to the same age, but I think I may know a little more about this life than you do. Don't even consider living with this Ted or even with your other friend, what's his name. You are not ready to commit to either of these guys as a partner. You are still in the exploring stage and enjoying it. The moment you move in with one of them, it gets serious and it could turn into disaster."

"Juan, I don't want to just be with one guy or girl, yet I am not sure what I want."

"Si, amigo, that is what I mean. I remember in PR when these two guys were lovers and the one guy that we knew was very flirty, he ended up making out with another guy and his friend found out. He was only 17 and his lover killed him and then himself. "

Carter was astonished to hear that a gay relationship could get that serious.

He said, "I know that Tommy would never do anything like that he would just find someone else, and as for Ted, he's already engaged and will probably get married soon. This is just sex for these guys. As for me, I think if I end up with anybody, I want it to be Tommy."

"But wait, you just admitted that you feel more for Tommy than the other two. That is what happens eventually, you will decide he is the only one and I believe with him that is already how he feels about you."

"I know that Tommy says he cares for me, but I don't think it's love, and each time I'm with someone else, I feel guilty but then I think I'm trying to prove that I can just do it for kicks."

"Oh, my friend, you are so young, and maybe you are really in love with Tommy. I have not gotten serious about anyone yet. Johnnie back in PR is just a passing fancy. I think I keep him around because sub consciously my family would not approve of my being with him, and by the way, he is good in bed. I also have had a few goodies here at Penn State, so I'm not judging. Let's go downstairs, your roommate is probably waiting for me to leave. You can tell him later I think he is HOT and I approve."

Later on, as Juan and Carter sat in the dorm's community lounge Carter saw Ted peering into the room and then disappearing into the hallway leading to the stairs. Carter was anxious to get back upstairs to the room to reassure Ted that his secret was still safe. He finally told Juan he had to go upstairs and they could talk about the plans more the next day.

When Carter went back to the room, Ted was sitting on his bed looking depressed. Carter explained right away that Juan understood and would not mention what happened to anyone at school because he was Carter's good friend.

Ted replied, "I don't care. I'll just deny it if he does tell anyone. I only care about it getting to the Dean or someone in authority. If your other buddy finds out and wants to talk to me, I will have to beat his ass."

"What do you mean my other buddy?"

"You know who I mean, your weekend lover."

"Ted, why are you talking this way? You said tonight would be our last time, now you're talking about beating people up and all kinds of craziness. You are engaged and you will be getting married, so you don't have to worry about beating anybody's ass."

"I'm talking about what has already happened. I may look him up and tell him myself."

Carter was becoming quite upset; he had no intention of ever telling Tommy about his escapades with Ted. After a lot of thought, he had decided he would not admit to any other sexual experiences with anyone.

He sat on the bed next to Ted, saying, "Ted, you're going to be happily married and I will still be this confused guy maybe all alone. Why don't we just forget what has been happening between us and I'll move over with Juan for the remainder of this semester. His roommate stays with a girlfriend and is never in the room. Next semester we're going to find an apartment off campus anyway. Juan is my friend, there's no physical stuff between us, we just see eye to eye."

Ted sits there quietly for a moment before he speaks, "I don't want you to move. I don't know what I want, but I know I don't want you to move. It's not your fault, I'm in it just as much as you are. I promise I won't bother your buddy as long as he doesn't bother me or you."

Carter is still not sure if he should just let this opportunity to get out pass he keeps quiet. Ted starts to put his arm around Carter, but Carter stands up and goes over to his own bed.

Ted says, "I said tonight was the last and it's not over yet."

"No," Carter replies.

"Carter, we had our last time already." Ted got up, took his clothes off, and got into his bed. In a way, Carter is disappointed, he almost wanted Ted to try harder to get him into his bed. Finally, he, too, undressed and got into his own bed.

When Friday arrived, Carter was very nervous about seeing Tommy after more than a week. They met at the bus stop in State College. Tommy was beaming and Carter felt like grabbing him in a hug, but they were standing there on the sidewalk. Tommy had parked his car around the corner, thinking they would have dinner at The Tavern or the Allen Street Grill.

Carter said, "You look well rested, you must be relieved when I'm away."

Tommy laughed, "I spent the whole time watching games on the TV and thinking about today. Do you think your mother would mind if you spent time at my place this summer?"

"I plan to find a summer job maybe at the Shore."

"Why is it always away from me?"

"I don't want to be away from you Tommy, but how do I explain staying with you instead of being at home? Let's talk about it later."

They decided to get take out and to go to their room at the motel. After Tommy had signed into the motel and they settled in the room, they left the food for later and sat talking. Carter was anxious to make love to Tommy. He wasn't fooling himself anymore; he had missed Tommy and he wanted to show him how much. The other experiences had just served to convince him that Tommy was the person he wanted to be with. Tommy was asking him how much he had enjoyed Puerto Rico and what it was like. He was telling Carter he had never really traveled any distance away from home and he wanted to hear all about Carter's trip. This actually made Carter nervous. He was sure if he started talking too much about his visit to Puerto Rico, he would stumble over the time he spent with Louis, and Tommy would sense something.

He remembered Tommy saying he didn't want to know about others and that helped him justify not blurting out the truth.

Finally, Tommy said, "Let's just go to bed." Carter didn't wait for another suggestion, he became the aggressor and Tommy submitted willingly. The food they had bought earlier went untouched that night.

The rest of the weekend was spent watching the TV and talking. Carter felt safe and relaxed; he was thinking, it would be nice to be with Tommy all the time at his apartment, but that can't happen yet. He watched Tommy moving around the room and he felt like he was overcome with caring for Tommy. How did this happen? Neither of them had any difficulty with women. They could easily find females who would be glad to be with either of them. But now there was no doubt about it. Tommy and Carter were lovers.

Finally, it was summer. Carter had succeeded in getting a 3.8, and though that was considered a darn good average, Carter wasn't that happy with the achievement. He wanted a perfect 4.0 and he felt that all of the confusion in his life had caused him to fall short. He applied for and got a summer job at a guest house in Atlantic City. It paid a small salary and a room in a cottage at the back of the property. Carter was better off than some of the other acquaintances that he made who had similar summer jobs but who either shared a room or slept in barracks like conditions with four to six other workers.

When his boss the owner realized that Carter had a friend who came down from Philadelphia every weekend to spend his free time with him, he told Carter he understood and it was okay for Tommy to stay with Carter in his room. That was when Carter became aware of the gay world that existed in tandem with a straight society. Herb, his boss, was obviously partnered with Ronny, who was the combination chef bartender at the guest house. Their quarters were separate from the guest area and consisted of a very nice apartment on the top floor.

Now that Herb had determined the depth of the relationship between Carter and Tommy, he became more like a guardian for the two boys (as he called them). He and Ronny invited them to dinner in their quarters and they enjoyed conversations and Carter discovered that he and Herb liked a lot of the same things. They were able to enjoy classical music together and Carter's suppressed appreciation for art. These preferences had not been enjoyed since his grandmother's demise.

Tommy wasn't that interested in art or classical music, but he became accustomed to both because he wanted to please Carter. Their relationship with Herb and Ronny served to help them with accepting their feelings for each other. Over that summer, they began to feel more and more like a couple and Carter no longer felt that he could be interested in anyone but Tommy. Tommy in turn was completely in love with Carter and only wanted the best for him. He had made up his mind; he would never stop wanting to be with Carter.

It was in that August when Herb announced that he and Ronny were giving a party and there would be friends coming from New York, California, and Florida. The guest house was booked for the week with friends and others would be staying in nearby hotels and houses. Of course, Carter and Tommy were invited not as help but as guests. Tommy was reluctant about being included in what he assumed would be a gay party. Carter was excited because he felt it would be a classy affair with New Yorkers and other sophisticated types.

Tommy commented to Carter the night before the soiree, "I'm not sure I will feel comfortable at a party full of gay people. I'm not like you, I don't know anything about composers and artists and I'm not cultured. These guys will look down their noses at me, I never went to college or anything."

Carter answered, "Don't be silly, who said this was a gay party? They said it's a party. That doesn't mean it's got to be a gay party because they are gay. Besides, even if it's all gay, I'm sure knowing them they would not tolerate anyone who would snub another invited guest. The other thing is if it's all gay, I will have to watch out because somebody will try to take you away from me. Do you realize how sexy and handsome you are?"

Tommy replied, "No, I'm the one who will have to watch out because they will be after you."

The house guests started arriving early the next morning, and just as Carter thought, there were guys and girls, some of whom were couples. Like he expected, they all seemed to have class and sophistication. After Carter had everyone that would be staying at the guest house signed in, he and Tommy went out to the beach at Kentucky Avenue. There wasn't much for him to do at the guest house since the guys hired special help for the weekend to take care of everything. Herb had informed Carter that normally summer employees were expected to work on a party weekend, but he and Ronny had taken the boys under their wing and they wanted them to meet some of their friends and to enjoy a good party. Carter had become quite fond of Herb and Ronny. They were always so cheerful and full of stories about their travels to places all over the world.

Over time Carter found out that Herb was from one of the wealthiest families on the Main Line in Philadelphia, and Ronny's father was the head of a very prestigious law firm in New York. The two had met at Harvard, and from there, the rest was history. They had discovered their preferences together and decided it was a permanent alliance. By the time commencement arrived for both of them, they had moved to an apartment off campus and declared themselves lifetime partners to families and friends. It didn't go over so well with Herb's family at first, but he resisted any warnings about reputation and family tradition and finally his father appeared at their apartment to ask them to be discreet and not to come back to the family home.

Herb, now at 39-years-old, laughs, saying, "Dad was willing to continue my allowance and to provide money for travel, this guest house, and the property in Fort Lauderdale. Of course, when I reached 25, I received access to my trust fund left to me by my grandmother. Plus, we have Ronny's house in the Hamptons; we only go there in the fall when most of the summer types are gone." Carter thought, No wonder you're so happy all the time. You don't have to worry about income. With Tommy and me, it's different, but I think I would like being with Tommy with no questions asked.

When Carter and Tommy went out on the beach, they walked down toward the ocean. Halfway down Carter heard someone calling his name. He looked over at a crowd of young people sitting on blankets and towels. There among them was Denise, Alice, and Louie. Carter went over and Denise stood up and hugged him, kissing him on the cheek.

Denise exclaimed, "Oh, Carter, we haven't seen you since summer began. What are you doing out here? I heard you and Anita are not together anymore; we've missed you." Carter was at a loss for a reply to Denise's questions temporarily. He felt caught off guard being seen with his friend Tommy by members of the so called "in crowd." He knew Denise couldn't wait to get back to Anita with this info.

Finally, Louie chimed in, "Hey, Cart, come join us, what's happening with you, man?"

Carter found his voice and answered, "I'm working down here for the summer at a guest house over near Ventnor."

Denise said, "Carter! In Atlantic City? Why not Cape May or Ocean City? There's lots of summer places down there. Atlantic City is so wild for a young innocent boy like you. By the way, who's your friend?"

Carter answered almost too quickly, "My ex-boss Tommy from the stables."

Denise replied, "Well, another cute friend, hI, Tommy." Tommy stepped up and Denise hugged him, too, which right away put Louie on guard.

Denise commented, "Oh, muscles, my goodness." Tommy responded with another hug and Louie stood up, putting his arms around Denise to show his ownership.

Denise ignored Louie, continuing with her chatter, "Anita is devastated, you know, she and her family are up in 'the ink well' for the summer with all of the old stiff folks. I think she is now seeing John Somebody from Alabama who is an intern at Howard's Med School."

Carter decided not to comment on the Anita topic; he knew it would get back to her with some embellishments.

Carter said, "We have to get back to the house, we were just taking a break."

Denise protested, "Oh, come on, you can sit with us for a while. I want to get more information out of you about what you've been doing for the last year. I know you're at Penn State, Anita told me that, but I was sure you two would be together forever."

Carter replied, "I'd love to sit and chat, but we really have to get back to work."

He and Tommy walked off, waving to everyone in the group.

Tommy spoke when they had gone a short distance out of earshot, "They are an attractive group. So, those are some of the "in crowd" you associate with." Carter was a little disconcerted; he felt exposed in a way and also sad that he was no longer a part of the old group. If Tommy hadn't been with him, he would probably have joined them.

Tommy added, "You pretended that I was working with you or something, like you didn't want them to know I come down to see you. I guess you're ashamed of me because I'm white, I don't have class, and I'm not the college type."

This statement snapped Carter to attention, "Tommy, I'm not ashamed of you and I don't care if they see you as some white guy. I see you as the person I care about as much as any member of my family. By the way, you are a really handsome guy and I'm proud to be with you. Also, they would probably believe that you are a classmate from school if I had thought to say that. You look as young as me. They wouldn't have known the difference." Tommy grabbed Carter's hand and squeezed it. Carter pulled his hand away, saying, "I didn't mean that I want to advertise to the world."

Tommy said, "I like being with you at the beach; someday we may own a beach house with a private beach where we can walk however we please."

Carter was thinking, I wonder if we could eventually be like Herb and Ronny with property together? Of course, we don't have money to start."

Tommy said, "Let's go back to take a nap. This sea air makes me sleepy."

"Ok," said Carter, "but are you sure you want to sleep?"

Tommy replied, "Let's find out." When they got back to the house, they went straight into Carter's room.

By 6:30 PM, the house was alive with activity. The main location for the festivities was the guys' apartment on the top floor, but the caterers set up bars and refreshments in the main floor dining room and out on the back lawn of the house. In the upstairs apartment, the furniture had been moved out of the large living room and the study where there was a huge buffet that stretched from one room into the other. Carter had instructed Tommy on attire, but it turned out that Tommy didn't have white trousers, so Carter had taken him up to one of the shops on the boardwalk and they had bought a pair of linen pants for him to wear. When Tommy put his new pants on, Carter thought, oh, no, everybody at the party will be after Tommy in these pants.

At 7:00 PM, they went up to Herb and Ronny's apartment. There were already a few couples there drinking and talking. They were from New York and the girls were all extremely chic, some of who were with guys or other girls who were obviously not the truck driver types. The guys were all attired in similar outfits, lots of linen, and some khaki but all white and beige. There was already a blend of all kinds of people, Asian, colored, and Hispanic, etc. The apartment began to fill quickly with more guests. Among the new arrivals were quite a few show people, in fact one very well-known female movie star and her young escort came in, causing a stir among some of the others.

Carter felt very proud when he checked out his partner Tommy. Tommy stayed next to Carter and seemed to be trying to let everyone that they were introduced to by Herb know that Carter was his special friend.

Herb announced to everyone, "These are my beautiful young children, they are very innocent, so be nice." The movie star laughed when she heard the introduction and said she would like to borrow the gorgeous blond stud for an evening. Tommy blushed almost purple and Carter actually felt pangs of jealousy, but he knew he didn't have to worry. Tommy made an obvious gesture at that moment by putting his arms around Carter.

In this group, it seemed that Carter and Tommy's relationship was totally acceptable, in fact some of the other guys and girls seemed to be congratulating them on their alliance. There were of course other gay couples, guys and girls, but as Carter realized almost no one was what he would have described as obviously "homosexual." The few "campy" types were holding their own in the "straight world" successfully. When the party had been in full swing for an hour, the hors d'oeuvres were replaced on the buffets by main course fare. All kinds of meats, poultry, and fish were there for the choosing. Carter was thinking, these guys really know how to give a party.

After most of the guests had eaten and drank their fill, Herb announced there would be music for dancing out on the back lawn where a small band was playing. Carter got the chance to dance with some of the gorgeous women when they discovered that he was a very good dancer. When several of the guys asked Carter to dance, Tommy bristled, but Carter was quick to politely refuse. The other thing was that Tommy was also asked to dance by guys and girls. Tommy simply explained that he was not a good dancer, but this served to ease some of the anxious moments.

The champagne was flowing and Carter was indulging with gusto.

Tommy pulled Carter off to a quiet area on the side of the building and said, "Carter, you are drinking too much and that stuff will sneak up on you." Carter laughed at this, stating that he had plenty of champagne in Puerto Rico and he could handle it very well.

Tommy answered, "That makes me wonder what you did in Puerto Rico when you were drinking." Carter wasn't alarmed at all by Tommy's remark. He felt so good and so sure of himself that he didn't worry that Tommy might be suspicious of his actions on semester break. It dawned on him that he would have normally felt guilty but why? He wasn't committed to Tommy or anyone else. In spite of his thoughts, he did slow his drinking down and this helped him to actually last through most of the party.

Things were beginning to die down, a lot of the partiers were drifting off to some of the clubs that were very prevalent in AC at the time that featured big entertainers, like Sammy Davis, Frank Sinatra, Ella Fitzgerald, Dean Martin, and Jerry Lewis. Kentucky Avenue's Club Harlem had Dinah Washington, Sarah Vaughn, Moms Mabley, Redd Foxx, and Nipsey Russell, etc. Carter was now feeling the champagne. He was sitting on the steps that led back into the house. Tommy was standing next to the steps. He had tried earlier to get Carter to go to his room to sleep, but Carter insisted that he was fine. Tommy had thought to himself, if all of these people weren't here, I would pick him up and carry him inside.

Finally, Carter got up and made it to his room with Tommy close behind him. He just fell on the bed fully dressed, so Tommy turned him over on his back and started undressing him. Carter was looking up at him as he pulled the clothing off.

Tommy said, "I told you to lighten up on the drinking."

Carter threw his arms around Tommy's neck and mumbled, "I love you, make love to me." Tommy tried to resist, but Carter kept pulling him down on top of him and finally Tommy gave in, saying, "I'm crazy about you."

The following day, the caterers were back serving brunch to the guests who remained in the house. There were individual tables set up café style in the first-floor dining room. Tommy and Carter were seated at the table with Herb and Ronny. Again, the caterers did an excellent job with the food.

Carter commented, "I hope in the future I can learn to give parties like yours' last night; it was wonderful."

Ronny answered, "It was good because of you two and the other guests. The people make the party."

Herb added, "Yes, maybe we should always have you at our parties as our professional party boys."

Carter replied, "There were quite a few others at the party that would qualify for those positions."

"Yes, but they are not unique because they are at all of the parties," answered Herb.

Ronny agreed, "There is one very rich Haitian at the table over by the window who is still here who can't keep his eyes off of Carter. His name is Lucian and he is very interested."

Tommy spoke up with, "Carter is not available."

Ronny laughed, saying, "Of course not, but we are just being campy and he obviously has eyes for our young friend here. But even if you two were not an item, I would caution Carter about him. He left Haiti rather hurriedly to avoid being arrested by Francois Duvalier's police force. The rumor is that he threatened to kill his ex-lover who cheated on him. There is more violence associated with his family. His father shot and killed himself while on the phone with his wife, Lucian's mother, on the other end. She is remarried to a very important ex-Diplomat from the previous government who has also sought asylum in the U.S. They say he is still not safe in the U.S. because Poppa Doc has put a contract out on him."

Carter said, "It sounds like the movies."

Herb added, "Ronny, stop scaring our boys. Carter is not ready for all of this drama. Lucian is very handsome, but he is also a possessive, jealous maniac and we are not going to let him near our children."

Carter added, "I'm not interested in anybody but Tommy."

Tommy said, "That's the first time you ever said that in front of anybody." He was looking at Carter with that dreamy look again, and this time, Carter loved it. He meant what he said and now he was admitting that he and Tommy were lovers.

When brunch was over, everyone started thinking about their plans for departure. Most of the remaining guests were New Yorkers with a few exceptions, like Lucian who lived in Washington D.C. When Carter thought about it, he realized that, even at the big party, there had been only a few Philadelphians. It brought to mind the story about Herb's father's financial terms. Welcome to the real world. It must be hard to completely isolate oneself from home, friends, and family for love and a way of life.

Carter and Tommy went out on the beach; it was late afternoon and almost time for Tommy to leave for Philadelphia. Carter was surprised to admit that the thought of staying in Atlantic City without Tommy made him sad. After all, it was only for four and a half days, but he was getting so used to being with Tommy that he missed him when he was not around.

Tommy asked, "Why are you so quiet?"

He answered, "Oh, no reason. I was just thinking about the weekend."

Tommy sensed the truth and he said, "I can stay and get up real early and go straight to work from here."

Carter said, "That's going to make you tired all day at work and it will be my fault."

"No, it won't; one of my employees drives up from the shore every day and seems to be fine at work."

So, it was decided. Tommy stayed over until Monday morning and left for work at 6 AM just to make sure he would get to the store on time.

Carter was dealing with his chores at the guest house, checking the rooms after the cleaning crew was finished to make sure all were in order when Herb came upstairs to find him.

"Carter, your mother is on the phone."

"My mother what's going on?" He was looking at Herb and he could see that Herb was upset. Herb said, "Come on to the office." He put his arm around Carter's shoulder.

Carter picked up the phone in the office, saying, "Mother, is everything alright?"

His mother sounded very upset, she replied, "Carter, there's been an accident, it's your friend Tommy." Carter felt like he had been hit by a bolt of lightning.

He responded with, "What do you mean, where is he?"

"He is in the hospital in New Jersey. They contacted the store from his identification in his wallet. Your dad's old boss called me because they can't find anyone else to contact."

Carter said, "I've got to go there. Where is the hospital?"

His mother said, "I understand, Carter, but I don't want you driving when you're upset. I'll call your Cousin Henry or maybe Steve is back in town from his father's."

"Mother, don't worry. I'll be careful. I can't wait for anyone to get here from Philadelphia, I need to go there right away."

"Please be careful, dear," his mother said.

Herb put his arms around Carter, trying to comfort him, and Carter lost it; he wept uncontrollably.

Herb said, "Come on, I will drive you to the hospital." Carter allowed himself to be led out to Herb's car.

Ronny came out still in his chef's apron and grabbed Carter in his arms, saying, "Don't worry, he'll be okay." They drove off to the hospital, which was in Camden. On the way, Carter was now quiet and under control.

He finally said to Herb, "I think God is punishing me because I have been running around with anybody who asked and Tommy just waited for me to wake up. Now he's going to be taken away from me."

"But, Carter, he will make it. This doesn't mean this is the end."

When they arrived at the hospital, Carter went up to the nurses station on the floor they were directed to.

He said to the nurse who was there behind the desk, "We're here to see Thomas McCullough."

The nurse answered, "Mr. McCullough is in intensive care and can only be visited by family members."

Before Carter could reply, an intern who was at the other end of the desk checking patient records said, "Follow me, I'll take you to him." The nurse protested, but he quieted her with, "I'll take responsibility for this." On the way down the hall, the doctor explained that he was glad someone had come to see Tommy because his condition was not good.

Carter had a strong feeling of doom; he could almost hear Tommy telling him to hurry. They entered the room. It was dim and quiet, except for the sound of the oxygen that was pumping into the tent that was draped over Tommy's upper torso and the beeping of a heart monitor. Carter took Tommy's hand in his and Tommy opened his eyes, which immediately brightened at the sight of Carter.

He struggled to speak, saying, "I'm sorry."

Carter replied, "Tommy, it's okay. I'm here, you're going to be okay."

Tommy simply smiled, saying in a strained voice, "No, I messed up." Herb was standing in the corner of the room; he turned and went out into the hallway to find the doctor. He found the doctor back at the nurses' station and asked him for the prognosis on Tommy. The doctor stated that that information should only be given to next of kin.

Herb became incensed, replying, "That's his next of kin in that room with him, he doesn't have anyone else." The doctor took Herb's arm and led him away from the counter.

He spoke in a hushed tone, "Look, my name is Richard Boston. I know exactly what you are trying to say, believe me, I understand. I have a lover. I will make sure your friend is treated fairly in this situation. Is his name Carter? I will put his name on the final papers since there are no other relatives present. When they brought the patient up to the floor, I was checking his vitals and he was asking for Carter."

Herb calmed down now, exclaiming, "Final papers? What are you saying, he won't make it?"

The doctor answered, "No, he won't. I am surprised he is still with us. His chest was crushed in the accident and we were afraid to try surgery because he won't survive it."

"Oh, God," said Herb, "Carter is so young, he will be devastated." With this he went back to the room and realized it had already happened. Carter had lifted the flap on the oxygen tent and he was laying half on the bed with his face next to Tommy's. The doctor had followed Herb back to the room and he came in, shutting the door behind him. He told Herb to help him get Carter off of the bed. Herb took Carter's arm, and with the doctor's help, pulled him off of Tommy's body. Carter was like someone in a trance; he sat down in the chair next to the bed.

The doctor went into action, and as a crash cart arrived with nurses and another intern, Herb and Carter were told to wait in the hallway. Carter got up and woodenly walked out of the room followed by Herb. Herb tried talking to Carter, but Carter was not really responding. Herb finally just decided to hug him. In a short time, the crash cart was wheeled out by the staff and Dr. Boston came over to Carter and Herb, telling them they could go back in to sit for a while.

Carter went directly to the bed where Tommy lay with all of the tubes removed. He looked very peaceful, and to Carter, very beautiful. Carter did not cry, he just leaned over and kissed Tommy's lips. The doctor had come back into the room with them.

He took Carter's hand and said, "I will help you in any way I can. We will make sure his body is released to you or to wherever the final arrangements are being made." Carter was completely confused about what to do. He knew he wanted to take care of Tommy's affairs and his final arrangements, but he didn't know how he would do it.

Herb spoke, "Yes, we will call the mortuary to have the body picked up." Carter turned to say something to Herb, but Herb stopped him, holding up his hand.

The doctor continued with, "I'm sure there is no need to consent to an autopsy since death was caused by auto accident. You can pick up his belongings at the information desk in the front lobby. They'll have them there by the time you get downstairs. Carter, I am Richard Boston, here is my card. I want you to feel free to contact me if you need more information or just to talk. I am so sorry for your loss." With that, the doctor left the room, closing the door softly behind him.

Carter said, "I don't think I will ever get over this."

Herb answered, "Go ahead and mourn your friend. It's the best way to survive, and after you get used to his absence, you will move on."

Carter sat in the chair next to the bed and occasionally he would stand and look down at Tommy's face, touching his cheek with one hand. He couldn't cry anymore; he just felt that somehow Tommy's presence was still in the room with them and he could convey all of the feelings he didn't get enough time to tell him about. The morning slipped into evening and finally there was a knock on the door, snapping Carter back to reality. Dr. Boston came in and informed Carter it was time to take Tommy down to the hospital morgue. The attendants were in the hallway with the gurney. Now Carter panicked.

"What do I do now?"

Herb stepped in, saying, "What we have to do now is take you back to the house to pick up your things and I'll drive you over to Philadelphia to your mother's house. Ronny will drive your car up, so you won't have to worry about that."

Herb went over to say something to the doctor and immediately came back, putting his arm around Carter, leading him down the hallway, saying, "You don't need to watch them take Tommy away, you've said goodbye."

Carter said, "I need to talk to my mother about helping me make arrangements. She had to do all of that for my dad, so she will know, and I guess she will be able to call his boss because he knows her from my dad."

Herb ushered Carter into his car, saying, "Don't worry, I already contacted the undertaker, Baron's Mortuary on City Line in Bala Cynwyd, they will handle everything."

"Herb, I don't know what Tommy had insurance wise or in savings and I don't know how I can get access to them, so I need to ask my mother to help with money. I can't tell her I picked an expensive undertaker; she would probably choose our family's undertaker."

Herb quieted Carter, saying, "Ronny and I love you two, and especially you in the short time we've known you, we have come to think of you like our young brothers. I have a lot of money and so does Ronny; we don't want you to worry about anything. If it turns out we have to get our lawyer to see that you get whatever Tommy left behind, we will take care of that, too. He would want you to have it I'm sure." Carter was overwhelmed with gratitude.

"I don't know what to say. I have my scholarship and the stipend my dad's company gave me. I know my mother would help me, but she has to take care of herself and her home."

Ronny came out to the car when they drove up to the house. He grabbed Carter in a tight hug and Carter had to fight back tears again.

He said, "I think I got all of your things into your bags. You can check the cottage to see if I overlooked anything."

Carter answered, "Thanks, Ronny. I think Tommy left some of his things here, too."

Ronny replied, "I put everything in your bags and your portable stereo is in the backseat of your car, don't worry, our house is open to you anytime. After a while, you might want to come back for a visit."

"Well, yes, the summer will be almost over after everything up in Philadelphia is done. I was supposed to meet with Juan to go to State College to sign our apartment lease next week. I might put that off."

In Philadelphia, they went first to the funeral home where the owner took them into his office. Carter was thinking, this place represents the kind of service wealthy people require, even in death. I feel some comfort in having Tommy's service at one of the best since he never got the chance to know how much I wanted to give him in life. As it turned out, John Baron had been a childhood friend of Herb's, and though he was married to a beautiful woman with two children, he understood Herb's lifestyle and didn't judge. Herb spoke freely to him, explaining that Carter and Tommy were partners in life, so Carter had to approve the arrangements.

After they decided on clothing, coffin, nad burial plot, John led them to the morgue where Tommy's body had already arrived. Now Carter looked at him partially covered by a sheet. He still had the peaceful expression on his face. Carter again felt like he was hearing Tommy telling him not to be sad, that he was okay. He wanted to go home now to be alone, to think about Tommy and to mourn his loss.

Herb seemed to be reading his thoughts, saying, "Alright, John, we'll leave everything up to you. If the service is going to be on Saturday, we had better start sending announcements out by tomorrow."

Carter said softly, "We don't have many people who were our mutual friends, maybe the guys from the stables, and Tommy may have wanted some of his current co-workers and his boss to come. I will call my Priest to ask him to conduct the service for me."

John said, "That's right, was Tommy Catholic?"

Carter answered, "We never discussed his religion; he knew I am Episcopalian, along with my whole family. His parents were killed in a car accident and he didn't have other family living. I guess I will have to ask his ex-boss if he knows of anyone else to notify."

They left the funeral home, and as they drove to Carter's home, Herb was talking, "I know you are very confused now and you are nervous about having your family involved because of your relationship with Tommy, but when I called your mother, she was very upset for you. She said, 'Oh, Carter will be devastated; he loves Tommy very much.' I believe every mother knows her son."

Carter answered, "I don't know how I feel about the gay life right now. I only feel angry that Tommy has been taken away just when I had accepted the fact that I cared deeply for him and I could be with him without shame or worry about being gay."

When they arrived at Carter's house, Ronny had already parked Carter's car in the driveway. When they looked inside the car, it was empty.

Herb exclaimed, "Where is this wild person? He was supposed to wait for us in the car." Carter already knew he was probably inside where Lila had invited him, and sure enough, when they entered the house, there he was sitting at the kitchen table drinking iced tea, with Lila sitting across from him with a dainty handkerchief dabbing at her eyes. As soon as they entered, Lila stood and rushed to Carter, enfolding him in her arms. Carter completely lost it; he wept in his mother's comforting arms.

Herb and Ronny also ended up holding each other and just standing there so overwhelmed with sorrow and no words. Carter was sobbing and pouring out his heart.

"I think I'm being punished, Mother, just because I don't treat people right. I don't return their affection, I don't act like I care, I betrayed Anita. I'm just worthless. But Tommy was just so determined and patient to be my friend."

Lila said, "Hush, son, you're upset now, don't blame yourself. God knows you're good, that's why he gave you these wonderful friends who care deeply for you; don't blame yourself for this. Maybe Tommy was sent to just make you know how deserving you are. Go up to your bedroom and get some rest. We'll be down here when you are ready to discuss your plans."

Carter went upstairs and collapsed on his bed. Even though he was exhausted emotionally, he felt he would never sleep peacefully again, but he did finally fall asleep. He was dreaming, Tommy had entered the room and was standing there looking at Carter with a sad expression.

He spoke to Carter, "I'm so sorry I had to go, but I will still be with you all the time, don't be sad." It was so real that Carter sat up reaching out, but of course, Tommy wasn't really there. He decided to return to the kitchen where his mother still sat now with his sister Catherine, who had come in from her ex-in-laws', and Herb was still there.

When Carter came into the room, the conversation they had been having ceased. Carter strangely enough was feeling better and more in charge.

Catherine spoke first, "Carter, I'm sorry to hear about your friend."

"Thanks, sis, it was a shock."

"Mother tells me there are no known relatives."

"Yes, that's right, we are handling the arrangements."

"Who's we?" Carter was ready for his sister's sarcasm.

He answered, "Herb, Ronny, and me, we have already made the arrangements for the burial." Carter's mother spoke now, "Yes, it seems that Tommy had Carter as his next of kin. I spoke to Addison, Tommy's boss, and he tells me that Tommy had Carter on his insurance and his savings plan."

Catherine replied, "That's ridiculous insurance companies don't pay claims to survivors who are not related to policy holders."

Lila said, "Addison told me not to worry, he would see that Carter gets payment."

Catherine did not comment after that.

Carter said, "I've got to call Sam, Jack, and Troy to tell them about Tommy." He went back up to his bedroom to find his address book that might contain the phone numbers of the people he wanted to call but finding only the phone number for the stables. He wasn't sure it was even still at the same location. He went back down to the hallway phone and called the number. A female voice answered the phone.

Carter asked for Troy, and to his surprise, the woman said, "Just a minute, he's outside."

Troy's voice came on the phone, "This is Troy, how can I help you?"

Carter answered, "Troy, it's Carter, remember me?"

"Of course, I remember you, college boy. How are you? What's happening? You coming out to see us?"

"Troy, I have some bad news."

"What's up?"

At this, Carter answered with a quavering voice, "Tommy was killed in a car accident. I wanted to let you, Sam, and Jack know about it."

"Oh, no," said Troy, "where and when?"

"He was on the way back from the Shore this morning," said Carter.

"Hey, Carter, I know how you guys felt about each other. I'm really sorry to hear this. I'll let the bosses know, they were crazy about Tommy. I've never been able to come up to their opinions of Tommy."

Carter gave Troy the details of the planned service on Saturday, asking him to pass the information along to the others who might want to come to pay their respects to Tommy. After hanging the phone up, Carter sat there next to the hall phone, remembering the days at the stables. Now looking back, he thought those were really happy but confusing times that actually signaled the path his life would take. He knew now how much he had come to love Tommy. He thought then he had all the time in the world to play games, never realizing that time was of the essence. Now with Tommy gone, he felt like his chance to be accepted and understood was over. Now he would go back to being, quote unquote, "normal"

Carter went back up to his bedroom without thinking of Herb sitting in the kitchen with his mother and sister. He laid across his bed and turned his Blaupunkt Radio on to his favorite jazz station. Herb came up knocking on the door jamb to the room.

"Carter, may I come in?"

Carter sat up immediately, saying, "Oh, God, Herb. I'm sorry. I didn't mean to leave you down there with my sister."

Herb answered, "Carter, don't worry, you need to grieve for your lover, you know that's who he was. This is probably your second most traumatic experience after your father. Your mother told me about your father." Carter snapped to reality. Tommy was his lover, Herb was right. He hadn't really accepted that fact before now. He had come out as a gay person.

Herb was so great with his caring and understanding, he told Carter he was going back to the Shore, but he would be back the next day and he and Ronny were going to be using a friend's apartment in town on Delancey Place until Sunday after the funeral and Carter could spend time there with them, so that he could be free to be himself.

He said, "Carter, you are still so young. You have your whole life ahead of you and Tommy would want you to move on and to be happy. Eventually, you will meet someone else and you will be able to love someone as much as you did Tommy."

"I will never love another guy the way I love Tommy. I don't even want to think about being gay. I'm going to get my degree and I will become a Journalist. I'm never going to be with anyone else."

Herb finally had to leave. Ronny came back to pick Herb up for the drive back to Atlantic City. He had been making more arrangements for the Saturday service. When they were gone, Carter remained in his bedroom. His mother came into the room

"Carter, are you feeling better? I have your dinner ready if you want to eat now."

"Mother, I'm not hungry, but thanks."

"Oh, my darling son, I'm so sorry you've lost your friend. I mourn for him, too; he was such a wonderful person and I know he loved you. I called Steve. He wants to talk to you."

"You called Steve? He's in Tennessee at Fisk. I haven't talked to him lately."

"Yes, but he had called last week because he didn't know how to reach you at the Shore. He is in Philadelphia at his mother's house."

Carter woke the next morning, thinking, was it all a bad dream? And finally facing reality, Tommy was gone. He sat on the side of the bed, staring at the wall as if in a trance.

His mother knocked on his bedroom door, saying, "Steve is on the phone for you." He wanted to say I can't talk to anyone now, but he knew he would have to talk to Steve eventually and he didn't want to make his mother worry more about him. He put on his dungarees that had been thrown over the chair and went down to answer the phone.

"Hey, Steve."

Steve on the other end said, "What happened, was he drunk?"

"No, he came down to visit me at the Shore and he left to come back in the morning."

Steve said "You two had become real close, huh?"

"So, what?" answered Carter.

"Hey I don't mean anything strange, I just was asking, that's all."

"Steve, I know you, remember?"

"Yeah, you should; we've been best friends for a long time and I'm still your friend, so you know I'm not trying to be smart with you. We got to have a talk."

"You haven't been here. I have a lot of new friends. You go to Fisk and I'm at Penn State. We don't talk to you southern snobs," joked Carter.

Steve laughed, "At least you still have a sense of humor."

Steve told Carter he was actually going to drive over to pick Carter up in the Cadillac. His step-dad was letting him use his car for the day. Carter went up, showered in his mother's bathroom, ad got dressed. He went down to the kitchen where his mother was fixing breakfast.

"Mother, Steve is coming over to pick me up. I'll just have coffee."

"Oh? When did you start drinking coffee?"

Carter answered, "I've been drinking coffee a lot when I study, and down at the Shore, I had coffee every morning."

"I guess that's one more thing that shows I haven't realized my son is now a young man."

"Mother, drinking coffee doesn't indicate my achievement of manhood." He was surprised that he was able to banter with his mother like everything was normal. He actually felt guilty for being able to joke with his mother when he should be sad. His mother seemed to read his thoughts; she commented that things will gradually get back to normal. It's not disrespectful to add a little humor to your conversation.

Soon Steve was knocking at the back-kitchen door. Being like one of the family, he had driven right up the driveway and come to the door that Carter and the rest of the family always used.

Lila called, "Come in, Steve," hugging him as he entered the kitchen. "Oh, Steve, you boys are growing to be such handsome young men, I'm so glad to see you. How is your mother? I haven't talked to her in ages." Carter was slightly amused because he knew that Steve had always admired his mother. He would always talk about her looks and how much class she seemed to have. These were important attributes to Steve; he said it was obvious that she had Caucasian in her background because of her facial features and complexion.

Carter would always joke, "What happened to me?"

Steve would laugh, "It's your father. He must be very dark. But you just make it because of your mother." Steve had never met Carter's father. Now with Lila hugging him, his ears were turning red. When Lila released him, he seemed to regain his composure.

"Mother is feeling great now; she was under the weather for a while after my grandmother passed away, but she is back to work now, running things in the shops."

"Oh, Steve, I didn't know your grandmother passed, when did it happen?"

"Oh, Mother went down in March to look after her and she died a month later. Everything happened so fast, so when Mother got the call that she was very ill, she left for Florida right away."

"I will call Jasmine today. I'm so sorry to hear about her mother. I'm just getting back to normal myself after the loss of my Bob after more than a year."

Steve said, "Well, it seems like the old adage that things come in threes has some truth to it because here we are with news of another passing." Carter was jolted back to reality now with his best friend Steve standing there, refer-ring to the loss of his beloved partner. He saw sympathy on Steve's face as if he knew exactly the kind of loss Carter was experiencing.

Carter turned away, saying, "Well, let's go riding in your Cadillac, Steve." They left the house and went out to the car.

"Steve, this is a new 1956 Coupe Deville, you didn't mention that Benny got a new one. The old one was only two-years-old," exclaimed Carter.

"Yeah, well, you know he has to have a new car every two years," answered Steve. "Well, he must feel that you've really matured to be trusting you with his brand new Caddy."

"No, he's just trying to convince my mother that he doesn't make a dif-ference in his son and me. If he thought we were going out to an affair with our girls, he would have sent Jerk Off to drive us, so that he could horn in and try to be socially acceptable."

They drove off with no particular destination.

Steve started the conversation with, "I know you are having a hard time right now."

Carter answered, "Yeah, I'm upset because Tommy was a good friend."

"Just a friend, huh?" said Steve.

"Of course, we had become really close friends."

Steve said, "Okay, remember you and I have been friends since junior high school, so I think we can cut to the chase. I know what was happening with you two." Carter was astonished by Steve's frank attitude and he was at a loss for words. Steve continued, "Before you start going off on me, let me tell you James has been doing me for a long time. I thought you would have guessed by now."

Carter was completely unprepared for this revelation; it had never oc-curred to him that grumpy James was gay or straight or anything but grumpy. In addition, he had always considered Steve to be what is known in junior cir-cles as a "cunt hound."

Steve went on to say, "I certainly wasn't in like with him or anything like that, he just gave a good blow job. But at school, I met someone that I really care about. We've fooled around a lot, and when I'm not with my girl Carol, I'm with him. His name is Bruce Medford; he plays on the basketball team. His father is a big-time surgeon in Chicago. We're going to be roommates this semester. I like him almost as much as I care about Carol." Carter was still speechless; he was trying to digest all of this, and in a way, he was beginning to feel relief. Steve was still his best friend and now he wouldn't have to hold back anything in their discussions.

Carter finally found his voice, "It never dawned on me that you and James were into anything like that. He doesn't act like he's gay or anything, but it's beginning to make sense because he must have been jealous when I was around. He never needed to worry. I care for you like a brother, not a lover."

"Don't worry, I feel the same way and I tried to tell him that along with he was not special, except for the head he gave," said Steve.

"He was your Ann," answered Carter.

"Very funny, but that is a good comparison; as for Bruce, it's different. I feel good telling you about it. I know how you feel about Tommy. I guess I was envious of you before because he obviously liked you and I always thought he was hot. It was frustrating because you didn't seem to know or care. I kept thinking you were definitely not gay."

Carter answered, "I still am not sure I'm totally into being gay. I still like girls, too, but Tommy is not the only guy I've been with. My roommate Ted and I have done it a few times and there was Louis in Puerto Rico, plus my cousin Peter."

"Hey, you are not only gay, you are a ho," laughed Steve.

"I'm being sincere and you're making fun of me. I still feel guilty because I started to feel like I was cheating on Tommy and I had just decided it was only going to be him. Now it's too late and I can't make it up to him. I feel awful," said Carter.

Steve countered, "Look, you are just finding out what life is all about. I know because I think I realized what was happening with me a long time ago. I've looked at guys that way ever since I can remember, even when I was a little kid."

"If I had those urges, I told myself it was just a normal reaction to someone I admired. I kept telling myself that it was okay to think another guy was good-looking and had a nice body," said Carter. "But I really started wanting Tommy to do things to me even before he told me he wanted to, and I think I just fell in love with him. I will never forget him."

"No, you won't, but you got to move on, friend. He would want you to."

They drove around for a while, just talking about everything that came to mind until it was almost dark.

Steve drove up to Carter's house, saying, "Let's get together tomorrow and maybe go to Smokey Joe's or Pagano's for pizza. We can chat some more then."

"Yes, tomorrow, my friends Herb and Ronny will be back up from A.C. I want you to meet them."

"The guys you worked for, right?"

"Yes, they are definitely your kind of people, you will like them," answered Carter.

Wednesday morning dawned a beautiful August day. Carter had finally been able to sleep through the night, enjoying a dream of Tommy, who seemed happy this time, full of memories of their days together. Again, it was like Tommy was really there and talking about their future together. Carter felt better this morning as a result of getting rest and realizing he had his friend Steve to confide in who understood what he must be feeling. He knew he had the ordeal to go through on Saturday, but he felt he would have more moral support now with Steve, who understood his loss. Also, Herb and Ronny were like his guardian angels, giving him strength and determination.

After sitting in the living room talking with his mother, Carter decided to go over to Steve's house. Before he could leave, the phone rang. Herb was calling to tell him to come down to visit him and Ronny at the apartment on Delancy Place that they were using for the week. He informed Herb that he had intended to spend the day at his friend Steve's house.

Herb said, "Oh, bring Steve with you, we'd love to meet him." This idea pleased Carter; he had wanted to introduce Steve to his new friends.

When he arrived at Steve's, he found him sitting in the kitchen where he had been chatting with the family's housekeeper.

Steve commented, "You look better than you looked yesterday."

Carter answered, "I feel better. I slept through the night and I just feel stronger."

"That's good," said Steve, "you want to call some girls and we can go to a movie or something?" Carter told Steve about Herb and Ronny's invitation. "Oh, great. I want to meet these fabulous friends of yours, forget about the girls."

"Listen, they are not the effeminate types; they have plenty of female friends, they are just two guys that decided they were into each other. They wouldn't care if we brought girls with us or not."

"Oh, my poor friend Carter, you have a lot to learn. I don't want to take girls. It's ironic that you are so naïve and you are always first to go all the way."

"What are you talking about? I'm not effeminate either."

"Carter, I'm not talking about how gay you are. I'm saying gay is gay. There are no in-betweens. Look, you've already had a lover, you didn't just jump in and out and that's why you are grieving; you lost your lover, accept it and remember him and miss him, don't think about how you can hide it."

Carter replied, "When did you become this great counselor?" Carter realized these words had struck home; he felt tears welling up again and he panicked. He was in the company of his best friend and his feelings were taking over, but he was comforted by the realization that Steve understood, in fact he was telling him to let it out.

He continued with, "I don't know what to do now. I felt that Tommy would always be there for me no matter what. I would look after him and he would look after me. I had decided I didn't care what other people thought. I can't believe my life is over at 19."

"Are you crazy? This isn't the end, it's the beginning; he would want you to move on after you cry a lot. This whole episode served to make you know yourself. There's a whole world out there full of people like us. When it happens again, you won't waste time accepting it. I've known I'm gay since I was a little kid and I've enjoyed it. Do you know how lucky you were to have this great-looking guy fall in love with you and to have him give up everything for you?"

Carter regained his control, saying, "Let's go. I want to get my mind on something else."

Delancy Place is one of the most exclusive addresses in Center City Philadelphia before Society Hill the Rittenhouse Square area, which Delancy is a part of, was the area in town. Herb and Ronny were occupying a two-story apartment in a townhouse (Mansion) that once belonged to a well-known writer. The place was beautiful.

Herb hugged Carter and turned to Steve, saying "We've heard a lot about you being the lady killer, it's nice to finally meet you."

Steve answered, "I'd rather be known as just the killer, but I'm very pleased to meet you two also."

Ronny chimed in, "We'd rather have the lovers here than killers. I'm Ronny." Steve was immediately comfortable with Carter's new friends; they had a very nice afternoon with open conversation.

When Steve and Carter were on the way back to their homes, Steve said, "They are great people; you have again just managed to be at the right place at the right time. You have made friends with the cream of the crop of the gay world without even trying, what a way to come out." Steve got out of the car at his house, telling Carter he would call him the next day. The following Thursday and Friday went by with Steve and Carter spending a lot of time together.

Saturday morning began overcast and muggy, a typical late August day in Philadelphia. Carter felt real dread thinking of saying farewell to his Tommy. He had slept fitfully and again dreamed that Tommy was still with him but was telling him to walk away and leave him standing at the bus stop in State College where they used to meet. When he was dressed and on going down to the kitchen, where he found his mother and sister sipping coffee, dressed, and waiting for him, he realized they planned to accompany him to the service.

His mother said, "Carter, I was going to come up to check on you. The limousine will be here in 30 minutes."

"Limo, what limo? I don't need a limo. I can drive my car," answered Carter.

Catherine spoke, "Carter, it's customary for the family of the deceased to ride in the limo and you're the only family he had. You are the one who is making the arrangements."

"Herb and Ronny are paying for this. I don't need a limo. I don't want to take advantage of their generosity."

His mother said, "Carter, this is part of the services included in the contract. You remember the arrangements we made for Bob, it's all included and they don't want you having to drive when you're upset." Carter responded to his mother's input with quiet acceptance.

The front doorbell rang and Carter's tension increased. He was visibly shaking; his mother was aware of his anxiety and she felt helpless to do anything to help him. She could only walk to the car beside him, conveying her moral support. Inside the plush, limo it was quiet when the attendant closed the extra heavy doors after assisting his mother and sister into the seat next to Carter. He felt like he was in an oppressive dream that he couldn't wake from and could not halt its inevitable ending. He told himself he was being too dramatic, but it wasn't an act.

It seemed like the next thing he was conscious of was the big car pulling up to the cupola over the side entrance to the funeral home. The driver got out of the car and the attendant also got out of the passenger seat and stood by the car door to wait for the signal from the undertaker inside to open the doors to help Carter, his mother, and sister out. They could hear organ music coming from inside when the attendant finally opened the car door. Catherine was helped out and the attendant reached in to take Lila's arm, so that she would follow. She took Carter's hand and squeezed it as if to encourage him to be strong and then allowed the attendant to help her out. Carter followed her out before the attendant could reach in for him. He suddenly felt strong and calm; he had acquired that strength from somewhere as if his grief was private and he would not expose it to others.

John Baron stood just inside the entrance. He escorted Carter and his mother down the carpeted hallway to the main chapel past several other slumber rooms whose doors were shut. They entered the chapel where Fr. Jefferson stood waiting and who turned walking in front of Carter, Lila, and Catherine down the aisle, reciting, "Jesus said, LET NOT YOUR HEART BE TROUBLED." Herb and Ronny had been standing across from Father Jefferson and they fell into step behind Carter and his family. To Carter's amazement Jack, Sam, Troy, and most of the stable's guys and girls were seated in the chapel. The other surprising attendees were some of the people that Tommy and Carter had met at the parties at the beach, including the gorgeous movie star who had so impressed Carter. He was sure Herb had persuaded some of his friends to come for "the boys" bene-fit. Of course, his best friend Steve was there and that probably was the most important attendance.

The service was handled with grace and in good taste. When Carter got to look at his friend Tommy for the last time, he imagined that he saw a smile on his face. Lila took care of the satin blanket, which she covered Tommy with inside his coffin. Carter wanted to do it himself, but because of appearances, he asked his mother to do it. The burial followed, and afterwards, Herb and Ronny arranged a catered repast at a well-known French restaurant on Walnut Street in Center City Philadelphia.

Carter and his mother circulated among the guests, thanking them for coming to pay their respects to Tommy. Lila was the epitome of class; she ex-plained that Tommy was like her older son. Herb and Ronny took care of ev-erything, and when Lila went again to thank them, they told her how much they, too, had grown to love and admire her in the short time they had known her. She never questioned their attachment to Carter or their motives. Cath-erine was so impressed by the guests and especially the movie star that she was very nice throughout the day. When Lila and Catherine left, Herb and Ronny told Lila they would look after her beloved son, and Steve also promised he would stay with Carter and see that he got home okay.

The repast was over. Herb and Ronny invited people back to their apartment on Delancy and left with Carter and Steve in tow. When they arrived back at the apartment, the caterers had set up a bar and buffet for the people who had decided to come by after the services. Of course, they were mostly the friends of Herb and Ronny from New York City and Washington D.C. The actress was accompanied by a very good-looking guy who was obviously her latest love interest.

When she introduced him to Carter, she laughed, saying, "He is the replacement for my last husband." Carter remembered when they met at the beach, she had been alone and flirting with Tommy. She had just divorced her third husband. This new affair would probably be just a fling. Everyone knew that she and her ex had been mentioned in all of the gossip columns as the two off and on lovers.

She hugged Carter and kissed him on the cheek, saying, "I know you two were very much in love." Carter had to contain his shock at her frank statement and he realized it wasn't said with sarcasm or viciousness; she was being sincere. The "gay" aspect was not a problem for her, it was just about two people who cared deeply for each other. Steve had been standing there next to Carter and he was obviously speechless with amazement and admiration. She was an example of the kind of sophistication that this group of worldly people possessed.

After she moved on to chat with Herb, who was nearby, Steve said again, "I repeat, you are so fortunate to have met these fabulous people. You need to always stay in contact with them; they have all of the important connections and they have all of the class."

Carter answered, "I know the class part means a lot to you. The kindness and real affection means the most to me and the fact that you came and you are here makes me feel so much stronger."

"Hey, don't start getting mushy with me."

Carter continued, "No, I can't begin to tell you how much it has helped me to realize that you might have the same things going on in your life that I have been experiencing and you are already my friend."

Steve replied, "Yeah, well, I'm going to try to get Bruce to come for a visit before we go back to school and you can meet him, so you can ask him what his intentions are, ha-ha."

By the time evening set in, Carter felt really exhausted and ready to get back to the refuge of his home. So many of the people he and Tommy had met at the beach had spoken their condolences to him and he had become weary of keeping a strong façade and not losing his composure. Herb insisted on sending Carter home and Steve back to his car in a rented town car driven by a hired driver. When Carter got out of the car at his house, Steve told him he would call him in the morning. He went inside and was about to go up the front stairway when his mother called to him from the living room where she was sitting in her usual chair next to the front window. For some reason, he had dreaded his usual chat in the living room with his mother. He knew his mother was too careful to actually come out and ask him questions about his relationship with Tommy, but if she did, he would not be able to avoid telling her the truth.

Actually, when Carter went in and sat across from his mother, she simply said, "He was a wonderful friend and it will take some time to get over his loss, but you must remember he would want you to go on and have a happy life. You and your friends honored him today. I'm sure he knows how much you cared for him." Carter remembered what Herb had said about his mother and he realized it was true his mother was the best she knew her son. He stood and leaned down to hug his mother; she patted his shoulder.

Carter went up to his bedroom tossing his suit jacket on the chair. He then collapsed on the bed after turning on his favorite Temple Jazz Station. Miles Davis' "Castles in Spain" was just ending. Next, Sarah Vaughn sang "Imagination" softly. Carter wept softly, thinking of his lost friend Tommy.

The rest of that August went quickly and it was time to return to school. As planned he and Juan rented an apartment off campus. The apartment consisted of two small bedrooms, one bath and a kitchenette, dining area, living room combination. Juan had a friend that visited often, and at first, was reluctant to allow Carter to know what was happening between him and Juan. After Juan explained Carter's tragic loss to the friend, he relaxed his uptight act.

He was walking across the quad when he ran into Ted.

He said, "Hi, Ted," and kept on walking, but Ted turned and called to him "Is that how you greet an old friend?"

He stopped and answered, "I'm sorry. I was on my way home to work on a paper. I just got my outline together and I'm ready to get it started." Ted was smiling at him and he remembered their last time together with a little bit of caution.

"Why don't you have a beer with me and fill me in on your summer," said Ted.

Carter answered, "I really ought to get back to the apartment and work."

"Ok, can I come with you, I've got some time to kill? We can pick up a six pack."

"I don't drink beer."

"Since when? Oh, that's right, we never actually socialized together."

"I think we decided we wouldn't socialize anymore if that's what you call it," said Carter.

Ted laughed, saying, "Relax, Carter, that's all in the past. We can at least be friends." At this point, Carter decided it would be ok to just have a drink with him. They stopped at the Delicatessen and picked up sandwiches and beer. Carter drove his car and Ted followed in his Austin Healy.

At the apartment, Carter led Ted inside. The apartment was empty. Juan had started staying at his friend's place and wasn't at home very much. Carter thought to himself, did I plan this on purpose?

Ted said sarcastically, "A nice little love nest."

Carter responded, "I thought we were just going to have a friendly drink and catch up on summer vacation!"

"You're so touchy, I'm just kidding. Are you still screwing that other clown who came up every weekend?"

"Don't call Tommy a clown. He's not here to defend himself."

"Call him up and tell him I'm here and what's he gonna do about it?" Carter is suddenly overcome with renewed grief.

"Tommy died."

Ted is transfixed, "What happened?" Carter, regaining his composure, explained what had occurred with the car accident and all.

Ted was apologizing profusely with, "Oh, God, Carter. I'm sorry. I'm sure he was probably a really good guy if you cared for him as much as you did. I know he must have been ok because it's easy to understand how he fell for you." He grabbed Carter in a bear hug. Carter felt like he was really going to cry.

He pulled away, saying, "Thanks for caring."

Ted said, "You know why I'm here, Carter. I think about you all the time. I think about how we enjoyed each other and I was glad to run into you today."

Carter answered, "But you're engaged or married for all I know, and besides, I can't forget Tommy. I finally made up my mind that we were special together and then he was killed. I think I am being punished because I fooled around with you and others."

Ted continued with, "I may have to rethink marriage right now. I don't know if I'm going in another direction or what."

Carter asked, "What do you mean by going in another direction? You know you will only be happy in the future with a wife and family."

"Right now I want to find out if I'd rather be with you. I told you I've been thinking about you all the time and I don't mean to be crude by saying it's not just to get a blow job."

"Look, Ted, I'm not ready to get involved with anyone else yet. I just want to remember my friend Tommy and maybe figure out where the rest of my life is going."

"Oh, come on, Carter. I didn't think you were a drama queen or something. We are young guys in the experimental stages of our lives, don't give me this bullshit about being in mourning for your lost lover. Besides, I'll bet if he could tell you what to do now, he would say move on."

Carter got glasses out of the kitchen cabinets and they sat at the little café table there and ate their sandwiches. He had turned on the stereo player and his favorite Dinah Washington record (Love Walked In) was playing.

Ted spoke after a long silence, "So, what's it going to be? I'm here and you're here, so now what?"

Carter almost could hear Tommy saying, "Enjoy your life." He looked at Ted again, thinking how good-looking he was and actually very sexy.

"I don't believe it's possible that I keep getting these really good-looking guys interested in me." Ted reached across the table and pulled Carter toward him, kissing him first on the cheek and moving his mouth around to finally cover Carter's. This resulted in them standing and holding each other tightly. Carter was completely overwhelmed with passion and he led Ted into his bedroom.

After that time in the apartment, they became closer and closer together through the rest of that semester and on through the rest of Carter's time at Penn State. As it turned out, Ted finished undergrad a year before Carter and was accepted at U of P Law School, so that he and Carter managed to get together at least two weekends a month mostly in Philadelphia.

Suddenly, it was 1957 in the month of April. Carter would be receiving his degree in Business Administration since he had changed over in his junior year after being convinced by an advisor at Penn State to choose business for better opportunities in the future. He often thought of that decision later with regret; he would have rather continued on to a Journalism degree and a Master's Degree in Communications later. It was true there was considerable demand for business majors with so many companies opening offices in Philadelphia and the vicinity. The area was becoming extremely White Collar with many opportunities for ambitious trainees. As it turned out, many of those positions were not necessarily open to Carter.

Steve came home from school for each semester break, holidays, and summer vacations. He and Carter had met many really nice people through Herb and Ronny from the gay and straight world, but all of whom seemed to be free of hang ups and prejudices. They spent a lot of time with show people who were not just the actors but also producers and directors of shows. They found themselves included in parties and invitations to the Hamptons in New York and plus even to San Francisco, California. Steve enjoyed all of this. In fact, as it turned out, these contacts were eventually instrumental in his successes in life. Carter also made some pleasing alliances that lasted through the years. One friend who Carter became very close to was a very good-looking guy who was also a Penn State alumnus and five years Carter's senior. He had his Master's and was working on his PhD in Social Administration.

Roger and Carter became best friends. Steve was very often not in town and Juan had transferred back to the university in San Juan, so Carter ended up telling Roger all of his secrets and thoughts. In fact, when he finally told Roger about Ted, Roger asked Carter to bring him by for his approval. By this time, Ted had an apartment just off of U of P's campus and Carter had a key, so that when he came in from State on weekends, he could go directly to the apartment and his family didn't know he was in town. Carter was very fond of Ted, but after the loss of his first partner, he wouldn't let himself really love Ted. Besides, he kept expecting Ted to tell him he had decided to marry the hometown girl and it was over between them.

Ted and Carter were talking about Carter's approaching commencement when Carter mentioned his conversations with Roger about their relationship.

Ted reacted at first angrily, "Since when have you gotten so close to this guy Roger that you tell him all of our personal business?"

Carter answered, "Roger is like the older brother I don't have. He is five years older than me and I have a lot of respect for him."

"Oh, yeah, respect, is that all? No sex?"

Carter replies, "What are you talking about? You don't understand; just because Roger is gay, it doesn't mean that we can't have a plutonic friendship. He knows I'm with you and that he and I are just friends. He is not interested in going to bed with me. Just as Steve, Herb, and Ronny are all my friends and all are just friends."

"How do I know you might be fucking around with all of them."

Carter became very angry, replying, "Well, maybe you are suspicious of me because you are doing it with anybody who wants you. Besides, you will probably finish law school and marry what's her name back home in New York." Ted was immediately sorry he had accused Carter. "I'm sorry, Carter. I don't know why I get so upset when you tell me about being friends with other guys. I have trouble understanding gay stuff." Carter softened; he knew that Ted was being truthful. Most people don't realize that gay people can have friends just as straight people can have friends who are not sex partners or love interests.

"I was getting around to saying Roger wants to invite us over to his place for drinks."

Ted answered, "Listen, I don't really have time to socialize. I have a bunch of cases to read and I want to just spend these weekends with you. You mentioned Roz back home. As it stands, I think about eventually joining a law firm here in Philadelphia and we can live together."

"Ted, I don't know what I'm going to do after May 28th, my commencement. I don't know if I want to live with you or if I want to commit to anyone. My mother probably expects me to live at home until I'm established in a career and am on the way to living on my own. I know I care about you a lot, but I'm afraid if I let go and be with you all of the time, something will happen to change things."

"Carter, you are right. I'm not sure either, but I do know if I didn't have you, I don't know what I'd be doing. I know I'm not going to change my mind about Roz, but I don't know if I want to live my life in a completely gay world. I also know I want to have you as part of my life. I think I am in love with you, and as I said before, it's not just the sex. You don't have to worry about grabbing the first job you come to. You can take your time to find something that pleases you because I already have an income from my family, so you don't need to go back to your mother's to live. We'll live here until I finish."

"Ted, let's wait until the time comes to decide. I do want you to meet my friend Roger and then the others, too; it means a lot to me."

Ted seemed to visibly give in, saying, "Okay, Carter, if that will satisfy you, I will. Just make it next weekend not today."

They were invited to Roger's apartment in Center City. Roger had already gone from working as a Social Worker for the state to Temple University's School of Social Administration and was in line for Asst. Dean. Ronny and Herb were also invited and Roger's new friend from New York, John Lawrence. At first, Ted was very uncomfortable because Herb and Ronny didn't hold back on just being campy and discussing gay topics. Much of their conversation was about show business and who's who in the gay world. Although Herb was very astute in his knowledge about the arts and written classics, the topics were: Guess who is doing so and so plus the fabulous movie star whose husband was caught in a raid on a gay bar. Ronny was the more grounded of the two; he would just agree that this is what he had also heard.

Roger's friend from New York fell right in to the conversations seeming to enjoy it immensely. Carter had always enjoyed their stories but leaned toward being more of a listener than adding to the commentary. He had met some of the people they were discussing through the guys, but he wasn't up on their gossip and news. Roger went out of his way to make Ted relax and enjoy the evening; he kept refilling his glass even when it was half full. Carter was surprised to realize that he was becoming a little perturbed by Roger's attention to Ted. He was actually a little jealous and he tried to tell himself that he had nothing to worry about, but he saw that Ted was loosening up and laughing at the jokes and friendly banter that was also coming from Roger.

They had a great dinner and more drinks afterward. Herb started talking about Tommy and how he had been such a handsome kid who really loved Carter. This made Carter uncomfortable and he tried to signal Herb to change the subject, but Herb seemed determined to talk about his deceased partner. Ronny even tried to talk about something else, but Herb persisted and Carter could see that Ted was becoming angry and starting to glare at Herb. Carter decided to announce that it was time for him and Ted to get back home.

As they were about to go out the door, Herb grabbed Carter's arm and pulled him aside, whispering, "I don't like this guy for you."

Carter answered, "Why, he's ok?"

Herb replied, "He was certainly enjoying Roger's attention and he seems uptight." Carter was a little surprised that it maybe wasn't just his imagination since Herb had noticed, too.

He said, "Well, we're not the same as it was with Tommy and me."

Herb went on, "Well, give me a call. We're staying on Delancy this week and we'd like to have you over."

Ted stood waiting in the hallway as Carter joined him; he said, "What the fuck was wrong with that guy, is he jealous of us or something?"

Carter answered, "No, he is my friend, I told you that before."

"Okay, why the hell was he harping on your Sweet Tommy? Was that for me?"

"I don't know he and Ronny liked Tommy, they called us their kids," said Carter.

"Well, I didn't feel like sitting there and hearing how wonderful your ex-lover was. I think he was doing it on purpose."

"It seems to me you didn't even notice it, you were so busy grinning all over yourself at Roger," said Carter. By this time, they were at Ted's car and Ted went to the drivers' side to get in.

Carter said, "I'll drive you had too much to drink."

"What? I'm not high! I admit I was trying to make you jealous; you were looking at your buddy Herb like you were worshipping an idol."

Ted got in the car and reached over, opening the passenger side door, saying, "Get in." Carter got in and they drove off in silence.

Back at Ted's apartment, Carter sat in the living room and Ted went into the bedroom. When Carter didn't follow, Ted came out and stared at him, looking hurt. Carter pretended not to notice and Ted went back into the bedroom. Carter sat there thinking, I guess I really do like him a lot. I was jealous when I thought he was flirting with Roger. He got up and went into the bedroom. Ted was lying across the bed and Carter lay down next to him.

Ted rolled over, putting his arm around Carter and putting his face against his, saying, "I told you I'd rather just stay at home with you. I'm not ready for all of the gay social stuff that guy Roger is supposed to be your friend and I think he was coming on to me."

Carter answered, "Yes, I didn't like that either. I guess he assumes we're just buddies."

"Bullshit, he was trying to show you up or make me look like a cheap twit."

"Then why did you play along?" said Carter.

"Because I told you I wanted you to be jealous," answered Ted.

"Well, guess what you succeeded now, are you happy?"

"No, I don't ever want to make you uncomfortable. I'll never do that again, and besides, that guy doesn't appeal to me at all in the old days. I would have told him to fuck off."

Carter decided to end the conversation by initiating sex and it turned into one of the best times yet.

Afterwards, when they were both calmly lying there and Ted whispered, "I've made up my mind whatever you want us to be is okay with me."

Carter answered gently, "Oh, shut up, stop trying to put it in words. It's like those guys tonight would say, we are lovers."

It was finally the month of May and commencement had arrived. There was a lot of excitement among the graduates and Carter's mood was one of elation, too. At the edge of happy feelings was a pang of sadness as he thought of Tommy and how much they had looked forward to this day. His mother, sister, Herb, Ronny, Roger, and of course, Ted were all there.

After the commencement exercises, there was a reception where everyone got the chance to congratulate each other and introduce families to families. Ted spent a lot of time talking to Carter's mother and sister. He made a point of staying away from Roger who had made several attempts to engage him in conversation.

Herb mentioned jokingly to Carter, "You must have read the riot act to your friend; he is definitely behaving himself today." Carter simply smiled at this remark not commenting. Herb continued, "I like him better today, he is courting your mother and sister to win them over. It's obvious that he really cares about you."

The transportation back to Philadelphia was prearranged by Ronny for Carter's mother and sister. They rode in Ronny's car. Carter's apartment had been vacated the week before, so he and Ted drove back in Ted's Austin Healy.

Ted was in a great mood; he pulled off of the highway on the way back onto a deserted road, saying, "I want to give you your graduation gift now."

Carter responded, "What are you doing? We can wait until we get home."

Ted stopped the car and leaned over kissing Carter and saying, "I told Roz I can't marry her because I'm in love with you." He opened the glove box in the car and took out a watch case that he gave to Carter. Inside the case was a beautiful Cartier Tank watch. Carter was overwhelmed with affection for his now friend. It dawned on him that Ted had said he told Roz what was happening between them. He was thinking, it's all out there now. He told someone we are gay. What will she do? Will she tell Ted's family? They will probably try to change his decision.

Carter finally said, "Ted, you shouldn't have told her about us. You could have just said you didn't want to get married now or something."

Ted answered, "First of all, I didn't want to make her think she was to blame, and secondly, I don't care who knows how I feel about you." Carter was speechless; he didn't have the nerve yet to actually tell anyone, who was not gay, how he felt about another guy in fact he was not able to say, "I'm gay," to anyone who was straight. At first, he felt ashamed and then he felt warm all over because he never thought he would ever find another person who could say he was really in love with him. The other part was this was another beautiful guy who was sincere.

Back in Philadelphia, Herb and Ronny had invited them to dinner at their Delancy Place loaner. Of course, Roger was there with another young guy that he had been seeing who worked at the Stock Exchange. Roger seemed to have gotten the message about possibilities with Ted. He was his usual friendly talkative self but definitely not directing his comments only to Ted. The evening was very pleasant until Herb announced that he and Ronny had a gift for Carter. It turned out to be to accompany him and Ronny on a trip to France and Italy, all expenses paid.

Ted spoke up immediately, saying, "That's a great gift, but the time is not right because I can't go at this time because of my internship at the law firm and Carter is not going to Europe without me. I will take him to Europe or wherever he wants to go when I am free."

There is a stunned silence after this and Carter himself is speechless at first, but he recovers his composure by lying.

"Ted and I had been talking about going to Europe, the first time for me, together so that he can show me around since he has been there before."

Ronny cut in, "No problem, we can arrange for both of you to go the next time. We can put it in writing, so that it is still classified as our commencement gift to Carter." The statement from Ronny saved the night; it was obvious that Herb was about to retaliate with some very nasty words for Ted. Roger now decided it was time for his announcement of two front row tickets to see West Side Story at the Forrest Theater. After that the tension in the room abated and Carter was thanking his friends for their gifts and affection. He also made clear his respect and love for Herb and Ronny, who he deemed his loving guardians in this new world of adulthood.

Later when they were back at Ted's apartment, Carter brought up the European gift.

"Ted, that statement about my traveling to Europe was uncalled for. You could have left it up to me to accept it and maybe later we could have discussed it between us."

Ted answered, "I don't like the way they act as if you have to do what they want you to do all of the time. They make the arrangements and you are supposed to follow along with no consideration for our plans." Carter didn't want to have a dispute at this time with Ted; he was feeling very happy after his completion of school for now and about his burgeoning affection for his friend.

He replied, "I was going to thank them and say I would like to take a rain check on the trip so that I could go out on a few interviews for a job."

"What about saying you wanted to be with me?" replied Ted.

"That goes without saying, Ted, I want to be with you, and as for Europe, I will wait until we can go together."

Ted grabbed Carter, hugging him tightly, saying, "You fucker, you have me so crazy. I'm jealous of everyone." Carter responded by hugging him back but thinking, maybe I shouldn't let this slide. I should let him know that he can't tell me what to do either. They sat up half the night drinking vodka and talking about their lives before their meeting at school. Carter drank enough to make him very mushy. He told Ted he had really cared for Tommy, but now he was really falling in love with Ted.

Carter officially moved into Ted's apartment, telling his mother it was probably best that he started being on his own and sharing a Center City Apartment would be super convenient since he planned to get a job in an office in town. His mother had finally agreed since she had taken to travelling with other members of her club. Several of them were also widows who had lost their husbands. In fact, his mother had become very social again and also volunteered much of her time with church charities.

After interviewing at several companies, he decided to take the government FSEE Middle Management Exam, which he passed with a decent grade and he was hired as a management trainee GS5 with an automatic GS7 in six months. Procurement School was a requirement, which usually had to be attended in Ft Lee, Virginia but fortunately for Carter and for Ted, classes were given for six weeks in Philadelphia at the US Army Signal Corps Building.

Federal Government clearance for secret was required for upper level positions in procurement at that time and Ted and Carter were living together as housemates. This did not present a problem for them; they had become known for great parties and lots of girls in and out of their now rented townhouse. The girl traffic had started with Ted bringing home female colleagues and returning to sexual episodes with them. One of the females he explained to Carter was his law professor who would give him great grades and references. As it turned out, she tried to talk Ted into moving into an apartment she would pay for away from Carter, whom she didn't like.

As for Carter, he had continued to party with his friends Herb and Ronny, plus he and Roger became good travel buddies and were very social with some of the friends that Carter had known back in high school. Also, whenever Steve was in town, he and Carter dated lots of girls and went to parties. Ted became very argumentative, and in fact. one night when Carter was on his way out, Ted told him he should stay home. This resulted in a serious confrontation.

Carter said, "I am going to a party in West Philadelphia."

Ted responded, "No, you are not." In the end, this resulted in Ted striking Carter and Carter storming out of the house swearing he would never return.

Steve was still Carter's confidant and he advised Carter to get the Hell out of the situation with Ted. That night they just sat around Steve's house and didn't go to the party as planned. Steve told Carter he had heard of some nightmare things that happened to other friends who hooked up with other guys and Carter remembered the story of Juan's friend in Puerto Rico.

"That's not going to happen to me mostly because I still care for him. I'm not going to leave. I will go back and we will have a talk. I know he didn't mean to hit me and I'm not going to accept him hitting me again, so I'll tell him that."

When Carter got back home, Ted was asleep on the couch in the living room. Carter went into the kitchen and Ted came in after him.

"Carter, I'm sorry. I don't know what to do. I don't want anyone touching you, but I still want these women and I know that's not fair to you. I know I love you and I don't want to let you go. It's funny if I thought anyone else ever hit you, I would kill them, but I hit you and I am so ashamed."

Steve and Carter went to a party in Atlantic City given by one of the guys from Carter and Steve's group of friends. It turned out to be a great party with people from Philly, New York area, and of course, New Jersey. One of the girls was from Morrisville, New Jersey. Ironically, her name was Maria like the leading lady in West Side Story; she was a gorgeous girl with lots of personality and an entrancing laugh. Carter was immediately smitten, but Steve being the charming lady killer decided she was going to be his. He spent a great deal of the night dancing with her and finally getting her number, so he could contact her again to ask her out.

By this time, Steve was working in Pittsburgh after graduating from Fisk University with honors and he was only in town for the weekend. After trying several times to contact Maria, he had passed her number to Carter asking him to set up a double date with him and Maria and Carter and Crystal, whom Carter had been dating off and on. Carter followed his best friend's request and first called Maria to ask her to go with Steve to see Johnnie Mathis, who was appearing at the Latin Casino in Cherry Hill, New Jersey.

Maria answered, "I love Johnnie Mathis, but why don't just you and I go to see him?" Carter was surprised at this response; he had never thought this gorgeous girl would ever consider dating him, although Crystal, whom he had been dating, was also very pretty. He just still couldn't believe these beautiful popular girls would be interested in him.

He answered, "Uh, yeah, that would be great since the two of us are real Mathis fans."

She said, "Yes, and maybe we can get to know each other." Carter was ecstatic; he felt this was probably the girl he had always dreamed he would end up with. In a way, he thought this was the kind of girl his mother had been in her youth. He completely discounted his relationship with Ted; he thought, after all Ted is now seeing this girl who is a fellow ADA where Ted now holds a position.

Maria normally stayed with a friend in West Philadelphia when she came for a weekend, so Carter made arrangements to pick her up there and he traded cars with Ted, who now had an XKE Jaguar coupe. Carter's new convertible Pontiac Lemans was very nice, but he wanted to really impress Maria, so he talked Ted into trading for the weekend. Ted did ask why this girl was so important, but he consented because he usually let Carter drive his car whenever he wanted it.

The show was fabulous, and Maria and Carter fell in love to the music of Johnnie Mathis. A favorite was "Chances Are;" they sat at the small table in the club holding hands and listening to what became their theme song. This was the beginning of a true love affair. Carter had deep feelings for Maria and he decided he would be true to her. In other words, no more guys he felt he cared enough for Maria to forget about Ted or any other guy. This, however, should have been a problem since he and Ted lived together, but Ted was so involved with his colleague that he and Carter hadn't been intimate for a while. Carter had actually considered moving because this Sue, who Ted was seeing was often at their house or Ted was staying at her apartment. So, Carter had begun to feel like the outsider. To be truthful at times, he had wanted Ted, but there hadn't been opportunities for them to be together and Ted almost seemed to be teasing him at times.

Carter and Maria were constantly together after the Mathis date and eventually Maria asked Carter to come to her house in Morrisville for a weekend. Johnnie Mathis was due to appear at the Latin Casino again and they could drive down from her home to see him. He could also meet her parents since Maria still lived at home.

Carter took the train to Trenton, New Jersey since it did not stop in Morrisville. Maria had arranged to pick him up at the station and to drive back to her home, which of course was on the outskirts of Morrisville. When they got back to Maria's house, they had a few hours to relax in the family room on the lower level. The house was the typical Suburban two-story colonial found in most areas. Maria's mother was just wonderful. She and Carter hit it off right away; they found that they had so much in common, good books, music, and politics. She was the epitome of class, and by the way, she loved to dance, which Carter had become pretty adept at. Maria's father was a chemist and he, too, immediately liked Carter, in fact they became buddies.

It seemed that this was going to be a perfect match. Maria's parents announced that they were driving into New York City to meet with Mrs. Norman's sisters at the Sugar Hill Club in Harlem. As it turned out, her sisters were both married to big band leaders, who happened to be the House bands for the Harlem Club and the Sugar Hill Club. This meant that Carter had another connection to celebrities who frequented the famous Harlem clubs and many of whom were friends of the Normans.

Maria and Carter were invited to go along with her parents to New York in fact this had been prearranged, so off they went. When they arrived at the Sugar Hill Club, it was very festive.

The Normans were super impressed when the famous movie star that Carter knew from his days in Atlantic City was arriving at the same time, and upon seeing Carter, she rushed over and hugged and kissed him, saying, "Carter, my darling, how nice to run into you here. Let's get our table together."

Carter introduced her to Maria and her parents, saying, "We are already supposed to be at the table with Maria's aunts."

She answered, "Well, maybe they will excuse you and Maria. I want to have you with us." She was referring to her escort, who was of course another very handsome hunk and who was her latest dalliance.

The Normans insisted that Maria and Carter consent to sit with Carter's fabulous celebrity friend "You can't refuse this gorgeous lady," said Maria's father. "Go on, we'll be fine." Carter was a little dubious because he wondered if his celebrity friend would mention his other life. As it turned out, he admonished himself for thinking that way.

We will call her Betty did not allude to his loss other than to say to Maria, "Carter and I have so much in common; we lost a dear friend from our days of partying in AC."

Another problem arose however, Betty's handsome friend was staring at Carter during most of the evening and his knee was uncomfortably pressed firmly against Carter's under the table. The worst part was that Carter didn't pull away, and as the night went on, it became more and more clear that if the opportunity had presented itself, they might have ended up together. Luckily, this was not possible and the only contact was between the knees and an occasional touch of the hands. The show was terrific, and after the show, there was dancing on the small dance floor that was cleared in front of the stage. Carter found his determination again while gliding around the floor with his Maria. He told himself she was the most desirable person in the world for him and he was going to be faithful to her.

When the night was over and they returned to Maria's home, they spent the balance of the evening in the family room listening to music and smooching. There would be no sleeping together in Maria's parents' home, especially with them upstairs in their bedroom. By the time the weekend was over, it was a foregone conclusion that Carter and Maria were expected to announce any day that they were engaged.

After that, Carter and Maria spent most of their weekends together, and during the week days, they spoke on the phone every night. Carter was truly in love with Maria and she returned his affection in kind. This continued, and at the same time, Ted had become very close to a girl that he had met through one of his old classmates from U of P and he was spending most of his time with her. Ted and his new girl Gina were often sleeping together at the house Carter and Ted shared. Evidently, Gina had two roommates and it wasn't always convenient for Ted to stay at her apartment. Carter became a little distressed at the arrangement between Ted and Gina, but he was so occupied with Maria that he didn't address it.

However, Ted did not discount Carter's attachment to Maria. He commented several times about Carter being on the phone with Maria, even when Gina was present. It finally came to a head when Carter mentioned that Maria would be coming to stay with him for the weekend. Ted came into the kitchen where Carter was sitting at the table eating a sandwich and snatched the sandwich plate from the table.

Carter exclaimed, "What's wrong with you?"

Ted answered, "You're not bringing anyone here, woman or man, to sleep with you."

Carter said, "Are you crazy? I can bring anybody I want, I pay rent here just as you do."

"Do you think I'm going to let you fuck somebody else in our house, in fact I don't want you fucking anyone else anywhere."

Carter answered. "You never cared how I felt with all of the people you brought here. I was sleeping in the next bedroom with you grunting and yelling with your latest lovers."

"They were not my lovers. I told you I still liked women and you understood."

"Wait a minute, you decided I understood. I never said I did."

By this time, Gina hearing the argument came into the kitchen.

"Carter, are you ok?" Carter was stymied; he didn't know what to say, here was Ted's girlfriend obviously knowing what was happening and asking if he was alright. He left the kitchen and went upstairs to his bedroom as he heard Ted yelling at Gina, telling her to stay out of it. He was totally confused and slightly disgusted. He was thinking, I must be lower than low to get to this point with this situation. Ted came into his bedroom and closed the door. Carter didn't know what to expect next.

Ted seemed calmer now; he spoke, "Carter, Gina knows how I feel about you and she accepts it. I told her I've got to have you as my friend and it doesn't mean I don't care about her. She knows." Carter was more disgusted by Ted's revelation.

"Ted, I'm going to move. I can't be part of this weird stuff. Just let me move out and you can get back to normal."

"What do you mean weird? She understands I'm bisexual and I love you. You fuckin' belong to me and I care for her, so if she wants me, she has to understand. In fact, she and I are going to get married, but that doesn't mean I'm not going to be with you, too."

"Wait a minute, what you are saying is what you want. What about what I want? I want to be with Maria and just Maria."

At this Ted went into a diatribe about Maria, whom he hadn't personally met.

"I don't like this, Maria. She sounds like all she is looking for is some guy to take her off of the market and marry her, so that she can be taken care of, and you mentioned something about her goal in life is to get a mink coat. She has to be the most shallow person you have ever met." Carter lost his temper, "Don't you talk about Maria. The girls you have been screwing around with, except for Gina, are not even good enough to polish Maria's shoes. Maria and I joke about the mink coat. If that was all I could give her in life, it would be a sad situation."

Ted sat down on Carter's bed and covered his face. Carter was thinking, oh, no, don't start trying to get pity after the way you have acted. But he realized how confused Ted was and that he was sincere when he talked about how he felt. This didn't make Carter feel better, in fact he felt worse because he blamed himself for everything.

I'm just messing up everybody's life, Ted's, Maria's, Gina's, and mine. I don't even know if I can be what Maria deserves. The next guy that comes along and shows interest might just snap his fingers and I will fall over. Thinking that way made him admit that he was very much in love with Ted and he was actually trying to get back at Ted for his thoughtless actions.

Carter stayed home that evening. He and Gina fixed dinner together, she did the salad and Carter broiled steaks on the grill in the backyard. It was like the two of them had some unspoken agreement to cheer up Ted.

Maria and Carter decided to spend that weekend together at another couple's house at McGuire Air Force Base Housing development. The wife was one of Maria's best friends whose husband was an air force pilot. It turned into a great weekend until while playing a game that required their telling the truth about one of their fondest wishes, the wife confessed that she wanted to kiss

Carter and she proceeded to do so and then ran from the room with her husband right behind her, asking for an explanation.

Carter and Maria were left to decide what should happen next. So, the weekend ended rather abruptly on that Saturday evening. Carter was totally confused, but Maria was not. She explained as they drove to her parent's home that Delores (the wife) had expressed her desire for Carter if she weren't married.

"I guess the wine loosened her inhibitions," said Maria. "She has always been funny about what she wants to do. She just does it and that's that. But I never thought she would just kiss my honey right in front of me and Gus (her husband)."

They spent the rest of Saturday night at Maria's house, and on Sunday, Maria decided to take Carter to her church for Sunday services. When they got back home, Maria announced that she was going to call Carter's mother to tell her she had made Carter go to church. When Lila answered, Maria had Carter pick up the extension so that he could hear the conversation.

"I took your son to church this morning."

Lila answered, "Oh, that's wonderful; he hasn't been going to church like he used to when he lived at home."

Carter interjected, "Mother, I still go sometime."

"Baby, is that you? I know you haven't been coming to our church. Father Jackson asked about you."

At this reply, Maria exclaimed, "Baby! Ha-ha, he is pretty big to be calling baby. I have a new pet name for him now."

Lila continued, "You're a sweetie, welcome to the family, Maria."

When they ended the call, Carter said, "You have made brownie points with my mother, now you can do no wrong."

"I know what I'm doing. I intend to marry you."

Carter was still thinking about what Maria had said after talking to his mother as he drove back to Philadelphia Sunday Evening. I would like to marry Maria, but I don't know if I could be faithful to her if an opportunity to be with Ted or even another interested guy presented itself. I already know that's what Ted expects and I still feel tempted to be with him.

Maria and Carter continued on as an item for some time. Ted and Gina's plans for marriage also progressed. Carter remained as Ted's housemate, and eventually he began to have Maria come to spend weekends at their shared townhouse. Ted never really warmed to Maria. Most times he spent in the second floor sitting room when the others were on the first floor in the living room and he and Gina usually went out in the evenings.

Ted was also becoming a very successful attorney with a heavy case load. He and Gina had set a date and Ted had asked Carter to be his best man. A little bit of irony. Carter had finally confided in his friends and Herb, Ronny, and Roger all responded with similar comments.

"How can that big jerk be so cruel? You were his partner and lover and he wants you to stand up there and watch him marry someone else."

It was November 1963, Ted and Gina's wedding day had arrived. They had decided on a small ceremony at Gina's parents' home. Ted's parents and a few other family members from both sides were in attendance. Ted's mother had been disappointed that the marriage would not take place in a church and that it would not be a large society affair. Gina's mother had tried to protest the small arrangements but had finally accepted the plan for a formal reception at a later date, perhaps in the spring of the following year.

Carter had been fortified with lots of alcohol beginning at a hastily arranged bachelor fest the night before. Herb, Ronny, and Roger had taken care of most of the plans, but it was a very straight affair because of all of the other lawyers and staff from Ted's office who attended, along with old U of P classmates. The bachelor party had had three times as many guests at the marriage ceremony. The bachelor affair had been held at Herb and Ronny's place on Delancy. During the marriage vows, Carter felt that he wasn't going to make it; he fought back tears throughout and he felt that all eyes were on him, and when he was supposed to present the bride's ring, the Minister had to ask several times.

Ted, on the other hand, seemed oblivious of how Carter might feel until the minister announced that he may kiss the bride. Ted kissed his new wife and held her for a moment and then he grasped Carter's hand tightly as he and Gina turned from the temporary alter that had been set up in the large living room. Gina's mother had arranged for a sit-down luncheon in the dining room of the house. A caterer was hired to serve the guests and there was abundant champagne. Carter and Maria excused themselves after the meal was over. Carter had become quite intoxicated after five champagne flutes added on to what he had drank the night before and pre-marriage vows.

They drove back to Ted and Carter's house. As they entered, the phone was ringing and Carter answered. Herb was on the other end.

"Carter, how are you?"

Carter replied, "I am numb. He is really married."

"Ronny, Roger and I want to see you. Can you come over?"

"Maria is with me, I'm ok."

Herb said, "Tell Maria to come with you, it sounds like you don't need to drive."

"Ok, I will tell her," said Carter. When he hung up the phone, he asked Maria if she would go with him to Roger's apartment on Pine Street. Maria seemed to sense that he didn't really want her to go.

She answered, "I will drive you over there and come back here. I just want to relax. I can come and pick you up when you are ready to come home." He was overcome with feelings of gratitude and affection for Maria; she was being so understanding. On the way in the car, he tried to tell her how much he cared for her, but she hushed him, saying, "Wait until tomorrow when you are sober and tell me then."

At Roger's, he walked in, his three friends encircled him in a hug and he lost it completely. He wept.

Herb spoke, "The unfortunate thing for many of us in the gay life is the unacceptance by society. It causes us to live under a cloud of deception made unwittingly by ourselves. We try to cover our true selves with false desire for what is considered 'normal.' In so doing, we make our lives miserable striving to please everyone else. We also need to be careful not to choose someone who is caught up in this make-believe bullshit. Oh, Carter, I ache for you. You set out as a truthful soul finding yourself and falling first for a wonderful guy who was that determined to be with you and then losing him so tragically. Now your heart is broken by this confused insincere person who thinks he can have it both ways no matter how much he hurts you and that naïve woman he just married."

Ronny said, "Oh, Herb, now is not the time to tell this kid about his mistakes, now is the time for the three of us to be here for him and to tell him he will get over this and move on."

Herb added, "Yes, but it is also the time to reiterate my warning about what he is thinking he should do and that is to try to go straight with this girl he is seeing. This is all probably in retaliation for what that mixed up jerk that he is in love with has done."

Carter gathered himself, saying, "Herb, I really do love Maria. She is just a perfect person. She even sensed how I felt today and she decided to let me come here alone to be with my friends." Herb answered, "Yes, but shouldn't that tell you that she doesn't deserve to be in a relationship with someone who isn't being truthful to himself about his needs?"

"Herb, don't be angry with me. I just need to have a stable future. I don't want to go from person to person or to this and that. I care for you guys, but I am in love with Maria and I think I can be with her and be content." Carter says this, but he is actually thinking about how he feels about Ted, and even if it's not Ted, he fears there will always be some other guy. This thought makes him feel worse.

The friends' night of mutual commiseration ended when Maria called to say she was coming to pick up Carter. When she arrived outside, she tapped on the horn to let them know she was there and Carter made his way out to join her in the car. They drove back to Carter's place in silence. The next morning was a bright, sunny Sunday. Carter and Maria decided to go out to the City Tavern for Sunday Brunch. After a pleasant meal and a couple of Bloody Mary's, Carter felt renewed and they spent the rest of the day wandering around Head House Square and Penn's Landing. Carter drove Maria back to Morrisville and returned to his empty townhouse.

The last few days of November included Thanksgiving dinner back at his mother's home. Maria and her mother and father were invited, and of course, his sister Catherine and her children, plus his Aunt Aida. His mother was able to pull out her very impressive china, crystal, and silverware; the table settings were beautiful, complete with candelabra and decanters. His aunt was her usual self. She dominated a lot of the conversation with much information about all of the prominent people that she normally socialized with, and of course, how she was glad that her nephew Carter had aligned himself with a nice girl from a good family. She was so upset when she learned that he and his previous girlfriend Anita, who was from one of the families in Yeadon, had broken up.

Carter was very disgusted with his aunt's performance and would have countered her remarks if his mother hadn't signaled several times with just a look for him to let his aunt's comments pass unchallenged.

However, his sister Catherine did not pay attention to their mother's plea and she said, "I for one was happy that my brother didn't end up with someone from that Bourgeoisie crowd." This retort precipitated a heated discussion between Catherine and Aunt Aida, which had to finally be interrupted by Carter's mother.

"Carter makes his own decisions and he has matured considerably; so has Anita. Theirs was a high school affair, and by the way, Anita's mother was a good friend of mine, so I would not label her or her husband as Bourgeoisie. Certainly, I am sure Maria is not interested in Carter's teenage affairs."

As always Carter was pleased with the way his mother could always handle uncomfortable situations with quiet control. His aunt was known for her outspoken opinionated remarks that mostly had dual purposes of sarcasm and criticism. Other times she would ask Carter directly when he was getting married or if he ever would. She would often exclaim that her two sons should have had his opportunities.

Maria and Carter had reservations to see Mathis again at the Latin Casino in Cherry Hill. When they arrived in the XKE Jaguar that Carter had taken over earlier that year, one of the owners of the club was outside the entrance and he commented to the attendant, who was taking the car to park it in the lot, "Be careful with that beautiful car that belongs to that beautiful couple." Carter and Maria got in line behind other people who were waiting to be admitted to the club.

The club owner pulled them out of line and told them they would be seated at one of the tables up front because he liked their looks. Maria had been chatting with the couple in front of them and she asked if they could be seated with her and Carter.

The owner answered, "Of course." The other couple was very attractive, but the guy was very good-looking and smiling at Carter a lot. Almost immediately, there seemed to be some signal of interest between Carter and the other guy, and again, once they were seated, there was the knee action under the table plus prolonged gazes.

Before the main part of the show. the band was playing during the intermission and the girls decided to go to the powder room.

Don, the other guy, said, "So, why don't we go to the restroom also?"

Carter said "Right," and they went to the men's room where there was an attendant, which was a saving grace. However, in the long hallway leading back to their table, Don grabbed Carter's arm and they were suddenly hugging each other. The vodka that they had been drinking aided in removing a lot of the inhibitions on both sides and they ended up with their faces touching briefly. Carter finally came to his senses and pulled away, embarrassed and shaken.

"I can't, I'm sorry, my mistake," murmured Carter.

Don answered, "What do you mean you can't? You were into me just like I'm into you."

"No, I mean I can't do this to my girlfriend, she doesn't deserve this."

"Look, man, we can't do anything here anyway. I'll give you my number and you can give me a call sometime."

"No, I can't; you're ok, but I'm not getting into anything like this." Don simply shrugged and walked down the hallway back to the table. When Carter returned to the table, the girls were back and chatting back and forth. Don looked up at him as he took his seat and then looked away. It was very hard to enjoy Johnnie that night. Carter's mind was in turmoil; he realized that he would never be able to live the straight married life, even though he cared deeply for Maria.

Carter began spending more time with his good friend Roger attending parties and other affairs given by friends that they had become aligned with at daily cocktail hours at The Drury Lane, an upscale bar in Center City that appealed to the after work crowd. Roger and Carter were constantly together at both gay and straight happenings. This eventually annoyed Maria. She finally asked Carter why he had to bring Roger around all the time. She said he was being jokingly called Carter's shadow. Carter hadn't realized that this was becoming an issue since they were all part of a group that was together just about every weekend.

In April when Maria was down for a weekend, she told Carter she would stay at her friend Adele's apartment in West Philly. Carter went over on that Friday night to take her out for drinks and dinner. Maria met Carter at the door. She looked sad, it was obvious she had been crying. Carter was alarmed. He asked her what was wrong.

Maria answered, "Carter, I came down to Philly this weekend to tell you in person that we had better call it off."

"Call what off, going out tonight?" asked Carter.

"No, I mean us, call us being together off. I care so much for you, Carter, but I think that our being together will not work." Maria now has tears streaming down her face as she continues. "I was going to wait until we went out tonight to tell you, but I can't prolong this. I can't do this and I think you know it's got to end. After a while, we can just be friends but not now."

Maria went back inside, closing the door behind her. Carter was left standing there, feeling like he had been hit by a ton of bricks. He returned to his car and sat staring at nothing. He knew Maria was right, it had to end and she had been the one with enough courage to say so. Now he had to face the truth; he should realize it's just like Herb had said, he should consider how much hurt he would cause for Maria and also for himself. He started the car and drove off.

Instead of going home, he parked in a Center City Garage and went to Maxine's, a gentlemen's bar where most of the patrons were of the more mature ilk. The bartender there was someone that Carter and Steve had met at one of the gay parties that they had gone to. The bartender (Sam) had taken to the boys right away and had sort of looked after them against any of the more forward older men.

Sam talked to Carter between making drinks and telling jokes to amuse others who sat at the bar. Carter was confiding in Sam about his attempts at going straight.

Sam smiled at him, saying sadly, "Honey, you're a young, cute kid and butch to boot, but I think you and your other buddy are definitely 'club members.' You're considered 'young trade' right now, but that is just proof that you're on track to being exclusively gay. Listen to your older sister, I mean this affectionately."

Carter was not offended by Sam's banter because he knew Sam was not being vicious like some of Queeny types that frequented the gay bars. His other friends were always telling him to stay away from most of the gay bars; they were pick-up spots for the one-night stands and promiscuous types. Carter had felt he needed to talk to someone and he knew what his other friends would say good riddance. He wanted to get understanding from someone outside of his immediate circle of friends. Subconsciously, he was relieved that Maria had made the break so he wouldn't have to.

As Sam moved away to wait on another person at the bar, Carter became aware of another man sitting on the bar stool next to his. Actually, the guy was crowding him and almost banging his leg against Carter's. Carter moved slightly away and the man, who was obviously drunk, grabbed his knee.

Carter pushed his hand away and the man started loud talking Carter, saying, "Who do you think you are, you piece of shit? You don't belong in this bar, you only came in here to try to get picked up by one of us white guys, so don't try to be grand with me."

With this he was kicking at Carter's leg. Sam rushed down from the other end of the bar, but before he got to Carter's end, Eddie, the owner of the club, was there.

Eddie spoke very quietly and forcefully to the drunk, "You have to leave and don't come back, you are permanently flagged from this establishment."

The man protested with, "Eddie, you mean you are putting me out because of this." He never got that insulting name out. Eddie forcibly took him by the arm and ushered him out of the bar area. The whole incident happened so quickly, most of the other patrons of the bar who were nearby didn't realize what was happening.

The hat check girl, who was nicknamed Mary the Hat because she always wore elaborate hats topping off her chic outfits and who was also affectionately thought of as a "fag hag."

That name was self-explanatory, came over to Carter, and hugged him, saying, "Darling, that old fart knows he will never even get a chance to even kiss the heel of your shoe, don't be upset." Carter was saying, "It's okay, I considered the source." Most times he didn't think about the race thing; as far as he was concerned, gay was gay and he, Steve, and Roger had socialized all across the board.

By this time, Eddie was back and apologizing profusely, saying, "Please don't worry about that jerk. You and your friend Steve are welcome here any time. Get in touch with him and tell him you two are invited here for dinner on me whenever you decide. You know our chef is excellent. You guys are an asset to this place." He added, "Sam, give Carter another drink and run a tab on me."

Sam answered, "I hear you, boss."

Carter settled again on his bar stool at the end of the bar.

When Sam came back with his Johnnie Walker Red and soda, Carter said, "You all are embarrassing me."

Sam laughed going into his act, "Listen, honey, Eddie knows you and your friend Steve light this place up when you come in here. Some of these old queens and also the younger ones wouldn't mind having some young exotic stuff. I should become your manager and take orders." This campy chatter really cheered Carter up. He even felt a little better about the ending with Maria. The wonderful thing about some of the gay acquaintances he had been fortunate enough to make had been their ability to make lighthearted fun of some of the serious events in life.

Carter remained at the bar for most of the rest of the night. At almost closing time, two of the guys he had met at one of the parties that his friends Herb and Ronny had given came into the bar. Paul and Jack were lovers who had been together for five years. Paul was Carter's age but had come out when he was still in his teens. He had met Jack who was from Holland and who had met and married a girl from a very wealthy Pennsylvania family that owned hotels and an old guard nationwide lumber company. Jack was a concert pianist and his wife Julia was at the Sorbonne in Paris, France when they met.

Jack saw Carter at the end of the bar and he and Paul came and greeted him, "Oh my, what are you doing here all alone?" said Jack, "Herb is always bragging about you being with a friend and not circulating on the gay scene."

Carter answered, "I just decided to come in and chat with my friend Sam."

Jack said, "Oh, are you here to drown your sorrows and confide in the bartender? You are too young to have problems."

Paul spoke, "Jack, don't poke into Carter's business and don't loud talk him here in this bar full of gossips."

"Oh, Paul, stop being a prude; these people don't care what we're saying, they're too busy trying to outdo each other."

Jack always did most of the talking. Paul was normally quiet, except to agree with whatever Jack said. Herb described the couple as the master and his pet. Jack always let everyone know how lucky Paul was to have latched onto him. Jack's family lived far outside the city, but he had purchased a spectacular townhouse in Center City where his lover Paul lived and he visited often. He had an understanding with his wife and family, which seemed to run very smoothly. Certainly, that wouldn't have been the kind of arrangement that Carter would have wanted with Ted, he attributed the set up to the Kinky Rich.

Jack announced they were having a party and they wanted Carter to come.

Paul said, "Feel free to bring someone with you or just come alone, there will be couples and singles. From what we hear, you need to get out and find someone new." Carter was not upset by the knowledge that Herb had probably told them his story because he knew that Herb didn't intend it viciously.

Jack added, "Definitely don't get all tied up with anyone too soon. Take your time."

Carter replied, "Everyone seems to worry about me."

"Seriously, Carter, you are special to a lot of people who think you deserve to be happy," said Jack.

"Jack, I am so fortunate to have been lucky enough to meet so many great people, they include you and Paul."

The night ended with Carter promising to come to their party the following week on Friday. When Carter got home, the thoughts of Maria returned. He knew their break up had been inevitable, but he actually fantasized about them being married with kids. What would it be like to have a daughter or son looking up to him as their father? Then that thought is interrupted by maybe him being attracted to another guy and cheating on Maria with that person, perhaps ending up hurting her and losing the love and respect of their children. He rationalized that he hoped Maria would find someone who would treat her well as she deserved.

The following week passed quickly with Carter engrossed in his work. Friday arrived and Carter went to Jack and Paul's party. He took his travelling buddy Roger with him. As promised the party was great, his other friends Herb and Ronny were there, of course. They were glad he had come out again and this time without their coaxing. There were three floors of fun and Carter had developed a devil may care attitude, so he danced with several people, no longer feeling up-tight about dancing with guys. After a while, as he circulated around from floor to floor and groups of people, he noticed everywhere he turned there was this blond-haired guy smiling at him.

Finally, Carter was standing and watching Jack and Paul doing a parody of a dancing duo doing a tango. Everyone was laughing and enjoying their act. The blond fellow had moved next to Carter and he spoke.

"How does one get to talk to you?"

Carter replied, "Hi, I suppose we just start talking, my name is Carter."

"Okay, my name is John, how about a dance?"

Carter answered, "Well, we don't want to interrupt the show."

"We can go upstairs, there is nice dance music up there," John replied.

"Okay," answered Carter.

Barbara Streisand is singing "People from Funny Girl," and John and Carter joined other slow dancers on the upper floor. The lights were low, and with a few drinks added to the effect, Carter began to feel very warm toward John and it was obvious that John was getting the same vibes.

When the music ended, John and Carter talked for a while. John asked Carter if maybe they could get together for lunch sometime since they both worked in Center City at offices that were near each other. Carter agreed to have lunch with John sometime and he gave his number to John, who explained that a friend of his was due to arrive at the party shortly and that this friend was just a friend whom he dated sometime. Carter didn't really consider this as a deterrent to being friendly with John or having lunch with him in the future.

Jack came up to the first floor where John and Carter were talking and whispered to John that his friend Wayne had arrived and was downstairs in the rec room looking for him. John excused himself and Jack took Carter's arm, pulling him aside.

"Carter, you need to be careful not to take John seriously; he means well, but Wayne is his lover and he lives at John's house over in the Art Museum Area. They have a stormy relationship because John is a free spirit and Wayne was just a trick that John met who didn't have a job and who jumped at the chance to move in with John. John has sponsored his acceptance at the exclusive French Cuisine School in Philadelphia and paid his tuition."

Carter answers Jack's concern with, "Thanks, Jack, but I'm not looking to get hooked up with anyone. I haven't had a lot of luck with that sort of thing so far."

Jack continues, "If John does get serious about someone, he will make a perfect match because basically he has a lot of class. He runs and is now the CEO of his father's company, which has the whole east coast distributorship of car batteries. His father also owns a Pontiac dealership in Miami, Florida." Carter is nonplused by Jack's description of John's possible wealth. He really felt more excitement about what he sensed about John and his compatibility, but hearing that John had a lover made that excitement diminish; he had always promised himself he would never get involved with anyone who was married or in partnership with anyone else.

Carter is not offended by Jack's idea of what makes someone a good catch because he knows Jack feels that money is the most important part of a successful life. The party continues full force. John is on the lower level when Carter goes down. John's friend Wayne is standing next to him and John introduces Carter to Wayne.

Right away Wayne asks, "How do you two know each other?"

Carter answers, "We just met, Jack and Paul are friends of mine."

"Well, I don't remember seeing you around here before."

Carter simply smiled and said, "Nice meeting you."

Roger and Carter are talking when they notice that John and Wayne are obviously having a heated discussion.

Roger says, "You can tell that your new boyfriend is sick of his friend."

Carter answers, "I can tell you one thing: I'm not going to be involved in that, he doesn't have to worry." As they are secretly watching, John and Wayne leave the party. Paul drifts over to where Roger and Carter are talking.

He says, "Well, Carter, you caused an uproar."

Carter answers, "What do you mean? I didn't know about his friend. I only chatted with him for a while."

Paul said, "John is a nice guy, but he has a wandering eye and he and Wayne argue all the time. To tell the truth, Wayne was just a wild number until he met John and they had a weekend together. We were surprised when John informed us that Wayne was moving in with him two years ago. John confided in Jack last week that he wanted Wayne to move out of his house."

After the party, Roger and Carter went back to Roger's house. Roger brought up John and Wayne again.

"Carter, be careful with that guy John. First of all, that other one seems desperate and trashy, so he won't get out of the way quietly. I hear your friend John is well fixed and that other one thinks he hit the jackpot, plus he might really be in love with John."

"I don't know why everyone thinks I will jump on the first good-looking guy that comes along. I think John is a real fox, but I don't want to mess with someone that's all tied up in a mess, especially if he's hooked up with someone who is desperate like you say."

"Okay, Carter, you know we all want to look after you, so you know I say this with love, be careful."

On that following Monday, Carter's office phone rang. On the other end was John from the party.

"Hello, Carter, can we do lunch today at 12:00?"

Carter felt that tinge of something again and he bantered, "Do lunch, aren't we formal?" and in spite of all his talk about not interfering in a partnership, before he could think, he answered, "Okay, where should we meet?"

John said, "What about that nice Italian restaurant on 19th between Chestnut and Market? We don't have to have reservations there."

"Okay, I'll see you there."

At lunch they talked about themselves and their families. John was especially open about his upbringing as his father's favorite of two sons. His father encouraged him to join the soccer team and participate in gymnastics at Penn Charter where he matriculated up to grade 12 and then to Princeton University.

Carter described his young life, and for the first time, actually admitted his love for his lost friend Tommy to someone other than a member of his close circle of friends.

In fact, during the conversation, he felt himself becoming really emotional and he could tell that John was sincerely full of empathy for his loss. He was opening up to John more than he had with anyone else and he felt that John wanted to know everything about him.

When he thought he was actually going to lose control, he said, "I guess this heavy stuff isn't luncheon conversation."

John replied, "I want to know all about you and I want to tell you all about me. I can't say I've fallen in love before now, my coming out happened during my service in the Peace Corps in Kenya. I actually had several affairs with girls there. In fact, it was more like one-night stands until I dated one of the daughters of an actual chief of a tribe I was working with. She took our alliance seriously and became very possessive. She asked her brother to befriend me so that he could look out for me, but in truth, to make sure I wouldn't cheat on her.

That turned out to be a serious mistake. His name was Kennata (Ken). We spent every day together and each day we would go for a swim in the river. It was very hot and swimming served two purposes: cooling off and washing away the sweat and grime of the day. Naturally, we swam in the altogether and eventually it turned to making love. If we had been discovered, it would not have turned out well for him. His position in the community as the son of a chief was respected by everyone and being found to be gay could have had serious repercussions.

When I finally told his sister I was not in love with her, she told her father I had taken advantage of her and I had to leave the village rather hurriedly overnight. Of course, I never saw Ken again, and after that, I served the rest of my time in Nigeria working out of an office with other Caucasians like myself who hoped to help the less fortunate others."

John went on with, "I continued with more experiences on the gay side, plus a few heterosexual episodes. It seemed I was like the climate there, constantly hot, and the guys and girls there seemed to be fascinated with my blond hair. When I got back home, I was still not ready to join my father's company; instead I became a member of the Young Republicans for Nixon in D.C. and became a Page in the Senate. Finally, I was called home. My mother had passed away, and during that same week, my father suffered a heart attack. My brother was in the service and planning to join a law firm after his discharge, so I was the designated CEO of my father's company with him as the Chairman Emeritus. That's mostly my story up till now."

Carter spoke now, "You said that's mostly your story. You did not include your relationship with your friend Wayne."

John answered, "Yes, I did not include that because that is ending. I won't go into details now, even though you are entitled to ask about it since I'm asking for us to get to know each other. I will tell you about Wayne and me, but let's save that for dinner tonight." Carter was dubious about the alleged ending; he thought to himself how can I be so goody two shoes when I'm sitting here having lunch with this guy who I am very attracted to in spite of knowing he has a lover.

It dawned on Carter that John had mentioned them having dinner that same night. He knew he should have said slow down, we need more time to decide if this is going to be a thing between them. It was apparent that John was used to having his way, but Carter was not the type to be controlled. He decided to go along with the plan for dinner that evening; in fact, he suggested that John come to his place instead of eating out. He detected a look of satisfaction on John's face, realizing that had been his intention. Carter was also thinking this is probably what John does when he is planning on a one-night stand. It makes sense he is not asking Carter to come to his place, of course because he and Wayne are still together.

Later when Carter was walking home from the office, he decided to stop at Genuardi's Supermarket for Porterhouse steaks and salad fixings. He didn't consider himself a gourmet cook, but this kind of meal usually was pleasing to almost any dinner guest.

When John arrived, he brought a bottle of wine that happened to be a Moscato, which in a stretch could go with beef, but Carter had a bottle of burgundy that was left over from the Ted days that went well with the meal. John was surprised and impressed that Carter seemed to know appropriate wines.

Carter responded to John's comments about the wine with a simple answer, "My ex and I were really into wines, not that I'm a connoisseur, but we liked good wines."

John replied, "I guess I'm in for a lot of surprises with you."

Carter said, "I'm just a regular 20 some-year-old who has likes and dislikes like any other guy. Maybe you didn't know that some 'colored' guys like good things."

John was upset, "Hey, wait a minute. I didn't figure you as one of those angry African-Americans. I just meant most young people don't get into good wines and top shelf drinks. Are we getting off on the wrong foot?" Carter had even surprised himself with his own defensive attitude.

He replied, "I don't know why I got up tight with you, maybe it's because I think you are used to pushovers and I'm not a pushover."

The night turned into a pleasant visit for John and Carter with the added influence of a few cocktails before dinner and the wine during. They ended up in bed in spite of Carter's intention to go slow. In the morning, John asked Carter where his razor was.

He said, "I can see you don't have a heavy beard, but you must have to shave sometime."

Carter went to the cabinet in the bathroom and took out his electric shaver, saying, "I have this, but it causes my skin to break out with ingrown hairs, so I use a depilatory and a table knife. That has helped to clear the skin on my neck."

John answered, "Hey, that sounds great. Let me try it." After they had both showered and dressed, they left the apartment to walk to their offices.

During the day, Roger called Carter at his office to say that everyone was meeting after work for cocktails at The Drury Lane as usual. This was normal, at least three nights a week the usual crowd would stop after work. When Carter arrived, he was immediately teased by Herb, Ronny, and Roger. The word had spread that he and John had been together. Carter was perplexed at first and then he found out how the news had spread so quickly. It seemed that Jack had called Herb to say that he had seen John at lunchtime and John's face was a bright red. It wasn't a sun burn. John had reluctantly explained that he had used a depilatory to shave that morning. After further questioning, he had admitted where he had shaved that morning.

Everyone decided that white guys should not use "Magic Shave." Carter was embarrassed at first and then he found himself defending the product.

"It can be used by anybody, it isn't just for people of color," he protested. After that the joke was on Carter and John's first union for a long time.

Carter later learned that night was the end of John's House Mate's stay at John's place. It seems there was a huge blow up regarding the red face, and of course, John's staying out all night. By that Friday, when Carter saw John again, the face was back to normal and John had called to ask Carter to go to

New York with him for the weekend. He had a whole itinerary planned, which included visiting special friends of John's, having dinner at the top French restaurant, and attending the opera Faust at Lincoln Center.

The weekend in New York was great, even though Carter had no great love for Faust. His favorite operas had consisted of Carmen (of course), Madame Butterfly, and La Boheme; in fact, Carmen had been the only Grand Opera he had experienced in person. The lavish production was impressive and he did enjoy it. John informed him that he had season's tickets to the opera and he would like it if Carter would come with him to each production. Carter decided that he and John were probably now partners.

The rest of the year commenced with Carter and John being together every day either at Carter's or at John's townhouse in the Art Museum Area. Finally, John asked Carter to move into his house. This brought forth a great deal of thought. Carter decided he wasn't ready to officially move in with anyone again just yet, so he told John he needed more time by himself. As it turned out, he was glad he had decided against it.

It was spring again and some of John's friends from New York came to town. Jack invited everyone out to his estate in Bucks County, Pennsylvania. The pool house and a huge barn were away from the main house. Jack used those areas for himself and to entertain his friends. The barn was larger than most houses and it contained Jack's concert grand piano. When Carter and John arrived with their New York guests, Carter was surprised to see John's ex-friend Wayne sitting with Paul next to the pool. It seems that they had remained friends and kept in touch.

Wayne was instantly very snarky.

"Well, if it isn't the two new lovers, hi, guys."

Carter simply answered, "Hey, how are you?" John ignored him.

When Carter sat down, Wayne snapped, "I guess by now you must know that your lover is a tramp."

Carter shot back, "I like tramps."

Wayne continued, "Ask him what he does at lunchtime most days."

At this Paul interceded, "Wayne, if you are going to carry on like this, you can leave now." Wayne said, "Thanks, I think I will." At this he got up and walked off toward the cars that were parked in the driveway.

Paul was instantly very apologetic, "I'm really sorry, he just suddenly came out here uninvited." Carter answered, "No problem, he doesn't bother me," but as he was saying this, he was remembering what Wayne had said about John's lunchtime activities. For the rest of the day, they enjoyed drinks and conversation. Jack took them into the barn/practice area and played the piano for them. He didn't normally play just for friends, but they had all requested that he play just one short piece. He ended up playing for at least an hour. It was quite a treat.

Arriving back in the city, Carter told John he would go home to his place since there were four guests who would be staying at John's and Carter felt that John's would be crowded and he hadn't really taken on the role of a co-host at John's place yet. Two of the guests were a couple, a really nice African-American guy Tony, who taught at NYU, and his partner Edmund, who was from Paris, France. Carter had really hit it off with them. They had shared stories of their experiences growing up, going away to school, and finally "coming out" with each other. It was decided that Carter would come early the next morning (Sunday) and they would all go to brunch at The Fountain Room before the visitors left to return to New York.

When Carter arrived the next morning, John fixed Bloody Mary's and they all sat talking before getting ready to leave for brunch. When they were ready to leave, it was decided to take two cars since John's car was a convertible with limited space and Carter's XKE was certainly not a spacious limousine and there were six of them. Edmund and Tony squeezed into Carter's car with Tony sitting sideways in the rear jump seat.

On the short drive to the restaurant, Edmund leaned over and said, "My good friend Carter, you are too trusting and nice."

Carter replied, "What do you mean?"

Edmund continued, "Your lover John made sure we were all comfortably ensconced in our rooms last night after you left and immediately went out. When he returned, he was not alone. He had some other person with him and they went into his bedroom, closing the door behind them. This morning before you arrived, he and the other person left and he came back alone. I am telling you this because I believe in honesty in a relationship and you impress me as someone who feels as I do."

Tony protested from the rear, saying, "Edmund, you have no right to say this to Carter."

"I feel that I do have a right to inform someone whom I already feel a kinship with that he is being cheated on," said Edmund. For the rest of the ride, there was silence in the car. When they got to the Fountain Room, they were seated at a table next to the floor to ceiling windows looking out on the Parkway.

Brunch was very pleasant. The setting was a casual but tasteful buffet with several choices of breakfast and luncheon dishes, which patrons were free to choose from at will. Champagne was served as part of the fare. Other cocktails and wines were extra. John picked up the tab for the group. Carter sat through the meal silently, thinking John wasn't trying to impress anyone, this just came naturally to him. Also, he was most attentive to Carter as if what had happened the night before was natural and had no effect on his feelings for Carter. He decided to tell John later that he was aware of what had transpired the night before and that he couldn't accept that kind of thing again in their relationship.

When brunch was over, the group returned to John's place where the New Yorkers had left their car. Carter said good bye to all of the visitors, to Tony and Edmund, he promised to be in touch. John and Carter went inside. Carter was anxious to discuss what Edmund had told him about John and his guest the night before.

"He should never have told you that," said John when Carter brought it up.

Carter answered, "That's beside the point. The fact is I thought you and I were, uh, something, maybe together and would only be with each other."

"Oh, please, Carter, that guy didn't mean anything to me. You decided to go home to your place and I felt like having sex, so I went out and got it. I care very much for you. I want you to be my partner, but I know I need other activity now and then; like I said, it doesn't mean anything, it's just a release."

Carter was flabbergasted; he couldn't believe that John treated this so casually.

He said, "Okay, if you thought it wasn't important, that means now you know it is important to me. So, if you and I are partners, you won't just jump in bed with someone else."

"Okay, now I know I will try to remember."

"Let's finish the discussion by saying you are free to do whatever you want and when you want, but we now understand what that means."

The relationship continued with Carter and John being together most of the time. In the summer, they even traveled to the notorious Fire Island, where they stayed with friends at their beachfront house. Basically, even though the island is known for a large percentage of its visitors' promiscuity, John paid attention only to Carter. Carter found himself thinking John's attention to him was mostly because the pines in Fire Island was predominately Caucasian and

John's preference was black. That thought annoyed him most because of the stereotype of "dinge queen" that was often attributed to older gays who preferred dark trade. However, John could not be classified as older; he was the same age as Carter.

Carter under estimated his ability to attract a partner who was actually sincere. He was not seasoned enough in the gay world to understand that some individuals did not feel that being monogamous was an indication of caring deeply for a partner. In addition, people were being infected all around them with the deadly Aids disease that was rumored to be the result of promiscuity. He didn't really think of that as a paramount reason for his resentment for John's episodes, but that was definitely a minor part. Carter was used to novices like himself who had just had new experiences or even experiments with a buddy. The Plague had become the topic among all segments of the gay world and being careful was paramount.

Meeting for drinks after work with his other friends at The Drury Lane continued for Carter most days. Most of the other people who also came for cocktail hour were those from offices in Center City, quite a few were professionals lawyers, interns, nurses, and even college students of legal age. The Drury Lane was a more upscale cocktail lounge, no underage people were allowed. It was not considered a pick-up bar, so most of the more flighty types were not welcome. If they happened in, they were mostly ignored.

On one Wednesday evening, Carter was talking to his friend Roger when Roger lowered his voice, saying, "You know there's a very handsome guy who is sitting across the bar from us and he is definitely looking at you. I've noticed him in here several times before and I've tried to give him the eye, but he is only looking at you."

Carter responded, "Oh, give me a break, Roger. You always have your mind on making out with somebody; that guy is probably not thinking about me or you. He is probably just having after work drinks just like us."

"Listen, I know what I'm talking about, he is very interested in you," said Roger.

"Well, guess what," said Carter, "I've got enough trouble on my hands without taking on more problems."

"Are you serious, Carter? There's nothing wrong with a little extra activity to keep you in shape. You can at least smile at the guy, and a little flirting never hurt anybody." Carter stole a glance across the bar and was surprised to realize that the person Roger referred to was looking right at him and smiling. Carter wasn't used to cruising (the gay slang for flirting), but he smiled back. This response caused a reaction on the other side of the bar. The good-looking guy got up, made his way around to where Roger and Carter were sitting.

"Hey there," he said to Carter, "I'm Carl, and you are?"

"Carter, and this is Roger, how are you?"

Carl answered, "I'm fine now that someone in this place is being friendly."

"Oh, have other people been unfriendly?"

"Well, not necessarily, but actually I haven't tried to find out if anyone else is friendly."

"I am sure if you had tried, they would have been friendly."

"I wasn't interested until now or maybe it was a week or so ago. Let me buy you two a drink."

After Al the Bartender brought their drinks, the three of them talked for a while. It turned out that Carl was from Hersey, Pennsylvania and he had attended Syracuse University. He had settled in Philadelphia two years ago and he was a counselor in the Board of Education. His father owned a well-known breakfast cereal company. He joked that his father had told him to get out of Hersey because he liked boys more than girls. Carter thought, oh, no, another castoff." Carl was not the typical nice guy, but he seemed to definitely be into Carter. In fact, as the bar began to be more crowded with the before dinner crowd, another guy accidently stepped on Carl's foot; he told the man to get the fuck off of his foot, "they're for me to walk on, not you."

During their conversation, Carter determined that Carl also had racist tendencies. Several times he cast disparaging remarks about other people in the bar, such as, "That one looks like he just left the cotton fields." Carter immediately made it known that he found Carl's remarks unacceptable and distasteful. In fact, he controlled his desire to retaliate in kind by telling Carl to fuck off in the Upscale Drury Lane.

Instead he simply said, "All people of color didn't come from cotton fields, and even if we did, it's a sign of strength and endurance."

To this comment, Carl replied, "I don't care where you came from. I'd like to take you out to dinner. I want to get to know you."

Roger broke in with, "You mean you'd like to get him in bed."

Carl ignored Roger's sarcasm, continuing to wait for Carter to accept his invitation.

For some reason, Carter answered, "Okay, when?" He was thinking about John and his promiscuity and the feeling of getting back at John for being unfaithful. He also wanted to have the pleasure of later telling Carl he would not be interested in making out with him.

Carl answered, "Let's go now. I have an open reservation most nights at 'Bon Appetite.'"

Carter said, "I didn't think you meant tonight, but okay, let's go." Roger was obviously surprised that Carter was consenting, but he had just been teasing Carter about living a little.

Carter said, "Roger, I'll call you tomorrow" and he and Carl left the bar.

At the restaurant, Elaine the owner greeted Carl with great affection, "Darling, where have you been? I haven't seen you for ages."

Carl answered, "I haven't been in the mood for fancy cuisine."

Elaine replied, "So, you must be trying to impress this handsome young man tonight."

Carl agreed, "Yeah, I'm going to wine and dine him, so he'll give it up." Carter was a little shaken by Carl's frankness; he hadn't ever admitted to being gay to a woman before, even with the very sophisticated types that his friends Herb and Ronny had introduced him to or to the famous actress who was so fond of Tommy and him.

Elaine seated them at a table very near the bar at the rear of the restaurant. It was one of the more private tables in the place.

When she had left them with a flourish promising to check back to make sure they were enjoying, Carter said, "I'm not used to being campy with a woman."

Carl replied, "Oh, don't sweat it. I've screwed her and her boyfriend. She doesn't think twice about it. Once she found out that I would rather be with someone like you, she simply wished me well."

Carter asked, "What do you mean by 'someone like me,' someone of color?"

Carl said, "Look, what I mean by someone like you is someone male and sexy and someone I want to fuck." Carter was flabbergasted, but he contained his surprise at how abrupt and rude Carl could be. He chalked it up to his being raised as a spoiled brat in a small-town affluent environment. Unlike Herb and Ronny, who had been in affluent households but who had developed kind and thoughtful personalities.

At this point, Carter thought maybe it was time for him to come down off of his judgmental cloud and to be real. This idea that everyone should have gentility like that taught by his mother does not apply to the real world. He started feeling drawn to Carl; in fact, Carl's attitude made him kind of desirable.

The meal was great with good wine and after another drink (Brandy). Carter was feeling warm and he decided that maybe he would with Carl. They left the restaurant and Carl suggested another drink at his place. Carter agreed. They went to Carl's apartment in The Philadelphian on the Parkway.

The doorman at the entrance to the building greeted them with a smile, saying, "Hello there, Mr. Mueller, how is your day going?"

Carl answered, "As you can see, pretty well. This is Carter. You'll be seeing him a lot in the future." Turning to Carter, he said, "This is Harry, my favorite doorman. He keeps me informed."

Carter said, "Hi, Harry," trying not to show his embarrassment at the obvious innuendo.

When they entered the elevator, Carter asked Carl what he meant by Harry keeps him informed. Carl answered, "I have this friend who I've been seeing for two years now, and if he comes while I'm entertaining someone else, Harry will signal me on the house phone." This almost made him lose his composure again. After all, he was there to possibly cheat on his own friend John, but it just didn't seem as disrespectful as the way Carl was viewing his attachment with his friend. To have the doorman watching out for his lover to make sure that he would not be caught with some other guy he had just picked up. The worst part was he was the pick-up. These thoughts seemed to seal his determination to reject this guy Carl.

The apartment was on the penthouse level and decorated in exquisite masculine taste. Carl was obviously a reader. There was a wall of bookshelves in the den full of many books that Carter himself had read and enjoyed. Carl asked if he would like a drink and went behind a built-in bar that was well stocked with all kinds of liquor. He fixed himself a scotch and soda and Carter said he would have the same. He came around and sat on the barstool next to Carter.

Carter mentioned the books and Carl replied, "You really are different from other colored guys I've met. Most are only interested in giving me a blow job or getting fucked, by the way which I prefer."

Carter decided he had had enough so, he said, "I have to go in to my office early tomorrow, so thanks for dinner and the drinks."

"What! Why the fuck do you think I brought you here to give you a free drink?" answered Carl. So, Carter simply stood and put on his suit jacket as he went out to the foyer of the apartment. By the time he was opening the door to leave, Carl started yelling curses at him and following him out to the elevator.

He literally screamed, "You nigger bitch," as the elevator doors opened. There was an older gentleman in the elevator who was ready to get off. He looked totally shocked by the language that was being hurled at Carter and he glared at Carl with disgust.

Carter took the elevator to the lobby of the building where Harry the Doorman now sat behind his desk. He looked at Carter with understanding.

He said, "You don't have to sign out in the guest book, you came in with a resident. Would you like for me to call you a cab, son?"

Carter answered, "No, thanks, I can walk." He went out and walked down the Parkway toward City Hall. He was thinking about his life so far as a gay man. So far there seemed to be a lot of differences in comparison to being straight.

Maybe it wasn't that different though. A lot of the so called normal young people he knew were just as promiscuous and unsettled as a lot of the gay people he had met. He thought about his friends Herb and Ronny. They seemed to be the perfect couple. He was almost sure they did not fool around on each other, but was that because they essentially came out together? Unlike Paul and Jack, who had been partners for five years, but who Carter was not sure were faithful to each other. Also, it might be that their relationship would be classified as a sponsorship with the older wealthy person supporting the younger one in comfort. The latter arrangement would not be his thing. He believed in love whether it was gay or straight.

He was almost home when his thoughts painfully went to Tommy. His Tommy, oh, Tommy if only I had been more mature and if I had been able to accept reality before I finally realized you were the person for me. I am sure by now we would have worked it all out and we could be like Herb and Ronny. As he arrived at his condo, he almost felt like Tommy was there with him. He felt sadness that seemed to permeate the air around him as though Tommy felt his sorrow and was equally sad.

On that Thursday, when he got to his office, his assistant told him he had messages on his desk. Roger, John, and of all people, Carl had called. After he had attended to some of the folders on his desk that contained offers from venders and manufacturers for open contracts that he was managing, he called Roger.

"Hi, Roger, I'm still alive after going to dinner with that crazy person."

Roger answered, "I really thought you would tell him no when he asked you to dinner because of his attitude and the fact that he's a nasty snob and a racist."

"Yes, to put it mildly, I was so intent on getting back at John that I went with him."

After his conversation with Roger, he returned to answering quotes from the venders and manufacturing representatives. Alice his assistant called in that there was a call waiting from Carl Mueller. Carter picked up the phone, ready to inform Carl that he had no desire to talk to him again.

At the other end, Carl immediately said, "Carter, I am so sorry. You made me so angry because you just didn't realize how much I like you and how much I want to spend time with you." Carter was astounded by the change in Carl's tone of voice and his genuine sounding apology. He simply replied, "You obviously have issues. Certainly, you must know that your true feelings about race are very transparent. I guess it could have something to do with your upbringing. We all know that very few people in this country are completely without some kind of prejudice, but you come right out with it."

Carl actually laughed at Carter's response and jokingly said, "I thought I was just talking like a lot of the big queens that frequent a lot of the colored gay bars in town."

Carter replied, "Look, you are obviously suffering from an extreme misconception of what all people of color are like, so I would suggest that you go to those bars you speak of to hunt for your trade."

"Oh my, my, aren't we smart using all of this high and mighty terminology?" said Carl. This retort was the last straw for Carter.

He exploded, "Listen, you ignorant asshole, don't ever call here again. In fact, don't ever call me anywhere again." With that, he banged the phone down.

Alice came into his cubicle, saying, "Was that one of those crooked salespersons that insist they deserve a contract because they are a white American, even though they are not a fair priced bidder? I will screen his calls in the future."

Carter lied, "Yes, he was. Thanks!"

Just before lunchtime, John called, "I'm downstairs, let's have lunch." Carter was still a little shaken from his telephone conversation with Carl, but he said, "Okay."

They went to Torrello's, where Carter ordered his favorite, Deviled Crab with Pasta. John was looking at him with an intense gaze.

"So, Carter, where were you last night?" he asked.

Carter responded with, "As usual, Roger and I stopped at the Drury Lane for drinks after work."

John added "And after that?"

Carter continued, "Oh, I went to dinner with another friend Carl Mueller."

"After dinner, did you go home with this other friend?" asked John.

Carter replied, "Yes, we went to his apartment for another drink."

"Okay, you went home with this guy that you just met. I guess that means you probably went to bed with him and that's why you weren't at home when I kept calling you."

Carter answered, "I was thinking about going to bed with him, but I decided not to and I walked home."

John said, "Then I guess being faithful doesn't apply to you, just to me," sarcastically.

"Wait a minute, John, you said it's okay to go out with someone else because it doesn't mean anything, it's just sex. The other thing is I didn't know we were lovers and also how did you know Carl and I had just met?"

"First of all, I thought it was understood that we were lovers, remember I asked you to move in with me. Secondly, a friend told me you had left the bar with someone you just met."

Carter thought to himself, I know Roger didn't tell John about last night. It must have been Al, but that's surprising because he seems a lot more discreet.

He said, "I wouldn't have gone with Carl if I thought you would care, and if you had told me, you would not go with anyone else either. But you didn't, so here we are."

"I am not saying I will not be with anyone else, but I am saying that I want you to be my special someone. Nobody else can touch the way I feel about you in spite of my being with them."

"Well, John, I will try to understand how you feel about our relationship, but I have to tell you I am not your property, and if you are going to sleep around, I will do what I want when I want also, even though that's not my style."

John and Carter continued as undeclared partners for a while longer. One of Carter's friends, who spent a lot of time in New York, called Carter, saying he was having some people in and some of the guys he would visit in New

York were coming. He told Carter he should come and feel free to bring his friend John. Carter accepted the invite and he and John went to Edward's apartment on Lincoln Drive for the gathering. There were a lot of Edward's friends from out of town. During the gathering, there was a lot of conversation and good music. There was a lull in the party chatter and the stereo was in the midst of changing an LP when John's voice was heard by everyone asking a fellow he had been talking to for his number, so that they could get together.

It seemed that all eyes turned to Carter to see his reaction.

Carter simply said to Edward, "Thanks, Ed; we have to get back in town. We have another party we promised we would go to." They left in John's car in silence.

Finally, John spoke, "Whose party are we going to?"

Carter answered, "There is no other party. I'm going home and you can go wherever and do whatever you want to."

Right away John replied, "Carter, I was just being friendly. I wasn't going to call that guy." Carter said, "Listen, John, you and I are nothing anymore. You can do whatever you want to. Just don't bother me."

"So, you mean we are through just because I talked to someone else at a party?"

By this time, they had arrived in front of the gate leading into the court-yard of Carter's condo. Carter opened the car door and got out of the car, walking through the gate into the courtyard and to his apartment. He was so angry, he couldn't utter another word. Inside when he was able to calm down, he realized he wasn't really that upset. This situation had been inevitable; he had known subconsciously that the affair with John had to end. Carter was not the type to accept everybody feeling sorry for him. While his so-called lover, partner, or whatever slept with every Tom, Dick, or Harry, especially with this new "gay disease" killing off people. The other thing was that this person had no respect for him and his feelings.

Suddenly, his life again included time with Ted and Gina. Ted was calling him to have lunch with him on several occasions and Carter consented. Carter knew it was probably not a good idea to spend time with Ted again, especially alone time. They went to lunch at Torrello's and other times at The Milan. Ted talked about his success and often mentioned how it would have been great if they were still sharing their townhouse in Center City. He and Carter could still have time together when Gina was out with her girlfriends or at her mother's. Carter was constantly saying nothing would happen between them again now that Ted was married.

As it happened, Gina called Carter and asked him to come to dinner at their house in Bryn Mawr. He thought to himself, oh, well, with Gina there, nothing could happen with Ted and me. So, he accepted the invite. When he got to their house, Ted was not there yet. Gina said he had a very important client that he had to meet before coming home. Carter and Gina reconnected. It was like the old days before Gina and Ted got married. They made martinis together and chatted about everything that came to mind.

Gina finally said, "I don't think Ted is happy being married to me."

"Why do you say that, Gina? He tells me he likes married life," said Carter.

She answers, "I often catch him looking sad in a pensive mood."

They had been sitting in an area off of the kitchen dining area that looked out over the garden. In walked Ted, looking great in his Brooks Brothers Suit, smiling brightly.

"Hey, you came. It's about time you decided to come to see your boring, married friends."

Carter stood up, saying, "Well, I was finally invited." Ted hugged Carter tightly and Carter pulled away a little uncomfortably. He almost felt embarrassed thinking Gina could see his weak knees and how he almost responded by returning Ted's hug with a strong embrace. Ted read his thoughts as he continued smiling and looking intently at Carter.

He said, "I'm going up to change into my soft clothes, so I can get comfortable. I'll be right back shortly." He left the room.

Gina exclaimed, "Now he's happy because you're here. I don't get those kinds of smiles normally when he comes home."

Carter responded, "Oh, come on, Gina, you know you are the most special person in the world to him."

Gina changed the subject with, "Help me make a salad, Ted will do the steaks on the grill outside."

Carter was slicing tomatoes and cucumbers when Ted came back into the kitchen.

"Hey, even in my house you're in charge of the food like old times."

Carter answered, "Evidently, that was my only purpose in the old household." He was immediately sorry for that comment. He didn't want Gina to think he was giving some message that he felt used and discarded. He had meant the comment to be a joke about Ted's lack of cooking prowess. He sensed that Gina always seemed to feel that she had interfered in Ted and Carter's relationship. Hence the reason for her earlier statements about Ted's moods.

Ted turned out to be very proficient at grilling steaks, maybe because he was a steak lover Porterhouse, T-bone, and rib were his favorites and a good sirloin cooked to perfection in a big iron skillet was also on his list. Of course, Carter was reminiscing about the days with Ted.

During dinner, conversation again flowed smoothly between the three of them. Gina mentioned that she had suggested that they should have told Carter he could bring a guest with him to dinner, but Ted had said it would be like old times in Center City with just the three of them. By this time, Ted was obviously feeling the liquor he had been consuming to supposedly catch up with Gina and Carter.

He said jokingly, "Carter belongs to us; he isn't allowed to bring a guest to our house."

Gina covered with, "That's right, she or he would feel like an outsider."

After dinner, they had more drinks and Carter was beginning to feel like he was not going to be able to drive home safely. Gina seemed to read his thoughts.

"Carter, you should stay over and leave in the morning. You need to be careful driving and drinking. Even if you think you are alright to drive, the police might pull you over and detect liquor on your breath."

Carter answered, "I'll be fine. I will just drink water for the rest of the night. That's supposed to slightly nullify the effects." Gina was not really satisfied with Carter's decision, but she went on to say she was going to bed and she wanted to give Ted and Carter time to catch up.

Carter became very alert at this and he said, "I have a busy day tomorrow, so I should leave." Ted spoke now, "Sit down, Carter. You're going to spend the night here like Gina said." Carter was saying no as Gina left the room and headed upstairs. Ted rose from his chair and came over to the couch where Carter was sitting. He leaned over, placing his hands on either side of Carter on the back of the couch. Carter started to try to stand up, avoiding Ted's attempts to keep him on the couch, but Ted had not lost any of that old strength. He held Carter's shoulders and his mouth clamped onto Carter's mouth. At first, Carter turned away, but Ted persisted and a passionate kiss resulted with Ted on top of Carter on the couch.

Carter finally collected his senses, pushing Ted off of him and rising from the couch; he moved toward the hallway.

"Ted, you are crazy. You have no regard for anyone else's feelings. How can you try to do this with Gina in the house?"

Ted responded, "I told you a long time ago Gina knows about us. I was honest with her from the beginning. I promised her the only one I would want besides her was you. That's why she has already gone up to bed, so that we could be together."

"Ted, you are disgusting. You don't even think about anybody but yourself. You are willing to make Gina feel like crap so you can indulge in all of your desires, probably with other women, too."

"Carter, you can call me names. You can tell me I'm disgusting or whatever, I'm still going to be me. So, if you think I'm disgusting, I don't care, and if Gina wants me, she has to put up with it."

Carter felt completely sober now, so he said, "Okay, I'm leaving. You can tell Gina I appreciate her offers, but I'm just fine." Ted stood up and came toward Carter.

"If you don't promise I can come over tomorrow, I'm going to make a lot of noise so that Gina will hear us now."

"Okay, you come to my place tomorrow when you're sober and we'll talk," said Carter. He went out quickly to his car and drove out before Ted could collect himself enough to catch up.

On the way home, he was asking himself why he had consented to have Ted come to see him the next day. The answer, of course, was he wanted to be with Ted again, even though he knew that Ted was never going to be faithful to anyone, man or woman. He felt so sorry for Gina, but he lied to himself, saying if it's me, at least I care about her feelings. Once he arrived, he went straight to bed exhausted.

The next day was a Thursday and normally Carter would have been meeting with venders or salespeople since Thursdays seemed to be one of the more favorite days to call on buyers and purchasing departments. Today was quiet and Carter was able to work on sending contracts up for signing by his contracting officer.

A call came through from Ted, "Hey, Carter, should I just come to your place, or do you want to meet first for drinks?"

He answered, "I didn't think you were serious about today."

"Oh, come on, you knew I was serious. There's no reason why we can't get together now and then," said Ted.

"Okay, come over to my place but just to talk. I'm not sure I should even be considering any kind of alone time with you."

Ted simply said, "I'll see you later." Carter found the rest of the day really slow and he realized he was anxious to see Ted again at his home. He left his office at 4:30 on the dot. That was unusual; he would normally never leave before 5:00 PM, and often when not meeting his buds at the bar, he wouldn't leave before 7:00. Tonight was different; he went straight home to his place on Lombard Street. He had become a real Absolute Vodka drinker, so he put a lot of ice cubes in the ice bucket on the coffee table in the living room with two Old Fashion size glasses and a bottle of that liquor.

Ted arrived shortly after Carter had changed into jeans and a T-shirt. He came into the living room and commented on the new couch and side chair with the ottoman that Carter's mother had purchased as a gift for Carter.

"You always had good taste, even when we didn't have much money for furniture," said Ted. "Well, your priorities were different from mine," replied Carter. Again, he thought to himself, why do I have to come off being so judgmental when I talk to him? Ted didn't seem to notice. He took off his jacket and helped himself to ice in his glass and poured vodka over it. He also fixed a drink for Carter in the additional glass.

Carter could now look at Ted without being aware that Gina could see how much he cared for Ted. He was a really good-looking guy and now fit the part of a young successful lawyer, and in addition, Carter knew that he would always be in love with Ted no matter what. So, now he felt like he could hardly restrain himself from just going over where Ted sat and pushing him back on the couch while just making love to him. The interesting thing was Ted always seemed to be able to read his thoughts. He was smiling and gazing back at Carter.

He said, "So, are we going to talk or what?" Carter sat in the chair across from him and diverted his eyes away from Ted's.

"Ted, I wanted to talk about Gina. I don't think it's fair to her to even have you here. I know you keep saying you told her in the beginning, but it's cruel."

Ted answered softly, "Well, what do you want me to do, leave her?"

"What! Of course not, I don't want to be responsible for breaking up your marriage I'm saying you decided to get married, so I should let you live your life and move on."

"Carter, I told you a long time ago that I'm always going to be your friend, even if I'm not your lover, I'm your friend. I'm here now, so if you want me, I'm here." This made Carter even more nervous, and when he looked up at Ted, he saw that Ted still had that smile on his face.

Carter stood up and said, "Let me show you what I've done with the bedroom." Ted got up and walked past Carter up the stairs to the second level. In the bedroom, they sat on the side of Carter's bed and finally Carter just pushed Ted back. The kiss boiled into passion, especially for Carter, he had really missed Ted.

So, it started all over again. Carter and Ted were together at least once a week, mostly mid-week, early evening, and after they were together, Ted would leave to return home to Gina. Carter was experiencing serious pangs of conscience, but he couldn't bring himself to stop Ted's visits. The only person he could confide in was Roger, who continued to tell Carter it wasn't his fault.

"If Ted insists on seeing you and you still care for him, you should keep on seeing him."

During one of Ted's visits, he mentioned that Gina had confronted him about his coming home late some nights during the week.

When Carter responded with, "Maybe we need to think about not seeing each other quite as often."

Ted replied, "I think I'm going to leave her." Carter was immediately torn between being pleased and guilt. He had been a willing participant in the break-up of a marriage between two friends. In a way, he thought it's probably a blessing in disguise for Gina. In time she could move on and she might realize that she should never have married someone as conflicted as Ted.

On the other side, this would bring back the old feelings of being uncertain about Ted's faithfulness.

Carter told Ted, "I don't want to feel guilty for being responsible for breaking up your marriage to Gina. I care about Gina. She is one of the most understanding and caring people I've ever known."

Ted answered, "It's not just you, it's also mostly because I don't love her, I just like her."

"My God, Ted, how can you be so cold about your feelings?"

"I'm not cold about you. I never lied to her about you."

"Stop talking, Ted, you're making it worse."

As it turned out, Ted and Gina separated, and after a few months of Ted living back in town in his own apartment, they decided on a divorce. Ted had wanted to move in with Carter, but Carter had reminded him that this would give Gina grounds for a quick divorce with Carter named as co-respondent. Ted had responded as a lawyer in Pennsylvania; there are never usually divorce filings with named co-respondents. Usually an unnamed individual would be mentioned. Carter was uncomfortable with the whole mess; he told Ted he could not move in as long as he was still married to Gina.

In the meantime, he and Ted were together every day at his condo or at Ted's apartment. Carter began to believe that Ted had finally matured and wanted to be with only him. It had taken a while, but now he actually felt confident about Ted's feelings for him. Carter had his friends Roger, Herb, and Ronny to confide in for advice. They often had dinner at each other's homes and Ted had become more amiable in their directions. He seemed to always be trying to prove to them that he was good for Carter.

So, life was again filled with Carter growing more in love with Ted. The problem was that Carter believed in being absolutely faithful to this alliance and Ted, like many others in the gay life, felt that occasional dalliances with others (male and female) did not count. This meant that they were again headed for disaster.

Ted had finally moved in with Carter and they even went on vacations together. One of the destinations was Carter's favorite, Puerto Rico, where they visited with Carter's friends. After a long period of contentment, Ted brought home a really attractive girl for dinner one night. Her name was Angela. She worked with a social welfare organization as their Legal Counsel. This was not unusual since both Ted and Carter often had colleagues over for impromptu dinners. This time Carter sensed a rapport between Ted and Angela that seemed intrinsic. Almost from the beginning, Carter knew there was something happening between them.

He went out of his way to be gracious to Angela, but he knew that she and Ted had been intimate. She seemed not to be aware of Ted and Carter's partnership. To her, it was very "normal" for ex-college roommates who were unmarried to share a dynamite condo in town. So, this was the beginning of the Ted and Angela period. Somehow Carter had been expecting a new affair for Ted. There never seemed to be a lessening of Ted's desire for being with Carter, but Carter just knew that Ted would always eventually need female contact. It wasn't something that Carter felt Ted did to their relationship on purpose, it was just part of Ted's makeup.

Again, his confidantes were his friends Roger, Herb, and Ronny. As usual Herb was the one with the most advice.

"This time tell him to decide if he wants to be with you or this Angela. If he wants to continue with her, tell him to move out now and avoid a repeat of the last fiasco. I don't have to tell you how I've always felt about him with you. He only cares about himself and he will break your heart again." Carter feared Herb was right and he wished that he could garner enough strength to follow Herb's advice, but instead he and Ted continued on as part-time lovers with the extra added Angela on the side for Ted.

One evening Carter had worked a bit later than usual, and when he got home, Ted was waiting for him.

"Where the Hell were you? I came home ready to have a good evening with you and you're not here. I think you're cheating on me." Carter was flabbergasted. Here was Ted accusing him of cheating and he was the one who didn't seem to have any respect for their relationship. He simply looked at Ted with amazement and went to his bedroom to change out of the suit he had worn to work. Ted followed him into the bedroom. When Carter was out of his clothes, Ted grabbed his arm and pulled him toward the bed. Carter was usually ready and willing any time Ted deemed to give him attention, but the way Ted was acting was a turn off and he pulled away. Ted swung at him with his fist, which Carter was able to avoid by stepping away from him.

Carter responded with, "I think I told you before the hitting will never be accepted again, so I guess you are signaling that we are over." Ted immediately went into his apologies and regrets.

"Please, Carter, I'm sorry. I wasn't really going to hit you. I just can't stand thinking you are maybe with somebody else. I get so confused. I love you so much, but I just can't stop with the women and then I think you are going to leave me." Carter found himself softening in Ted's direction and he actually put his arms around him and they ended up on the bed. After a lot of passion between them, Carter came to the realization that he needed to end this relationship for his own benefit and Ted's.

For days after that, Carter was purposely late getting home after work. Ted responded by spending even more time with Angela. This is what Carter had hoped for, it would make it easier for him to suggest that he and Ted should break it off again. However, realistically, he was dreading the finish. He had gotten used to Ted being with him and he really didn't know what his life would be like without Ted. He was spending those hours after work with his friends and their moral support had been most welcome. Ted had even called Roger several times asking for Carter, and Roger had been forced to lie, saying he hadn't seen Carter that day.

Finally, after Ted had not been at home for three days, he came in without a word about where he had been. Carter decided to ask him where he was for three days. Carter went into the kitchen where Ted was making himself a vodka martini.

"So, Ted, where were you for the last three days?"

"Angela and I were organizing her new condo."

"Oh, did she buy or is she renting?"

"She bought it, I helped her a little."

"Oh, I see, so you are planning to move in with her?"

"What are you talking about? I live here with you. I told you I want to stay with you," answered Ted. "Ted, I care for you and every day that we continue living together makes me care more. But I can't go on living this way with you. I think we should realize that we don't belong together as partners. Maybe we should just be friends. Not right away but in the future after we get used to not living together." Carter didn't know what to expect this time from Ted since his reactions previously had been extreme to Carter's statements about their breaking up.

He was surprised when Ted answered, "Okay, I'm tired of fighting and of your possessiveness, so be it."

Carter was amazed, but he decided not to contest Ted's reply. He knew if he did, the situation would become untenable.

Ted continued with, "I'll make a deal with you. Let's go to bed and you can decide if you want to change your mind later."

Carter answered, "No, thanks, you are acting like this is a joke to you. I am serious, Ted." Now Ted takes a sip of his drink and looks at Carter for a prolonged few seconds.

"Carter, I think you are right. We should end whatever this is that we have because you won't accept me with my needs. I told you I have to have a woman in addition to you."

Looking back, Carter is remembering the days of his initiation into the world of love and loss in the gay life. Overall, he has had a full life of wonderful times mingled with some heart break, but when those heart breaks were happening, they seemed insurmountable.

CPSIA information can be obtained
at www.ICGtesting.com
Printed in the USA
BVHW040959040321
601621BV00002BA/10